TUNNEL
TO
GLORY

TUNNEL TO GLORY

A Novel by

F. L. Kafka

LYFORD
Books

This is a work of fiction. Any resemblance between characters in this novel and persons living or dead, other than historical figures, is coincidental and unintentional.

LYFORD Books
Published by Presidio Press
505 B San Marin Dr., Suite 300
Novato, CA 94945-1340

Library of Congress Cataloging-in-Publication Data

Kafka, F. L., 1926-
    Tunnel to glory/ F. L. Kafka.
      p. cm.
    ISBN 0-89141-442-8
    1. Petersburg (Va.)—History—Siege, 1864-1865—Fiction.
2. United States—History—Civil War, 1861-1865—Fiction.
I. Title.
PS3561.A3627T8 1992
813'.54—dc20   92-12078
                                    CIP

Typography by ProImage

Printed in the United States of America

To Barbara, who always believed

CHAPTER 1

Petersburg I:
Whitworths for Breakfast

Some said it was the rain (seasonal for northern Virginia); some said it was the plan (nothing else had worked); some said the tunnel was too long (it reached its objective); some said General Grant was drunk and couldn't give the proper orders (it wasn't Grant); some said it was the timing (the sun rises, even without plans); some said the Rebs were waiting for them all along (it had crossed their minds); some said they should have questioned the regiment afterwards to isolate the factors for the records (the regiment advanced beyond the need for records); some said they were stubborn damn fools ("War is hell").

The sniper's ball splintered the long telescope in his hands. His fingers went numb even as he pushed himself back off the parapet, sprawling onto the shoulders of a surprised private, who thought him dead. He tasted the mud that had saved his life and blinked his eyes.

"Whitworths up there somewhere," he said through the blinking and tasting to the soldier and to anyone else who might be awake for a summer's dawn. "I can smell 'em as plain as I can taste the guck in me gullet."

"You all right, sir?"

"Changing the muster status of Michael Curran, the oldest second lieutenant in the Army of the Potomac, is an honor I reserve for General Grant and not some stray Reb bucko who's probably been stalking me all week and has now blown it proper."

"Glad, sir. We lost Lieutenant Evans two weeks ago to a sniper. He liked to look around at sunrises, too."

"No need to be maudlin, lad. Do me a favor, now. There should be a stub of a pencil sticking out of me top pocket, and me map board should have tumbled down with me somewhere nearby. Open up the map, and I'll show you where to mark where I think the Whitworths are today. Me hands are a bit thick as yet."

Following instructions, the young soldier made a pair of tick marks some two hundred feet in from the eastern perimeter of the small plateau identified on the artillery map as Petersburg.

"Your name, lad?"

"Private Bunko Terry, sir."

"Well, Private Bunko Terry, you are looking at the shortest route to the end of a very long war. Do you feel prescient?"

"No, sir. Unless that means scared, which I've been ever since joining up at Cold Harbor."

The officer laughed, deep, throaty gulps of laughter that seemed to bring the feeling back to his fingers as he snapped the hinged map case together with a crack, startling the section into grumbling wakefulness.

"Coffee, that's what we need. Come with me. The Whitworths will be chewing soon enough. But not this morning. This glorious sunrise belongs to the 48th Pennsylvania cooks. Their coffee is good for boils, bunions, skitters, trench foot, the vapors, and mud in the beard. Petersburg, is it? A saintly name for a place in which we'll soon be shakin' hands with the devil."

Several months earlier 2d Lt. Michael Curran had watched his wife fold his dress uniform blouse carefully into his carpetbag. He admired the ease with which she could stow it away so that when he returned to his post with the Army of the Potomac the blouse would be as crisp as her careful ironing had just made it.

They were finally alone in the big sitting room of the new house in Philadelphia that his grateful partners had found for him after luring him from Wales. The fire in the grate needed stirring, and the French clock on the mantle reminded him that his train left in just over an hour. He knew it would be on time.

His knees were slightly stiff from the weight of his two small daughters who had refused to get enough of his reading of the stories they all knew by heart. He had carried them up to their beds and covered them while they were still in their clothes after they had finally fallen asleep against his chest. He was putting the big picture book back on the shelf in the sitting room when he saw his wife tuck his dress blouse so neatly into the carpetbag.

"You really don't have to go, Michael," she said with sudden firmness. "Two years of doing nothing down there with those fancy generals is long enough service in Virginia for any man. Especially one who's been a second lieutenant the whole stupid time and has watched all his associates become captains or better."

She tried to smile at the family joke about being a second lieutenant so long, but her eyes blinked, and she knew the corners of her mouth were probably trembling.

"Cushlamacree, darlin'. If I had known that General Burnside himself was behind me on his gilded, gun-shy filly, I'd not have waxed so eloquent in front of the men on the futility of whisker-combin' compared to Reb-chasin'. Besides, being the oldest but highest-ranking second lieutenant in the entire Union army is something of a distinction. So many people know me."

He saw no need to mention the half dozen from his officer training class who had already perished from fever, wounds, and poisonous rations.

"You and your Dublin blather. All I'm asking you to do is to put it to some good use and write General Burnside a genteel note of resignation. You should be back in the job you know better than anyone in America: finding and transporting coal for the Union trains that seem to flit in and out of here every ten seconds. And I'm no 'heart of your heart' if you leave us to go tripping over your saber again on some idiotic parade ground just to prove that you're a man. I've had enough of foolish games."

As she turned from him to fold away the ironing board, he stepped softly behind her and put his arms around her waist. He kissed her earlobes and then the back of her neck.

"It would seem, Cush, that I have been home once too often as it is," he whispered, gently rubbing the subtle swelling that was just beginning to make the bright silk dress a little too tight around the middle.

She held his hand over her abdomen and leaned back against him. There was no fight left in her; she knew he was going no matter what. "Maybe we'll have a little boy this time. A little boy to howl sweet demands at me all day long, while his old goat of a father is chasing lead-footed Southern belles through the back streets of Richmond five years from now as the oldest-ranking second lieutenant in the world. Now will you please let me put this ironing board away!"

His arms unfolded slowly, and he turned around to look into the dying fire. "I don't think so, Cush," he said evenly. "They gave us this leave because President Lincoln has replaced 'Old Brains' Halleck with a wee terrier of a general named Grant. Comes from the western armies. He's the man who took Forts Henry and Donelson, turned the Rebs at Shiloh, and captured Vicksburg. I think we'll be striking tent poles and doing what I'm being paid me glorious salary to do fairly soon. From what I hear, the little man chews black powder for breakfast and pees grapeshot for tea. What are you doing?"

This time she was smiling. She had come back to stand in front of him and was lifting her hair high up over the back of her neck so he could see the long row of buttons on the back of her dress.

"Why, Lieutenant, sir! What kind of a question is that to ask a married woman whose husband is off to the wars? We still have over three-quarters of an hour before you have to catch your train."

CHAPTER 2

Petersburg II: Tactics

The cigar had gone out. Using it as a pointer, General Grant mashed the cold ash into the map of Virginia displayed on a tripod in front of his staff.

"Petersburg is a boil. When we lance it, General Lee will have nowhere left to go but up the Appomattox River, and it will be finished. We haven't endured Chancellorsville, Mechanicsville, Cold Harbor, Malvern Hill, and Spotsylvania just to grovel in front of one last miserable pimple.

"Sherman is moving toward Atlanta pretty much as he pleases by now. Sheridan has them looking up their own tailbones to the west. Jeff Davis hasn't even seen his mail for two weeks. Petersburg is the key to the last lock. It's as simple as that."

He started to relight the cigar, thought better of it, and again touched the map with the cold tip.

"That's what's so wonderful about simplicity," he continued in a lower and grimmer voice. "The Rebs know we have to attack here, too."

He checked a sheet on his note board.

"General Burnside. Your brigade is placed in the exact spot for the attack, including the 48th Pennsylvania and the 365th Colored Sharpshooters. We can concentrate the fire of over five hundred cannon in that area. Send the 48th in two mornings from now. We'll begin moving the guns over to you tonight."

"But that will leave our flank—" began Burnside.

"Quite vulnerable, General. By the time General Lee realizes that, he'll be heading the other way too fast to have it make any difference. Movement is what this army has been doing best for nearly half a year,

General. I don't propose to change that just when we can end the whole war. Any questions?"

From the rear, where the junior colonels were standing, came a soft voice with just the trace of a drawl.

"General, sir, what's this 'Colored Sharpshooters' unit you mentioned?"

"A good question, Colonel. It's a designation we've given to an all-Negro special-attack battalion fighting under Colonel Ashley, who is standing two paces to your right."

Nearly all eyes swung toward the stocky, fiery-eyed young white colonel who met all gazes full on.

"Oh," said the soft voice with the drawl.

"Oh what? We're fighting for 'em, aren't we?"

"Yes, sir. It's with 'em that burdens me."

"Suppose we leave that to Colonel Ashley. You may learn a thing or two. All right, get ready to move those guns out as soon as it gets dark. Colonel Zaretski of the 48th Pennsylvania will now take over the meeting. His men are dug in less than five hundred feet from the hill."

"Might as well eat it," said Sergeant Wendermuth, looking around at the drawn faces of his platoon as the evening soup carriers made their way along the forward trench. "There'll be nothing in the morning to be proud of. Come on, Bunko, dig in."

"Lieutenant Curran said the same thing. But I can't seem to find the stomach."

"Get the swill down whenever there's time is still the best advice in the army. Did that crazy artillery lieutenant say anything else worth sharing with your comrades in arms?"

"I don't think he feels we have much of a chance."

"I'm glad he's doing you such big favors. Look, lad, and the rest of you, too. Nobody is promising you a waltz in the garden tomorrow, but ain't none of us ever heard so many cannon firing behind us, neither. Just keep moving forward, and the whole thing will take care of itself."

"That's what I said to him this afternoon, and he said to me in that funny way he has, 'Ah, true. Ammunition we have; 'tis the brains that are a bit in demand.' "

"What did he mean by that?" asked Sergeant Wendermuth, putting down his spoon.

"That's what I asked, and he asked me if I had heard any Reb shells lately, which I haven't."

"They ain't got any powder. What's so bad about that?" offered a voice down the line. Sergeant Wendermuth noticed that a few more of the new men were now eating.

"I said the same thing," continued Bunko Terry, "but he just shook his head and said they were dug in so well that we've just been blowing dust up there."

Sergeant Wendermuth made a mental note to have a word with Colonel Zaretski about allowing officers to talk like that with green troops before an attack.

"He still talking about his tunnel?" he asked, to change the subject.

"That's about all he ever talks about, Sarge," answered Corporal Bielecki, picking up the cue.

"He is kinda funny about that tunnel," conceded Bunko, as surprised by all the attention as by the discovery of a real piece of meat in the soup.

"Barmy, not just funny," chimed in Jones, the platoon messenger. Jones was entrusted with carrying the bright red flags used for adjusting the artillery fire during an attack. "Did he give you the nigger bit?"

Bunko Terry stopped eating.

"Well, he did say something about wanting the likes of someone as black as those troops on our flank out there right now hitching his backside up a dark tree alongside of their artillery so he could hang up something that would reflect the sunlight in the morning."

"What good would that do?" asked a tense voice up the trench.

"My dad was in the artillery, and he was always talking about triangulation to get proper range."

"Maybe," interrupted Sergeant Wendermuth, "but it's us who do the real fighting, so don't let all that cross-eyed arithmetic bother you. Wars may sound different, but I'm telling you nothing ever changes. The officers talk and we do the fighting. Anything else, son?"

"Yes. Lieutenant Curran said that if he could triangulate the position of the Confederate battery, he could build his tunnel and end the war."

"He won't have to; we'll hand him Petersburg in the morning. General Grant says we'll be home for Christmas," laughed Corporal Bielecki flatly.

"Lieutenant Curran said one more thing," added Bunko.

"What?" asked a dozen voices together.

"He said he'd be coming with us tomorrow to handle the artillery flags."

In the ensuing silence Sergeant Wendermuth's quiet follow-up carried a long way along the trench.

"Anybody got any letter-writing to do better get to it about now."

Col. Anton Zaretski's headquarters tent was as spare as the man, as ordered as the best legal mind in western Pennsylvania. The colonel still looked more like a bespectacled barrister than the commander of a regiment of former coal miners. He was used to taking command of a discussion by clearing his throat with a slight cough, as if he were about to begin an argument for a client. He walked with long, deliberate strides, often hunched over with weighty thoughts. He wasted no movement. He listened to all arguments with equal intensity, as if he were practicing for a higher office. In less than twenty-four hours he would be ordering his regiment, the 48th Pennsylvania, into a frontal assault. He hoped he could get the attack launched before the regiment came under the command of Brig. Gen. Edmund Service, who was expected any hour.

Colonel Zaretski knew from the balloon observer's drawings made the previous week that the Petersburg trenches, only some five hundred feet away, were probably impenetrable. The trenches, which snaked above them on the Petersburg plateau, were zigzagged in such a clever order that each trench protected the one before, and direct passage was impossible. Abatis of pointed wooden shafts made them nearly impenetrable by infantry, and heavy earthworks protected the occupants from anything other than a direct hit by cannon. He had planned a heavy barrage through the night, and then the 48th would race across the bare fields, possibly penetrating the outer positions. Then it would be hand-to-hand and numerical superiority. Everyone knew the attack would depend on good artillery, as well as speed and courage that had to be dredged up from sources yet untapped.

His musings were interrupted by the arrival of Lt. Michael Curran, a new forward observer who, instead of bothering to salute, handed him a most welcome cup of hot coffee.

" 'Tis terrible, I know, sir, but it's full of sugar, and I've brought some currant buns from my dear wife who fears for our digestions in the midst of all this army mollycoddlin'."

Colonel Zaretski grinned his first grin in three weeks and waved the new arrival to a seat at the small camp table.

"You may not have heard, Lieutenant, but this regiment is about to go on the offensive, not to a tea party. But thanks anyway, they're awful good. My wife worries about the same invariables. The Reb wives probably worry the same. Now, why this buttering up when I've got another twenty-four hours of planning and checking and coordinating to do in less than twenty?"

"Posterity, Colonel, mindless and simple. If I should happen not to come back tomorrow, I wanted you to have the key to the future in your own hands. I could see in me telescope how well dug in they are over on the mound and how merry a jig we'll have to play them before the dance is over." Noting the sudden suspicion creeping into the colonel's eyes, Curran came immediately to the point.

"I hold here in me hand the basic scheme for a tunnel that goes from our house to their house. I asked for this forward-observer assignment because this is a regiment of volunteers from Pennsylvania. A natural-born lot of professional diggers. Well, sir, diggin' is me business, and pending a few inconvenient measurements, we could soon be beginnin' the one sure way of getting beyond all those blind-alley trenches up there."

Curran slowly turned over his map board and slipped out a sheet of engineering draft paper. On the draft paper was laid out, in overview and profile, a tunnel from the Union lines up the mound ending under the forward trenches, the regiment's goal for the attack planned for the next morning.

Colonel Zaretski looked at the drawings in astonishment. He polished his glasses, he coughed quietly, then he harrumphed a time or two. From under darkening brows he asked, "Are you a Reb spy or simply a tail-twisting clairvoyant? For someone but lately come to the regiment—"

"No spy, sir, I assure you. I've been here two days now, and it's been a bit quiet, so I did some doodlin'. I imagine the Rebs have been thinking about the same thing. And although some Celts do seem to have the gift of second sight, I'm no more clairvoyant than General Burnside, whose imagination doesn't quite make it to the latrine, beggin' your pardon, sir."

Colonel Zaretski recognized immediately that the tunnel was the work of a masterful engineer. It was, he was about to tell Lieutenant Curran, exactly what his staff had been badgering him to allow them to do for several weeks. But priorities called.

"Curran, this is excellent work. But we're going to take the mound in the morning, and there'll be no need for this sketch. However, I'll keep this, if I may, and you had best be reporting to Major Harrington at the artillery command post for his wishes."

"Not to worry, sir. The good major and I have already passed the time of day, and I'll be out with the lead elements wigwaggin' the artillery fire so there'll be no chance for anything going astray. Thanks for listening. I'll tell me wife you like her baking. And we'll talk again when it's more convenient to your busy schedule."

He lifted his empty coffee cup in symbolic tribute. Slowly, Colonel Zaretski did the same. Curran's eyes confirmed everything Colonel Zaretski feared for the morrow. He gave the husky lieutenant the empty cup and eased the sketch into the drawer of the table as the engineer–cum–artillery-fire–director left the tent. Colonel Zaretski returned his full attention to the details of the infantry and artillery coordination, ammunition supply, signals, morale, resupply, and tending of the wounded. He wrote everything down in long lists and then, almost as an afterthought, he added burial.

It wasn't until late afternoon that he reexamined the proposed tunnel. The sketch went back into the drawer with SECRET written across the top. God help us, he thought, if we ever have to get into Petersburg by tunneling.

Lieutenant Curran returned to his post near the front lines and seated himself on an old ammunition box. There was better lumber in the box than in some of the cottages he had seen on the outskirts of Dublin while growing up. He spread the map case across his knees and on a clean sheet of paper began making a list of the things he needed to know about the tunnel:

1. Exact distance from the lead Union trench to the base of the Petersburg mound.
2. Height of the mound.
3. Location of the Confederate batteries on the mound. Whitworths? Left to right and front to back.
4. Soil composition (how deep would the tunnel have to go?).

5. How many feet per day could the digging go?
6. Ventilation (invisible to Confederates?).
7. Secret removal of dirt each day.
8. Shoring.
9. Number of diggers (the more the merrier).
10. Size and shape of the glory hole (saucer, platter, bowl?).
11. How many tons of powder?
12. Transport.
13. When to detonate?
14. Fuzing.

Even as Lieutenant Curran wrote, he began to recognize the old familiar demon of planning. Each question gave birth to five more questions. Yet a deep satisfaction started to grow as he began the detailing of what would probably be the only way to conquer the mound. From his map, the importance of Petersburg itself soared. All the railroad lines supplying Richmond from the south and west met in Petersburg. Once Petersburg fell, Richmond had to collapse like an indulgent mother's anger before her son's mischief. He added to his list:

15. Shovels and picks.
16. Ladders.
17. Wheelbarrows.

With enough heavy thoughts to hold him for the morning, he slipped the list into the map case and tucked the case under his arm as he went off in pursuit of Major Harrington to confirm his assignments for the next day. He had volunteered to direct fire. To Curran, the only real problem lay in staying alive long enough to use the flags. He also hoped the overused, ancient Parrott ten-pounders could be relied on to lob their shells up over the attacking forces once the mound was scaled. He would have worried less if Major Harrington's batteries had Whitworths. He also knew that any Confederate sniper still alive after the initial assault would be watching for his flags.

From Major Harrington, Lieutenant Curran got the use of eight men, who swiftly followed him to the quartermaster's, where they picked up shovels, hammers, boards, and nails. About a hundred yards back from the front, where pine trees and thick laurel bushes gave partial protection from Confederate telescopes, he organized two outhouse-digging parties. Six of the men worked on two separate holes, digging for half a day. The other two assembled the outhouses. There were no complaints. As in any army, busywork was preferable to the endless routine of waiting for a dawn with the bite of shrapnel in it.

After digging down some six feet, Curran found about what he had expected. Under the fourteen inches of gumbo-gritty topsoil, both teams had run into sandy soil that his men found as easy to dig in as fine Swiss Gruyère. Progress would be easy for a tunnel through such soil if he could get enough shoring. He was bothered only by the high mound of excavated earth next to the holes. It was yellow and very easy to see for a long distance. He would have to find a way to hide every shovelful.

He marched the eight men back to the quartermaster's with their tools and then released them to their own units for supper. The usual miserable fare would probably be better tonight, with only hard-tack and water in the morning. There would also be hot, screaming metal, breath-sucking explosions and the odd million incongruities of slaughter that rob men of their sanity. He left his map case and tele-scope with Colonel Zaretski's aide and returned to the batteries to claim his red flags.

General Grant's headquarters area was as Spartan as Colonel Zaretski's. Members of Grant's staff moved quietly and efficiently in the heavy June air of Virginia. Since early spring the Army of the Potomac had advanced in the costliest campaign of the war. Seemingly endless levies of recruits plugged the gaps left by the fallen, a fact ruefully noted by the South, for whom such gaps remained unfillable. Grant's full support of his staff inspired the best. Although Grant hardly ever apologized, lives seldom stood in the way of an opportunity to exploit an enemy error. But beneath the apparent efficiency and peace of the evening, the commanding general's mood was anything but tranquil. He was looking over the staff report on Brig. Gen. Edmund Service.

"We're a big army, but I don't see where there's any more room to hide this sonovabitch," he said to no one in particular. An orderly brought a lantern into the tent and set it gently on the portable staff table.

"Mr. Lincoln sent him along to us with a personal note, sir," offered an unhappy personnel officer.

"I know, Mac, I know. We get these bastards all the time. But this Service is the only real mistake I've known the president to make in his whole campaign. I know the man paid a fortune to support Lincoln in the election coming up this fall, and he's probably going to make a big difference in Indiana, but political generals are nearly as big a pain as ol' Johnny Reb himself. And I'll take Johnny anytime. At least I know he only wants to kill me. These leeches want my balls for lapel ornaments. I haven't heard one good word about the man since he started soldiering."

He held the dossier up to the lantern light again and then dropped it in disgust on the table. He reached into a footlocker for a bottle of whiskey. He moved with catlike quickness to the tent flap and called easily into the darkness.

"Harry, mugs all around, please. These gentlemen get pretty thirsty listening to me use so much fancy language."

After the mugs had been brought in and generously filled, Grant passed out cigars before continuing.

"These records show that Ed Service has already cost the Union over twenty thousand lives, give or take a few thousand men we can't even find. Cold Harbor, eight thousand men in a charge after I told him to hold his position. Six thousand lost at Spotsylvania holding steady when I told him to fall back. Nearly got us all killed, remember? At least another six thousand lost three weeks ago when the Rebs overran his positions on the Chickahominy because he couldn't be bothered to post enough sentries on a Saturday night. Anyway, gentlemen, I want to put this bastard where he can't do any harm for a while. If he pulls any more of his goddamn stunts, I'll blow his brains out myself!"

Cautiously, the personnel chief offered, "The 48th Pennsylvania, General, might be a good place to stash him, sir. They're a solid bunch of volunteers from the central and eastern part of the state. Decent boys, good officers.

"Or," he added, trying to catch the mood of the informal gathering, "maybe we could send him over to Colonel Kalanyi's sweet Hungarian hussars and let him ride up and down the Shenandoah where General Sheridan can help keep an eye on him."

"Phil's got enough problems this summer with ol' Jubal Early. He doesn't need both Kalanyi and Service as allies. Well, the 48th Pennsylvania sounds OK to me. Send him over there tomorrow morning."

The personnel chief rose to do as directed, then paused even as he was writing himself a short note. "There's one small hitch, General. Could we make it the day after tomorrow?"

"I don't care, just get him out of here. That's right, the 48th is leading the attack on Petersburg tomorrow morning. Colonel Zaretski doesn't need anything as sudden as General Service tomorrow. Make it the day after, then. Who knows, if Zaretski gets lucky, we'll be following right after. Service may have to ride all the way into Petersburg to take over his new command, and he'll miss all the fun. And now, gentlemen, let's review the artillery procedures for this goddamn polyp once more. I wish we had a couple more batteries to handle those zigzag trenches. They're really something. The Rebs can't keep this up much longer. By now they know that our Kilkenny cat has the longer tail!"

"Let's hope so, sir," answered his de facto chief of staff, Gen. Thomas Johnson.

Grant nailed him with a look. "Why don't we see how the Pennsylvanians do tomorrow with all the extra artillery support we've sent them, and maybe the light of revelation will shine for all of us."

The answer was milder than anyone had expected. Some, remembering the calm before Vicksburg a year earlier, glanced nervously about for others who remembered the awful price of Grant's tenacity.

On top of the Petersburg mound, Confederate Maj. Gen. William Mahone studied the Union positions through his telescope. With casual indifference to the pleadings of his staff to be careful of exposure to Union snipers, he moved the scope slowly from camp fire to camp fire hoping to get an inkling of the morrow's problems.

"Well, gentlemen," he allowed as he scanned, "'pears to me there's a mite more activity tonight than usual. I can hear artillery being dragged all over the place. Damn Yankees know we can see right into their outhouses from here, but I don't think they reckon how far we can hear. You all hear what I'm hearing?"

Lieutenant Pierce, in charge of the main Whitworth battery since May, answered, "They've moved six batteries into the area in the past forty-eight hours. If the tubes are still in good shape, that extra amount of artillery could be big trouble soon. My guess is they'll try something within twenty-four hours."

"Can we hold 'em?"

"Yes, sir. We really have all the advantages. And we've been hoarding shells and rounds like the ladies in Richmond hoard tea. We'll make it plenty hot for them until you can get some more ammo up to us, General."

"Good, Lieutenant. Ah, those bluebellies. It must be nice to have so many cannonballs that you can fire until the barrels melt right off their carriages." He collapsed the telescope carefully and handed it to an aide.

"We'll get more ammo up to you tonight. Don't be bashful about asking for more. We got to hold this hill no matter what. We can plug any gap the way we've got the reserves placed, so keep friendly. How long have you been a lieutenant?"

Startled, the young artillery officer had to think a few seconds about something that really hadn't concerned him. "About a year, sir. Maybe a year and a half. Our records aren't too good with all the fightin' since April, and rank doesn't seem to mean too much up here, anyway."

"Good, good. Bullets don't have much respect for a man's rank, either. I'll be sending you some captain's insignia in the morning, anyway. These positions are terrific, and the morale of the troops is the best I've seen all along the hill. Somebody's doing something right."

"Thank you, General."

Mahone turned to look back over the five hundred or so feet separating him from the Union lines.

"You know what I'd do if I were these goddamn Yanks?"

"No, sir."

"I'd build me a tunnel, blow this mound to glory, and run five thousand men right through the gap so fast our hats would spin. Do you think they've thought of that yet?"

"Probably, sir. Only there haven't been any diggin' noises out there yet. And nobody's been seen getting rid of any of that yellow earth yet, either. And if they ever do get up the nerve to try tunneling over here, we'll just look for their ventilators and then dig right under them and blow their tunnel up at the right time. It's an old game."

"Well, keep me informed."

"Yes, sir, and please, sir, stand back a little from these parapets. They've got some powerful good snipers."

"So you've said, Captain. They've been missing me for nearly four years—on foot, on horseback, on belly, on backside, in the dry and in the wet, on parade and in my drawers, in the daytime and at night. I'm still here, and I don't believe they'll be doing anything tonight, either. However, if it'll make you feel better, I'll go home. Sure wish we had a few more telescopes; funny what they can tell us. For instance, it 'pears to me like them bluebellies don't eat no better than our boys, and they sure don't understand greens. Some war. I can see right into their field kitchens. Tell you what I can also see from here."

"Sir?"

"When they finally do decide to pay us a visit, they'll be enfiladed pretty quick when they get to the bottom of this hill. Be sure you have your best men in the forward trenches. And if you see any teams carrying ladders or long planks, shoot them first. Well, thanks for the tour. You got your scouts out yet?"

"They'll be leavin' just about now, sir. The Yanks send theirs out about the same time. The scouts talk to each other sometimes."

"When they come, it won't be for tea."

"Yes, sir."

CHAPTER 3

Michael Curran

To Michael Curran, third-year engineering student from Dublin Technical Institute, the creaking wheel of the mine-shaft elevator keened a dirge. Its theme was loneliness; apprehension its counterpoint. The earth gives up her treasures dearly, he remembered. What a way to make a living.

"Does it ever sound to you like music?" he asked the stocky Welshman next to him in the rapidly descending cage.

"Trust an Irishman to ask a damn-fool question at five o'clock in the morning. Of course it sounds like music—every time we come up. But going down is different, except for a young fool who still has hope instead of a callus to sit on."

Curran let it go. They were all the same, the men and the machinery. Tired. Philosophy came after hot tea, not before. At the thousand-foot level the cage came to a jangling, knee-cracking jolt. The cage door opened, and he moved into the receiving room with the other miners. Small sputtering lights did little to push back the heavy darkness.

"This is as far down as it goes, Mick," said someone. "From now on it's dig 'til the tons fall out or the roof falls in."

"Or the gas creeps up your pantaloons, dearie," proffered another.

"Or until I tell you to do something else," said the brittle, no-nonsense voice belonging to the hulking shape that loomed in front of him. The shape carried a clipboard. The foreman.

"I'm Owen, the in-charge. I don't know what daft reason you have for stealing bread out of an able-bodied man's mouth to take his place in this crew, but by Christ you'd better be prepared to earn it even if the earl himself is married to your sixth cousin or some such muck. Can you use a pick and shovel?"

"Aye. I've been in the mines since I was six. Only never so deep. My father had a job about as cush as yours and measured all things against the weight of his fist."

Something flew out of the black before him and cracked against the side of his head. He sprawled numbly on the wet floor while sudden laughter rippled around him. Slowly he got to his feet. It was an old game.

" 'Tis a sweet left hand you have there, Mr. Owen," he said with great care so as not to slur a syllable while his head cleared and his eyes focused. "I came to dig coal, not fight. I'm not challenging your authority, man. And there's no sixth cousin. Just an underpaid professor who writes good letters. Now give me the tools, and I'm good as money in your pocket."

"Save us the blarney, Mick. That's all we get. The real fighters need air and the smiles of their whorey colleens."

Owen's mock condescension changed to a sudden intake of air as Curran's toe caught him in the groin in a short kick of such force that his feet left the ground. Clipboard and lantern clattered to the tunnel floor as he put both hands over his paralyzed middle, and an involuntary cry filled the cavern. As Owen lay facedown on the wet floor in his own vomit, Curran moved over him with a short pickax he had picked up from a pile behind the now-prostrate foreman.

"My father, Mr. Owen, as I tried to explain, was just such a man as yourself. Some of his little benevolence rubbed off, you see. If you'll be telling me in which direction to go, I'll be off without bothering to nick the top of your head with this wee lancet of production."

He swung the pick as suddenly as he had arched his kick a minute earlier, sinking its tip deep into the soft Welsh coal. The tip pinned the short bill of the foreman's cap to the floor. The circling crowds were silent.

"Number four, and go to hell in it," groaned Owen. "Williams will show you. And watch yourself, you black Irish bastard." Owen tried to sit up but fell over on his side. Curran noticed that no one bothered to help him.

A hand picked up a lantern and signalled him to follow. The rest of the onlookers broke up to get on with the business of the mine. Williams turned out to be a slow-moving, gentle hulk of a man who allowed neither the time of day nor the tide of man's foolishness to sway him very far from the modest path of his destiny, the digging of enough coal to please his pride and feed his family of eleven. Nothing else made much difference, except the weekly rehearsals and occasional performances of the church choir.

"Number four it would be, lad, after a kick like that. Aye, but Black Owen has had it comin' for a long time. Took a stranger without his proper ration of brains to take care of it for us. Much obliged. But be careful; he's a mean one. I guess it will go hard with everyone for a while, but pay no mind. Best look to yourself outside of the mine for a bit, too. He has relatives all through this valley. But then so do all of us. I'll pass the word."

They walked along a narrow-gauge railroad spur for nearly forty minutes, stooping lower and lower every few hundred yards. At last the big man could go no farther.

"You'll have to work this stope alone from here on, Mick. I'll be back up the tunnel a pace. You'll be able to see my lantern. The walls here are good cannel bituminous and will split easily when you get your back into it. You'll learn soon enough. The shoring gang will be by sometime today to give you room enough to stand in. Just pile the coal up near where you're standing, and the boys with the carts will be along soon enough. Be sure to keep proper count. Get a slip from the boys each time. The boys don't mind fooling a new man, believe me. Drive a man daft, do those youngsters. Still I hate to see 'em down here, I do. I started the same way, and I don't like thinking of my own flesh doing it all over.

"Every once in a while you'll hear an explosion. Pay it no more heed than in any other mine you've worked. Just the powder crews blasting a new seam. We don't use much powder at this level, mainly muscle. Well, to it—at least a carful by tea."

The big man was gone, leaving him fully exhausted for only six in the morning with twelve hours still to go before quitting. Although soft from the past nine months of university life, his heavily gloved hands found familiar comfort in the rhythm of the pick. It didn't take him long to get the proper heft again. The height of the stope bothered him more than the actual work. In Scotland and the English Midlands on previous summer assignments he had been able to stand erect. He didn't know whether to blame a parsimonious mine owner or the peculiarly narrow seam in tunnel number four for the awkward angles.

His solitary labors were broken twice. First came the boy with the donkey gondola. Hard work without the track. "Is that all you've got for half the mornin', Mick?" taunted the boy. His jeer changed to a smile when Curran tossed him a paper-wrapped peppermint.

"You've handled your share of donkeys, I can see, lad. And please be sure to leave me the slip of paper for the filling of the cart."

A look of understanding passed between the two, and the slip was quickly handed over. Later in the morning four burly men made their way into the room that he was opening in the seam. They pulled a work cart piled high with studs. They dropped off a pile with casual ease.

"Here, Mick, we'll be givin' you a hand while you muck off for tea. The engineer seems to think there's more coal than he estimated in this vein, so we're going to shore it up a bit after we give it a taste of powder. You'll probably want to hold your ears—and don't forget our percent of the load when you scoop up the blessings of modern science. We're Jones Number Seven's crew. Lucky for you, easy to remember. See you back here in about half an hour. You won't know the place. It will be a palace of production, man."

"Can I watch, Mr. Jones?"

"Mister Jones is it? For sure, boys, we have here a proper trained lad even if he was brought up on peat and mealy potatoes. No misters in this crew. Just call me Jones Number Seven, and all will go well, Mick. As for watchin', you're welcome, eh, lads?"

Grunts and murmurs and multisyllable blabberings suggested Welsh approval to Curran. He wondered if they traveled in fours for safety, efficiency, or by some special clause in the contract that permitted or insisted on the privilege of singing in quartets.

"Have you not seen this before, laddie, or is it that you have a true sentiment for craftsmanship?" asked Jones Number Seven. Grumbles, nudges, and twinkles from the chorus.

"In Newcastle and Edinburgh they spoke of the Cardiff collieries as the seat of true learning about explosives, Jones Number Seven."

"Well, Mick, there's got to be some truth in that boast, or it wouldn't have traveled as far as all that. Talent does have a way of emerging, even from a thousand feet. But 'tis dangerous stuff, the powder. Not for the amateur, you might be saying. The work pays a premium, which is small comfort to the widows and orphans of the valley, but it does get the wrinkles out of the bituminous for sure. Shall we demonstrate, lads?"

The men surveyed the room off the main gallery where Curran had been working. Then they looked across the gallery into the small room that someone had started earlier. A leathery older man, who had not spoken a syllable to Curran the whole morning, emerged from another room nearby, shouldered his pick, picked up his flask of hot tea, and shuffled back up the tunnel toward the main gallery.

At last the quartet agreed on a spot, and drilling equipment was extracted from the all-purpose cart. Within a half hour the quartet, pounding the long drill bar in time to rigorous work chants rendered in intricate harmonies, had pierced a neat hole some four feet deep into the outer face of the small room in which Curran had been working. From the box at the rear of the cart one of Jones's crew took several sausagelike sacks.

"The devil's dingus for sure, Mick," said the man who handed the casings over to Jones. In turn, Jones slipped them gingerly into the long, narrow hole. Fuze lengths were attached deftly during the process, and the whole sausage train was tamped home continuously with a wooden poker that resembled a broom handle.

"Now there's the whole trick, boy," puffed Jones Number Seven as he spliced the fuze lines together at the mouth of the hole and began extending the line out of the small room into the longitudinal gallery. "Pack the powder tight, make sure it's dry, don't use too much, and make sure the fuze lines all get to the mark at the same time."

The team pushed the cart back slowly as the fuze line played out. At the first substantial shoring stud, the men stopped the cart while Jones Number Seven went back a few feet toward the room to cut the fuze line. He checked with his crew to make sure the powder keg was covered; and then after holding his miner's cap at several heights quickly, the big man struck a match and lit the long fuze.

"Stay close to the cart, Mick, and keep a hand on the man in front of you," Curran heard someone say as the crew pressed around him and the cart.

"Fire in the hole," shouted Jones Number Seven as soon as he was convinced that the fuze was burning. Jones jumped with surprising nimbleness to join his crew in the gallery. Curran was fascinated. He knew that deep-shaft blasting, traditional to Wales and popular in America, was thoroughly feared throughout England. The sputtering white fuze lashed along the mine floor with Promethean singleness, seeming to gain momentum with each scorching foot.

"Straight to mother," he heard the man ahead of him whisper.

"Burn, you darlin', burn," he heard Jones Number Seven grunt.

"Your ears, Mick," the voice behind him said suddenly just as the flame left the floor and skittered its way up the wall of his workroom toward the hole. The men crouched even tighter together. He clapped both hands over his head and ducked lower just as the blast went off. He felt himself lifted from his knees, his arms were flung apart, and then he was tumbling backward against one of the gallery walls. He opened his eyes just in time to see his workroom flying apart in orderly decomposition as tons of coal slid off the face of his inner wall. One of the sides collapsed as well, bringing down several feet of ceiling. When the ceiling fell in, the stud in front of the powder wagon split. He felt himself picked up and thrown backwards, away from the cracking timber, and then, for the second time that morning, things grew very fuzzy indeed.

The murkiness slowly left him as the hot tea reached his throat. The black dust was beginning to settle from his eyes and from the gallery as he became aware of the surprisingly gentle giants who were kneeling around him.

"See, lad," he heard Jones say as he opened his eyes to blink away some of the grit, "it's just as I was telling the boys. It's a fortunate thing we were here when an Irishman goes into a wall headfirst."

He swallowed a few more sips of the hot, sweet tea from the flask. "A myth, Jones Number Seven. An Irish head may be flinty, but these Welsh farts are the hardest weapons yet known to the collieries of the world. Look what you did to my stope!"

"You're lucky, Mick," said a soft voice nearby, "your coal is in good chunks, and they'll be having the tracks completed to you by tomorrow. We'll replace the stud that split and be on our way. We'll leave you a few extra studs in case you make any progress this afternoon."

"Oh my God," said Curran suddenly.

"What now, man, you hurt?" asked Jones Number Seven.

"Me dinner pail, Jones. It's under the careful mayhem created by your talents in my room."

"Aye, we saw it but figured you'd be wantin' the lesson. The three Gs of mining haven't changed in a thousand years, as your professors might have had the decency to tell you."

"Gas, grub, and get out fast," chorused the four. Grunts and mumbles. Laughter. A still-warm pasty pressed into his hand, his hat set right on his head, and the cart slowly creaking back up the gallery from which it had emerged.

His head hurt the rest of the day, and he asked himself a thousand questions as he splintered away at the huge blocks of coal loosened by the explosion. How does a man keep both his ears covered while holding onto the man in front of him? The work was so demanding, he soon forgot time, fatigue, and the pain in his hands, raw in spite of the thick leather gloves. Sometime during the day he remembered the pasty. He ate it with such hasty relish that it caused him agony the rest of the afternoon.

When the closing whistle sounded, he made his way up the gallery to the central assignment room. He noticed Owen checking out the teams and tallying the day's production. Owen turned his back. In the lift he felt a bit of jostling around him as he stepped in. In later trips it was always the same. He began to recognize the faces around him. My God, he said to himself, a bodyguard for Michael Curran, the fool of the hour.

On the way to his lodgings that first evening, he was thankful for the peaceful walk of two miles that let him stretch cramped muscles and breathe clean air. He could not help but notice the stares cast at him from under hat brims and bonnets. But he wasted no time on them; he thought only of the hot tub that his landlady had promised would be waiting. Twice he turned his head to catch little groups whispering after he had passed. He concluded that Owen the foreman had made his share of enemies. Perhaps, he concluded further, these people are already making bets on my time of survival in the mine.

"They have pierced my hands and my feet; they have numbered all my bones," came to him from the litany of the mass he no longer attended. Maybe he would drop by this Sunday.

A rock whistled close by his head and cracked off a wall behind him. He ducked and ran until he turned the corner of a better-lighted street. That was the only incident in the pleasant walk home. The tub was waiting as promised. A deep, old tub, so long that he could stick his legs straight out in front and not touch the other side. And then there was a dinner of beans and creamed eggs with fresh, warm bread and sweet butter brought to him by his smiling landlady. There was also a tall pint of the best ale he had ever known. Ah, he thought later as he eased himself down into clean sheets, there are worse ways to end a day of honest toil.

He wasn't so sure the following day. In the stope a crackling like bacon frying was his only warning as the left-side shoring beam suddenly splintered, bringing the roof down into his room with a ton or more of loose coal. Only instinct had made him dive for the door-way and ball up into a tumbler's roll. The little man from across the gallery was out of his hole and by his side in an instant. When the dust had settled, they cleared the gallery and began clearing out his room.

"'Tis odd now, Mick," said the little man. "That was a new bit of shoring Jones Number Seven plugged in here yesterday for us. But this bit of timber is as rotten as the devil's spit."

Curran looked at the ancient timber and then put several of the larger pieces aside.

"And 'tis another dinner pail, too," he grinned at his sinewy neighbor. Another pasty found its way into his hand, but this time he remembered to eat it slowly.

"A great invention, the pasty," philosophized his neighbor as they ate together after setting up the new shoring. "Fills the stomach, warms the heart, comforts the soul, recharges the testicles, and keeps the doctor climbin' sour apple trees."

At the end of the shift he hefted the rotted timber sections back to the elevator. Owen, as if expecting him, was surrounded by a dozen tough and determined-looking miners. The cart boys must have passed the word of the cave-in. Curran felt eyes watching him closely again as he made his way into the assembly room. As he approached Owen, one of the toughs stepped in front of Curran, a sunless smile on his face and his hand covering the glint of a blade tucked carefully into his sleeve. It was an old stance. Curran had seen it in every mine he had worked. He knew that his best weapon was surprise.

"Mr. Owen's busy, Mick," said the bodyguard, pushing him back with a jolting straight arm.

Curran dropped the rotted pieces of studding, grabbed the wrist stretched out in front of him, dipped his right shoulder, turned, and heaved with all his strength in one sudden motion. The man arced over Curran's back, screamed briefly as his shoulder dislocated, then fell silent as his head met the floor in a squashy finality that brought gasps from the onlookers. Curran picked up the knife that had slipped from the unconscious man's sleeve and stuck it into the largest of the rotted timber sections at his feet.

"Mr. Owen," he said evenly, "bad timber in place of the good left by Jones Number Seven and illegal knives are two causes for discipline in most mines. I came to Wales to learn deep-pit mining. I'm not sure I can take too many more of your lessons. Any more, mind you, and only one of us goes back up the shaft."

He dropped the stud on the floor and turned to head for the elevator. A quiet phalanx shuffled in behind him. No one spoke during the long, rattling ride to the surface.

"I'm sorry, Mr. Curran, but I can't be lettin' the room out to you anymore," said an embarrassed and slightly gaunt Mrs. Picks. "After Saturday, I'd appreciate it if you'd be lookin' elsewhere."

He nodded and went up to his bath. The temperature of the water was so perfect that he nearly fell asleep in the long tub. He couldn't blame Mrs. Picks. His fight was more trouble than anyone in the valley needed. Cleaned by the water and rubbed red by the huge, nubby towel, he found a beef stew waiting for him downstairs in the small dining room. The stew was so delicious that he felt he would have to be carted away to his room before he would ever admit he'd had enough. A trifle with fresh raspberries and sweet whipped cream finally brought him to surrender.

"Beautiful, Mrs. Picks, absolutely beautiful," he groaned appreciatively.

"You'll not be leavin' this house hungry, Mr. Curran," answered an unhappy Mrs. Picks as she gathered up the plates. More groans from Curran and Mr. Picks.

"Another mouthful, Mrs. Picks, and I'll not be leavin' at all, that bloated am I. But don't worry. I know that words have been passed about my conduct at the mine, and I'll not be havin' any harm come to you because of it."

As he rose to leave the table the doorbell rang. A look of apprehension passed between the Pickses before Mrs. Picks went out into the front room to answer the forceful jinglings. A short, thick man with a trim red beard and a tweedy look of brisk independence stood on the doorstep. He bunched a green felt hat and a riding crop in his left hand.

"Good evening, Mrs. Picks. Forgive an uncouth man for calling without your leave so late in the evening. But could I please be having a word with you and your good husband?"

"Why, Mr. Morgan, welcome you are and you know it. Come in, come in. Willum," she called over her shoulder to her husband, "it's Mr. Morgan."

Royalty, thought Curran. A few thousand Morgans in the valley, but this one was "Mister."

"I'll be runnin' along, Mrs. Picks," Curran said, rising from the table.

"Please stay, son," said Morgan with a smile. "You're part of the reason for my unmannerly call on these good people."

Curran joined the others in the front room, leaning easily against the mantelpiece while the robust visitor began again.

"I'll get right to the point, Mrs. Picks. As the purveyor of all live-stock to the mines of this valley, I find myself short of a jackass. I'm wonderin' if you could be loaning me Mr. Curran, here, as a boarder?"

Picks hooted and stamped both his feet as he laughed loudly enough to rattle the windowpanes. Mrs. Picks ducked her head into her apron, her shoulders shaking. Curran blushed as the anger rose quickly up the back of his neck. He tried to smile politely as Morgan looked up at him with plump elfin innocence. Before Curran could say anything to ruin his chances of going, Mrs. Picks came to his rescue.

"Quick, Mr. Curran, go up and get your trunk. You're saved. There'll be no incidents now, and you'll be exchanging a cottage for a man-sion. You'll be having hot water, servants, and . . . and . . ."

"And it's time we were leaving and not botherin' the privacy of good folk such as yourselves." Morgan turned to address Curran who hadn't decided whether to go for his trunk or not. "Please forgive my pro-clivity for a modest jest, young man. We would be most pleased to have you join us."

Curran, knowing that Mrs. Picks's judgment was beyond question, and liking the husky visitor besides, hurried to his room to pack his trunk.

"Don't worry about your laundry, Mr. Curran. We'll be bringing it by in a day or two," Mrs. Picks called to him as he made the short climb to his alcove.

He was back in ten minutes to the sound of more laughter and the clinking of teacups. The best ones.

"I put the room money on the washstand, Mrs. Picks. If it is not enough, I'll make it up on payday. I feel like a coward, but I've no mind to bring trouble into your home. Thank you for the great feast and for all your kindness."

He turned to the half-smiling visitor. "I can only pay what I'm paying here, Mr. Morgan. I'm on student permit in the mines, which is high on experience but somewhat low on compensation. I'll be happy to help around your place on Sundays to make up the difference."

"We can discuss it later, lad. Not to worry."

He rose carefully, put down his teacup, bowed affectionately to the Pickses, took Curran by the arm, and led him to the door.

The matched bays standing in front of the light wickerwork pony cart caught his eye immediately. They were stocky, with broad, sturdy chests and an unusually dignified way of holding their heads, even at rest. The smooth start as Morgan signalled the driver soon gave way to a full-headed trot as lively as any he could remember.

"These are very special horses, Mr. Morgan," he remarked as they rattled off the cobblestones onto the country road leading away from the mine area.

"They're from New York state in America, Mr. Curran. Took a fancy to them, I did, when I saw them in Paris. They call them Morgans, and I was hooked fair and square."

At that pace the trot up the switchback took a steady hand on the reins. Curran admired the skill of the slender driver as much as he did the matched beat of the trim bays. In fifteen minutes they wheeled up in front of the house. Mrs. Picks had been right; it was a mansion. Lights shone from many windows and grooms came quickly to take the horses and Curran's trunk. Things could be worse.

"A fine lad you have at the reins, Mr. Morgan," said Curran as he climbed down into the courtyard to survey his new good fortune.

Morgan laughed and signalled to his driver. "Mr. Curran thinks you're a fair hand at the reins, lad!"

The driver took off the low-crowned tweed driving cap, letting the long brown curls fall about the shoulders of the driving coat. She gave Mr. Morgan a kiss and Curran a smile. "Thanks, Dad. Gwen Morgan is always glad to help the cause." She vanished in light steps and laughter into the front door of the house.

"Even smoother than these Morgans are *the* Morgans, sir," answered an embarrassed Curran as he followed his host up the same stairs.

Morgan chuckled. "Come in, Michael. We'll have a pipe and a glass, review the bidding, and then we'll let you get to bed. You can drive down to the mine with me in the morning. I'll have you there in time to start your shift proper, don't worry."

The pipes turned out to be long Cuban cigars and the glass a decanter of Irish whiskey. Mr. Morgan waved him into an armchair by the fire and filled two crystal tumblers. Curran could soon feel the apprehension fading as he looked into the fire, leaned back, and enjoyed the Irish. Holding the heavy glass reminded him that on this day he had finally put aside his gloves.

"Irish, Mr. Morgan? You must have known I'd accept your invitation."

The quick eyes twinkled back at him. "Michael, you're too valuable to mining and to the safety of this valley to allow for nonsense. I'll be having a word with the mine owner, who's a neighbor, and Owen will be bothering you no more."

"I can fight me own—"

"Of course, my boy, of course. That's understood. But here, where everyone's related to everyone, nobody has a chance to fight his own fights. Besides, he's been building a savage name for himself, and the owner has about had enough. Especially since you're his pet experiment for the summer."

"I didn't know I was his pet. But I do know from the feel of my hands that I'm earning my own way in spite of all the pamperin'."

"Of course." Morgan poured another pair of drinks. Standing by the fire seemed to give him the privilege of relaxing his jolly demeanor. Talking to no one in particular, he said quietly, "Here in Wales we have a saying that there is no unemployment because it takes two men to fill every miner's job; one to break out the coal and one for the pits to keep. This village has paid its share. Yes, I am a little curious why a Dublin Institute man would want to dig coal for a living. It's none of my business, mind you, Michael Curran. Absolutely none."

"Pride, Mr. Morgan. Stubborn pride. I watched me father cough out his lungs for years before he was lucky enough to have a shaft cave in on him. Can you believe I thanked God for the peace that such a miserable death gave him? 'Tis a terrible thing to say, wishin' a man dead, but me father would have understood well enough. So now I'm at the Institute studying to make the diggin' safer and the production higher. And if I learn well, there won't be the Welsh kind of unemployment, either, just drier and safer mines for everyone. And you know we've just begun to use the power of coal. Also, I can see a time when we won't have to blast so much. Did you know there are some places on this earth where the coal is just waitin' to be scooped off the surface? Then watch the money roll in! We'll stoke all the ships and fuel the world's production. It will be a long time before the world gets tired of coal."

"Michael, you're way ahead of a tired horse trader, but I will say one thing. I'm really not sure if you want to be the best coal man in the world or just earn the honor of dying like your father in the pits."

"Good night, Mr. Morgan. Many thanks for the hospitality."

"Good night, lad. James will show you to your room. Morning always comes too early in a mining village. The porter will call you, and we can have a cup of tea before Gwen drives us down to the mine."

In the pit the next morning, Owen greeted him with passable cordiality that rang a trifle off-key as the foreman said carelessly, "This morning your education will be continued in a new form of exercise, Curran. You're assigned to powder crew number two with those fellas over there by the carts. We're a bit shorthanded, and a spry lad such as yourself will be of service. Besides, you can't learn too much about powder handling in a mine, can you?"

"No, sir," he answered, going over to the powder team. He introduced himself to three men who could easily have doubled for the taciturn giants of the Jones Number Seven crew. He was told to load new studs onto the cart. In short order the crew was pulling the cart down a narrow track into another of the countless warrens of the thousand-foot level.

He helped set two charges that morning, watching carefully as the cotton sausages were assembled, noting intensely how gently and selectively the charges were eased and packed into the holes for blowing. At the start of the second blowing, the leader broke the morning's silence.

"The secret is there's no secret, just patience. Everything depends on how the fuze and the powder get along. Changes every day. Watch well and you'll live long enough to hear your grandchildren's prayers of an evening. Muck it up and you'll watch your bowels ooze out on the floor. Ask anything you like as we work. If it makes sense we'll answer. But for today just watch."

As before, the crew gathered in a knot behind the cart as the leader lit the fuze. The flame ran a sputtering path to the hole and left a week's work for two men. Curran dropped off four studs as directed and followed the team to the next blasting site. This is a soft one, he said to himself. I'll be needin' me gloves again when they put me back with the picks and shovels.

At the next stope he was allowed to help pack some of the charges from the cask of black powder that rode in the well-packed box in the center of the cart. Only the leader, however, was allowed to coax the elongated charges into the hole superbly drilled by the other two crew members. It amazed him whenever he watched a drill team how completely one man could put his fate in the hands of another. The two men usually took turns on such teams, one holding the star drill while the other swung the heavy sledgehammer. He never saw a miss. Jones Number Seven once told him that a man's swing was his signature. He could tell the location of every team on the thousand-foot level by the rhythm of the sledges.

When the fuzes were installed and trailed out to the gallery for lighting, the crouch-and-seize routine began again as the leader struck the flame to blow the charge. As the fuze caught he grunted "fire in the hole" and ducked in behind the cart next to Curran.

"Sput," said one of the crew about half a minute later.

"Spit," continued an equally unhappy mate.

"Shit!" summed up the leader as he looked around the corner of the heavy cart to where the fuze had stopped burning halfway up the wall to the hole.

"That'll take a pair of heels. Here, Mick, let's see if your balls are for real. Go relight that fuze. Scoot for here as soon as she sputters. You're the quickest of the four." He handed him the matchbox.

Curran took the matches and walked slowly toward the dead fuze, watching it like a snake to make sure it didn't suddenly sputter back into life. After reaching the far wall of the stope, he looked back to mark his exit run, noting that one of the crew had edged over to make room for him at the corner of the cart nearest to the impending explosion. He was grateful for the courtesy.

"Strike and git," shouted the crew leader. Curran held the box up to the cold fuze at about eye level and struck one of the heavy matches. The whole wall seemed to shudder in front of him; his ears were suddenly overwhelmed from the rolling shock waves that rocked him backwards and then upwards. He lost track of movement as the roof splintered above him and the great stillness changed to a concussive roar. Who was doing that screaming?

Then there seemed to be a second explosion, sharper than the first, coming straight at him, sucking the air out of his throat, hurling tons of coal at him like hailstones, but probably saving his life as the force lifted him straight back into the gallery and the protection of the studding just as the roof dropped in on the stope.

Hands were groping for him in the gallery and he was conscious of a harsh whistling in his ears. His legs were numb, and he suspected that his work jacket was in shreds. He couldn't focus his eyes, and his mouth was full of coal dust. The crew all seemed to be talking at once, but he couldn't hear a one of them. He knew they were lifting him up on the cart, then nothing.

He was unconscious up the long elevator ride to where the company doctor and an ambulance were waiting for him. The company infirmary was not staffed for such an explosion. He was still unconscious when they put him on the train to Cardiff and the Royal Hospital by the sea. The company doctor shrugged his shoulders when Morgan and the mine manager met him at the station as he was climbing aboard, "Double concussion and half the tunnel fell on him. We're in for a long night."

Back in the assignment room at the end of the shift, Owen became conscious of an unmoving circle of men around him. No one spoke. Abruptly the heavy form of the leader of powder crew number two was kicked into the center of the circle next to Owen.

"Up the shaft, all of you," snapped Owen. "If you delay the night crew, it'll come out of everyone's pay."

There was no movement and still no sound.

"He'll have the best care in Cardiff."

"A question, Mr. Owen," said Jones Number Seven very deliberately.

"We'll have no questions. I said get back to work, the lot of you."

One of the other members of crew number two bounced like a sodden football into the circle and lay where he had been tossed. He lay quietly until a low groan finally escaped from his bruised lips.

"A question, Mr. Owen?" repeated another voice as the crowd grew and the circle tightened. Only the winch could be heard in the heavy silence.

"All right, ask, damn it, and let's be done with it!"

"It's Harnish Number Two I'll be asking."

"It could have been any one of us, Jones."

"The question, Harnish, is why did you let a new man light a burned-out fuze instead of doing the job yourself like all the other crew leaders and like you've always done before?"

"He came to learn, and I thought the experience would be good for him."

"Did you teach him to test for the gas, Harnish?" rasped a voice from the thickening fringe.

"Of course, but you know how no one can teach a university man nothin'."

One of Harnish's crew members shook his head from his place on the floor. His mate, on his knees nearby, seeing the head shaking, began to do the same. There was a buzzing around the circle.

"There seems to be a slight difference of opinion, Harnish. If, by chance, you neglected to tell him to check for the methane, it could have been at just the right height when you gave him your matches. And where were you when the first explosion went off?"

"There was only one explosion, Jones. And we were all behind the cart, same as your crew would have been."

Murmurs and the shuffling of heavy feet. Then the voice of Jones Number Seven again.

"You're a liar, Harnish. I never told the Mick much about the gas when he was with me, and you didn't have time to train him overmuch, if at all. He ain't learned about life down this deep yet and don't know about the gas flowin' all about us. I promise you, Harnish, if the lad don't come through this, look to yourself. Find work away from the valley and don't even think about coming back down here."

Grunts of approval echoed around the circle. Belligerently, Owen sought to resume command of the shift.

"Up the shaft, the lot of you; the new crews are waitin'. You get paid to dig, not talk. This will be the worst production day of the year for all this blatherin'."

"Owen, you black bastard, the warning goes for you, too," said a sharp voice from behind him in the shadow-wrapped circle.

"Who said that?" shouted the foreman, turning toward the voice as if to tear out the tongue of the speaker.

"I did!" shouted a voice from the other side of the circle.

"I did!" echoed another from the flank.

"I did!" shouted a third from nowhere in particular just before the whole ring took in a breath to hurl as one indictment, "I did!"

Owen froze as the circle around him wrinkled and then slowly broke, the men heading for the lift and the final chores of the day. A length of fuze whistled through the air and landed at Owen's feet. There were indentations all along the line. Jones's voice followed the fuze into the faint circle.

"When a man knows his trade, there's no problem to stoppin' a trail wherever he pleases. Pity we can't find the one that quit."

Michael Curran proved to be as durable as his boast, and the hospital agreed to let him go after only three days of rest and observation. He had cuts aplenty and battered ribs that were so painful he could hardly stand the train journey back to the Morgans'. It would be too embarrassing if he fainted. His left leg was strained, and a light cast was put around his knee to give the ligaments a chance to heal. His doctor marveled at this quick recovery in the hospital.

"You're a lucky man, Michael Curran. One hears a bit of talk even in the hospital. You have made some good friends in Wales, which is one of the true pleasures of this earth. The Welsh are demon-good haters, too, you know. You seem to have come through enough concussion to have killed six crews, and just by the skin of your teeth. You may not get all of your hearing back in that right ear; we'll just have to wait a bit to see. And I'm not at all sure that a few more things aren't torn up inside. We'll have to watch your stool for signs of blood. I'll stop by daily. Then you'll need a long rest; maybe as long as a month. Your own doctor can take the cast off in ten days."

"I can't rest a whole month, doctor. I'll never manage to get through the university without colliery money. A week, maybe, but no month, please, sir."

"Didn't you know that here in Wales mine insurance will pay you an average wage during recovery as well as my fee? So rest easy, lad, and enjoy the few good days that Wales has to offer you."

"Tush, man, it's not fair; and think of the Morgans having a cripple about their grand house."

"Well, at last, some less-than-selfish sense from the somnolent scholar," piped Gwen Morgan behind a huge bouquet of mixed flowers. "You'll be coming home in two days, and you will be no bother to the Morgans. We'll fatten you up and bring your hearing back to normal with the reading of good Welsh poetry. After a month your leg will be so strong, you'll be jumping for the town in the Valley Games."

He looked at her numbly. She and the flowers seemed to fill the room with good sounds and smells and more colors than his eyes could consume. She looked a lot different from the groom who had driven them up the hillside that first evening not so long ago.

But she had even more directions for his recovery, about which she seemed completely at ease. "And the doctor has given me full authority in his absence, so there'll be no nonsense about bedpans or bandages or drinking your broth."

She looked meaningfully at the doctor, who nodded in helpless agreement. Neither one of us can make the weight in this division, concluded Curran.

"You'll just rest with us and get well in the good Lord's own good time. If you're real good you can walk around the garden with me in about ten days on your hopping sticks."

She was smiling and bubbling busily, but the way she looked at his bruises made him look at her eyes. He realized, with a jolt, that she had probably been crying just before she came into the hospital room. Now why should she be crying?

In two days the trip back to the Morgan household was endured on the train. He was carried up to his room by strong and gentle hands. A marvelous air of imperceptible efficiency permeated the looking-after of Michael Curran, so that he found his convalescence anything but boring.

First, two of his textbooks appeared from Dublin with a get-well greeting from his major professor. With the texts came assignments and the offer of special credit for a paper on the use of explosives at great depths. Every day, beguiled or blackmailed explosives experts found themselves, all nervous smiles, in his bedroom unburdening themselves of the subtleties of deep-shaft explosives while failing, nine times out of ten, to balance a teacup and a cake. His notebooks were also filled with observations on steam-power management, hoist control, digging strategies, the vagaries of deep-mine seams, coal quality, stable management, accident procedures, and methods of improving the efficiency of the work force. On the first Sunday afternoon after the accident, Jones Number Seven and his crew came for tea. They were finally coaxed into telling him about testing for methane gas before firing a charge.

"The gas can set off an explosion all by itself, just from a spark, Mick. As good a blast as ever any of us has rigged." Mumbles, slow slurps, and head-nods from the chorus. "You've got to hold your lamp to the level of your charge every time. 'If it glows white, don't light,' we say in the mine. My fault, really, Mick. I thought you'd be with our crew a bit longer. I'd have been telling you all about the gas in a day or two. And a new man never even lights a fart for four years in our shop! Beggin' your pardon, mum."

Curran choked over his cup, but the restraint hurt far worse than the laughter, so he howled his approval until his ribs hurt so that he could hardly breathe. Gwen took his cup and looked at him pensively. The pain eased quickly.

"Mr. Jones, you and your crew are the greatest tonic a man ever had. If I can survive the cure, you'll make a deep-pit miner of me yet."

"Aye, Mick, the best. Well, the lads and I are expected home. Thank

you for the splendid tea, Miss Morgan. He's a bit slow, yet, but I predict
he'll make up for it with luck and diligence."

"The more diligent he learns to be, Mr. Jones, the luckier he ought
to get, wouldn't you say?" answered Gwen with a warm thank-you
blooming in her cheeks as she escorted the four ponderous miners down
the long flight of stairs to the door.

"He thinks the fuze was purposely crimped short," said Curran as
Gwen returned.

"And so does the whole valley, Mickey."

"You know, that's the first time you've done that."

"What, expressed the sentiment of the valley? Surely you must
have sensed—"

"No, called me Mickey."

"Well, Mr. Curran is a bit formal with a man for whom you've been
changing bedpans for a week, so take no offense, please."

" 'Tis not mine to take, only enjoy."

"Well, Mickey, me boy, open your big mouth because your medicine is ready. Then we'll all have a bit of blessed silence while you
take the rest we all need."

A week after returning to the Morgans, Curran was back on
his feet, bobbing quite well on crutches even on the stairs. In ten days
he was able to walk with only a cane and a sturdy, shapely shoulder for occasional extra support. At such moments he felt that he
could almost fly. That was when Gwen suggested a picnic for a change
of scene.

They left the matched bays browsing in the shade and walked slowly
to the hillside from which they could look out over the entire valley,
the mine at one end and pastures at the other. He was able to manage
well enough, although it bothered him to let Gwen carry the heavy
picnic basket. She knelt in the lush grass and spread a soft tablecloth
in front of the basket.

"Come and sit, Michael Curran of Dublin town, and join a country
lass for a spot of alfresco dining."

"Sweet Gwen Morgan," he said softly, almost to himself, watching
her put out the very special cold meats, the fresh bread, and choice
fruits of their repast. The people he grew up with never saw so
much fine food in a year, let alone at a casual picnic on a hillside.
"You make too much of me." He gently took the chilled bottle of white
wine from her.

"Here, now, that's a talent I will own up to." He eased himself off

his awkward position with his cane and sat down beside her to open
the bottle. "Gwen, you know I'm not to the manner born. Look at these
heavy calluses. I come from plain country people much like these in
the valley. All such people want is strength for the day, a little peace
in the evening, and no surprises that could make things worse. I'm at
the Institute because the mine where my father died is paying for its
shame in my education to avoid a bad siege with my father's lawyers.
I'm taking the education to avoid a long siege with their lawyers. For
six years I've known only work and study, and then study and work,
until now that I can see me degree but a semester down the tunnel, I
can scarce breathe for thinkin' on it."

"No time for anyone special, Mickey?"

"No; I'm really a dull one, I tell you. I have no way with the girls.
A bit of surface blather for the passin' of the time of day, but underneath you see a true social coward who still has to look around to see
which fork to use."

Accepting a large napkin, he tied it carefully around his neck.

"An advantage of dining 'alfresco,' as you call it, is that 'tis only
God's knives and forks we employ, and proper order is providential.
Your glass, mine hostess fair."

"Am I?"

"Are you what?"

"Fair?"

"Aye. As fair as anything I've ever known. It's really a good thing
I have a cane, because even with two good knees I'm a bit weak when
I think how truly fair."

"Why, Mickey, that's quite gallant."

"Well, you had to ask a simple man such a complicated question.
I'm not one to hold me tongue in the face of the obvious, woman."

She laughed with him as they touched glasses of the cool Moselle.

"That's very nice, Mickey."

"Aye, a very tingly wine for one used to stout and dark bread."

"No, silly man, not the wine. I mean being called 'woman.' You've
made me feel very much a woman ever since you came to the house.
And I like it ever so much better than being a stable hand."

"You were pretty cute then, too, you know."

"Were you surprised?"

"And then some."

She laughed softly again as she handed him a plate of cold chicken
and grapes and broke a piece of soft bread for him. She buttered it.

"Gwen, I'm not used to such. It's me leg that's weak, not me hands."

She placed her hands over his, which were holding the plate, and looked full into his eyes. "I know, but strong as you think you are, you are my patient now, and you'll answer to my mother's ghost if you struggle just one smidge and break that heirloom plate."

He kissed her very gently on the lips. Her hand squeezed his in surprise. Had he gone too far? He opened his eyes to see her face, immobile, lifted up to him, eyes closed, her breathing scarcely audible.

"Gwen," he whispered, "forgive me if I startled you."

"Startle me again, Mickey."

He kissed her eyes, her cheeks, her neck quickly and tenderly but with growing force until, when he kissed her lips again, her arms came up to encircle his neck. Because of his awkward balance he rolled over on top of her as she embraced him with all her strength.

All time and earthly complications stood still as the full bursting of emotions overwhelmed them both in immense waves unknown to either before. Later, as she lay in the curiously conscienceless security of his arms whispering "I love you, I love you, I love you," he placed his free hand gently over her mouth.

"Gwen, heart of my heart, I'm such a clumsy man. I tried to warn you; please forgive me. I know little enough of women and nothing of love, I . . . I . . ."

"For an ignorant man, you're a good teacher. But I will confess that I'm the one who cleared the way to the garden path."

"Gwen, I've no right to you. I'm nothing. Worse, a stranger. A guest in your father's house. How can I face him?"

"Easily. Tell him I seduced you with sliced chicken and gallons of Moselle. Tell him I saw the way to your heart reflected in the heirloom china you just tossed so skillfully into that rock pile."

He started to chuckle, then, clasping her tight to him, he lay back and gave himself over to full roars of contented laughter.

"Gwen, marry me and you'll never know peace, you know that don't you?"

"I love you, and you're right—you don't know anything about women."

Time stopped ticking during the remaining two weeks of his convalescence. Love grew in dozens of tiny delicious ways: a look, a smile of understanding, an agreement over the weather, an absorbing interest in the valley and its people.

On the evening before he was to return to the mines, they were walking on the flagstone terrace overlooking the valley. Mr. Morgan sat inside at his desk by the open French doors. Occasionally he waved to them.

"Gwen," Curran broke the stillness reluctantly. The contentment of walking beside her in the soft evening air was more conducive to the eloquence of silence than to the incidental chattering of a man whose heart was too full to make sense of miracles. She took his hand.

"Gwen," he began again.

"I love you. Does that help?"

"Forever, Cush. In a month I'll be going back to Dublin. Four months after that I'll be graduating and setting out to make me own way. I've a hankering to try America where there's more coal than they know what to do with and not that much talent for getting it out. And they've not had time yet to work out feelings about strangers. A man like me could make a good living in America. Good enough to afford a family."

"Yes, Mickey, you could make a good living in America. But you could here, too, and have loving family and good friends ready-made."

"And all the methods and thinking as clumsy and ancient as the daily shift whistle! I'm a man who's been held under water for almost six years. When I come up for air, it's gulps I'm needin', not sniffs."

"You'll need more than your work, Michael Curran. Have you considered a nice Welsh bride who can cook, sew, ride, gossip, scheme, connive, and love you, love you, love you?"

It was too much. If their all-consuming affection was a secret to anyone but themselves, he gave up caring as he suddenly wrapped his arms about her and kissed her lips.

"Yes, I need you. I adore you. I need you more than anything in my life. More than my life. I was a full, happy man when I came here. Now I'm all empty whenever you're not near me and full miserable if your hand isn't in me own." She squeezed his hand and led him back across the terrace toward the house.

"Will you want to be talking to my father, sir?"

"Of course. But I can't. Not yet. To him I'm only a burly school-boy with me books tucked under me arm and not a penny in me pocket. What kind of a catch is that for the beauty of the valley?"

"Why don't we see?" she answered with a neat toss of her head as she brought him to the French doors. He stopped and let go of her hand.

"I'll see your father man to man, as is fittin'. Please wait, darlin'. I'm sure your father would appreciate it."

She stood on tiptoe to kiss his cheek and then left him in the loneliest position of his life. He knocked on the French doors, which were quickly opened wide to him.

"Come in, Mike. A man who looks like he's obeying a summons to the gallows deserves refreshments. A glass of port?"

Was he so transparent? Might as well out with it as soon as possible.

"Thank you, sir. A glass of port would be fine."

As he accepted the glass, still fearful that such a fragile thing would break of itself as soon as he touched it, he blurted out his message.

"Mr. Morgan, I would like to marry your daughter. I love Gwen more than I know how to tell you. And she loves me, sir. I've got nothing but the future to offer her, but she'd never know want, and I'd never let any harm come to her."

Mr. Morgan was smiling. "Here, Mike, hold up your glass a bit, and I'll put a little more port in it. It seems to have splashed about some in that great speech." He poured and then gestured toward a pair of wing chairs near the unlit fire.

"Everyone in the household, and probably most in the valley, knows that my Gwen and you are the coziest, most self-contented, purblindest lovebirds of the year. Frankly, I wasn't quite sure you'd even bother to go through this ancient formality. I'm as nervous as you, so why don't we both sit down?"

They sat in the big chairs.

"Surely you must know, Michael, that Gwen means more to me than any other treasure of this life. When she's gone from this home it will change back into a cold house with nothing but echoes and memories to fill the emptiness. Most of the brave lads of the valley have been by to pay their respects, and some from other valleys as well. But she would have none of them, and I was beginning to fear I had ruined her chances for happiness. Then you came to learn about deep-pit mining. If she loves you then you're the man for her, and I'm happy as punch for both of you."

He raised his glass.

"Here's to you, Michael Curran, and to Gwen, and may God bless you both."

Curran raised his glass in return, his mind racing with the abundance of good news he was hearing.

"However," continued William Morgan, "I'm assuming you mean to settle nearby so that I'll be seeing a bit of you and Gwen from time to time. Why not make it a bit easier on yourselves and make the guest cottage your first home until time and nature burst its walls, and then we'll swap. I'll go into the cottage and you and Gwen take over this house. Rent-free, of course, as a sort of wedding present."

"Mr. Morgan," began Curran, thinking of America, groping for the words that would ease the agony of the older man's coming bout with loneliness, "I—" The wineglass collapsed in his grip.

"Don't bother to thank me, Michael. I'm probably thwarting plans you already have begun to make on your own. One gets a trifle self-ish in the face of reality. I am bribing you, and it's not fair. But Gwen has always loved this place, and I hope you will give it a chance to become a wee part of your lives. It's solid stone, and there's distance enough so that conjugal disparity remains within private walls. Shall we call her in?"

Morgan stepped to the French doors to call her name into the twi-light, as if he knew exactly where she would be waiting. She came running and gave him such a hug that the glass flew from his hand and splintered on the terrace floor. They both laughed and said as one, "It's good luck!"

They came back into the room arm in arm. She flew to Curran's side, however, when she saw he had cut his hand crushing the fragile wineglass moments before. She sent for soap and water and soon had his hand bound in her handkerchief.

"Your father's been too kind, Cush. I'm afraid I forgot me manners again."

"Nonsense," answered Mr. Morgan benevolently, "merely offered the bride and groom the guest cottage for a wedding present."

"But, Da, Michael and I are going to be living—" she started to answer before Michael put his hand on her arm.

"In more luxury than her coal-digging man has ever known. Your father is being most generous, and there's much to be learned about mining here if they'll take me on."

She flashed him a look of complete confusion, which changed abruptly to understanding and then grew into a "we'll-talk-about-this-later" expression.

"And when," continued the beaming Mr. Morgan, "are you think-ing of getting married, Gwen?"

"Right now, Da," she laughed.

"After graduation; about five months, sir," said Curran, taking her hand again.

"Michael, you know I won't be able to stand it, being away from you for all that time. All those pretty colleens will be making doe eyes at you while you're trying to study, and you'll forget me. Why don't I come to Dublin and keep house for you? We could get married before you leave, and then after graduation we could come back here to live. Oh, I can hardly wait to hang your diploma over the mantel!"

"Gwen, I'd never be able to concentrate on me studies with you in the room. Besides, I'm too poor to afford decent enough digs for a bride. I can't even give you a ring for your hand to say I love you to the whole world."

Smiling as if Curran had reminded him of something, Mr. Morgan opened the small central drawer of his two-tier desk. He withdrew a jeweler's box and laid it on the table between them.

"Open it, darling," he said gently to his daughter.

"Da, I can't," she began in a nearly breathless whisper.

He kept smiling and nodding. At last she opened the box, her eyes glowing with expectation through the tears that were brimming up. Curran found himself staring at the largest and loveliest diamond ring he had ever seen, even in the windows on O'Connell Street in Dublin. They all stared at it.

"Your adorable mother wore it for too short a time, angel. From heaven I know she would be asking you to wear it for Michael and as a pale reflection of her love for you. Come, see if it fits."

He gave the box to Curran, who lifted the ring carefully from its satin pillow and turned to guide it onto her left hand. It was a perfect fit. She drew in her breath sharply.

"Oh, it's so beautiful. So splendidly beautiful."

"It's a good omen, Mr. Morgan, even if I shouldn't be taking such a fortune from your hand."

"The treasure you take from this house, Michael Curran, has nothing to do with jewelry. And now, may God bless you both. All this happiness is too much for me. Please excuse me while I retire a bit early."

He got up and walked slowly to the door. He turned around, smiled at them, then hurried back to embrace them both.

The day after his graduation, Michael Curran of Dublin became the safety engineer and advanced mining methods director for the valley colliery. Two weeks later he and Gwen Morgan were married, and he began a life that was infinitely more satisfying and complicated than anything he had ever imagined. The cottage, complete with maid, was luxurious compared to anything Michael had ever known in his twenty-five years. His bride seemed to anticipate his every whim and loved him so thoroughly that he quite forgot all about his original plans for emigration to the United States. His duties at the mine paid him well, and there was much to challenge him professionally. Michael also discovered that he was very popular. He drove to work each day with William Morgan amid many hearty greetings. He carried a lunch that would have done justice to the whole crew of Jones Number Seven. He shared most of it. But he often walked home alone because interest in his work absorbed the clock.

Curran learned how to control explosives by charge size and position and by fuze length. In three weeks he could estimate to the half-ton the leavings of any blast. Even Owen stopped bothering him as the production rate climbed and the accident rate dropped. He opened up half a dozen highly productive seams in the next seven months and received permission to conduct safety classes on company time, with compensatory benefits paid to the men attending.

When their daughter Sheila was born, Curran took two weeks off "to get in the way." He was fascinated by his eight-pound delight. Every cry sent him into near panic, and he would wake up to keep his wife company for every feeding. Finally Gwen had enough.

"Mickey, you big puff of a man. This is not your work. I can take care of a little girl while you get some sleep. It's not love you're giving her; it's colic from too much nervousness. And I'm about to find the Welsh equivalent of a shillelagh if that's the only language you will understand."

Seeing the sudden look of hurt and disbelief come over his face, she ran to him and clung to him.

"Forgive me," Gwen said. "Please, sweetheart, please. I'm really so happy you love her that I have no right to complain. At heart, you see me for the fishwife that rests in the soul of every weary new mother. I truly hate myself when I'm like this."

She started to cry. Sniffles at first, but when he put his arms around her she broke down into deep sobs, the deepest he had ever heard. What had he done?

"Oh, Mickey, forgive me," she said finally as she calmed down. "Woman do queer things like this after giving birth to their infants. But not to worry. It's just that having two infants around so much of the time is too much for me today. Why don't you begin work on the article you've been talking about these many months about explosives in the mine, like your thesis, and we'll send it off to a good publisher. You write and I'll copy for you. We'll get it done quicker than you think."

And so peace returned to the Morgan cottage as Michael devoted three surprisingly grueling days of his time off to the hardest work of his life, an article on handling, not explosives, but water in the mine. It was Institute precise and Jones-Number-Seven pungent. It was also Curran optimistic. Of particular relevance was his study of the effect of water pressure at various levels as deep as one thousand feet. Once Michael had his beginning in hand, the words poured from his pen with the ease of good conversation. Gwen came in to leave him food, but he hardly noticed. She left him to his thoughts. At the end of the proposed article he described the diversion channels he had designed and built at the thousand-foot level in the valley mine. He then went to bed and slept for sixteen hours. On the fourth day he revised his draft and read his manuscript to Gwen while she fed a very contented daughter. In two days she had copied it for him.

The mine superintendent was delighted with the article. He went with Curran to Cardiff to the offices of the trade quarterly for Wales. One look at the manuscript, and the editor bought it on the spot. Curran also sent a copy to his professor in Dublin, whence came a request to publish concurrently with the Welsh quarterly. The articles ran in April 1855.

Response was immediate, and it came from around the world, wherever coal was dug. He was soon granting editors permission to print in German, French, and Russian. Two American periodicals also received his permission to print.

The Currans's second child, Julia, was born a year after Sheila. This time he really was needed at home because of the strain of the second delivery. He stayed by his exhausted wife's bedside for four days before she even knew him or her father. At the end of two weeks, however, they were walking the green hills together again.

"Are you disappointed, Mickey?" she asked when they stopped to sit near their picnic area.

"Because I now have two daughters? What kind of a question is that to ask the proudest father in the valley?"

"I know you wanted a son. Most men do, and—"

"Cush, darlin'," he interrupted, "most men make a lot of noise. I'm so relieved you are mending and the little ones are healthy and as beautiful as their mother that there is nothing in me but gratitude."

She smiled a bit thinly.

"You know there probably won't be any more?"

"Aye, the doctor put the possibility to me."

"And?"

"And I love you."

She put her head in his lap and cried. The cries soon turned to sobs and then almost to a keening. He held her while she moaned and shook. After a while she quieted down, the wildness left her eyes, and they walked home across the meadow hand in hand.

The making of Curran's fortune came unexpectedly. It didn't take him five minutes at the thousand-foot level the next morning to realize something was terribly wrong. The entire noise pattern was turned around. He hurried over to the foreman.

"Owen, by any chance have you been sending crews into Fifteen and Sixteen South?"

"Aye, professor, and bringing in record hauls ever since you went home to hold hands with the missus and whatever stray housemaids you could find in your mansions."

"Later, Owen. Look at me report on your board behind you. Those shafts in the southern quadrant are all condemned. I told you and the manager I could hear water running on the other side of the walls. It's roaring out there! For all I know we could be hearing the sea this far down. But good coal or not, we can't risk it. Now call the men in and stop this blasting."

Owen smiled as he held up a note from the office. It was a scribbled congratulations from the superintendent on his record-breaking production for the past week.

"Why don't you go home and write another fancy paper while the real men dig out the coal, Mister Curran of Dublin?"

"As safety director, I'm orderin' you to stop blastin' in those two tunnels right away, Owen."

Owen laughed. "Orderin', is it? Orderin'! There's no orderin' down here except by me. The likes of a stranger like you cut no dust down here, Mick!"

Curran knew he was wasting time. As the staff engineer, he had to go through line channels to get anything done. He would have to go back up the shaft, find the superintendent, present his case all over again, and then pray for sanity to prevail over greed. He feared what the answer would be.

"For once you're right, Owen. But your cheap coal is going to come dear, and we both know it. I'll have another look before digging me way through the channels of management to hang you proper. Who's working fifteen and sixteen?"

Owen looked at his clipboard with mock formality. "Jones Two, Six, and Seven, and about sixty picks, all gettin' rich. Look, you, we have a lively thing going, and no one is going to take kindly to you stoppin' it, or even trying to."

But Curran was already off at a dogtrot for another look at the southern quadrant. He hadn't condemned those shafts lightly, and he felt the air tingle with apprehension as he got closer. From time to time he pressed his best ear against an outside wall or thumped the ceiling with a pick handle. He grew more worried as he approached the blasting area. When he rubbed the sides of the mine his hands came away wet. As soon as he could, he gathered the blasting teams together to explain the danger. They refused to believe him since they had all worked near rushing water and wet walls all their lives.

"Mickey, these are the sounds of prosperity. During the past two weeks we've been takin' home nearly double wages from the thickness of this seam. 'Tis Owen who is right this time, and you know it."

Grunts, noddings, and garbles of approval.

"Jones, my very good friend. I know the coal is good, but the seam is much thinner than you know. And that water isn't burbling on the other side of the wall, it's howling. Put your hands on the wall with mine; you can feel it heaving. The water's strong. So strong it scares the bejesus out of me. It could drown us all in seconds. Now if you won't stop blastin' because you're all getting so rich, at least hold it to half charges for the rest of the day. You'll still get plenty of tonnage and reduce the chance of a breach. If you'll do that for me, I'll be back up to the office to change this madness."

Conference. More grunts, wobbles, and shuffles. The crews prepared to move on as Jones Number Seven turned back to Curran.

"Sorry, Mick. We have our orders, and things oughta stand as they are. That's how it's always been." The crews moved on to the next stope.

Curran stood in the gallery, watching the lights grow dim down the long corridor. He waited for the next blast, dreading, for the first time, the familiar rhythms of the drill crews at their work. He moved only when the squeaking of the rails warned him of the approach of a pony cart coming to haul out the treasure. When the blast came he heard a scream, the lights vanished, and then the flood struck him with its full impact, hurling all before it. It was so strong that Curran felt he had been blasted off his feet again as he concentrated all his strength in spastic attempts to keep his head above the furious current.

He tried to work his legs downstream even as he kept bobbing to the mad surface of the flood. He knew there was always an inch or two of air between the top of the flood and the roof of the tunnel. It was an even gamble, he reflected as he gasped for air, between drowning and bashing in your head. Tumbling antlike at the whim of the current, he derived momentary comfort from the hope that his two steel safety doors were automatically sliding into place near the center of the thousand-foot level, isolating the southern quadrant. He gasped a prayer that his diversion channels would be able to handle this torrent, taming at least part of what seemed, at the moment, untamable. He had never known anything as terrifying and powerful as the angry blackness that flung him about so easily. In spite of his efforts to get his feet forward, the crest tumbled him every which way. He had no concept of up or down and no strength. Miraculously he seemed to bob to the frothing surface often enough to gulp the precious air.

The force of the flooding reminded him of the power of Niagara. At the thought of the world-famous precipice, he began putting his hands out carefully in the hope of catching onto an outcropping of coal or a sturdy piling. He knew that underground rivers had a history of finding the weakest part of a mine; it was sure death for anyone swept down through the hole. Only his ears would be able to save him, but the warning would probably come too late. He had to stop his passage right away.

Even as his ears tried to catch any change in the roar or tempo of the water, and his lungs fought for precious spasms of air, the flood hurled him into a wall where the gallery made a sudden right turn. His hands scraped past timber, and he flung himself backwards to wrap both arms around the sturdiest oak he could ever have wished for. His chest ached, and his arms were already so tired they barely did as he asked of them. But while he clung to the post, he found his strength ebbing rapidly as the river tried to tear him away again. It became a nightmarish struggle as each new wave tore at him with what seemed like personal vindictiveness.

Realizing that the current would win shortly, Curran grasped for the miner's scarf at his throat and knotted it with nearly frozen fingers around the post and his left wrist. The loop allowed him to rest, to bring his breathing down to normal, and to begin thinking himself through the disaster.

But the water battered him like a block of sodden wood, and he lost all sense of time in spite of his efforts to concentrate. In between intermittent spells of fainting, he sensed only essentials: the bruising strength of the river, never abating; the endless fighting for air; the fear that the post would crack; and the life-draining cold of the deep water.

Sometimes a form would brush against him in the angry darkness. He called out but never got back an answer. Were they men or some deep earth creatures never even seen by men? Once he heard a groan, but even as he called out, the groan fell silent and vanished. Once he felt an arm across his back. "Hold on," he gasped, but the arm slid away even as he turned his free, numb hand to help.

Battered, nauseated, too tired to care about air except for the pain of deprivation, his ears suddenly began telling him that a change was taking place. The roar was diminishing. He could breathe without lifting his head, and soon he found that he could actually stand. He could hear the vibration of the pumps somewhere beyond, and he blessed the diversion channels. He braced himself to try to catch any more miners who might come floating past in the waist-high water. In due time he rescued three, who gathered in three others soon enough. But that seemed to end it.

Heavy, matted, sausagelike lumps kept bumping into his legs before turning the corner into the next gallery as he gathered the six around him.

"Leave 'em be, Mickey," said one of the six. "Them's rats. Some of 'em may still have a bite in 'em."

"Jones Seven?" he asked in disbelief.

"Aye."

"How did you manage?"

"The cart, lad, the cart. It wedged into a stope, and we clung to it like flaming barnacles. I've got the crew with me, along with Williams Two and Five."

Heaves and grunts.

"Anyone hurt?" Curran asked.

"Jones's arm is broke from the catching of all of us. The cart weren't as strong as he was," said a voice wearily from the dark.

"We're all goners, Mick, what's the use?" groaned one of the others.

"The use is yourselves. The good Lord has spared us so far, so from here on out I think we can help ourselves. You can feel how the water has gone down. The diversion channels must be doing some good. You can hear the pumps somewhere out there. I suspect the breach is being shored up right now way back behind us. They'll soon be making their way down looking for us. We'll do what we can about our breaks and bruises, and then I propose we head upstream toward the assembly room, gathering anyone we meet along the way."

"Usually we sit tight, Mick, and let the rescue gang get to us. We'll hear them calling soon. There were a couple dozen of us went under."

"Agreed, Jones, except for two things. First, the river swept everything out so fast there's no way of our knowing where we are, or for the rescue workers to estimate where we are. Not only that, I'm sure the river made its own gallery, so there are places to search that no one even knows exist. And second, we're freezin' to death in this black piss, and a stretch of the legs will help get the blood moving."

He assumed the low wheezings were semiconvinced expressions of approval as he reversed the line and headed out of the life-saving bend in the gallery that had suggested to him they were not more than a mile from the assembly room. He knew of only one such bend in the entire south quadrant.

Sloshing slowly back upstream through the gallery, Curran noted that the water had dropped to knee level. Just as the steady progress of the group of survivors and the receding of the water began to bring hope, he bumped full into another wall. Turns to left and right brought only more dead ends. The only bit of encouragement that came with the realization of their entrapment was a piece of board that he salvaged to make a support for Jones's broken arm. The man had yet to utter one word of complaint.

They tried knocking all along the three walls in front and to their sides, hoping for answers, praying for weak places through which they could knock a hole. But the only sounds were their own breathing and the current. The water seemed to be holding steady at just below knee depth, which told him nothing. Faintly he thought he still heard the thudding of the relief pumps.

"Best rest awhile, Mick," said one of the crew. "They'll come; they never quit trying, believe us. Our big worries now are grub and gas. Cave-ins often bring the gas."

They did stop, and Curran tried again to reconstruct the topography of the south quadrant to link probabilities of location in his mind. His original estimate was now very wrong. He had no idea where they were. Perhaps he should have gone downstream as some of the others had suggested. To lead is one thing, to be a pigheaded fool is another. He thought again about the wall that had halted their apparent return to safety. It was sheer and solid, meaning that the conformation of their tomb-to-be had been made by man before this disaster. But if the wall were already made, how did the other miners get in? The same way the water was getting in, he concluded, through a passage near his feet. He returned to the wall and shuffled along its width until he found the source of the flow, a second tunnel at his feet dipping downward.

"The gas and no grub mean we have to keep heading back toward a place where they'll find us. We have to keep moving before we lose the little strength we have and collapse in a feeder gallery like this one that not too many have cause to remember. The water is coming in through a hole right by me feet. If we had a rope I could try swimming through the tunnel that this hole represents, and when I'm safe I could signal you to join me one at a time, like mountain climbers do. Since we have no rope, I'll give it a go both ways and then we can move together in bunches. If I don't come back by the time you count to five hundred, one of you will have to try it. But we can't stay here."

"Mick, I've got a bit of rope," said one of the men from Jones's crew. "One of our bunch always carries it. I've got twenty-five feet of good mine hemp wrapped around me, and you're welcome to it." The man unwound the rope from his ample waist and felt his way along the wall until he could put the cordage into Curran's hand.

Curran quickly set up a series of rope signals with Jones. One pull, let out more rope. Two pulls, all is well. Three pulls, pull the swimmer back in as fast as possible. Four pulls, follow.

Curran tied one end around his middle and put the other into Jones's good hand. He dropped to his knees to feel into the hole and then slipped headfirst into the river. As he had expected, the hole was bigger than it looked. How else could they all have passed through the opening earlier without breaking their heads? After a short drop he found himself at a new level. Air again permitted him to breathe against the roof of the stepped-down passageway. The current was far stronger in the narrow tunnel than in the gallery just departed. When he came to the end of the rope he found that he could just stand in the tunnel with water around his neck. He gave the rope four strong yanks.

The wheezing and sputtering were the music of the spheres to him a few minutes later.

"Right cozy, Mick. Where are we now?" asked a gasping baritone from the swirling black near him.

"Haven't the foggiest; but we're going to move forward twenty-five feet at a time until we're out of here. I don't think you have to be afraid of the gas while the water is this high. Just stay together and keep alert for my signals."

In three more stages Michael Curran brought his six miners into a great echoing chamber. Instinctively he made them all stay flat against the wall as they emerged into the great void where the water, once again, only reached up to their ankles.

"Jones," asked Curran listening intently to the odd echoes that elaborated each simple sentence, "what do you know of a great emptiness smack-dab in the middle of the whole mine?"

"Only rumor, Mick, but I'd almost rather be dead than in the Great Vault. The story's been around as long as I have about a great cavern that will someday swallow up the whole mine. They say there's no bottom to it, but who's to know, since no one has ever come back who's seen it. But everyone knows about it just the same—like heaven and hell."

"That's what I thought. The echoes are a bit bothersome. I think we're on the ledge of just such a pit, so stay close to the wall. At least now we know what happened to most of the water. When it ran into this place it just fell away to join another, deeper source. Some of it ran along where we're standing in a sort of natural viaduct. All we have to do is follow the water back. Be real sure of every step you take. Don't trust your weight to anything until you've tested it. Here, someone pass me a piece of coal."

When a piece the size of a cricket ball finally reached him, he edged his way gingerly to the rim of the shallow viaduct and pitched the coal into the void. He counted the seconds until the faintest of splashes reached their ears.

"Oh, my God," said several as one.

"It must be a wee bit over two hundred feet," said Curran slowly in the overwhelming silence. "Well, if it can save the mine, it can save us. There's no gas here; it's all down in the hole. The river's path must have broken through walls already weakened by the explosions and eventually come crashing out through here. Which means we've been heading in the right direction and we're going to keep on doing so. Hang onto the man in front of you and follow me. We're going to inch along this rim until we find how the water got into this place, and we're going to follow the stream home. Here, I've got an idea. I'll tie us all together with the rope in case there are any shaky places."

As he passed the rope back he heard Jones calling up to him weakly. "Lad, here we are, blind as bats, and you're leading us around as if you had a private lantern. Careful, now, it's no good getting too comfortable in a mine."

"Aye, lad, aye," echoed the others.

"Good advice, Number Seven. I'm getting light-headed from carrying so much fear around. But I will promise you one thing. No one from this gang is going to die today. So just keep together and follow me. And hang onto this wall as if it were the great mother tit of salvation itself."

They were out of the cavern in less than half an hour. Two hours later they heard a search party on the other side of a passage wall. Hearty blows from many willing picks demolished the thin wall between them. The thin rays of the rescue party's lanterns seemed brighter than any sunrise any of the rescued had ever enjoyed.

The news was appalling. Of 116 miners trapped by the water only 19 were rescued. Twelve pony-cart boys were drowned, along with William Morgan inspecting his most neglected line on a disastrous day. Most of the other bodies were never found.

Curran discovered that he was famous. His diversion channels and steel safety doors had saved most of the mine, and his own exploits made good tabloid churning. London and Cardiff papers, as well as Reuters, wanted interviews. He gave them short shrift upon learning of his father-in-law's death. Gwen was waiting for him at the shaft head; she clung to him so fiercely he was breathless from the strength of her.

She had no words as she hugged him, aching for him and yet agonizing in the pain she knew he carried. But her tears were short lived as she supervised the distribution of the dry clothes and blankets and steaming hot soup she had organized for all the survivors.

"Da?" he finally asked her.

Woodenly she led him to the few blanket-wrapped bodies that had been recovered.

"He had two of the little lads in his arms when they found him. He was trying to keep them afloat. Some job for a man fifty-four years old who couldn't swim a stroke. I'm numb, Mickey. I can't believe I'm holding you. I can't believe Da's gone. I can't believe all those good men and poor little boys are gone. Let's go home."

"Aye. Only two questions, please. What's the time and what day is this?"

And that's how Michael Curran learned he had been fighting the water for two and a half days. He was asleep before the cart reached the cottage, and he slept the clock around twice.

Families buried their dead with Welsh stolidity and mine-town forbearance. There had been worse mine disasters and there would be others. Since most of the victims were to be buried in the same graveyard, a traditional single service for most was agreed to. William Morgan was buried next to the gentle wife he had mourned for eleven years. The singing in the six-hundred-year-old church flooded Curran's eyes with unashamed tears, even as Gwen sat dry-eyed beside him. He put his hand on hers when they read off the names of the dead, and she squeezed his fingers so hard that his arm went numb. The two girls cried when he cried, knowing, but not understanding, that "Granda" was not to be with them ever again.

The mine was cleared and ready for work in two days, but Michael stayed home for a week. During that time he was able to read the disaster report from the superintendent wherein his diversion channels and safety doors were given full credit for saving the entire thousand-foot level. The superintendent attached a small note: "Sorry about William Morgan." He crushed the note into his wastebasket but filed the report in his desk. During the next few days he had plenty of time for reporters who gave full attention to his theories on deep-mine safety after the superintendent's report became known. He found himself a celebrity, thanks to the number of miners saved, his own heroism, and the originality of his thinking.

But even as fame swirled around him to deaden the void of William Morgan's death, and the deaths of all those swept away by ignorance and greed, he realized he had one vital act to complete. He slipped off to the mine after a week of recuperation and descended to the thousand-foot level. Those who knew him sensed the reason for his early return and went about their business without comment. He heard the heavy, grating voice even as the car doors clattered open. As Curran walked into the lantern light, the big foreman nodded as if he were expecting him.

"So you're a big hero, Mr. Curran. A big, internationally famous engineer. Why don't you go back topside and autograph hankies while the men and I earn our bread in peace?"

"Here or upstairs after work, Owen?" he answered.

"You're a fool, man. I can take care of you after you've had your rest."

"Then let's do it here, Owen. Look to yourself."

The fight nearly ended before it began. As the two men circled each other, Curran made a dangerous discovery. The expected spring in his legs was gone, lost in the swirling icy currents of last week. He should have waited a bit, he thought to himself even as Owen's first blow crashed heavily against the side of his skull and sent him reeling backwards to the floor. It was a solid enough blow to end any fight. He was paralyzed, and everything blurred. Again it was his ears that focused for him. The roar he heard was the great bellow of triumph from Owen as he walked over to crush Curran's face with his boot heel in the best tradition of mine fighting.

He tried to hold an arm up in front of his face and then suddenly rolled to one side. The kick missed by just over an inch, and pain shot up Owen's leg as he encountered flooring instead of Curran's face. Curran managed to get to his feet while Owen shook off the pain. As he turned toward Owen, the engineer tried a kick of his own, catching Owen just behind his right elbow and numbing it. Curran followed up with a series of well-timed punches to the defenseless right side that fazed Owen not in the slightest. It was like hitting a well-packed sack of sand. Curran decided he would never win trading punches.

But as Curran's head began clearing, he made two other discoveries. The spring was beginning to return to his legs, and the reason that the foreman had always looked a bit odd to him became evident. His arms were a shade too short for his torso. Now Curran's strategy was simple: keep out of Owen's range and wear him down, the old game of the left jab. A big man like Owen was probably used to many

fights that ended with one punch after a short discussion, but a long
contest would probably prove that the man had no wind. Well, Curran
thought as he planted two stiff jabs to the side of Owen's neck and
jowl, there's probably not an Irishman in the world who doesn't know
how to jab and circle. He also knew he had to make Owen so mad
that the foreman would lose the good street sense he seemed to have
for such encounters.

"A hundred men, Owen, and a dozen of the cart boys. What will
you bet there were more? And for every man and boy there's someone like me who's going to make you pay. You'll never be free of us.
Never. So pay, you black bastard, pay!" he grunted as he landed lefts
and rights to the well-padded kidneys and ducked a surprisingly swift
roundhouse swing that nearly ended the fight again. As Owen spun
around from the missed punch, Curran leveled another mighty kick
into Owen's rump, nearly fracturing the Irishman's foot and bringing
hoots of laughter from the rapidly growing crowd of spectators.

"Get back to work," Owen shouted into the faceless mob gathering around them. As he took his eyes off his opponent, Curran flashed
a right hook over Owen's shoulder and caught the foreman full in the
mouth. To his credit, the foreman swung back, catching Curran in the
heart and backing him off. And so it went for twenty minutes, the men
trading blows equally, feinting, striking, circling, retreating, ducking.
Once Owen charged Curran, hoping to get both arms around him. It
would have been a fatal bear hug. But Curran slipped on the wet floor
and was able to roll away. As he bounced up he planted another kick.
More laughter.

Owen's swings were getting wilder: still lethal but no longer savage. Curran could hear the wheezing deep in Owen's chest, and his
eyes seemed to be getting tired. The man must be twenty years my
senior, thought Curran, he can't go on like this much longer. A sudden kick to the groin caught Curran unexpectedly and dropped him
to one knee in breath-sucking pain. He sensed Owen's rush and pushed
up from the floor with all his strength to catch the foreman in the stomach
with his head. They went down together. Curran found he could clamp
both hands around Owen's throat, which he did until the older man
gasped. He was tempted to hold on until Owen fainted.

"No, Mick, no," boomed a voice from the ring of the unseen. He
let go of Owen, rolled away, and got back up to his feet. As Owen
struggled to his knees and then into a crouch, Curran got off a solid

kick into his ribs, bringing a gasp of pain. Curran backed away and returned to his basic plan of circling and jabbing.

Although he suspected that Owen was hurt, Curran found he had enough troubles just keeping himself from falling over. If he went down again he knew he'd just have to lie there and let happen whatever came. Had he paid attention to the subtle changes in Owen, he might have planned his next move differently. He knew that an injured animal does things a healthy beast wouldn't. As he stepped in for a solid pounding to Owen's ribs, Curran just barely caught sight of the pick handle as it arced down on him. He had only time enough to duck his chin in behind his shoulder when the flat of the rough handle snaked over his guard and exploded against the side of his head. Curran went down again, this time in a pool of his own vomit. On his hands and knees, struggling to keep his senses, he waited for the second blow, the one that would kill him or cripple him for life. He only had time to curse himself for the ridiculous pride that had made him confront Owen in the name of all the dead miners. Nothing could bring William Morgan back to life, especially the split skull of Black Owen.

The second blow seemed uncommonly long in coming. As Curran gasped for air while his head slowly cleared he was aware of a dull cry of pain from his adversary as a hefty shard of slate skimmed in from the ring, thudding against the back of his neck.

"Drop it, Owen," commanded the darkness.

"Drop it, Owen!" echoed the chamber.

Blood covered the hand Owen clasped to the back of his head, but he dropped the pickax handle.

Curran found the unexpected strength to get back to his feet and meet the grim-faced opponent whose guard seemed just a shade lower. This had best be ended soon, Curran thought as he followed his life-saving jab with a solid swing to the stomach, producing a sudden deep groan. He swung again and again. Breaths were now rasps of agony for the Welshman. Curran gave him no peace. He rained body blows, avoiding the head shots that could break his knuckles. He knew some of his punches could be heard in the farthest corner of the assembly room.

Almost as if in a dream, Owen's heavy hands sagged to his sides. His eyes seemed to glaze as he coughed up a throatful of blood. He stumbled awkwardly to his knees mumbling, "Enough, enough," and rolled over onto his aching side.

A cheer broke out from the crowd.

"Fair and square, Mick!" He saw waves of excited faces, heard cheering voices and, quickly, felt helpful hands. But that was all he remembered until he woke up hours later in his own bedroom, a mass of bandages, thinking he must be black and blue from head to toe. He sensed that Gwen was by his bed.

"Cush," he tried softly through puffed lips.

"Oh, Mickey," she answered softly, exasperation creeping into her voice in spite of sympathy for his bruised body. "You foolish man. I can't bear to think that I've nearly lost you twice in ten days. And for what? They're all still dead. Da can't come back if you pummel a thousand Owens. My sweet fool, we love you, but no more of this madness. If you'll stop groaning for a minute, I'll call the girls. They're sure that you're dying."

"Am I?"

"No, sweetheart, you're a tough one for sure."

"Owen?" he ventured.

"His spleen ruptured. He'll be in the hospital a long time. You're a hero to the men, not just for your channels, but for their freedom from a petty tyrant. But I like my heroes home and free from suffering."

She opened the doors for the girls. The moment he heard the first soft, slightly hesitant "Daddy?" he started to cry. He knew he had soaked through all his bandages by the time he had been able to surround the girls with his arms. They were kissing his cheeks very gently as he fell into the deep sleep that was his best medicine.

Two months later Michael Curran accepted an offer to become a partner with a mining consulting firm in Philadelphia, America. "The pay is high and the mines shallow," he told Gwen. "Soon all the ships and factories in the world will be burning coal, not just the railroads. We'll have to build another house just to hold the money."

It was raining, but the hills never seemed greener than on the gray day they bid Wales good-bye.

CHAPTER 4

Petersburg III: The Attack

The Union artillery, silent since sundown, opened fire again at midnight. The long-barreled cannon were fired every five minutes. At four in the morning the stubbier field howitzers joined them at three-minute intervals. With the entire attack front covering less than half a mile, the effect of the concentrated cannonade was awesome. Over a hundred guns inched explosives up the hill, across the trenches, and into the reserve trenches and supply pockets of the Petersburg defenders. Then they inched back again. It was probably the most thorough preattack barrage of the Civil War.

At 3:30 A.M. the engineering platoon moved up to the front lines to remove the Union abatis. The constant fury of the barrage muted the bites of the axes and the crashings of the mauls. Black labor troops carried the heavy timbers and branches to the rear and helped shovel down the parapets to expedite the charge.

With the false dawn, the Confederate artillery responded for the first time. Shells with surprisingly low trajectories screamed into the crowded parapets or arced accurately into the overly concentrated batteries of the North. Not a shot was wasted. A few remembered, as they hugged the wet earth, what Lieutenant Curran had said about the well-protected enemy artillery. In the lurching of the earth, the term took on vicious significance.

Since midnight Colonel Zaretski had been walking the entire line, talking to as many men as he could, checking map positions and assignments with every officer, sharing a few cups of steaming tea.

"You'll be walking in like teatime, Colonel," Major Harrington offered brightly after the tour, just before dawn when all the guns made an answer impossible by flashing at a staggered two-minute pace.

Colonel Zaretski took off his sword and picked up the musket he preferred when there was real work ahead. The artillery officer saluted and turned back to his command post.

"Beautiful," growled Sergeant Wendermuth out of the side of his mouth to Corporal Bielecki as the first hint of dawn revealed the havoc wrought by the concentrated barrage. "If nobody breaks a leg stumblin' into those half million holes out there we may make it to the hill yet. Hope that crazy lieutenant remembers to bring Jones's wig-wags."

A whistle pierced the air.

"Let's go!" shouted Sergeant Wendermuth. He sprang up the ladder, running easily in zigzag strides toward the Petersburg mound. The new men shouted a variety of inanities to assure each other that they were still alive and followed. The veterans saved their wind for running.

The enemy artillery returned to life vigorously. In spite of Sergeant Wendermuth's skepticism, the shell holes offered invaluable cover against the scorching accuracy of the Whitworths. Moving rapidly, the soldiers advanced easily from hole to hole across the field. Nonetheless, the compact target of a thousand men crossing the narrow front gave the Confederate gunners an eagerly awaited advantage.

Colonel Zaretski, taking a final look through his telescope before following his men into the charge, noted that the Union artillery had successfully blown apart the first Confederate breastworks in dozens of places during the night. He doubted the possibility that many were still alive in those trenches at the top of the hill after such a bombardment. He noted that the new men were charging well and moved after them with the first feelings of optimism he had permitted himself to entertain since midnight.

Bunko Terry dogged the steps of Sergeant Wendermuth. Corporal Bielecki had disappeared. Bunko ran forward a few steps, threw himself to the ground, imagined a target in the line ahead, fired, rolled to his right, lay on his back to reload, then jumped up to go a few yards before once again hurling himself into the safe embrace of the tortured earth. At the bottom of the hill he passed Lieutenant Curran who was furiously waving the bright red flags that had finally raised the protecting fire of the Union artillery up to the top of the mound. From the time the troops reached the bottom of the hill the search for cover ended. Now speed up the hill was the only thing. He was grateful for one thing: he was now protected from the Whitworths.

Musket fire was negligible. Bunko had stopped firing until he could find better targets. The holes ripped by the Union artillery gaped above him, far bigger than he had realized. But halfway up the steepest part of the hillside, gray hats started popping up in the line above him. Blue uniforms began crumpling around him as he climbed. Some men screamed as they fell, some cursed, some sat down silently and rolled in awkward pinwheels back down the slope. Some pitched forward and tried to rise again. It wasn't until later that Bunko even remembered any of it. He kept climbing.

He was into the front trench before he realized it. He fired into one of the perspiring faces in front of him and then leaped in after his shot to swing the stock of his musket full into the chest of a ferret-quick sergeant who had come running at him with a bayonet. Without bothering to wonder where the other blue uniforms were, he set about flailing with the musket, hoping no one would be able to get a shot at him in the narrow trench before help followed.

Bones cracked and skulls splintered, but still he stayed on his feet until he heard familiar voices as the waves of blue spilled into the trench all around him. The Confederates broke, leaping over the rear of the trench or scurrying down shallow communications trenches to a secondary line of defense deeper on the plateau. At his feet lay a boy about his own age in a ragged gray uniform. The boy had lost his face but could still cry. As Bunko stared helplessly at the suffering of his enemy, Sergeant Wendermuth dropped into the trench and shot the dying defender. Lieutenant Curran stood on top of the trench and signalled the artillery to lift its fire another hundred yards onto the plateau. The lieutenant then loped on as the covering fire quickly responded to the flags. The trench was now swollen with dozens of blues, with hundreds following rapidly behind them. It gave Bunko a false sense of security, which Sergeant Wendermuth promptly dispelled.

"Can't stop," gasped Sergeant Wendermuth. "Even that blathery lieutenant knows that. Load as you run and keep shootin'. Follow me."

Although it was actually impossible to hear the lanky sergeant because of the exploding covering fire, his meaning was clear enough. The trench emptied again, filled again, and emptied once more in wavelike repetition as the regiment collected its second wind and followed Sergeant Wendermuth in pursuit of the early victory of Petersburg Heights. Amazed at the large number of his men who had made it to the top of the hill,

Colonel Zaretski sent his messenger leaping back across the battlefield to signal the cavalry to exploit the rent in the Confederate lines.
But even as the messenger began waving his signals for the horsemen,
the glorious adventure slowed to a painful halt.

The Whitworths were buried so that their long muzzles faced the
attacking Union troops at knee height. The commander of the battery
waited for the forward trenches to empty of gray uniforms so that the
plateau was thickly covered with bunched-up Union soldiers all in the
open. They then opened rapid fire, first with high explosives and solid
shot, then grape and canister. The breech-loaded Whitworths, when manned
by a well-trained crew, could spew out death at a rate of three rounds
to the minute. As he threw himself onto the ground, Lieutenant Curran
estimated that at least a dozen Whitworths must be firing into the
Pennsylvanians. The cannonade was so intense and the range so short
that the flat-trajectory shells didn't even have time to shriek as they
had in the night. As the range closed, the thunder of the guns combined with the shrieks of the wounded as thousands of pieces of grapeshot
and canister tore into the Union ranks at point-blank range. The two
perfectly placed batteries were able to command the entire plateau. The
ground offered scant cover as the shattering barrage ripped entire
companies to pieces in seconds. To compound the confusion, strate-
gically placed Confederate fire centers caught the attackers with musket
fire from the flanks. Every Confederate shot found a target. Completely
immune to the haphazard Union artillery fire, which could no longer
be directed, the rapid-firing Whitworths splattered bloody Union corpses
across the plateau like broken branches.

"Back, everybody back to the first trench!" shouted Colonel Zaretski.
"Back, everyone back!"

It was a useless command. No one could hear. Those without enough
sense to recognize the situation were already dead. The remainder of
the men were soon catapulted into full retreat. The day was saved from
total disaster only by Lieutenant Curran, who was able to crawl back
to the edge of the plateau to signal the Union fire down upon the regiment's
most advanced position, providing some protection through which a
few of the surviving companies were able to stumble back down the
hill to their original lines.

Not until the Union covering fire let up with the arrival of the shattered
survivors did Lieutenant Curran realize that blood was oozing from
at least a dozen small wounds and that his legs wouldn't respond. He

fell into a shell hole at the edge of the plateau, the red flags flutter-ing to rest over him. Sergeant Wendermuth helped a concussion-stunned Colonel Zaretski back to his command post. Bunko Terry, his scalp creased by a sniper's slight miscalculation, lay on the plateau in a shallow communications trench that had saved him from the Whitworths and his own supporting fire as well. He and Lieutenant Curran were 2 of the 118 prisoners taken that morning, and a part of the 323 casualties suffered by the regiment in the forty-three-minute assault that had netted not a single foot of ground.

CHAPTER 5

Bunko Terry

The audience was enjoying itself. The Confederate officer who kept tripping over his sword and swaggering into the sides of the barn and nearly bucketing himself into the well was a howling success. It was difficult for the audience to make the transition from him to the whimsical grandmother and then to the bumbling streetcar conductor in successive sketches, knowing that it was the same actor, their own blacksmith's son, Bunko Terry. At the age of seventeen, in the first year of the Civil War, Bunko Terry made the Monongamesh High School "drama gala" one to remember for a lifetime for all in the audience.

In his own eyes, it was Bunko's sole accomplishment in seventeen years. He never seemed to understand that his love for living and a talent as natural as breath made him welcome wherever he found himself. His love for small things such as time, energy, dreams, and the beauty of any day seemed particularly uneventful to him as the war progressed and he stayed home in western Pennsylvania.

His mother had been a gentle woman who devoted a lifetime that was short even by frontier standards to her blacksmith husband and her ever-cheerful son. In them she found the strength to endure without a single comment the malignancy that finally consumed her when Bunko was almost fourteen.

Bunko's father, former artillery sergeant Sean Terry, had handled a small battery of field pieces in Monongamesh's battle against Kills-the-Hawk. Pittsburgh-based Sergeant Terry had fallen in love with the Monongamesh Valley and had moved there after the campaign, when Bunko was barely nine. He had enjoyed beating swords into ploughshares as the village blacksmith. He found satisfaction in every day that allowed him to be his own man. People had just about forgotten what a professional fighting man he had been until the raiders whooped into Monongamesh one afternoon in the summer of 1858.

The raiders were only half a dozen men, but they carried good weapons and understood about protecting flanks and rear. They came peacefully, extolling the virtues of abolition, and demanding food, liquor, and "donations" to carry out John Brown's work. This work was a "God-directed" mission to arouse the countryside to the evils of slavery and the glories of honest wrath.

The sheriff was away delivering a prisoner to the county seat. He wasn't expected back for two days. There was no deputy. Mayor Zaretski was in Harrisburg on business. The town ran itself well enough, but no one had predicted this kind of emergency.

There seemed no harm in a little saloon boasting until the "donations" ceased being voluntary in spirit, if not in actuality. One by one the raiders visited the merchants, taking what they needed for the cause. They were so quick and efficient about their plundering that no one dared oppose them. The streets emptied, but storekeepers who attempted to close their doors soon found bullets cracking through them, and glass windows fared worse.

Bunko, who had watched everything from a hitching rail near the edge of town, ran to tell his father in the blacksmith shop, which was a quarter mile from the town. Former sergeant Sean Terry asked only two questions: how many and how drunk? Sergeant Terry took his shotgun from the wall and a box of shells from a kitchen drawer and then walked toward town to see the situation for himself. Were they handgun users or riflemen, he wondered. A quick reconnaissance from a rooftop showed him the major errors in the raiders' plans. First, they had wandered too far from their horses, and second, they had started to drink up their profits.

Looking behind him on the rooftop, Sean Terry saw Bunko, aged thirteen, climbing up to join him. Recognizing reinforcements rather than disobedience, Sergeant Terry dispatched his nimble son to the far end of the street to steal the horses.

Sean Terry waited a few minutes and then climbed down to the street to wait in the shadows for the first raider to notice a boy making off with their mounts. When that anxious raider came running around the corner shouting and waving his pistols and nearly tripping over his roweled spurs, Sean Terry stepped into his path and rendered him unconscious with the stock of his shotgun. Some men of the town, recognizing that a plan of help was afoot, dragged the unconscious raider into a deserted shop, took his guns, and tied him securely. The blacksmith then asked one of the less awestruck young men in the group to put on the raider's hat, hold a pistol in his hand, and whistle anxiously toward the second raider standing guard in front of the grocery store. When the second gunman replied on the run to the whistle and wave, he turned the corner to find himself looking directly into half a dozen shotgun barrels. He dropped his revolver and was soon as helpless as his companion.

"We've got to get into the store before the other four get the wind up," said Sean Terry to an informal council of war. "But I don't know how to get into the store with the one weapon that can handle a quick-draw bunch like that, my shotgun!"

In the long silence that followed the description of the situation and the possible solution, the popping of the umbrella from the display barrel was explosive. Sergeant Terry whirled around to see his son collapsing a large sun parasol popular with Monongamesh women. He then watched catatonically as Bunko slid the chunky barrel of the old army shotgun into the umbrella folds. The stock and trigger housing of the gun vanished behind the handle when held the way Bunko had chosen to hold the folded umbrella. There were little gasps from the circle of men. Sean Terry smiled.

"Dad, if you can wait a minute, I'll find a dress and a wig to get into this place. Then we can drive up to where those gunmen are as if we knew nothing about them. We can walk right in, with me carrying the shotgun for you in the parasol. When you want it, I'll hand it to you. When you shoot, all these men can rush the store."

"It's a grand idea, lad. But I'll not risk my thirteen-year-old's hide for such odds. If anything should happen to you because of this foolishness . . ."

But Bunko was already picking out a long gingham gown from a rack.

"Dad, no one is going to shoot an old lady carrying an umbrella. You'd better be sure to strap on one of these six-shooters so they can take it away from you and feel good."

Sergeant Terry held his peace. In a few minutes Bunko had turned into a sweet but doddering old lady, complete with spectacles, wig, and a hat with flowers in a cracked brim. The men had hitched up a farm wagon behind the store, and Bunko headed for it, followed by a very reluctant father. Signals for charging the main store were agreed to as Sergeant Terry at last climbed onto the narrow bench seat next to his son.

It was a resigned Sergeant Terry who whipped up the horses and ran them around the dusty back streets of Monongamesh. When he and Bunko pulled up in front of the grocery emporium in the center of the main street, the team and wagon looked dusty and tired. With great patience, the big man helped the fragile old lady down from the seat. She seemed tired and clasped her old parasol tightly to one side. Their conversation ended abruptly as they found themselves looking into four guns and what had become angry, rather than domineering, faces.

"Over there against the wall, Hayseed, and take your granny with you. First let me relieve you of that iron around your gut to keep down the stupidity. You wouldn't want to be stupid, Hayseed, would you? Right nice of you to bring us such a good-looking wagon for your contributions. If those two dung bellies don't get back here with the horses in a few minutes, we'll just pile our goods and services in the wagon and move out without 'em."

Sean Terry let the gun be yanked out of an ancient holster, and then he shuffled along with the old woman to the rear of the store, where he found eleven other hostages standing and sitting, not quite able to believe what was happening. One of the four Kansans evidently had the chore of guarding the hopeless bunch, a task he found boring and wasteful. The store was semidark to give the raiders the best possible view out. The street was still deserted. The hostages were silent. Just as well, thought Sean Terry as he placed himself so that he was next to the parasol arm of the old lady. He was amazed how well the stock of the shotgun blended with the clumsy wooden handle of the old parasol in the growing dark of the late afternoon. Bunko knew that the right combination of bunching up by the raiders, diverted eyes, and a clear field of fire were essential. He shuffled out into the middle of the floor, between the hostages and the bandits.

"Say, young man," began Bunko to the gunman who was supposed to be watching the hostages. "Why don't you and your friends get sensible and get out of here. I saw all your horses tied up around the corner when we was comin' into town. Besides, I gotta use the toilet something awful, and all this standing around don't help my bladder none."

The gunman howled with laughter and called his friends over to join him in the center of the room with the old woman.

"Old lady has to pee real bad," he coughed out between spasms of laughter. "She can speak to the yahoos slinking around out there for us, and we can get the hell outta here. She says the horses are tied up around the corner with Joe and Charlie."

"I think I wanta see 'em first, there's something—" began the leader of the raiders when Bunko cut him short.

"Now, Dad, now!" shouted Bunko, dropping flat to the floor and clamping his arms around his head.

Sergeant Terry knew it was the exact opportunity and fired as high as he dared even as his son's slender body hit the planking. At twelve feet the effect of the shotgun blast into the group of four was devastating. The nearest gunman was lifted off his feet and smashed up against the counter, where he died a few seconds later. A second screamed and staggered backwards, his hands around the lacerated belly that began spilling his intestines out between his numbed fingers. He sat down, paralyzed. The third, blinded by a savage head wound, pitched forward, drawing and firing even as he fell. He shattered the window and lay still on the floor. The leader of the raiders, however, standing on the periphery of the four, caught only the edge of the pattern of pellets. He shifted his gun from his bleeding left hand to his untouched right in an easy border shuffle and whirled to the sound of the explosion. Sean Terry's second shot hurled the leader straight backwards until he crashed through the front window, across the porch, and into the street. He never moved after he fell into the dust.

Sean Terry leaped to his son's side as other hostages kicked the guns away from the dead and dying thieves.

"Bunko, Bunko," he called fiercely, fearing the inevitable even as he knelt at his son's side.

"Dad, is that you?" asked the small voice from the floor. "I think I've gone deaf."

"It'll pass, son; it'll pass. That's an almighty noisy shotgun, and the concussion passed right over you."

Bunko heard only odd sounds as his ears refused to unplug. He suspected his father was explaining in the logical way he always did about things that hurt or bothered him. He thought he ought to say something to relieve his concerned father.

"Well, it was a good plan, anyway, Dad."

"No, son, it was terrible. We nearly paid much too high a price for the privilege of clearing out vermin. I don't know how I let you talk me into shooting so close to you. If your mother was here . . ."

Bunko felt his father's huge hand gently massage his shoulder muscles. His neck felt a little wet. Was his father crying? The floor shook suddenly and he looked over to see his father's inert body lying next to him. A closer look at the blood oozing through the back of the thin dress had proved too much for the hero of the shoot-out at the Monongamesh Emporium.

In later years, Bunko remembered the feel of his father's unconscious body sprawled next to him more than all the other vivid impressions of that violent afternoon. Sometimes he took time to wonder why he couldn't remember the force of the two explosions or the shrieks of the wounded and dying gunmen or the whimpering of the gunman who watched his life spilling out through his shredded innards or the ugly brittleness of the breaking glass or the sobs of the terrified hostages. These all faded as his eardrums cleared and the clatter of his father fainting dramatized the agony of the strongest man in the valley.

But recovery was sweet, and the two found the already-warm bond between them strengthened by deep mutual respect for their respective roles in the victory over the raiders. The citizens of Monongamesh regarded them with benevolent awe, and life grew pleasant for the blacksmith and his family.

Mrs. Terry died five months later, shortly before Bunko's fourteenth birthday. Bunko's hero-filled eyes were all that kept the blacksmith from turning the heavy gun on himself.

Sean and Bunko Terry had hoped the funeral would be simple and quiet. It was, but nearly everyone in Monongamesh came to the cemetery to stand silently with the two gentle strangers who had brought so much happiness and good sense to the valley in the seven years since the Kills-the-Hawk campaign.

"Dad, they loved her too," whispered Bunko to his father as he watched the restrained compassion of the hundreds who had come to the grave. It was so different from what the two had imagined might happen. There were no blubberings from semiprofessional mourners and no gentle shoulder squeezings from men who had hardly been able to pass the time of day with either of them before. The men and women of the valley made no sounds to confound the graceful benediction of the circuit preacher. Mary Elizabeth McAuley, representing Bunko's class, laid flowers by the grave. He smiled to let her know that he recognized the placing of the flowers to be the hardest assignment of her scholastic life. She really understands us, Bunko thought as their eyes met.

The blacksmith grieved for his wife for eleven days, hardly knowing what Bunko put before him at the table, unwilling to kindle his
forge, unable to talk to friends, walking the hills alone at all hours,
in all weather. One afternoon he came back from such a walk to find
Bunko struggling with flour, eggs, and milk in a disastrous mess. His
eyes asked why, and Bunko answered in his usual straightforward,
uncomplicated way.

"I'm fourteen tomorrow, and I'm trying to bake a cake for us and
maybe a few others. Sorry you came back so soon; it was going to be
a surprise for you."

The blacksmith looked at his son in bewilderment. Did a self-
pitying man deserve such a youngster? It was the boy's birthday,
and all he thought of doing was surprising his father. He looked
over the disorganized kitchen and the excited eyes looking hopefully
up to him.

"Do it, lad; do it! And I'll be back in two licks to share the fortunes of a willful oven with you."

The blacksmith ran from the house like Prometheus unbound. He
ordered the butcher to slaughter two steers and to begin roasting them
on the village spit as soon as the heat was out of the carcasses. He
shook up the baker and ordered cakes for five hundred people. He even
found a fiddler. He then returned home, gathered up his son, and began
knocking on the doors of all the homes in Monongamesh. All were
invited to a feast on the morrow at the village green to celebrate Bunko's
fourteenth birthday. In the process he remembered to order all the punch
the grocer could make. In each instance, as he plunked the cash on
the counter of the shop, it was gently pushed back to him.

Sean was amazed at the crowd. It was a glorious party. There were
games for the youngsters, competitions in strength and marksmanship
for the men, recitations and singing for the women. Then the fiddler
moved up, and the village caller soon had graceful circles and lively
squares bobbing happily across the green.

Wise heads arranged to have pies and breads and jams and gallons
of tea and lemonade added to the bowls and buckets of punch. Somehow there was enough meat and drink for everyone, and everything
seemed to happen so fast that there was only time to enjoy it all.

As the sun started to settle in behind the hills at the end of a long
afternoon, a still-exuberant Sean Terry stood up on a table amid the
applause of the valley. He spread his huge hands wide in a broad plea
for quiet.

"Good friends," he began. More applause. "I say good friends all. I am standing on a table making a big fool of myself because I want to make a very short speech, and I have no idea what I am going to say. But first, I want to thank you all for being with Bunko and me this afternoon. Can you believe I nearly drowned in my own tears before I realized that my clever son had somehow managed to sneak up to his fourteenth year? This means he is big enough to carry a musket, or maybe a shotgun [more applause] with the men of the town. He can handle a bucket in the fire brigade. Bunko's mother, not too well known to many of you, would have been ashamed of me.

"What Bunko's birthday means to me is the same thing that all these young people mean to all of us. The important thing about this valley is the future we offer to them. Not give them, offer to them. When I look at my growing son and think of my lost wife, I realize that we have all lost, and the lucky ones are those who can still hope. But I was selfish and forgot this until I came home yesterday and found my son covered with flour and eggs, trying to make a birthday cake for himself.

"From now on, our sorrows shall be private and our joys shall be shared. Thank you for sharing our joy today. Getting to be fourteen in spite of plague, hunger, flood, Indians, renegades, multiplication tables, conjugations, and the tyranny of the forge is feat enough for anyone.

"So, what I'm trying to say in this short speech that suddenly turned into a sermon is that we should remember this bright June day of 1858 as a quiet oasis in the middle of troubled times that may yet take us all. We have to remember that the hope of the future is more important than the pain of the past, and that there is high promise for anyone blessed with the good friends Bunko and I share today.

"That's it!"

Cheers filled the air above the village green. Bunko was embarrassed. But that day, the school play, and Mary Elizabeth McAuley watching him from under a bonnet that kept bouncing off were memories that never dimmed throughout the remainder of his life.

War came to Monongamesh three years later. Although the valley was never to know the shaking of thousands of marching men or suffer the searing concussion of artillery, the families of Monongamesh soon enough knew the agonies of waiting for the weekly casualty lists. There were calls for volunteers, which were answered briskly enough, and calls for hospital linen and calls for provisioners, and soon there were shortages of soap and gunpowder for hunting and sewing thread. Some of the more enterprising even found prosperity. Sean Terry brought home a small contract for nails and railway bolts from Harrisburg.

One evening Sean called his son to the smithy to show him a new railway bolt. It was strong for the size, a very clean design. His father observed to Bunko that the youngster held the key to the war's most lethal weapon in his hand. Did Bunko notice anything different about the bolt?

"Sure, Dad. It's got a left-hand thread," he said finally.

Sergeant Terry smiled warmly and nodded. "It's our secret, Bunko—and our fortune. I won the contract because it took an old artilleryman to understand the significance of the proposal. This bolt fits the extractor of a breech-loading cannon the English are selling to the Union forces. The cannon is called a Whitworth. Best breechloader in the world. Fires three rounds a minute, maybe more with a good crew. The gun is better than anything we can make over here. A real beauty."

"But why are we making parts?"

"Well, England is a long way away. The government has ordered hundreds and hundreds of these Whitworths, and wouldn't it be bad news if suddenly the parts supply should dry up? Can you believe the English are selling the same cannon to the Rebs? Now, the Ordnance Department wasn't born yesterday. The department is farming out contracts just like ours all over the country. No one knows what he's making, except maybe me. In a few months we'll be able to replace anything except the barrels. These bolts are nearly worth their weight in gold. We get paid in cash for as many as we can make that pass inspection. No one is to know what we're doing. I'm told that Southern sympathizers have ways of tracing such doings, and we could lose the whole smithy some night. So it's just you and me, Bunko, and no slips of the tongue. It's just railroad bolts we're turning out, right? I'll have to transport them to Harrisburg myself for a while, but I expect the government to work out a pickup system soon enough."

Bunko derived a sense of pride from the government's recognition of his father's talent. He was also proud that his father had taken him into his confidence. For a few days he stopped envying the boys from Monongamesh who came home on furloughs to strut their uniforms and turn the heads of the girls who wanted so much to have a man to

wait for. The element of secrecy, although frustrating in light of the
uniformed swagger, was a comfort in the following months when he
rose before the sun to start the forge fire or when he had to work late
at night with his father to finish a special Whitworth order.

As Sean and Bunko began putting in the extra hours to meet the
seemingly endless demand on their forge, the Ordnance Department
gave Sean a second contract for regular gunsight mounts to wipe out
any casual conjecture over the railway bolts.

"War is a funny thing," Sean observed wearily to his son one late
afternoon. "I've never had so much money in the bank and so little
time in which to spend it. Would you like to be an engineer? I think
there should be enough in the pot when all this is over to send you to
school for it, if you've a mind to go."

Bunko smiled back wearily to signify that pipe dreams were fun,
but the work of the smithy was challenging enough without thinking
of college.

In due order, as predicted, a nocturnal pickup by Ordnance Department couriers was established. There were code names for this business and passwords for the couriers, who also brought cash for the
previous collection's payment. The couriers changed often, coming at
different times in a variety of civilian disguises. It was very exciting
for Bunko; it was also very satisfying because he felt so needed. But
there were two cravings that refused to leave him in spite of the demanding work.

The first was a desire to join up with the 48th Pennsylvania Volunteer Regiment, now commanded by Monongamesh's former mayor, Col.
Anton Zaretski. It had been formed long before the war and over thirty
of the town's young men had gone with the colonel. The town and all
of Pennsylvania were very proud of the regiment. The second was Mary
Elizabeth McAuley, whom he had adored since coming to Monongamesh
while in the fourth grade. She didn't want him to join up. Her brother,
Sgt. Jack McAuley, had died at Gettysburg.

There was a big photograph of Jack in his sergeant's uniform in
the McAuley parlor. Seeing others in their uniforms seemed to terrify
Mary Elizabeth, even when Bunko was near. The family no longer talked
of the war. They often spoke of expanding the family's butchering
and provisioning business and of the future careers waiting for the
other three McAuley sons. But Bunko and Mary Elizabeth were talking of the war one evening at a Monongamesh social when he suddenly asked if he could walk her home. More and more, it seemed, as

the furlough men came home, Mary Elizabeth had been harder to find for a walk or a visit. She was changing, he had to admit, even as he wasn't. He still looked for the special gentleness in her eyes when she was near. But from a distance she looked like the most vivacious young woman in the valley. She had once been so easy to talk to; now things were different. She surprised him, as she often surprised him, by saying, "I would like that very much. I was afraid you'd never get around to asking."

He didn't really hear what she said nor remember what they talked about on the terribly short walk to her house. He only remembered the sweet glow in her eyes when she answered him. She invited him up to her front porch to rest a while before he trudged home to the smithy. When they were seated on the double swing she took his hand and rubbed the calluses gently.

"I thought so," she said. "Your hands are a knobby giveaway, Bunko. You've been working too hard with your father. Why don't you ask him for an afternoon off now and then so we can spend a little time together?"

"It's the war, Mary Elizabeth. All we ever seem to do is work and worry. But he'll not begrudge me time to see you. I've just been too worried to leave him all alone with so much to be done."

"Is there something the matter with him that you're keeping from me?"

"I don't know. He's just slowed down a lot in the last month, and he seems to forget things he never used to forget. He misses my mother more, too."

"I'm so sorry. I think he needs to visit Dr. Bailey, and I'll bet Dr. Bailey will tell him to take a rest for a few weeks. I think it's a good idea to stay close to him. I'll tell you what I can do to help. I can visit you in the buggy and we can cheer him up together. Maybe I can even talk Ma into cooking a few things for you so I can leave them. And I'm not that bad a cook myself. So just be prepared to have your bachelor tranquility shaken from time to time real soon."

Bunko smiled at her and then gradually became aware that he hadn't let go of her hand since she had first worried about his calluses and that she had made no effort to take it back.

"Since the fourth grade, Mary Elizabeth—" he began.

"I know, Bunko, I've said that to myself more times than you would believe. 'Since the fourth grade' you've been somebody very special in this household."

She rested her head lightly against his shoulder as they rocked gently on the swing.

He was so full of being near her that evening that he couldn't think of anything more to say. His worry was cut short by her father calling her to come in. They laughed together, and she gave his arm a gentle squeeze as they stood up. There was just enough light for him to see her eyes. She was so beautiful he thought his heart would explode. He bent down and kissed her cheek. She flinched from the sudden motion. He drew back, afraid he had offended her. She looked up at him, smiled, and then stood on tiptoe to kiss him full on the lips. He stood numbly, only vaguely aware that he was alone because he had heard the door open and close behind him.

He whistled and hummed tunes from the social all the way home. His feet never touched the ground during the entire mile. How was it that she always seemed to know his mind even before he did? He must have said her name a thousand times by the time he reached the smithy. He could see that his father was still working by the forge and that two men were with him; it must be another Ordnance Department pickup. It was a different team again, but he went in to say hello anyway. His father introduced him and asked him to help take the carefully packed bolts out to the horses. There he helped the two men stuff them into the saddlebags.

"We could have used these at Pittsburg Landing," said the senior agent as he mounted an excitable mare that was obviously built for speed. It was typical of Ordnance men to ride fast mounts. Bunko handed up the last package of bolts and then called over his shoulder to his father.

"Dad, can I have the shotgun tomorrow? Think I hear some wood hens out there."

Somewhat surprised, Sean Terry answered, "Of course, Bunko; it's in the same place as always."

"Thanks, Dad." After saying good night to the two agents, Bunko went into the house to see to the shotgun. He came back just as the two men were tipping their hats to Sean and turning their horses toward the road. Bunko moved carefully out of the light and into an open field of fire.

"Drop the reins, men. Hands over your heads. Get out of the way, Dad. All right, climb off your mounts and no funny moves toward guns or anything. Dad, when they're both down, get the gun from the back fella and cuff him to the forge. You know where."

"Bunko . . ." began his father, but instinct told him to hold his peace and do as directed. He headed around behind the horses toward the agent farthest from Bunko.

"Come on, kid, what's going on here? Look at my orders, for Christ's sake, and let us get on with our business. Here, lemme show you." The agent dropped one hand to reach into his inner coat pocket but spurred his horse straight at Bunko at the same instant. The other did the same, only he headed for the road, bending low over the neck of his mount. Bunko fired twice as if he had anticipated both moves. The first blast knocked over the first horse and hurled the rider backwards across the road, dead before he hit the ground. The second shot took the other rider out of the saddle as well, but his foot tangled in the stirrup, and he screamed as his horse galloped for the road. The horse went down a few seconds later and fell on him, struggled to get up, then whinnied in pain and confusion and terror until Sean Terry could run up with a pistol to end his misery. The man never moved.

Open-mouthed, Sean returned to where his son stared at the gore he had created with the two steady shots from the family gun. As he gazed at his son, Bunko answered the unasked question.

"They're Rebs, Dad. We knew it might happen someday. They were just a little faster than we thought. What that fellow called Pittsburg Landing we've been calling Shiloh. No Yankee would make that mistake."

Sean Terry put his arm around his son and led him back into the house. He took the shotgun from him and put it back over the mantel. He saw his son to bed and then went back outside to bury the evidence. It took him the rest of the night. In the morning he sent a telegram to Harrisburg asking for help. He also cancelled his contract. The next day Sean noticed that his son moved about the smithy with a quiet strength and firmness he had never shown before. Sean knew Bunko's days in the house were numbered.

Mary Elizabeth McAuley knew it, too, and it made her suddenly possessive of the precious few hours they had together. She watched Bunko watching the soldiers who were home on leave. She noticed how he seemed to make excuses to visit them. She was delighted when a great many of them admitted that soldiering was unbelievably boring and that there was very little fighting to match the large amounts of drilling.

"There, now, you've heard them for yourself," she said to Bunko one afternoon as they went for a stroll through the orchards above the valley. "What's so wonderful about being a soldier?"

"I don't know. But I do wish I were a part of all this instead of just a horseshoe bender. The most important thing that's happening to America means soldiering."

"Soldiers," she answered with disgust. "More like silly children with big sticks. This valley and all the people here are far more important than all this concern for a few slaves and for people growing cotton a thousand miles from here. They don't hate us and we don't hate them. So why all this killing?"

"It doesn't have anything to do with the hating. It has to do with keeping America together, just as Mr. Lincoln says. That's important to me. And that's not the way you used to talk back in school when you were the best Union preserver in the class."

She sat down on the long, warm grass between the trees and put her arms around her raised knees. He leaned against one of the trees and watched her.

"That's when I was very young and very idealistic. That was before Jack got killed and Larry Buetner came home without his arm and Eddie White's father just vanished at Gettysburg. Simply disappeared! If something like that were to happen to you, why think of all the people who would go crazy with worry!"

"There's just Dad, and he's a soldier and understands battlefields."

"Not quite, Bunko. You know very well there are others who would worry a great deal about you."

She smiled up at him, but her eyes blinked from the small tears that were trying to squeeze out. He laughed at her furrowed forehead and sat down next to her to keep the sun out of her eyes.

"Not me," he repeated.

"Oh, Bunko, you're a true idiot," she said, turning toward him so swiftly she knocked him over on his back. He groaned with pretended pain. "And don't play games with me, Mr. Actor, because I know you too well." She kissed him before he could answer, and then he had no answer.

"Bunko, would you take away all of a girl's pride by refusing to understand what I've been trying to say to you for nearly ten years?"

"Lizzy," he whispered, stroking her hair very gently, "I've no right to think of such things at such a time."

"I'm not 'such things.' I'm me, just me. And I can't seem to make you, just you, see more than fluttery excuses in the God-given business of just living with someone you truly love." She pressed her cheek gently to his. "Bunko, don't you like me even a little?"

"I like you more than anything in the world. A million times more. I like you so much I think about you even when I'm supposed to be working or delivering or listening to customers. I do lots of dumb things because I'm not listening to anything anyone is saying. Just last week I nearly ruined a horseshoe for Mrs. Zaretski because I was thinking of how you looked in that blue dress going to the party and—"

But he couldn't finish because warm tears were trickling down his cheeks, and hot, moist lips were being pressed to his over and over, and she was whispering breathlessly between kisses, "Bunko, oh, Bunko."

He stroked her hair and held her tight, never dreaming that one man could be at once so happy and so terrified.

"Bunko," she said quietly at last, kissing his neck between thoughts, "why didn't you say that to me before?"

"I thought you knew."

She nipped him. He held her closer.

"I've really been scared to, even though I've wanted to tell you ever since the fourth grade. But when you started getting so beautiful and all, and I'm just a shuffly kid in the back row, and I was sure one of these soldiers would just up and take you away from here before I was old enough to up and take care of you myself—"

She started to laugh to herself, and then her whole body began shaking so happily that she had to sit up to keep from choking.

"Afraid of me, Bunko? My sweet fool. Do you imagine I would let so much as a mosquito nip you without hating it the rest of my life? Look around you, Bunko. This valley has everything I could ever wish for. Good land, a steady river, four seasons, happy, good people, and room for growing. Why, this beautiful place is just crying out to grow. Don't you ever feel that you want to be a part of that growing? It makes so much more sense than drumming and marching about and killing strangers."

She wasn't smiling now. These were the words he used to hear from his mother, and he knew clearly enough why Sean Terry had left the artillery after the Indian Wars to settle in Monongamesh. Mary Elizabeth McAuley was the same beautiful person who had once brought flowers for her teacher, shared lunch with her seatmate, and found time to bandage a scraped knee for the new boy without causing anyone in the school to make fun of either one of them. Being beautiful became her.

"It gets lonely even in a beautiful valley, Bunko," she said.

"That's strange since you have so many brothers and sisters in your house. It gets pretty bad in our house. Dad sometimes gets out a jug and tries to pretend it's the cold; but it's being in that house without Ma. I never thought of you as being lonely. You're always going to socials, and those soldiers are always knocking on your door, and—"

"Hush, hush," she said, taking his hand to help her up. "The solution to loneliness isn't just quantity of attention."

"Well, I can't argue that, 'cause being busy doesn't solve missing you even if you are only a mile up the road."

They walked back to the McAuley home slowly, her arm tucked very carefully in his. Neither spoke as the deepening twilight offered dialogue enough.

A strange combination of excitement, serenity, and apprehension filled him as he walked home afterwards. The serenity part ended abruptly when he opened the door and saw his father's guest.

"Come in, Bunko," said Sean Terry in a jovial outburst a pitch or two above his normal manner. "I'd like you to meet Nora. Nora and I were married this afternoon. Our home is complete again, and you and I will shortly be living like lords of the manor."

He put his arm around the dark-haired, slightly fleshy young woman who smiled up at him from the couch his mother had brought with them from Pittsburgh. Nora extended both arms to him.

"Come over here, Bunko, honey, and give your mommy a hug." She giggled privately to Sean, who looked expectantly toward his son.

Bunko didn't move. He felt numb. How could he have been so dense? So this is what had been gnawing at his father. He had been trying to tell Bunko for weeks, but the dutiful son refused to notice or give him the encouragement he needed. He had seen Nora at some of the socials where he had watched Mary Elizabeth dancing with the soldiers on leave. Nora ran a small dress shop. Did well, he understood. Her husband had been killed at Chancellorsville. She seemed to attract plenty of company at a social. She seemed to like to stick out her bosom and make it shake when she laughed, which was nearly all night long. His dad must have been quite a suitor to get her away from those panting men. If only his dad had said something.

"Bunko—" he heard his father urge quietly.

"No thank you, ma'am," he heard a metallic answer clicking out of his throat, "my mommy died six years ago."

He stumbled out of the house even as he saw his father's eyes widen in shock and heard the high giggle start up again from the couch. He could make out only one sentence before the door closed.

"Let the boy go, dear; he'll be back by supper time tomorrow."

He never quite remembered where he wandered that miserable night. He knew only that he could never go back to that house, but he did. He knew that such deep hurt couldn't be endured, but it was. He knew that such a violation of his mother's memory was a crime against everything he felt was right about life, but he knew that he would try to see it differently for his father's sake. He knew that grown men didn't weep, but his cheeks burned from the welts of his tears.

Shortly after dawn he found himself near the orchard where Mary Elizabeth had talked about a future for them so recently. With the sunrise he began to stop feeling sorry for himself and went home. His father had left the latch off for him, which allowed him to ease his way back into the house and slip soundlessly into bed. Just before he fell asleep he thought of Mary Elizabeth. The contrast to the flamboyant Nora was so painful that in spite of his fatigue he found sleep eluded him. After what seemed to be endless tossing, one of her observations suddenly crystalized. He was upset because he had witnessed the descent of his father from hero to mortal, a man without answers in pursuit of ful-fillment. Mary Elizabeth was right; he had needed his hero father more than he realized. The thought brought him such comfort that he was soon in deep slumber.

In the morning nothing was quite as bad as he had feared. He apologized to Nora at breakfast. His father caught his eye over the coffeepot to say thank you. Nora seemed quieter and calmer also and managed to produce scrambled eggs, sausage, and griddle cakes for her hard-working family in a strange kitchen with no hitches. The coffee was the best Sean and Bunko had known for four years.

"Ain't nobody gonna be losin' weight around here, ma'am," said Bunko as he groaned away from the table toward the smithy. He still couldn't get used to the idea of seeing his father kiss her.

Pretty soon the yard began filling up with well-wishers, and the whole day turned into a continuous party. He enjoyed watching his father laugh so heartily at the crude compliments and knowing winks, which Nora pretended not to see. It was a good day, so good that he actually felt guilty about it. He was not even surprised when Sean announced that he and Nora were off to Harrisburg for a week of getting acquainted. When he told Bunko to keep the forge hot, Bunko was even feeling happy enough to suggest the same to his father. That seemed to put his father and Nora into a great mood, and they left the smithy in the trim buggy amid great laughter and hand-waving, quite oblivious to the fact that travelers didn't normally begin journeys at twilight.

Mary Elizabeth rode over the next morning. He left the forge and took her strolling down by the river. When she stopped to rest, he sat down next to her. When she looked up at him he leaned over to kiss her. She drew him backwards with her. Without knowing exactly how, he found his hand gently caressing her bosom. Her hand lightly stroked the back of his.

"I love you, I love you," he whispered. She pressed his hand tightly to her breast. Suddenly she gasped a little cry and rolled from him in the high grass. He knew she was crying.

"I'm sorry," he said. "Don't cry, Liz."

"I made you kiss me, you know that, don't you? That's why I'm crying. I don't know how I could do such a thing to you. I hate myself, Bunko. I could die. I mean it; I could just die!"

That was so unexpected he had no idea what to do. Robbery, extortion, spies were all things that made sense to him, but the tears of the most adorable girl in the world were too much. At last he blurted.

"Well, Liz, if you're going to die I guess it'll be by drowning. A few more minutes with tears like this, and the river is going to overflow."

She wailed all the harder into her handkerchief. He could see her shoulders shaking. Gradually he realized she wasn't crying; she was laughing. She put down her handkerchief and started to comb her hair, careful not to look at him. When she did turn to him, he looked so puzzled that she started to laugh again and then threw her arms around him.

"Bunko, I really am a little nit. If you can make me laugh when I've just told you I want to die, it just proves what I came over to tell you. I love you. Now, can you ever love such a wanton?"

"You know I have ever since Dad brought us here."

"You were always such a brave and thoughtful little boy. How come you were never brave enough to tell me you loved me?"

"I'm brave enough, Mary Elizabeth, just a little stupid. Do you think you could ever bear to live all your life with anyone so dumb?"

This time her eyes were shining with the deep light he had seen in them on the hillside. He got to his knees.

"I love you as much as a man can love a woman, Liz. While I'm alive ain't nobody ever going to do you harm. You'll never want, and I'll try to give you everything you ask me for. Now this is more talking than I've ever done 'ceptin' acting, and I'm about wore out with this heavy thinking. And I still have to talk to your father! Will he be home tonight?"

She leaned over to stroke his hair gently. "You know he is, and I suspect he may know what's on your mind, so don't worry too much. But just because I talked you into kissing me, you don't have to—"

His eyes made her stop banalities.

"I may have been a fool, but if I ever let you go now I'd deserve lockin' up in the looney house. I'll call on your pa at eight tonight."

"Come for supper at six, Bunko. You know we always love having you. Besides, that's what I told Mama I was coming over here to ask you."

They laughed together, and then she was gone. Bunko went back into the smithy to settle the fire for the night. The lightheartedness had gone out of him as he slowly realized the enormity of his words. Bunko Terry, student, blacksmith, actor, husband. Bunko Terry, husband, father, grandfather. He suddenly felt very old.

It was a bad time at the McAuleys'. Mary Elizabeth squeezed his hand when he came in, but he scarcely felt it. Everything felt wrong. The younger McAuleys sensed it, too, but it was so unlike Bunko that they quite refused to believe he could be out of sorts with them. He was so nervous that when Mr. McAuley asked his preference from the huge roast at the head of the table, he couldn't hold it back any longer.

"Sir," he said, "I'm not hungry. All I want to do is ask you if I can marry Liz. I love her, Mr. McAuley, and I'll take real good care of her." He turned to Mrs. McAuley and added, "I promise."

Before the startled father could even put down his carving knife and fork, the whole tableful of McAuleys exploded into whistles and hurrahs and shouts and high laughter and back-thumpings and handshakings and huggings in such abundance that an answer hardly seemed necessary. After a while Mr. McAuley gave up trying.

Bunko went home that evening engaged and scheduled for marriage in six weeks. He slept far better than he had expected. He had realized, finally, when he was climbing into bed in the lonely house, that being married to Mary Elizabeth McAuley would not only be the greatest adventure of his life, it would also be the most natural experience he could imagine. Feeling natural let him fall asleep.

His father and Nora came back from Harrisburg the next morning. When he raced out to greet them with his great good news, the smile on Bunko's face told Sean everything. The big man leaped down from the buggy to embrace his son warmly. There was no need of words between the two.

Nora smiled perfunctorily for him and went into the house where she made a considerable to-do about many little things. The men retreated to the smithy. By afternoon Bunko began to suspect that his father's good humor was a trace too hearty, his concern for his son's welfare a trifle too solicitous. He suspected his father wasn't quite sober. He concluded that it must have been a great week in Harrisburg.

But dinner that evening was a testy affair that left him bewildered. Breakfast was better because he and his father ate it alone. Bunko took a chunk of corn bread and a slice of ham to the river rather than face the tension at lunch. It must be his fault, he concluded, having heard that honeymooners often prefer their own company to anyone else's. He made plans to sleep in the smithy and went to considerable pains to explain the timetable for his wedding and his plans for a new house. He had already discussed the loan with the banker. After dinner his father handed Bunko the deed for the ten acres adjoining Sean's property.

"It's 'Terry and Son' from now on, if you'll accept it, Bunko," said Sean Terry a bit thickly. "My boy, I know I'm a bit in my cups, but I'm still able to think carefully enough where you're concerned. All of this will be yours one day. It's written down at the lawyer's. The ten acres have been yours since your mother died. The income from the rental of that good ground has been banked for you all these years. You can hire carpenters and have a fine home ready in just a few weeks. In plenty of time for the wedding. Son, I'm so happy for you I could bust; you know that, don't you? A good wife is the greatest undeserved treasure a man can ever claim. Your mother and I . . . well, we had something between us I can't really describe. But you know you grew up in a happy house, and that's something you can keep forever. Well, we can discuss it in the morning. A day's work after a week's play is the fiddler's due in spades."

Sean made his way to the bedroom. To Bunko it seemed as if his father's shoulders drooped slightly, and he seemed to sway a little as he walked. Bunko dried the dishes wondering what had gone wrong in Harrisburg. He was no closer to the answer when he blew out the light and fell asleep. Shortly after midnight the answer came with the scratch of a match.

He smelled the spring-flower perfume before he heard the soft, husky voice whispering his name. He felt a light weight being placed at the foot of his bed, and then he heard his name again. He opened disbelieving eyes to find himself looking at Nora, who was smiling at him. She was holding a small candle, which revealed that she was naked.

When she saw the surprise pop his eyes open, she chuckled softly and went away from him to stand by the foot of his bed so he could see all of her.

"Come now, Bunko. You must have seen a naked woman before. A good-looking young buck like you probably has more chicken feed on his hands than he knows what to do with. Don't be afraid to stare. I enjoy having you look at me like that."

"I ain't lookin' at you, ma'am. And you'll wake Dad in a minute, and he'll come in here, and then what? It ain't fittin', your being in here like this."

"Your daddy is so drunk he'll keep 'til noon. He's not good for much else, believe me. Seven blissful nights in that swanky hotel in Harrisburg and not so much as a decent tickle. Don't know what his problem is 'cause he isn't all that old. But little ol' Nora thought she might as well keep it in the family."

"Nora, please, ma'am, you oughta go. Please."

"Open your eyes, Bunko. I've been watching you watch me for a long time. You're getting married real soon, and you're going to be needing some training so that Mary Elizabeth will realize right from the start what a lucky catch she's got. A man's got to know about these things, believe me. I'm only doing my Christian duty in helping you along. You'll thank me one day."

"No, I won't. You better git, ma'am."

" 'Nora', not 'ma'am'," she smiled back, coming to the side of the bed. She glided smoothly when she walked, breasts high, hips flowing in the easy, sensual way that some women master with puberty.

"Women are soft, helpless creatures, Bunko, who need lots of affection to fill the unfillable bowl of life's desires." She slid into bed next to him, leaving the candle on the floor to cast a glow over the small room. She continued as she caressed his chest with one finger: "They can handle a plow, dress a chicken, dig a garden, sew a shirt, change a diaper, and tend a hot fire all day without a whimper if they know their man will kiss their heavy eyelids shut at night."

Her hand eased down to his thighs and then to his genitals. The practiced touch of her fingers came as such a surprise that he became erect almost instantly. She mounted him, easing him into her with careful undulations of her hips. She cupped her hands over his mouth to keep him from crying out. Her rhythmic response to his probing suddenly brought such an explosive reaction within him that he arced into her in spite of her weight across his legs. He felt that he was capable of lifting her to the ceiling on the power of his iron-hard penis alone. She groaned with pleasure as the hot, wet product of his orgasm filled her body.

Spent at last, he withdrew abruptly, hating himself, in spite of the newfound pleasure, for allowing her womanliness to gain control over him so easily. But she wouldn't let him go. Pressing herself close to him, she lifted his limp arm around her so that she could lie in the protection of his embrace. His hand fell across her breast. She held it there gently and kissed his neck. She sighed.

"It's been so long, oh, so terribly, terribly long," she murmured. She fondled his penis gently again.

"I'm not carnal, Bunko. I'm just a woman who needs to be needed. Someday you'll understand that a little better. You know, I had a little girl once. She was kinda sweet, and we were getting to understand each other in a way you'd think foolish. But I loved her. Fever took her when she was only two."

She began to cry. Bunko could feel warm tears on his chest where she laid her cheek. Before he knew it he felt a strong hunger for her rising up within him, and when he turned to take her, she was ready. It was so natural that he hardly knew if it was happening; his whole existence was concentrated in the huge throbbing rhythm that was as much a response as an action. When he awoke afterwards, Nora was gone, and the sun was shining into the house. He struggled somewhat automatically into his clothes as his nostrils caught the aroma of frying eggs and ham. His father stuck his head into the room and smiled.

"A fine pair of sleepyheads in this house for sure, you and me. Never happened before. We must be getting old, Bunko. Let's go. Smell those biscuits?"

"Dad," he began.

"Yes, son?"

"Nothing. Sorry I overslept."

"Privilege of owning your own business. Our customers will just have to get used to it while we wallow our way into bankruptcy."

Smiling at each other, they went into the kitchen together. Later in the morning he broke off his engagement to Mary Elizabeth McAuley, pledging undying love. He left his father a note saying that he had to prove he was man enough to be his partner as well as his son. Before noon he enlisted in Colonel Zaretski's 48th Pennsylvania Regiment. He was on his way to the training camp for the Army of the Potomac on the afternoon train. He wondered if they would consider him for the artillery.

CHAPTER 6

Petersburg IV:
The Shadow Charge

The night after the attack by the 48th Pennsylvania, the 365th Colored Sharpshooters moved its men into the front trenches for an assault on the Petersburg flank. The black troops had stacked blankets, knapsacks, overcoats, and even pairs of shoes in neat rows under the trees. Tense, black military police guarded the piles. Throughout the long night the soldiers moved into the assault trenches in silence, each man holding onto the belt of the man ahead. With no men held in reserve there was barely room for the attack troops to hunker down in the chilling mud of the forward lines. The 481 men carried only muskets, bayonets, ammunition, and water. The 365th Colored Sharpshooters were commanded by Col. Robert Ashley, and Sgt. Maj. Willie Washburn was the senior enlisted man.

About an hour before dawn, the advance raiders from the 365th Colored Sharpshooters squirmed over the parapets to eliminate the Confederate listening posts. Not a sound filtered back through the echo-choking mists as the scouts silenced the Confederate communications outposts. With the break of day, the black volunteers ebbed from the shallow Union trenches in waves, moving toward the Petersburg flank.

Slipping in and out of the thick whirls of lowland fog, the specially trained troops crossed over the entire battlefield to the shelter of the Petersburg mound unobserved.

Colonel Ashley had ordered the first part of the "shadow charge" to be made with unloaded muskets. Those who stumbled took their bruises silently, rose silently, and padded on silently. Sergeants with broad yellow Xs painted across the backs of their uniforms led squads by compass. The sergeants blessed the numbing fog for its protection even while cursing it for the confusion. Nearly a tenth of the sharp-shooters never even found their way to the Petersburg mound. One entire squad, after stumbling through the fog for over an hour, found itself back in the Union trenches.

At the foot of the steep rise to the Petersburg positions, the lead companies regrouped using hand signals. There they loaded muskets, posted guides to direct those coming after them, and began the scramble up the thorny hillside. The Confederate flanks, still weakened from the frontal attack by the 48th Pennsylvanians the previous dawn, were overrun with such swift fury that the defenders died almost without firing a shot along the entire line. The long, cold steel of vengeance-seeking bayonets, materializing suddenly without sound from the fog with grim black faces behind them, terrorized hundreds of Southern troops into stone as death lanced out for them. Within ten minutes, the 365th Colored Sharpshooters had overrun the trenches and captured the Petersburg flank. As the final platoons reached the captured lines, the main force prepared for the simple job of mopping up the exposed Confederate frontal defenses from the rear. Half the unit was dispatched to attack the front lines; the remainder turned toward the artillery position near the center of the Petersburg plateau.

The twelve guns in the center of the plateau, however, were commanded by a man who had seen his position overrun at Chickamauga, Pittsburg Landing, and Chancellorsville. He had yet to lose a gun. Up early by habit to look for any changes in the Union positions through his telescope, he heard the few shots on his right flank. Instantly realizing that the Union commanders might have enough initiative to try attacking in the fog on the lightly defended flank, he kicked his battery into life in seconds.

A plan practiced dozens of times during the do-nothing periods of life in the Petersburg trenches was instantly put into action as the six cannon not facing forward were hitched to caissons and then to horses quartered in underground stables near the ammunition. The horses were spurred some two hundred yards to the rear with the remainder of the crews running after them. Each man carried two self-contained rounds for the breech-loading Whitworths. The horses were cut free as the crews wheeled the guns into position aiming at the right flank. The first rounds were shoved home before the stragglers could get to their positions. As the first of the Negro troops broke out of the fog, three of the left-behind, dug-in Whitworths fired grapeshot at what was nearly point-blank range.

The guns behind the cannon, already wheel-to-wheel, opened up with high-explosive shells that neatly cleared the three dug-in weapons and exploded with high-shrieking violence into the advancing line. Although they had counted on speed of movement to get them across the open field, the attackers had never experienced a highly disciplined Whitworth battery in rapid fire. In less than a minute, three rounds had cleared each muzzle. In the compressed area of the attacking force there was no place to seek cover. There was no chance of any shell missing its targets. After the fifth volley, the attack faltered. After the eighth round, the entire wave staggered. Grapeshot exploded through the ranks from less than fifty yards. The artillery commander ordered half the guns pushed forward in twenty-five-yard increments while the other half continued firing. The maneuver was reversed when all wheels were again aligned. The shattered attackers piled up in front of the guns like ripped linen dolls. Surprise, the slender thread upon which had hung the entire gamble, had begun its swing from hope to holocaust. Back in position, the Whitworths, having staggered the flankers, now turned half of their firepower to the force that lay in front of them, attacking the rear of the exposed front lines. The slaughter of the flankers was repeated in the mayhem of the awakening dawn. The frontal forces, now trapped between the cannon and the alerted Confederate front, soon felt the fatal shards of grape, which left little smoke and deep pain.

The only men who could have brought the sharpshooters out of the disaster were Colonel Ashley and his staff. They were the only ones who would have had the courage to order a retreat. Colonel Ashley and his staff were wiped out in the first volley of the Whitworths, encouraging the sharpshooters, by their gallant deaths, to continue the attack. By the time the gallant deaths were recognized simply as deaths, there were over three hundred casualties on the field. When the artillery commander stopped firing to save his overheated guns from ruin, a few of the fortunate who could move managed to squirm their way back down the partially shrouded hill to the Union lines before the Confederate infantry could move in to dispatch the disabled and bury the dead. There were fewer than ten prisoners.

The Confederate forces were shocked by the fierce daring of so many Negro troops. The mass of torn bodies piled before the Rebel lines bore mute testimony to the Negroes' valor. When ex-slaves could execute that kind of attack, it would be only hours before every black under their command knew of it. Their real enemy would then be all

around them as the invisible tendrils of pride and hope and fighting
manhood awakened spirits too long crippled in bondage. The Confederates recognized the same fear in each other's eyes and made haste
to bury the evidence.

Among the survivors was Willie Washburn. He had been invited to
accompany Colonel Ashley to plead the validity of the shadow charge
before General Grant three weeks earlier. He had led the first of the
raiders onto the field to dispatch the Rebel listening posts. He had been
the first into the flanking trenches, and it was Willie who had separated the forces into the two groups that had begun the mopping up.
The premature lifting of the fog and the mobile tenacity of the artillery commander had crucified his dream on the calvary of canister fire,
three to the minute.

When the Southerners found him, he was the only man alive within
a radius of thirty feet. There was no blood on him, but his head was
sodden from the concussion that had leveled him. He was already feeling
the relentless agony of guilt. The whispered death gasps of every friend
he had known in the army were thundering screams driving devils of
madness through what remained of his consciousness. In a complete
daze he followed the line of prisoners to the rear.

About a mile behind the guns, the prisoners were herded into a
stockade that already housed the survivors of the attack by the 48th
Pennsylvanians.

"Here, nigger lovers, look after your black bastards," shouted the
sergeant in charge of the detail as he cracked open the stockade gate.
There was no shade, no water, no medicine, no latrines. Nearly a dozen
sentries patrolled the perimeter, daring any prisoner to bolt. During
the day the prisoners buried six of their own. That night Sgt. Maj. Willie
Washburn met Pvt. Bunko Terry, who introduced him to the oldest second
lieutenant in the Army of the Potomac. That night Willie Washburn
discovered a small shaft of light blinking at him from the end of his
long tunnel of despair. In the light was room for a man to die like a
man, like all the fallen men who had trusted in him. He slept.

CHAPTER 7

Willie Washburn

Willie Washburn liked being a house nigger on the Ballard plantation. None of his relatives, as far back as anyone in the slave cottages could remember, had ever worked anywhere but in the fields.

"Watch yo' britches, boy," old Moll had whispered when Ivy, the huge mother-hen cook, had brought word that he was wanted for an interview with the master. The true wisdom became clearer half a year later when he found himself the object of unusual attention from sixteen-year-old Angelica Ballard, which scared him numb. In the pseudoinnocence of her not-quite-decipherable smile he sensed the rasping bite of a hangman's noose. When it came to teenage white girls, there were no innocent niggers.

Ivy suggested that he get married. But Willie suspected that a little thing like a nigger marriage wouldn't mean much to Angelica.

"I is only twenty-two. Why don' she get married, and then her husband can worry about her somewhere else?"

He and Ivy laughed together. Willie went about his duties as assistant butler in the big house with added resolve to keep everything plain and simple and to guard his place as if his life depended on it. He was also number one silver polisher and number one footman. One thing about the Ballards, they kept wonderful horses. Sitting up behind Jimbo the driver when the twin bays were high-stepping made his heart sing. Roger Ballard taught Willie to ride so that he could accompany any of the members of his household should they choose to use saddle instead of carriage. Ivy taught him to seek safety in numbers. It worked for a while.

All in all, however, he liked being a house nigger. The rooms were cooler than the sun of the fields, even if he did lack for company.

The food was plentiful. Strangely, Willie liked learning the manners of the white folks. He liked to hear the important people of the county argue about the issues of the day. He gradually learned that most of them were fools. One of the few good things Angelica did for him was teach him to read. But she had an interesting attitude toward arithmetic.

In the early spring of 1858, when Willie had been working in the house for six months, Angelica strode briskly into the tiny kitchen sitting nook where Ivy was having a midmorning cup of tea with Willie.

"Saddle up, Willie," she ordered briskly. "We're going to learn to count this morning." She smiled at both of them, cracked her riding crop across the top of her boots, and then spun away to exit on light ripples of private merriment. He looked at Ivy, who shrugged back in a gesture of resignation that said everything necessary about the meaning of slavery and the significance of enduring.

"She probably gonna meet up wif her frien' Thelma Doolittle. Them two girls is pure tinderboxes just askin' for sparks wherever they can find them."

Willie and Angelica rode up into the lightly wooded hills behind the Ballard mansion toward the larger fields dominated by the gracious Georgian lines of the Doolittle plantation. He had ridden the long way around to the Doolittles' several times with Jimbo, but this was his first ride through the woods.

In a glade near the top of the hill separating the two estates they found Thelma waiting for them. She was all smiles and full of secret eyebrow-raisings for Angelica. Willie felt he was being looked over like one of the bays. Behind Angelica a tall, sturdy young Negro groom held the Doolittle mounts.

While the two very-much-in-charge young girls chattered, Willie climbed down and tried to catch the eye of the other groom. He got a knowing grin for his troubles, which confused him further. The two girls stopped talking at last, and Angelica turned toward the two grooms.

"Tie up the horses and come when we call you, hear? We're going to separate for a bit, so do keep your ears open. Willie, bring the basket to me first. Nero, I'm sure Miss Thelma would like hers too. My, that is handsome, Thelma. Nero, I hear you are pretty good at counting."

"I tries, Miss Angelica."

"That's the spirit. Willie, do you know anything about counting?"

"No, ma'am."

The two girls threw their arms around each other and began the giggling all over. Willie left them to tie the two horses in the shade where they could graze easily and returned with a large picnic basket for Angelica. Then the girls separated and disappeared along the faint but evidently well-known footpaths on either side of the glade.

"What goin' on here?" he asked Nero.

A grin. "Big game fo' dem, but you doin' it fo' every nigger on the plantation, remember that."

"Doin' what fo' every nigger?"

"Relax, boy."

He heared Angelica calling his name from down the footpath. There seemed to be a slight edge of mockery in the added sweetness of the call. Was she going to let him eat with her in the privacy of the woods? Obediently he followed the path until it seemed to disappear. He hesitated and heard Nero being called from the other side of the glade.

Angelica's voice came from his left. "Over here, Willie." When he turned he saw her lying motionless on a blanket under a shade tree. She was naked.

He stepped back, terrified. She laughed and put her hands behind her head so that her surprisingly full bosom rose and quivered. She laughed lightly again and gently lifted her breasts even higher with one hand that she took from behind her head.

"Don't be afraid, Willie. I'm the same sweet girl you've been devouring with your eyes for months. I just know how you've burned for me every time I've come close to you, and now you're going to have your chance. Come here, Willie."

He stepped forward numbly. She patted the blanket next to her and gestured for him to join her. Afraid to sit down, he compromised by kneeling near her. He avoided looking at her by lowering his eyes to the pattern on the blanket near his knees. Cooing and laughing at his embarrassment, she unbuttoned his tight riding britches. Before he knew what was happening she had his penis in her hands. "That's nice, Willie, that's very, very nice," she whispered.

Suddenly all his confusion and frustration and bone-deep anger seized him in a total passion he had never known before. His penis erected like a musket barrel. He spread her legs apart and thrust himself into her with a fury that drew a deep gasp from her, and then another, and then a stifled small scream as his thrustings seemed to drive her backbone through the blanket. As his passion finally spent itself and he started to back off, wondering if he had hurt her, he found her smiling up at him with genuine affection.

"Stay a minute, Willie," she suggested, and then added a word he had never heard from her before: "Please?"

Still kneeling, he bent over and kissed her breasts until the nipples rose again, turgid with anticipation. He felt her legs scissoring around behind him, urging him on as he felt himself growing hard within her again. With less effort now he seemed to penetrate even deeper. This time there were no deep breaths, just the full scream of primitive ecstasy, which she muffled by putting her hand to her mouth and biting the soft flesh between her thumb and forefinger.

"Oh, Willie, Willie," she moaned, and then another scream-moan burst from her throat which she didn't even bother to stifle. She almost seems proud to act like this, he thought. Exhausted, he withdrew. Gradually she opened her eyes and gave him her most gracious smile. As she handed him a tattered piece of linen with which to dry himself she asked, "Did you keep count?"

"Of what, Miss Angelica?"

"Willie, don't be so stupid after being so sensible. Of the times you made me come . . . you know."

"You mean when you moaned and such?"

Again the smile. "Those were the best, but the first times weren't so bad, either. So I guess that makes three for us."

She raised her voice and turned her head toward the top of the glade.

"All right, Thelma. Three! The sun will be going down pretty soon. You getting results? You ready?"

"Ready," came back a silver-belled voice from over the hill. "I hope he can make me squeal like that. We've got two here."

"Button up, Willie, and you go and be real nice to Miss Thelma. She thinks you're scrumptiously beautiful. And do tell Nero not to dawdle."

He got to his feet in disbelief, hitched up his pants, and stumbled back up the footpath to the hill. There he found Nero, waiting for him with the same fatuous grin.

"Fo' every nigger in the fields, Willie. But nothin' says you can't enjoy the sacrifice, boy."

Willie hit him with a wild left hook that broke Nero's jaw and rendered him unconscious for a quarter of an hour. Willie untied his mount and rode back to the Ballard plantation alone. He was sure he had broken his hand.

Ivy backed away from him when he strode into the kitchen. She had seen men with that wild look in their eyes before. No good ever came of it.

"Got to see massah. And I think I broke this han'. Gwine need some help later, I 'spect."

He found Mr. Ballard in the study. The door was open, so he walked straight in and began to talk without waiting to be given permission.

"Massah, you bes' shoot me or sell me off. I ain't no more use to you here."

Roger Ballard, no stranger to Negro tantrums, said nothing. This was the first time he had seen his steady second butler in a lather, and he sensed the cause was grave.

"Willie, go ahead and tell me what happened."

"Cain't, massah. You just have to get rid of me, that's all."

Out of the corner of his eye Roger Ballard could see Angelica riding down from the Doolittle plantation. She was riding hard enough to kill herself and her horse.

"Does it have to do with Miss Angelica?"

Willie stared at the floor without answering.

"Willie, I've been hearing stories about Thelma Doolittle for some time. I guess my friends have been too embarrassed to include my own daughter in the stories. From the looks of things, it's been all too true. They say Thelma is partial to that big grinning buck, Nero."

"Busted his head, massah. My han', too," answered Willie still looking at the rug.

"A wild filly is a handful for any man. The South is strewn with the mischief of bored high spirits. You go and get Ivy to take care of your hand; I'll take care of Angelica. Something I should have done years ago. Then you stay out of sight for about a week. Don't do anything foolish."

Willie backed out of the study before Angelica could reach the house and went out to the kitchen. Ivy already had a big bowl of warm water waiting for his hand. It was really beginning to throb. As he eased his left hand into the herb-laced water, he heard Angelica's boots in the hallway.

"Daddy, that no-'count nigger Willie Washburn tried to rape me!" she screamed.

"Come into the study, Angelica, and close the door after you, please," answered Roger Ballard. A few minutes later the hearty whacks of a long leather shoehorn against the shapeliest bottom around Roanoke,

Virginia, thunked through the house. Piercing screams accompanied
the blows, which were so vigorously applied that the air whistled with
the flailing of the shoehorn. Ivy smiled.

"Didn't think he'd really do it," grunted Willie with surprising
satisfaction as Ivy began packing his throbbing hand in a foul-smelling poultice.

In a quarter of an hour the screaming and wailing subsided into
heavy sobbing. Angelica crawled up the long, winding staircase to her
room, where she remained facedown on her bed for nearly a week.
Willie's hand took nearly a month to mend, but at least he knew he
could again hold field implements and make himself useful. But Roger
Ballard refused to waste good talent. In six weeks Willie found himself back in second-butler livery.

"I've asked Jason to show you about our accounts here," said Mr.
Ballard a few days after Willie's return. "Someday you'll be running
this household, and accurate accounts are the foundation stones of good
management. Know the facts."

"But, massah—"

"Don't worry about Miss Angelica. She'll be going to visit her aunt
in Norfolk next week. It'll be a long stay. My sister has much to show
a budding debutante. It really is high time that girl was making her
debut. Heaven knows there are enough young men panting along the
fence rail every time we go for a drive. I promise you Miss Angelica
will be far too busy to bother you any more."

Angelica took her meals in her room, and Willie didn't see her. He
found the accounts that Mr. Ballard had talked about very interesting.
Jason was a patient teacher and far shrewder than Willie had ever realized.

"Yeah, boy, facts are facts," smiled Ivy, "but ol' Jason, he know a
thing or two beside. That's even better than facts!"

But meaningful or not, counting always reminded him of Angelica,
and the discipline was painful for him.

Angelica was carted off as promised, and things settled down very
well for Willie. He noticed flickering glances of respect and wonder-
ment cast his way when the plantation people didn't think he was watching. He noticed them first around the slave quarters, but then the same
thing happened whenever he drove Mr. Ballard into Roanoke or to the
other plantations. Once he met Nero, but this time the glance was pure
hate. Thelma Doolittle, it seems, had developed a sudden yearning to
visit an older sister in Savannah.

But a woman scorned can not only hate, she can wait. Willie found out the deeper meaning of the expression early in the fall when Angelica returned from her aunt's and preparations for her debut began. Because Angelica had to have so many fittings in Roanoke, and because Mr. Ballard wanted to have her portrait painted before the plantation gave her up, she required a great many trips in the carriage. Every so often the footman assigned to her would be on other duties, and Willie had no choice but to climb up beside Jimbo and serve as before. The trips developed a pattern. As Willie stood by the carriage door, Angelica gave him her hand, smiled appropriately as she stepped into the open carriage, and said softly, "You nigger sonovabitch." When they returned, Angelica alighted, cooing gracefully, "Fuck you, Willie."

Once he laughed in spite of his better judgment. That's when she broke the parasol over his shoulders and he had to go back into the house for another one.

Willie's reckoning came on a crystal blue market day in early October when Mr. Ballard had ridden north to look over some property in the next county. Angelica decided on impulse to go into Roanoke, and the carriage was quickly brought around for her. Since her footman had stomach grippe, Willie put aside the silver polish and climbed up beside Jimbo.

Jimbo laughed quietly, "Well, you nigger sonovabitch, how you feelin' today?"

Willie grinned back, "Fuck you, Jimbo, you old black bastard. Ain't you never gonna get cultivated? Oop, here she come."

He climbed down to stand by the door as usual. This time Angelica refused his hand.

"Down to the market, Jimbo," she said casually.

Jimbo and Willie exchanged glances as Willie hoisted himself back up to the seat. None of the plantation ladies ever went to the market on the main market day. Too many people shoving, shouting, fighting, defecating, and all sorts of things it might be best for a young lady of highbred sensitivities not to brush up against. Dutifully, Jimbo drove the carriage to the edge of the great Roanoke Square where the colorful market was in full swing as a lively, lusty reminder of European and African commonality in customs too ancient for anyone to decipher. It was peaceful enough as Jimbo stopped the carriage.

"I'll be at the market about an hour, Jimbo. Some darling things to get for the party. Put the carriage behind the hotel and wait for me with the other drivers. Willie, you come with me."

"Yes'm," they both mumbled. As Willie helped her alight from the carriage, he brushed back against a gaunt white man who was strolling toward the carriage with a companion. Both men were strangers to Willie.

"Watch it, nigger."

He whisked his hat off and looked at the wood-plank sidewalk to which he had escorted Angelica.

"Yessuh." It was hard to go wrong agreeing with white folks. The man's boots, although well shined, looked well worn. Oddly enough, the handle of a knife stuck out from the right boot. No one in Roanoke he knew of wore knives that way. "Beg yo' pardon, sir."

"Willie, don't pay attention to this trash," snipped Angelica. "I've shopping to do."

"Oh, bless my Aunt Matilda's pox," observed the companion of the man who had spoken. "Here's one of them starchy plantation belles just made for a bit of ringing." Willie looked up to see the second man slip his arm around Angelica's waist and squeeze her breast. He stepped forward instinctively to protect Roger Ballard's daughter. A riding crop slashed across his face knocking his hat into the dust.

"Leave us alone," hissed Angelica, stabbing out convincingly with her parasol at the two strangers.

"Hoo-eey, honey. Your humble servant, ma'am. Forgive the intrusion," replied the man with the knife in his boot. The man doffed his hat to make an elaborate mock bow. Somehow in the sweep he managed to get hold of Angelica's hand, which he promptly kissed. He then proceeded to inch his way up Angelica's bare arm with further noisy kisses. When she beat at him with the parasol, he took it away from her and broke it against a post while the second man howled with laughter.

The howl was shut off abruptly as Willie's powerful arms encircled him from behind. The once-laughing man felt himself lifted, then whirled in a quick circle. His feet flipped up with the momentum in such a perfectly timed whirling that his boots clipped the hand kisser just behind the ear. The man with the knife in his boot sprawled into the dust and lay there. The man being whirled was flung loose, and his head cracked against the red brick of the Roanoke General Emporium. Willie led Angelica in unhurried steps through the muttering crowd of startled whites and blacks. Only after Willie and Angelica were through the crowd did Jimbo drive around the square to the back of the hotel. He would have felt much better if Angelica had decided to cancel the trip.

At the corner of the main part of the open-air market, Angelica thanked Willie for the escort perfunctorily. There was no mention of the two men.

"I'll be wandering around here for about an hour, Willie. You join the other plantation servants over by the big barns and join up with Jimbo by the hotel when the big clock chimes twelve. Good thing you know how to count, Willie boy. If I change my mind, I'll go to the hotel and send Jimbo to fetch you. Don't get lost now, hear?"

"Yes'm."

He watched her melt easily into the ebb and flow of the chattering market crowd. He turned to his right away from the square and walked the short distance to the rear of the block of shops that made up the east side of the town square. There was a large dusty area between the backs of the town-square shops and the long stable where the blacks traditionally congregated while their owners attended to the business of the day. Someone usually had a fire going and some ribs or chicken cooking, so a slave could do himself proud for a few coppers. Willie admired the shrewd business sense of the slave who did the planning for such a tidy operation. He was also grateful for the few coins Jimbo had given him to buy dinner for the two of them. He made a mental note to ask Mr. Ballard for some strolling money the next time he had to come into Roanoke on market day.

Since the meat wasn't ready, he squatted in the shade of the barn to watch the horseshoe game that always seemed in motion on market day. He was careful to keep his clothes out of the dust. The heat made him sleepy enough that he lost track of the time. It seemed he had dozed but a minute before he heard his name being called with conspiratorial urgency. It was Nero. In spite of the recently broken jaw, the grin was the same.

"Willie, this is your lucky day. Good thing I found you so quick. Come along wif me. I got us an arrangement that even a slow fool like you will like. Pick up yo' ass and follow ol' Nero."

"What fo', Nero? Ah knows already it ain't gonna be nothin' good."

"Willie, that's no way to talk. This arrangement is so special I'se afraid to talk about it right here on the street for every bush nigger in the county to hear. I cain't handle all dis arrangement by myself."

Reluctantly Willie unwound himself to get up and follow the man who couldn't really be as cordial as he was pretending. He was partially intrigued, partially bored, and noon was still a long way away. Nero passed the small barbecue pit where the aroma of the broiling meat seemed so perfect to Willie that he nearly called out to Nero to forget the arrangement. As he rounded the shaded corner of the stone barn to head toward the square, four white men grabbed him and threw him on the ground. They were so big and so purposeful that he was helpless even before the shot-loaded whip handle rapped against the side of his head. Dazed, he was only dimly aware that his feet were being tied to stakes driven into the ground. As his arms were jerked away from his body for similar treatment, the pain of being spread-eagled brought him back from the brink of unconsciousness. He could feel the ropes biting into his wrists. A sharp knife slit open his vest and shirt, baring his chest and stomach. The sun was so bright that he could hardly make out the faces of the men standing over him.

"My, my, Willie, you do look a bit dusty," he heard Nero say from somewhere in the blaze over his eyes. "We been savin' a cool bucket of horse piss to clear off the dust and give you some relief from the sun."

There was hearty laughter as the foul bucket was emptied into his upturned face. It was hurled at such a malicious angle that much ran up his nose, choking him. As he gasped and coughed, another bucketful hit him so that he swallowed in spite of his resolve. More laughter, but it sounded white rather than black, telling Willie that Nero was the only Negro betrayer in whatever was to follow. He knew that none of the other Negroes would dare to help him. Jimbo was all the way across the square at the hotel and wouldn't even hear the noise. Angelica was his only hope. He suddenly felt helpless. His eyes were now burning from the urine, but he was able to make out the form of the man with the knife in his boot who seemed to be in charge.

"Niggah, you're going to learn what it means to kick a white man into the dirt. Ol' Tom Jerrud don't forget such trifles, and he don't want you to forget them either, ya hear?"

Jerrud's associate went over to the barbecue fire and helped himself to the pot bubbling with the savory sauce. With a benevolent smile lifting the corners of his mouth, he began painting Willie's stomach with the oily mixture. The involuntary scream that broke from Willie's lips brought hearty laughter from those holding him down and from most of the several hundred spectators who had suddenly gathered for the sport. Willie vowed he wouldn't scream again, not even if they built a fire right on him. Which is exactly what they did.

" 'Pears to me this niggah sauce ain't hot enough," said Tom Jerrud. "We'll just have to bring the fire a mite closer."

Short lengths of white-hot wood were extracted from the fire and carefully balanced on Willie's stomach. The still-bubbling sauce was tilted over the smoldering embers, which caused them to flare instantly into flame. The crowd gasped, moved back, and then fell strangely silent. Willie strained to twist his torso so the flames would slide off his stomach. He strained so fiercely at his ropes that Nero felt obliged to kneel on his right wrist. Sweat streamed from his face as he smelled his own flesh burning. He knew that in a few seconds he would be screaming just as they wanted him to.

It sounded like a pistol shot. The fire on Willie's belly suddenly disintegrated, and Jimbo was kneeling over him brushing the remains of the fire from him with his bare hand. A wet cloth followed to wipe up the oil and blood. Another crack and the knife flew from Tom Jerrud's hand.

"Get away from my property, you no good trash," shouted Roger Ballard as he flailed about him with the fifteen-foot bullwhip that had been his trademark in the county for thirty years. "My property, do you hear?" The tip flicked out and snapped against the head of the man holding the pot of sauce, leaving most of an ear in the dust. The man sprang back. Nero jumped up and ran for the Negro quarter as the whip reached out and just split open his shirt. Jerrud reached for the pistol in the holster at his waist.

"Don't even think about it, sonny," warned Roger Ballard, cocking his whip arm. "When you injure a man's property in Virginia you bring down more law than you'll ever be able to handle. 'Sides, I'm just liable to cut your head off in self-defense. Now get out of here, both of you, and don't ever let me hear you've been back to Roanoke. I promise you that you won't be given a chance to leave a second time. And you, Angelica, stay where I can see you."

The crowd dispersed before the wrath of Roger Ballard, many of the onlookers now ashamed of themselves. Some, however, were disappointed that the fire had been stopped. A good lesson cleared the air every so often. Angelica stood in her tracks in the second row of spectators.

Jimbo cut the ropes with the knife that had been dropped into the dust and picked Willie up. Roger Ballard led him, with Angelica following dutifully behind, around the corner to the doctor's office. Somewhere in the short journey, and just after he had seen Angelica smiling at him, Willie fainted. That made it easier for Dr. Iverson to clean the burned area, dress the seared tissue, and bandage Willie.

"He's most fortunate," said Dr. Iverson to Roger Ballard. "That greasy mess the Negroes enjoy so much did most of the burning, not Willie. Oh, he's plenty sick, and if an infection sets in he could die easily enough. But I've seen these 'lessons' before, and this is the first student who's ever had a chance to recover. Why don't you leave him with me for a week and then send your driver in for him, Roger? I'm afraid a journey home now would really tear him up."

Roger Ballard agreed and left with Angelica in tow. Jimbo had the carriage waiting at the hotel. During the entire trip home, Ballard said nothing to his daughter. Angelica tried several times to distract him with the light talk that typified the charm of the young ladies of her set, but she gave it up after a few miles and waited silently for the inevitable. She knew her father understood that she had hired Tom Jerrud.

As she walked on her father's arm from the carriage to the house, Angelica heard her fate in soft, deliberate sentences that brooked no further discussion.

"I expect you to choose a man within the month. Within three months you'd best be married. After that you should pay close attention to your new home, because that's all you'll ever have from me."

She didn't insult his intelligence by feigning innocence, nor did she flaunt reality by threatening to leave immediately if she were no longer welcome at the place of her birth. She concluded that she was getting off lightly. Besides, Willie had nearly got his, so the gesture hadn't been a complete failure.

As Jimbo drove the carriage to the stable, he saw his course as a simple one, also. Nero would never suspect that a gentle darkey like ol' Jimbo could ever do him harm. It was to be Nero's greatest mistake. He was found a week before Angelica's wedding staked out in the woods. Foxes had eaten most of him, and the ants were doing their share. Nothing was ever done about it, since it was common knowledge that Nero had a great many enemies among the married men of the surrounding plantations.

Dr. Iverson sat up with Willie all through the agony of the long afternoon and the interminable first night. Willie passed out from shock on three different occasions; fever gripped him so that he sweated through the mattress. A good constitution and youth were his two major allies, Dr. Iverson later told Mr. Ballard. The pus-filled blisters began draining the next morning. The problem was to keep Willie from scratching at the unquenchable itch that crinkled the tortured skin and contracted the abused abdominal muscles. Through the shredded mist of partial coma Willie understood that Dr. Iverson was asking his forgiveness for binding his arms to the side of the bed. He lay that way for two more days, days that had no dawning or sunset, just rising or diminishing pain. Every time his head cleared long enough for him to recognize anything, he saw Dr. Iverson looking down at him. On the third day the fever began subsiding, the heavy sweating stopped, and when he looked up at Dr. Iverson, he was able to smile. The weary doctor smiled back and untied his hands.

"You're a good patient, Willie. I do believe, young man, that you're going to be all right."

"Yessuh, thanks to you."

"Thanks to Mr. Ballard. His timely arrival saved you from that trash that was after blood for sure. Something mighty funny about all that."

Willie shrugged, remembering the wild look of pleasure he had glimpsed in Angelica's eyes as she stood not quite hidden in the circle of spectators around his staked-out body. He said nothing, but he knew he could never again work in the Ballard household. He knew that Roger Ballard would have to sell him out of the state as soon as he was healthy. The poor man could not bear to look at him, the victim of his daughter's cruelty. He began making plans to escape to the North. The details filled most of his waking hours until Jimbo came for him at the end of the seven-day convalescence. The ride home was painful, but he was comforted by the inside details of Nero's disappearance and by the announcement of Angelica's engagement.

Willie's strength returned just in time to be of service for Angelica's wedding. She married a good-looking second son of a South Carolina plantation owner. The two of them thrived on the glorious succession of balls, garden fetes, hunts, races, bachelor parties, and bridal showers. Guests at the wedding were exhausted from the continuous merriment, but the bridal couple was as energetic as on the day of the announcement. Mr. Ballard began to entertain the possibility that Angelica had married her match in irresponsible endurance. The list of family items she had decided to take with her also suggested that his vivacious daughter had a very good sense of the worth of domestic property.

As the chattering, waving, smiling couple finally vanished down the road to the Roanoke railroad station with Jimbo at the reins, Ivy observed to Willie, "She be back soon enough. That boy can't keep up wif her fo' long."

Later in the afternoon, when all the guests had departed, Roger Ballard asked Willie to join him in the study.

"Thank you for helping out, Willie," began Roger Ballard.

"Yessuh. It was a fine weddin', massuh."

Mr. Ballard smiled and then opened the center drawer of his huge French country desk. Willie knew that drawer was always kept locked and contained some very important papers. Mr. Ballard withdrew a white, legal-looking document. He then got up and walked around the corner of his desk so that he could hand it to Willie.

"Willie, I know how hard it is for you to work here now, so I've thought of a solution. The solution bothers me a little, because you are the best man that's ever worked on this plantation, and I'm going to miss you."

Willie's heart sank. Mr. Ballard had beaten him to the punch. His escape plans were nearly in order, and now he was being sold to where it would be even more difficult.

"You're a free man, Willie. This paper says so for all the world to know. Take care of it, you may have to show it someday. But it's all recorded in the Roanoke Courthouse; anyone can write me for verification."

He placed the certificate of manumission and an envelope in Willie's numb hand.

"The envelope holds a railroad ticket to Philadelphia and a hundred dollars to help get you started in your new life. There's a train out in the morning, so why don't you take the rest of the day off for saying good-bye and putting your things in order. Jimbo will drive you to the train tomorrow. In light of the way things are going in Washington, the sooner we get you into the North, the better."

"Massuh?"

Roger Ballard smiled. He then put out his hand to Willie. Limply, Willie proffered his own.

"No more 'massuh,' Willie. From now on the law says you're as good as any other man. You know how I feel about that. One last thing: there's no such thing as absolute black and absolute white. Forgiveness is the great shade of difference."

As the good man's grip tightened in the farewell handshake, Willie found the courage to squeeze back. When the door closed behind him, Willie felt alone for the second time in as many months.

*   *   *

After serving a discouraging year as a stevedore, roustabout, mill hand, and slaughterhouse gutter, Willie found that the sound of freedom was worth every bit of the echo of deprivation. He even enjoyed the privilege of being fired. But he missed the company of the slave quarters back on the Ballard plantation when the day's work was done. One day he admitted something deeper to himself. He missed being known for what he was, a man to be reckoned with, a man with a future.

One evening in 1861, while walking the streets of Philadelphia, Willie read a poster that suddenly sent exhilarating vibrations charging through his spine. The federal government was recruiting soldiers. The poster showed a smiling white man with three large gold stripes on his blue uniform sleeve. The merry-eyed sergeant was gently encouraging a pair of gawky Yankee field hands to join up. Laughing colored mess attendants could be seen in the background preparing a hearty field stew to be served in the shade of nearby trees. Colored mule skinners could be seen driving army wagons. It looked like a good life. If a white man could wear gold stripes, why not a black? He knew lots of blacks wanted to fight with the North. Someday men with any kind of training would be needed. Today mules, he said to himself; tomorrow men.

Willie felt challenged in another way as he wandered around thinking about the poster. He heard white folks talking about the war every day. The black man, Willie felt, had some proving to do in his new country. The Negro had to prove he could fight. For all the crimes done to him, Willie felt that the Negro should have freedom, not because he deserved it under American law, but because he had earned it under universal law. When he shared his views at work, he discovered he was in the minority. "Get what's yours and git" is what he heard so often that he felt ill. Willie began to yearn for a chance to help with the proving of black manhood and loyalty.

About two weeks after seeing the poster, Willie made his way to the recruiting station. There were no smiling sergeants, but there were some looks of grudging respect when they asked him why he wanted to sign up.

" 'Cause you needs me."

"Oh?"

"Yessuh; and I needs you."

The recruiting officer smiled. "The federal government is not accepting any Negro volunteers."

"I know that. But I seen colored serving men and wagon drivers in your poster, and I wanted to do something. I can handle horses and mules. But I is a terrible cook."

"Well, that's good to know. Tell you what. This war ain't going to be over in one battle. If you're so all-fired anxious to be useful, come back here tomorrow morning at eight o'clock, and I'll introduce you to someone who might be able to make you an interesting proposition. If you can write your name, leave it with my sergeant by the table. If you can't—"

"I can write my name, and I can do sums—and I can fight! I'll be back in the mawnin'. And I'll bring a few others. The name's Willie Washburn."

The next day he was taken into a back room filled with over a dozen young black men and a red-headed white Union officer who introduced himself as Captain Ashley. Within half an hour the room was overflowing with black men. The captain took them out into a brick courtyard. He was followed by a sergeant who set up a small table and chair and then went back inside, closing the door behind him. Captain Ashley jumped easily onto the table and asked the Negroes to gather around him.

"Men," he began in a semiconspiratorial tone which instantly captured everyone's attention. "You're all here because you want to fight the Rebs. The government won't let you. Officially. But I'm here today to let you know there's plenty of ways of fightin' besides direct assault.

"You're needed out West in Kansas where I work for a general who has a man-sized job for men who like a little adventure in their lives. Nobody is going to know you exist other than as drivers and mess attendants—that's army talk for kitchen help. You'll get two sets of fatigues and a dollar a week for yourselves. That's about a third of what a private gets. We'll feed you. Some of it's edible. And we'll give you a tent and a clean cot with two blankets. But you aren't going to be doing much driving and no messin'. Your real job will be to go with me into Tennessee and Missouri and bring out any male slaves who want to be free. The more we bring out, the less will be left to work for the Rebs. And it's just a matter of time before we have Negro regiments that you and the men we free can join.

"Naturally, the Confederates know we're coming. Yes, I've been there before. The fun comes when we find the Rebs who are trying to find us. That's why we're going to give you muskets and teach you to shoot. The Southern states can't afford to lose their slaves."

A spontaneous cheer went up from the Negroes. This was more like it. Captain Ashley grinned.

"Oh, one final insight before you sign up. If we're caught, I'll get shot, but you will probably be made slaves. Possibly even branded or mutilated as runaways. I can guarantee you that you'll earn your dollar. Any questions?"

There was only one.

"Captain, does we get army shoes?"

"The best."

Willie signed his name and helped others sign theirs. Some fifty of them were on a westward-bound train that night. Next to leaving the Ballard plantation, it was the biggest journey of his life.

The chunky red-headed captain marched two hundred haphazardly uniformed black recruits into the shade of some tall trees along one edge of the windy, dusty drill field. Two other companies of Negro volunteers were drilling on the hot parade ground. Willie had been on duty for nearly a week, and it had been the greatest disappointment of his life. There were plenty of sergeants with big stripes on their sleeves, but there were no smiles. It was very warm for September, and Willie had begun to doubt that he had any cause to prove anything to anybody. The shade felt good. The stubby captain had the men sit so their backs were to the sun. He took off his hat to wipe his forehead as the company gathered at his feet in a large semicircle.

"My name is Captain Ashley," he began. He then repeated his name and had the company say it with him, like children. Willie felt insulted.

"Men, you're the first Negro volunteers from the eastern regions of the United States. I've just come from duty out West with an all-volunteer unit of cavalry. Those men believed that fighting Indians with anything other than cold steel was sissy stuff. That's how we're going to do it. Your backsides belong to me until you're killed or transferred. Don't ever doubt it for a minute. I'm the one who is going to order you into action, and I'm the only one who can bring you home, so when I tell you to do something, do it fast. Put all your trust in me, because I'm all you've got. Me and your training.

"The army still has to be convinced that Negro troops are good for anything besides carrying supplies, scraping roads, walloping pots, or stealing chickens. Now that the army sort of has you, you're going to prove I was right about every one of you. If I have to throw you into an attack by the balls, at least I'll prove to the army that you had the equipment.

"This shake-up between the North and South is going to be the meanest mess you ever imagined. It's going to take a long time, and you will remember that you signed on for the whole of it, even in those cases where someone had to witness your mark.

"Be prepared. People are going to hate you. The Southerners are going to hate you because you embarrass them and you cost them money, and because many feel you are biting the hand that fed you. Especially if you've escaped. Northern folks aren't going to be overly fond of you either, because their kin are dying for you. They'll look at you and wonder if the price is too high. Without you, their sons would be home. Other Negroes will fear you because you are calling attention to many who would rather remain in the shadows.

"So, why are you bearing all of this trouble? Anybody know? Raise your hand if you think you know; don't be afraid."

Willie's hand shot up. The captain nodded.

" 'Cause I'se good as any man!" He was half-proud—and half-embarrassed.

The captain seemed to make a mental note to himself. He unbuckled his belt, took off his blouse, and laid them carefully on a patch of grass beneath one of the large shade trees.

"You as good as me, nigger?"

Uniform or not, Willie knew the man was still Captain Ashley, and such talk could only get him into trouble. Back in Roanoke, such a challenge, if answered incorrectly, would be all the trouble a black man could handle. He had been told that, in the army, fighting with an officer could get a man shot.

"You deaf, nigger?"

"No."

"You good as me?"

"Sure. I said it, didn't I? But in the army I cain't—"

"You see any rank marks on me?"

"No, I don't see no marks."

The captain walked over to where he was sitting and cuffed him. Willie's cap tumbled into the dust.

"You good as me?" the captain repeated.

Willie stood up, his face burning from the shame of the blow and the badgering in front of his new friends. He put up his fists, and the two men began circling. The captain was very quick on his feet and he had a clever way of tucking his chin behind his forward shoulder so that Willie couldn't see much of a target. But Willie felt so much bigger that he was afraid he might do the officer some real harm. While Willie was considering the "what ifs," the captain planted two quick jabs into his midsection and then flicked upwards to catch Willie against the left side of the jaw. With the jarring punch, Willie knew he was up against a professional fighter. He ached down to his heels. Determined to end it quickly, Willie swung a heavy right at the bobbing figure. Captain Ashley let the blow slide over his shoulder, suddenly grabbed the overextended arm, whirled his back on Willie, and pulled forward at the same time. Willie sailed over the captain's back and slammed into the ground so hard and flat that the breath was knocked out of him. While he lay there gasping for air and fighting the paralysis in his chest, Captain Ashley calmly returned to the foot of the shade tree and put on his blouse. He returned his cap to its original jaunty air. As Willie slowly sat up, the captain extended his hand to help him to his feet and then turned to the company.

"That wasn't quite fair. What I just did to this man is part of a special kind of fighting you'll be learning all about very soon. Knowing this kind of fighting gives you quite an advantage. As you just saw."

He looked over to Willie who was brushing the dirt and dust from his uniform.

"By the way, it's 'sir' when you talk to an officer."

The captain seemed about to say more when he caught sight of Willie's stomach as Willie straightened out his fatigue uniform.

"What happened to your belly?"

"Dey built a fire on it."

"They built a fire on it, sir!"

"White folks built a fire on it, sir!"

"Where?"

"Roanoke, Virginia."

The captain paused. Willie picked up the cue.

"Roanoke, Virginia, sir!"

Captain Ashley turned back to his troops. He was smiling.

"Yes, sir, men, I think you are going to do just fine in this training program."

He never called any of them "nigger" again, and no one ever forgot to say "sir" when addressing him.

But the new experience gradually settled down into the tedious routine of basic military training. At the end of two months, Captain Ashley felt that at least he had parade-ground discipline to show for his efforts. The outstanding performance by the Negro troops in a Kansas City parade met with silence along the parade route. Yet the white audience broke into repeated applause for the colorful white marching units that came from many of the states. The significance of the coolness was not lost on Captain Ashley, who followed his unit along the route in civilian clothes. As he had warned, black participants were not acceptable, even as kitchen help. Only one test would make them so: combat. Only a brilliant combat record would permit the North to tap the large Negro manpower reserves. The only way to build a distinguished service record was through audacity and discipline. The soul of audacity was self-confidence. For the next month he would concentrate on tactical problems that his new command would help him solve. He brushed aside the knowledge that while audacity might bring victories, it always brought heavy casualties. He would then be ready to lead small raiding parties into Missouri to rescue slaves.

Considering his three companies as a battalion force, Captain Ashley built a model village at one end of the training encampment. He then had carpenters build a replica of the town and the field around it on a large sand table. He told the battalion to choose leaders. He then gave the leaders selected pieces of the problem, designing an attack upon the town. The new mess attendants and drivers welcomed the highly realistic approach to a "real" problem of war and plunged happily into their assignments in general strategy, communications, company tactics, route of escape, handling of military prisoners, treatment of civilians, attention to wounded, rearguard action, and overall critique. Captain Ashley and his staff kept out of all decisions.

To the practiced eye, however, the town was a perfect trap. The best approach for speed of movement was along a single dirt road. Along the way to the town, the road passed through lightly wooded hills, where the Negroes had been told the referees for the attack would probably position themselves. Beyond the town was a swiftly moving river some seventy yards wide. In front of the town flat fields offered no concealment except at night. If trapped between fields and river, the attackers would suffer annihilation. Captain Ashley intended to have the attackers discover the exigencies of combat early on. The selected leaders planned a three-pronged attack at night. The major force, some two hundred men, was to advance along the road at night until in position in front of the town, whereupon the attack would begin. On the night of the attack, Captain Ashley secretly moved artillery pieces up into the hills overlooking the road. White artillerymen manned the guns. Blank rounds were prepared and the guns pointed toward the expected route of march, the single dirt road.

The hidden artillerymen heard the first sounds of the infantry marching up the road at about 2:00 A.M. Guarding their lighted tapers behind blankets, the gunners waited for Captain Ashley's whistle. When it came, the guns all fired together. The crash of the combined field pieces seemed to explode from within the ears of the new troops. It was thousands of times worse than the worst thunderstorms any of them had ever endured. Some actually fell down believing themselves wounded. Many turned in terror and ran from the flashing muzzles. The attack came to a halt, faltered, and then simply melted away into a rout. Muskets and packs were flung to the ground as impediments to the more important task of flight.

There was no satisfaction in the knowledge that he had been right, but Captain Ashley believed that the early reality of battlefield terror would save the lives of his recruits in the long run. There would be many days of explaining before they would trust him again, and he needed their trust above everything. But the night held an unexpected denouement for Captain Ashley.

He should have realized that the order of the cease-fire for the cannon was slightly irregular. Although they were stopping before his whistle, he assumed that the gunners could see the flight of the attackers and were saving their rounds. When he went to investigate the cannon positions nearest his command post, he found the gunners tied to their pieces and all ammunition removed. By inching his way toward the road he could hear urgent, whispered commands regrouping the remainder of the attacking force. In less than a quarter hour nearly a hundred soldiers resumed their attack on the town, which fell with only a whimper to a flanking attack that bypassed the frontal breastworks thrown up after dark.

The referees declared the attack a "disastrous success." At the critique the next morning, Captain Ashley asked who had captured the guns and regrouped the attackers.

"Willie," laughed a dozen proud throats.

"Willie what?" asked Captain Ashley.

"Willie, sir!" chorused the battalion.

Washburn faded from everything but the pay records, and he was known as "Willie, sir" for the remainder of his military career. They even called him "Willie, sir" while he was sewing on the illegal bright gold sergeant stripes that night. Explain as he would that soldiers do not address sergeants as "sir," Captain Ashley found himself helpless before the explanation that "Willie, sir" was not a rank, just a name.

But that night spawned more than just a brilliant military career. From the hundred men who had regrouped with Willie came the legend of the Dark Rocks of Milliken's Bend in 1862. This legend finally brought Captain Ashley the caliber of recruits he needed for the crack Negro regiment that had been his goal. The legend actually brought him more good men than he could properly handle. At Milliken's Bend, Captain Ashley's "troops" had been among the few in the Union forces who had not fled from what was a near catastrophe. Sturdy as boulders, the black soldiers had helped cover a bewildering retreat. Milliken's Bend taught Lincoln to expect a long war. Milliken's Bend reminded Captain Ashley that while discipline can make good soldiers, the will to succeed can make great ones.

Under the wink-and-look-the-other-way orders of Major General Bell of the western armies, Captain Ashley's irregulars made over a hundred sorties into Missouri and Tennessee to encourage and guide "contraband" blacks to the safety of Union lines. Ashley estimated that between two and four thousand Negroes escaped slavery because of his men's efforts.

Some of the slaves even brought their families into the North, settled them, and then returned to volunteer for a fighting unit in 1863. One enfeebled old man was carried over three hundred miles by his family so he could die free, a privilege almost beyond dreaming. Babies were born on the furtive night marches. Ambushes and counterambushes became common. Punishment, as warned, was swift and brutal. The Southerners were quick to defend their property. A strong network of informers and night-riding avengers grew in efficiency and cleverness as the drain of Negroes intensified. Members of Captain Ashley's raiders soon discovered it was better to die defending their charges than to surrender to their pursuers. Captured raiders were often mutilated, maimed, blinded, or hanged (a favor returned when possible). Return to slavery, usually after a near-crippling lashing, was common for escapees and raiders, many of whom had been born free men in the North. Some of the raiders spent the remainder of the war in the Deep South shackled daily to vehicles of agricultural production.

Since President Lincoln had once proposed paying slaveholders three hundred dollars for each freed slave, Captain Ashley estimated that the raiders had cost the Confederacy over a million dollars in lost "property."

"Not bad for dollar-a-week mule skinners," said General Bell. His official report of his unofficial campaign eventually found its way to Lincoln's desk. General Bell strongly urged the incorporation of Negroes into regular combat units of the Union army. In Bell's judgment, the success of the repeated sorties into the South, and the performance under fire of Negroes at Milliken's Bend, were proof enough of black courage. Lincoln's note to General Bell expressed personal commendation and appreciation, as well as the news that in early 1863 all slaves would be proclaimed emancipated and blacks would be admitted into the army as part of the United States Colored Troops. He further suggested that Captain Ashley ought to be promoted.

The camp for the Negro regiment was moved to Pennsylvania. The gray-black symbol of Gibraltar became their first uniform patch, and the regiment was assigned a number, the 365th (C). The C stood for *colored,* and no protestations from now-Major Ashley could change it.

At the opening of the new camp, Major Ashley spoke to over two thousand recruits in his opening day address. He noted the difference in their eyes. He welcomed them with an exciting speech, paying tribute to the Black Rocks of Milliken's Bend. He brought them to earth with the reminder that the legend now belonged to history but their backsides belonged to him.

Early that evening, Major Ashley's aide asked if Willie could see his commanding officer. When Willie entered and saluted, the salute was returned and a chair proffered.

"Sit down, Willie. You didn't come by to discuss the usual lack of proper training facilities. What's cooking?"

"Major Ashley, sir, beggin' you' pardon, but I'm a little bit worried."

"About what?"

" 'Bout bein' a Gibraltar."

"Please, Willie, we've made this into a proud outfit with that story. Look at those new, good men out there, and more wanting to get in every day. Why would you want to change a good thing?"

"Because, sir, that rock means you is defending somethin'. Defense is not why these boys joined up with this here army. We'll finish all the basic training exactly like you says and then, wif yo' permission, sir, I'd like to show you the kind of fightin' these boys can really do."

Major Ashley was intrigued. He had never seen Willie like this.

"You're on, Willie. We have eight weeks to make soldiers. Then you have one more day to surprise me."

Willie nodded and left the tent. He was smiling. He knew the major would never believe the evidence even after he saw it happen right in front of him. Even after all their raids together.

The training of the new companies was even stricter than the agonies and torments endured by Willie's class the year before. The new black noncommissioned officers were tyrants. Most of the instructors were the survivors of Milliken's Bend, and they were dedicated to the practical commitment of weeding out the weak. The uniforms fit, the scheduling was prompt, and the food the best that Major Ashley could find. The only thing wrong, he concluded, was that the Union was losing the war.

Although the training went well, morale crumbled during the now-traditional night attack on the training town that had created "Willie, sir." This time Willie had positioned cadre infantry around the surprise cannon to protect them if anyone tried to duplicate his own maneuver. But not one of the recruits had the imagination or courage to conceive and execute Willie's original tactics. The attack failed.

The training cycle ended a week later. The night before the last day of basic training, Willie visited Major Ashley's tent once more. Again he was offered a chair.

"Major, suh. I came to ask permission to give you the demonstration we discussed eight weeks ago. I'd like to do it tomorrow night. We is so ready we don' need the extra day you offered me."

"All right with me, Willie. What will you need and what do you intend to demonstrate with your maneuver? I'm going to have to explain your purpose to the general who's coming here for the graduation. I'd like to have him stay over for this demonstration."

The presence of army brass didn't seem to faze Willie.

"I needs twelve Yankee soldiers wearing Confederate-gray coats and caps. The maneuver is gwine show you and the general how a battalion of niggers takes over an enemy position at night."

"You mean attack the same town the recruits messed up last week?"

"Yessuh."

"What do you want the twelve Yankees dressed in Reb gray to do?"

"We wants them to dig defense pits in front of the town and man them tomorrow night."

"And then?"

"And then, suh, we is gonna send three hundred men right through them into the town. If any one of the three hundred is caught, the whole bet is off."

"What bet?"

"Major, if we gets through, every man gets a three-day pass. If even one of the attacking force is captured we is gwine buy you the best soldierin' horse in Pennsylvania."

"Why, Willie?"

" 'Member what I said about not likin' the Gibraltar talk? Ain't our way to stand like rocks. Cain't rightly 'splain, suh, but it ain't our way. The way I sees this war, deys gonna be so many men and horses and cannon and such in the war before long that everybody's gwine to bog down from carrying too much. That's when somebody who can get through dem bogs is gonna be very important. Dat's us. You'll see."

Major Ashley thought about that. A war of movement was the only kind of war he really knew. Where did this semiliterate ex-slave get such depth of understanding about the strategies of the service? If the Union ever permitted the commissioning of a Negro, he wanted to be among the first to be able to salute "Willie, sir."

"What time do you want to start the exercise?"

"Ten P.M., suh."

"Very well, Willie, we'll start at ten o'clock tomorrow night. The signal will be a pistol shot from me up on the hill. You will then infiltrate three hundred men through the three listening posts into frontal attack positions in front of the town. Completely unobserved. The operation will end by 3 A.M. How wide do you think the infiltration front should be?"

"Would a hundred yards be all right, suh?"

"Impossible, Willie. You couldn't get three hundred shadows through a hundred-yard front, let alone three hundred men. Let's give you at least two hundred yards width, fair enough?"

Willie shook his head. Reluctantly Major Ashley agreed to the compressed hundred-yard front. As Willie was about to leave the tent, Major Ashley spoke.

"Forget the horse, Willie. I'll settle for a good pair of gloves. And it's every man or nothing, right?"

Willie laughed.

"Thas' the only way, Major!"

The ease with which Willie seemed to melt into the night as he left the tent suggested to Major Ashley that he had better select the twelve sentries personally.

The last day of training went so smoothly that Major Ashley realized the whole regiment was with the infiltrators in spirit. He surmised that they were probably with them to the full extent of a month's wages as well. He decided to sit up through the entire experiment to make sure that the decisions by the three majors who would patrol the field as judges would be accurate. He hoped the visiting general would share his curiosity. During the morning he picked twelve men from a neighboring platoon of white sappers for the sentry pits. He wanted men well versed in the sounds of the earth.

The graduation parade that afternoon was noteworthy for the vigor of the marching men and the imagination of the special drill team. Major Ashley smiled privately. From the news in Virginia and along the Mississippi, the Union forces would need all the optimism and panache they could muster. Even more, they would need discipline to hold fast in the midst of the savagery awaiting them. He wondered if these eager-eyed young men manifested only the semblance of discipline in the faultless straight lines of their parade.

"Amazing, Major, amazing," said the visiting general from Washington at his side on the reviewing stand. Between salutes, Major Ashley put forth his invitation.

"If you can stay the night with us, General Meade, I promise you a front-row seat on a field exercise you'll never forget."

"Why not, Major? You have no idea what a chaotic mess Washington has become. Give me a simple battlefield every time. Most of your enemies are in front of you in battle. You have no idea how lucky you are."

"It has been challenging, sir. By the way, tonight's exercise has been created by the troops. I'll explain it at supper."

At 8:00 P.M., when a heavy darkness had settled over the camp, Major Ashley met Willie and three of his sergeants, the twelve sappers, and the three majors who were serving as field judges. The general remained in the background, a heavy overcoat covering his rank. Major Ashley had drawn a sketch of the hundred-yard-wide battlefield on a large sheet of paper, which he tacked to an easel. He hung a lantern from a nearby tree branch. At one end of the sketch lay the target town, at the other the entrance road where the troops had panicked the week before. He pointed to the town end.

"The twelve sappers will head out now in three teams and construct listening dugouts somewhere in front of the immediate town perimeter. Sometime between 10:00 P.M. and 3:00 A.M., Sergeant Washburn will infiltrate three hundred men through the sapper listening posts and take up formal attack positions at the edge of the town. If Sergeant Washburn's men can all get by the listening posts, then we may assume the town will fall, and the attackers will be declared victorious. If any of you men in the pits hears or sees anything to warrant suspicion, call out "Halt!" If you prefer to fire because the enemy does not halt, you may fire your blank charges. If you catch or 'kill' a single infiltrator, the attack is a failure. Just one.

"Sergeant Washburn's troops are not to execute pretend 'kills' on the outposts. Their entire mission is total infiltration without detection. The attacking troops will not know where the listening posts are, other than somewhere in front of the town. We have drawn the side boundaries of the hundred-yard front into the grass with a mixture of lime and water. The three field judges are strangers to all of us, and we are guaranteed of their impartiality. They will wander the field all night. Their word is final. All right, let's get to it."

Willie followed the sapper teams into the dark for a few steps until he came to the start of the white lime line marking the rear edge of the attack area. Major Ashley watched as Willie knelt down to smell the mixture, rubbing some between his fingers. The way across the battlefield was simple, due south, with no turns. He gathered his sergeants around him and faded into the night toward the company area. Major Ashley knew that he would probably see Willie again around 3:00 A.M. in the attack line.

The night was heavy with dew and seemed unusually quiet. It was also unusually dark because of the new moon and the low-lying clouds. Chalk one up for Willie, thought Major Ashley, he sure picked the right night. Camp chairs, blankets, and a bottle of whiskey had been set up on the knoll overlooking the attack area. Major Ashley

and the general established themselves there at ten o'clock and prepared to let their ears tell them the story of Willie's infiltration demonstration. It turned out to be the most boring night of Major Ashley's
career. The whole exercise was soundless. Twice he dozed. Once he
was awakened by a discharged musket. Expecting the experiment to
end, he noted the sound in his log at 1:22 A.M. It was the only entry
in the book since 10:00 P.M. when he had assumed his watch. Nothing came of the shot, a mistake by a tired sapper. There were no other
sounds.

The general sat very quietly beside him, sipping whiskey now and
then as the early fall damp made them long for bed and sleep. Also,
every now and then, he chuckled softly to himself. It was so still on
the infiltration area that the sound of the three majors' boots could
be heard as they wandered their rounds. Voices drifted up to them from
the sappers in the listening posts.

At last the agony of the long night was over. Just before 3:00 A.M.,
Major Ashley and the general walked down from the command post
out onto the infiltration field. Two enlisted men accompanied them with
lighted lanterns. As the party approached midfield, Major Ashley heard
Willie's deep command.

"First platoon, light your lanterns. Second platoon, light your lanterns. Third platoon, light your lanterns."

Before the astonished eyes of the command party, two lanterns lit
up in left-to-right sequence in front of each of three perfectly drawn
up platoons. The town stood directly behind them. The listening posts
were between the command party and the platoons.

"Report," commanded Willie.

"First platoon all present," barked back a crisp voice followed rapidly by the other two platoons in sequence.

Major Ashley approached Willie, who did a precise about-face and
saluted.

"The company's assembled and prepared to attack the position, sir."

Both officers returned the salute.

"Amazing," said the general. "But do you think it would be possible to speak to the listening posts for a minute?"

"Yes, sir, but perhaps we could save the general a little time. We
has got a little evidence right here."

The general looked at Major Ashley.

"By all means, Sergeant Washburn," answered Major Ashley. "Please proceed."

Willie turned to face his platoons.

"Company, parade rest. Lantern carriers, on yo' way. Bring the sacks."

Soundless runners detached themselves from the three platoons with small bundles, which they laid at the feet of the two officers. The bundles were opened.

"Christ almighty; they're Confederate caps!" stammered the general.

"Yes, sir, General," answered Willie. "They're the hats from the listening posts. Why don' you all look over at the lanterns?"

The general stared into the night at the lantern-lit listening positions. Unable to believe what he thought he saw, the general headed toward the nearest post with Major Ashley, equally incredulous, trotting behind him. Suddenly the general began to laugh. He stopped walking.

"My God, Ashley, don't you see it? Those sappers are wearing red railway-porter caps and don't even know it!"

Then the laughter swept the field. The lanterns reflected the complete and happy triumph of the perfectly executed infiltration by the three hundred men. Major Ashley looked over at Willie. Ramrod straight, the big sergeant had tears of relief and joy running down his cheeks.

"Three-day passes for everyone," Major Ashley announced. As he walked back by Willie's position with the general, Major Ashley asked Willie to drop by his tent around noon the next day if he were still in camp.

"Never saw a single one of those goddamn coons," one of the referees said as he ambled over to Major Ashley when Willie had dismissed the company.

"Then you might wish to keep the ribbon with the little bells they tied around your boots, Major," replied a suddenly defensive Major Ashley. The general laughed again and returned to the command post.

"Ashley, there'll be a time for these men, and I'll never forget this exercise. My compliments to that sergeant of yours, and good night to you, sir."

"Good night, General Meade."

The next afternoon Willie and Major Ashley worked out a number of plans utilizing the unique skills of the Negro volunteers. To Major Ashley it was all too clear that the terror tactics of a successful night infiltration might give the bulky and balky Union army a little extra time to rouse itself. Time was the Union's most important commodity. He saw even the smallest battlefield triumph as an incalculable advantage to the disinclined-to-fight North.

To Willie, the "African tactics" for which he had trained his recruits were heady returns for the hours of crawling, crouching, sniffing, and creeping in the dark after an already-exhausting day of training. To Willie, a black man who couldn't move as well in the night as a white man in the day was only half a soldier. He got a chance to prove part of his case at Chancellorsville in 1863.

The brutal chaos of Chancellorsville resulted in a Union defeat. The Union losses would have been even greater had Willie's men not been able to work their way into the Confederate lines to discourage any thoughts of night pursuit. The Negro regiment also learned there were two sets of rules in the war. All of Willie's men who were captured were promptly hanged. In the chill light of dawn, Willie watched numbly as he counted fourteen black bodies swaying from makeshift gallows. It was a small comfort to Willie to know that many times fourteen Confederates had died first in hand-to-hand skirmishes throughout the night. The Union retreat had been without incident.

"That's the kind of fightin' I'se been talking about, sir," Willie said to Major Ashley a few days after Chancellorsville. "Our boys can do everything those Berdan's Sharpshooters can do, but especially we can do them in the dark.

"Those Rebs cain't hardly get no black men to fight for them. Every time a slave puts on a Reb uniform he jes' skedaddles over here to be with us. And when we goes callin', them Rebs don' know if they'se lookin' at one of they own or one of us. And if it's one of us, it's probably already too late for ol' Johnny Reb to do anything 'bout it 'cause he jes' died from being skeered to death. Also, we can learn what the Rebs is fixin' to do in time to stop 'em.

"What you say, suh? No more of this Gibraltar stuff. From now on we is midnight attack specialists!"

And that's how the 365th Sharpshooters (C) entered the organizational manifest of the United States Colored Troops. The gray shoulder patches of Gibraltar were replaced with midnight blue patches saying nothing. The "silent patch" of the 365th was the only Negro unit mark that commanded instant respect throughout the Union army. It was a short-lived distinction. After Petersburg, the 365th Sharpshooters (C) vanished from the Union rolls.

*   *   *

Willie's greatest contribution to the war, before the siege of Petersburg, came not very far from the Negro regiment's training camp in southeastern Pennsylvania. In 1863, near Gettysburg, the full might of both armies exploded for the three bloodiest days of the war. At the end of the second day, Willie and now–Lieutenant Colonel Ashley were sent for by the commanding general of the Union forces, George Meade.

The stench of death permeated even the high command's quarters. The urgency of suddenly changed orders and ultimate-effort demands was commonplace in the furious pace of the coming and going of exhausted aides and unit commanders who had already given their ultimate efforts. General Meade wasted no time when the two arrived at his tent.

"I need to know one thing, Colonel Ashley. Are they going to try it again tomorrow or are they going home? I've got some fancy-pants reserves coming about midday, but if the Rebs decide to come through early, they might just make it this time. We also have a chance to break them. One minute we were just tracking each other, and the next thing I know we're tearing at each other's bowels through the orchards. I'd feel a lot better about tomorrow if I knew whether they were charging again, digging in, or turning tail. My cannon are about worn out. If they come at us again, there's only one place for a real attack, and I'm going to have to put every good gun into that area before daylight. If they make it through us this time, we'll have to evacuate Washington. I believe they're as whipped as we are, but I've got to find out. I was at the Point with many Southern officers. Some of them are so brave they scare me. Can Sergeant Washburn and his men get into their lines, find out the enemy's intentions, and get back to me before dawn?"

"Yes, sir," said Colonel Ashley and Willie together.

General Meade nodded, pointed to his map of last-known positions, and then left his tent. Colonel Ashley and Willie picked entry points for six teams of three men dressed as laborers. They were to operate separately, reporting to Colonel Ashley at a central point on the way out. There was no time to warn the Union positions, so the infiltration maneuver would have to be successful both leaving and returning. Colonel Ashley set up his post shortly after leaving the command area, and Willie went to find seventeen volunteers to join him.

It took the six teams over an hour to pass through their own lines and infiltrate the Confederate positions. As General Meade had suspected, the bloodletting had been so fierce on both sides that the teams hardly felt they had exchanged one army for another. But all the overheard conversations led nowhere. The Negroes moved carefully, carrying ammunition, hospital supplies, or food from one dimly lit area to another, hoping eventually to work close to General Lee's headquarters. But they never found it. Twice Willie heard discussions of picket lines voiced with some anxiety. When Willie checked with his men, they shed even less light on the enigma, except for the same concern for their horses. Willie decided to follow his timetable and return with what he had so that wiser heads could interpret. He felt useless.

It was nearly 3:00 A.M. by the time the black patrols returned—all of them. Willie brought them all to report to Colonel Ashley. The results caused Ashley to wonder if he should even wake General Meade. However, it's a rare soldier who receives a reprimand for following orders, he concluded as he and Willie awakened the general's aide twenty minutes later. General Meade soon appeared carrying two cups of coffee. He gave one to each.

"Well?" he asked wearily.

"Nothing, sir. Everything over there is as confused as it appears to be here. Willie's scouts report lots of wounded but high morale. They couldn't get near General Lee's headquarters. There seemed to be a lot of talk about picket lines. Willie heard it, and several of the units mentioned it as well. But none reports seeing anything significant."

Meade quickly called his aide and issued the most crucial orders of what would become known as the Battle of Gettysburg. He positioned men and cannon to repulse a full-scale charge on Cemetery Ridge by the Confederate infantry reserves known to be under the command of Gen. George Pickett of Virginia, a former messmate of Meade's from the war with Mexico.

Pickett lost three-quarters of the last good reserve division in the Confederate army in three extraordinary charges that afternoon. Lee abandoned the field, and the military fortunes of the Confederacy drained with him. Willie Washburn became the first Negro to wear sergeant major stripes. Lieutenant Colonel Ashley won his eagles.

By the time Grant became Commanding General of the Army in 1864, there were eighteen Medals of Honor in the 48th Pennsylvania regiment, and the Sharpshooters' legend had grown. The legend emphasized doing the unexpected with style and courage. It became a tradition for the Sharpshooters to announce their presence in a new battle area by exchanging Rebel caps for Union caps in a trench, listening post, or picket line, killing just one member of the defending team in the process. Soundlessly. In over fifty raids, Willie had only lost two men: one through carelessness, one through disobedience. Again, both were hanged. But wherever Colonel Ashley moved his regiment, when the time came for a large-scale attack across an army or corps front, the Negro regiment usually led the way before dawn with devastating ease. The foe was generally exhausted from too many nights of terror-driven vigilance. Inexperienced Southern troops were often captured in a paralysis of fear. Capture was the surest way out.

On the second day of the Wilderness campaign, as Grant moved the once-sluggish Army of the Potomac into the attack, Colonel Ashley was wounded by a spent artillery round. It hurled out of the early morning fog of the James River and ricocheted off a pine tree. A shell fragment broke four ribs. While convalescing in a Washington hospital, Ashley often found himself sitting on a balcony watching the early morning sun burn off the bottom fog. The ephemeral scene gave him the idea of how his soldiers could infiltrate enemy positions even in the daylight in full regiment force. The effect could be spectacular.

Colonel Ashley shared his idea with Willie when he returned to the regiment a month later. Willie liked the prospect and tested the concept with a patrol-sized force on three different bivouac areas. Two were successful. A sudden lifting of the fog left the third patrol totally vulnerable. The most difficult part of the infiltration in force proved to be communications within the infiltrating unit. Willie suggested painting bright markers on the backs of every noncommissioned officer. Yellow seemed to do as well as any other color in the fog, and soon gallons of yellow paint found their way onto Colonel Ashley's supply manifest. Through the offices of General Meade, Colonel Ashley managed to arrange a chilly demonstration for General Grant. Grant was mildly impressed, not so much with the unit infiltration, which seemed to have too many reasons for failure built into the scheme, as with the spirit and discipline of the black troops.

"Someday, Colonel, maybe someday. Keep practicing. A fine group, by the way."

Practicing meant in one's spare time. In Grant's Wilderness campaign there was no such thing. Grant met the Confederate armies head-on wherever he could. His pursuit was relentless. Men, mounts, and cannon all seemed to speak in raspy degrees of exhaustion. But the enemy kept falling back as the brutal days of the Wilderness campaign began to bear fruit. Consistent victories, with persistent pressures following them, did what Burnside, Hooker, and Meade had not been able to accomplish. The war was now entirely in the enemy's camp.

"It would appear that I've finally found a general," Lincoln is reputed to have said.

The Union casualties were high, but the mileage was impressive enough to balance the record until Petersburg.

General Beauregard doubted that General Grant would send a third attack in on the heels of the other two, but he was not a man to be sloppy about possibilities. He ordered every available man assigned to burial duty. This was a fortunate decision for the oldest second lieutenant in the Army of the Potomac who, two days earlier, had discovered that the Union positions were just barely visible from near the location of the Whitworths on the plateau.

Knowing that, Lieutenant Curran had to solve only four simple problems and the Battle of Petersburg would be over: escape, placement of marking reflectors near the battery, return to the Union lines, and the building of a tunnel to the guns.

Escape was the simplest part of Curran's plan. That evening, when the soup detail arrived, a savage fight in the corner of the stockade took the attention of all the accompanying guards. One prisoner was killed by the exhausted, anxious guards. But by the time the squad reassembled after establishing order, Lieutenant Curran was wearing Confederate gray, and he was gingerly backing out of the compound with his fellow guards, musket and bayonet at the ready. That night he returned with the officer of the guard for that officer's first personal inspection of the compound interior. A cocked revolver went unnoticed under Curran's cape. When the two left, the officer of the guard bore a striking resemblance to a gangling Union private with a gift for mimicry. The officer of the guard had decided that a rebellious black sergeant in manacles had need of further discipline and was removing him. Somewhere between the prison compound and the first picket line the trio vanished.

The oldest lieutenant in the Army of the Potomac worked his way to the Confederate front lines. From there he volunteered for night-patrol duty, after which he vanished again.

A young Confederate officer coughed nervously at the entrance to the Whitworth battery compound on the Petersburg Heights. His uniform signified a staff officer from general headquarters, now located within a few miles of the battery. The staff officer was followed at a respectful distance by a muscular Negro orderly who hefted a large field sack over his shoulder.

"Beggin' the captain's pardon," began the staff officer in measured Southern politeness, "but General Beauregard sends his compliments for the 'extraordinary efforts of the day.' Them's his exact words, sir."

Not even bothering to return the salute or look at the speaker, the artillery commander slowly stuck bone-weary legs out in front of the ammunition box on which he sat and painfully made room for his heels in the dust.

"Thank the general for his courtesy."

"Yes, sir," continued the eager-voiced messenger. "The general sent along some Yankee telescopes captured two days ago. He thought you might like to look over a few." He beckoned his orderly forward with the heavy sack.

"Hold it, sonny!" commanded a voice from the shadows. "Put the bag down right there, boy," the voice ordered the orderly. A gaunt captain in a yellowed undershirt, with suspendered breeches flopping loosely over heavy field boots, stepped slowly into the half-light of the evening. A long cavalry revolver was held in a steady hand.

"Undo the bag right there," he said to the orderly.

After looking carefully into the bag and then feeling carefully among the wares, the angular captain broke into a slow grin.

"Right friendly of the Yankees to leave such good equipment around for their country cousins."

"Never mind," interrupted the battery commander. "I've already got a telescope. Ask General Beauregard if he can spare twenty-five casks of powder."

"Surely the captain knows—" began the young lieutenant, nearly tripping over his sword as he walked around to get into better position to speak to the commander.

"You goddamn right 'the captain knows'! but wipe your nose and ask the general anyway. How does he expect us to stop the next one, by throwing these optics at them?"

"No, sir."

"Never mind, lad. It's not your fault—or the general's. Thank the general and tell him I will relay his generous compliment to the men. It will be appreciated. We lost six, but the guns are all safe and fully operational."

"I'll report your thanks and the good condition of your battery as soon as I can get back to headquarters tonight. Would the captain mind if I took some of these telescopes to the flank over yonder? They're powerful good glasses, sir."

"So you've said. They're a mite busy cleaning up. Hope it doesn't upset your supper."

The lieutenant saluted and, followed by his orderly with the sack, withdrew to the flank area. They stepped carefully over the bodies of the fallen Negroes not yet collected into the common pits.

As the two moved off into the lengthening shadows, the captain with the revolver spoke again.

"I know that big nigger. Damn if I don't. And he wasn't so quick to jump when I knew him, either. Someplace around central Virginia when we used to have manner-teaching time every so often. It'll come by-and-by."

"Relax, Tom. That's the trouble with you slave wallopers. Suspicious of every big darky. To us mountain boys they all look the same. Tell you what, we got enough to worry about. General Beauregard was telling us, polite as always, to put a few more pieces on the flank, which we've already done. I suspect that's one of the things that boy is supposed to report on when he gets back. But if it makes you feel any better, why don't you go and keep those two company?"

"Think I will."

The captain caught up to the staff officer and his orderly at the edge of the clearing on their right flank, the area from which the Negro charge had exploded the previous dawn. The staff officer had given away three telescopes to junior officers in charge of restoring the trenches and was looking out over the valley. He saluted when he saw the captain.

"Good of you to come along, sir. Would you say that pine behind Timothy is the tallest tree on this flank?"

"Why?"

"Because the general gave us a small job, and I can't quite see well enough in this light. Do you think it's the tallest?"

"Probably."

"Thank you, sir. A most timely arrival. Timothy, climb up that tree behind you and tell me if you can see the Yankee lines from as high as you can get."

The black orderly dropped his sack and was up the tree in slow, powerful swings in seconds. Only a little hard breathing marked his progress after the first branches. From some forty feet up he soon called down.

"I can see some cookin' fires out dere, massah."

"Very fine. Come on down as soon as you count them."

"Lieutenant, why don't you just have the darky set up a telegraph line to General Grant's headquarters and bark a few times? Your voices go forever on a night like this. Even the bluebellies know enough to keep listening posts out there. Next time you have something to say to that big nigger, say it down here."

"Yes, sir. Wasn't thinking, sir. Sorry, awful sorry, sir. Won't happen again, sir. The general just wanted—"

"Oh, Christ!"

"Yes, sir."

The orderly was suddenly alongside the lieutenant, again shouldering the sack.

"Couple hundred, sir."

The lieutenant wrote the number down in a small booklet.

"Captain, would you be able to come with us over to the other side of the plateau? We'll need the tallest tree over there also."

"What for?"

"Same reason, sir," answered the lieutenant as they began working their way back toward the Whitworth area. "Beggin' your pardon, sir, but General Beauregard asked me to ask the battery commander if scouts were ever posted in the tallest trees flanking the battery at dawn to observe enemy movements?"

"The general asked that?"

"Yes, sir."

"Why didn't you ask the battery commander when you were talking to him with the 'general's compliments' and all that crap?"

"He looked powerful tired, sir. And I thought that if I could see for myself, I wouldn't have to bother him."

"Well, you're a thoughtful boy, sonny, but you might as well have asked. We don't post scouts in trees. We can see awful good right from here."

"Yes, sir. Oh, climb here, Timothy," he suddenly said to his servant. The captain stood back without an argument, his eyes twitching with apprehension.

"Only this time wait until you get down to report," added the lieutenant.

The eyes relaxed.

"Yessuh."

When the orderly was well up into the tree, the staff officer said, "Captain, the general asked me to ask the battery commander if he would mind posting a man in these flanking pines every night until we are out of these positions."

"You got that order in writing, Lieutenant?" asked the battery commander quietly walking up to the two men.

"No, sir, Captain. You know how the writing situation is these days. The general just said to put the suggestion before you."

The slave descended from the tree and stood waiting for his master to notice. The lieutenant nodded.

"See pretty good up there, too. Only not so many. Maybe half, suh."

He picked up his field sack and waited patiently for his next command.

Out of the corner of his eye, as if expecting a familiar movement, the captain glimpsed a woman weaving her way through the resting troops toward them.

"Laundry time," he said easily.

"Hell, Tom," answered the commander, turning away from General Beauregard's aide and dropping his voice, "why don't you do like I asked you and send that cheeky bitch packing?"

"She just delivers my laundry, sir."

"I know what she's delivering, Tom. It ain't exactly right for you to be flaunting your prowess with the camp-follower floozies in front of the men, you know. Rotten example."

"They like to see their officers makin' out, Captain Caitlin. Some of 'em even bet on it. Besides, that li'l ol' gal just loves it!"

"This is still a war, and if you'd pay attention to it there'd be no place for all these sluts with their screechin' and screamin'. I almost ache for another bluebelly attack just to keep them away for a few days."

"They've lost kin in this war too, suh."

The grudging acknowledgment of the commander was stifled by the arrival of the fleshy, disheveled laundress who had aged considerably before her time. Snarled, greasy hair clung to her face and neck. A torn blouse fell loosely off one shoulder. Her walk suggested a natural sensuousness that turned eyes as she glided toward the officers. She flipped the bundle of clothes to the captain, and as he reached out his arms to catch it, she whacked his backside. Then clutching his arm she chuckled.

"Honey," he whispered, "everyone's watchin'."

As she snuggled against him her eyes took in the two new arrivals. Suddenly she straightened and stared hard at the Negro. Then slowly the smile returned to her face as her tongue flicked out.

"Hello, Willie. What are you doing here? Father said you joined up with the Yankees. Tom, you remember ol' Willie boy? We once lit a fire on his belly to teach him manners."

The captain's revolver slid out again, noiselessly. The brittle voice broke off the words in splinters.

"Market day in Roanoke, nigger. Cocky you was then. Captain, we don't know what this darky's game is, but he ain't movin' 'til we check with headquarters. Something ain't right."

The heavy revolver slashed viciously toward Willie's head even as the sack caught Jerrud full in the face. He fired once in the direction of the broad chest bearing down at him. Willie's powerful arms wrapped around the captain, bending him backwards. He screamed as his back snapped and the revolver dropped from his hand.

The dumdum bullet intended for Willie tore a vicious hole in the middle of the laundress, who gasped and sat down suddenly. Slowly she put her hands over the blood which had started to spread over her dress.

"Oh, God," she said as she locked her fingers across her stomach. Stunned by the sudden tragedy, the circle of onlookers was silent. Willie shoved himself away from the paralyzed, dying Jerrud and crawled quickly to the laundress, who had now fallen into the dust. Gently he put his hands over hers. A hole the size of his fist marked the bullet's exit from her back.

"Miss Angelica, I'm sorry," he said in a low voice to the frightened woman who was suddenly staring death in the face.

"Willie," the word seemed to come from the bottom of her soul. "I'm the one who's sorry. Willie, I've been sorry for six years. And now

I'm going to be sorry forever. I'm going to burn for that fire forever. Oh, Willie!"

"Hush, ma'am. It's goin' to be all right soon as we can get a stretcher for you. And my stomach don't hurt none from that little fire. Don't fret. Yo' daddy gave me my freedom for it, so you done me a favor. I'll take care of you now. The bullet's gone clean through. That's good. Jes' hold on."

"Willie," her voice was growing softer and her eyes were starting to glaze. "Willie, put my hand on your stomach. Oh, my poor Willie. And. . . ."

"Yes'm."

"Put your cap on my grave, will you, please?"

"No need to talk like that. Doctor's coming."

"He'll not catch me. I can feel . . . oh, my beautiful Willie. I'm so sorry about what I did to you. Willie, you still there?"

"Yes'm."

"Willie," she hesitated, beginning to have trouble bridging her thoughts. "Daddy died last fall. Nobody to harvest the fields. Yankee soldiers everywhere. He had a stroke. Lay paralyzed for weeks and weeks. Everyday I asked him to forgive me, asked him and asked him. Know what he said?"

"No, Miss Angelica."

"Angelica, that's so much better than 'ma'am.' He didn't say anything, Willie. Not a thing. I don't think he even knew me. Willie, please forgive me. I don't want to burn. I don't want to burn!"

"Yo' daddy loved you, Miss Angelica. And you know he was mighty proud of how pretty you growed up to be. If they was any forgivin' to be done, you know he'd a done it if he could."

"I didn't deserve him, Willie. I don't deserve you, either. What made me so wicked? Can you ever forgive such a fool?"

Willie knelt beside her holding her lifeless hand until the stretcher-bearers arrived moments later to take the two bodies to the rear for burial. He went with them to help dig Angelica's grave. The weary diggers wanted to dump both bodies in the same shallow hole. Willie brushed the grave diggers away like spiders and spent the evening digging a deep pit for her, carefully marking the place with a sketch. He laid her gently in the earth as Bunko finally found him. They pounded a crude cross at her head, and Willie laid his cap on it as promised. While the two stood by her grave in the silence of the long Virginia twilight,

Willie said softly, "This war is gettin' to me. I'm gonna be mighty glad when it's finished."

"The general wants to see you two, if it's convenient," Captain Caitlin of the Whitworth battery said, walking quietly up behind them.

"Yes, sir," answered Bunko, pretending not to notice the two armed men who followed them unobtrusively to General Mahone, who was sitting on a stump overlooking the Union camps, where thousands of evening cooking fires flickered.

"These are the two, General," said the captain, saluting. Bunko and Willie saluted as well, standing at attention, much to the surprise of General Mahone.

"At ease, everyone," smiled General Mahone. "You two fellas have been having yourselves a time, running up and down trees and squeezin' folks to death. Understand you come from General Beauregard. Anything you want to share with me?"

"Yes, sir," answered Bunko. "We nearly didn't make it because of that fool captain with the pistol. But now that we are here, what we were told to say to you is supposed to be said to you alone."

"Mighta known. All right, Caitlin. These two are a little bashful now that they've torn up your camp and all. Maybe you could give us a few moments of privacy. Don't go so far away that you can't come back for a cup of coffee soon, hear?"

"Yes, sir, General." The three withdrew beyond earshot and took up positions of tense watchfulness.

"All right, boys," continued General Mahone, "you wanted to tell me something that General Beauregard hasn't had time to tell me himself? Who wants to start?"

The tone was congenial; the eyes were unwavering.

"Sir," Bunko began, looking for approval from Willie before proceeding, "what you see here is a charade, a scheme General Beauregard thought might get us through to you inconspicuously. Running into Tom Jerrud, who had tortured Willie six years ago, was a god-awful fluke."

"A charade, Lieutenant?"

"Yes, sir. I'm only a corporal. Willie, here, is the lieutenant. I believe, sir, that Willie is the first colored officer in the Confederate army. He's in charge of me. Everything you're going to hear is his idea. Willie, go ahead and tell General Mahone the plan."

"A colored lieutenant. My, my, this is interesting," said General Mahone.

"General, suh. I is awful new to this officer business. But I had me an idea a few weeks back, and when I 'splained it to General Beauregard he tol' me to come here and tell you. My idea is about colored deserters from the Confederate army, suh."

"Yes, Lieutenant Washburn, we have plenty—"

"Well, suh, there is a way to stop the desertin', a way special for colored boys. You know that lots of colored boys have been volunteering to serve. But lots of 'em have jes' been getting a uniform as an excuse to get off the farm and get close enough to the Yankee lines so they can desert. Lots of 'em then turn around and come back in blue to shoot the hand that fed 'em."

"An interesting way to put it. And then?"

"Suh, like I tol' General Beauregard, I believe we can skeer 'em into staying put by makin' sure they knows about us when they join up."

"Us?"

"Yessuh, the Colored Avengers of the Confederacy. Our job is to go on over into the Union side where the deserters are and quietly slit a few throats. The Yanks cain't tell one nigger from another, but the deserters can."

"An assassination squad!"

"Platoon, suh. The best men you could ever want to command."

"Sir," interrupted Bunko, "Willie's made nine trips behind the Union lines since Gettysburg."

"Nine crossings! That's im——"

"No trick at all, General," Willie smiled. "I'se black and I can sound awful dumb and agreeable."

It was General Mahone's turn to smile, a brief twitch. "That's a mighty bloody proposition."

"Yessuh, and we is probably too late. Maybe not. The Yanks is using lots of colored troops now, and we jes' gettin' around to understandin' the problem. Suh, Mr. Ballard freed me in fifty-eight and I went North. Nearly starved to death. I came home in sixty-one and worked in a whole passel of army camps as a cook, a messenger, and a transport skinner; and I'se even been a messenger in the fightin' from time to time. I picked up a musket and fought Yanks at Chickamauga and Stone River. Lots of colored boys with me, too. I guess that's how come General Bragg made me a lieutenant, and my idea of getting colored boys to stop desertin' brought me to you. This would make a good staging area for our platoon. With your permission, suh, I'd like to git back to Roanoke and bring the platoon up here for you to see. After we've been working this area for a few days, there ain't going to be any more nigger deserters."

General Mahone sat quietly for a few minutes; then looking absently into the sky he answered evenly:

"Tell you what, Lieutenant Washburn. Let's have a little test. I'll remand you and your white sidekick back to the custody of Captain Caitlin. Get to my tent and be in a position to slit my throat before dawn, and your platoon of Avengers has a job. Mess up and you'll have to stay with me and fight bluebellies in the normal way, or maybe we'll just have to hang you after I talk to General Beauregard. Ready to gamble?"

"Yessuh."

General Mahone waved Captain Caitlin back into his stump, explained the conditions, and had Willie and Bunko taken back to the Whitworth area. As they walked, Bunko remarked on General Mahone's five-foot stature.

"He ain't much of a man," answered Captain Caitlin, "but he's a hell of a general."

General Mahone alerted his sentries to be particularly watchful that night. Before going to sleep, he slid his revolver under his thin camp pillow. He smiled. Lt. Willie Washburn didn't know that Bill Mahone was the lightest-sleeping general in the Confederate army.

In the morning Captain Caitlin and the two guards were found bound and gagged a hundred yards from the Whitworths. Both "guests" were gone. Captain Caitlin reported the embarrassment to General Mahone immediately.

"I've been had," admitted General Mahone. "Conned by a goddamn nigger and a skinny boy." He continued getting dressed, but as he picked up his revolver he paused to note the difference in the heft of the familiar weapon. His eyes then fell on his gloves where he had laid them on the camp table the night before. In the palm of the right glove nestled the six bullets from the Colt. He looked at Captain Caitlin.

"And don't bother lookin' for them, son. They're back with the Yanks by now. Probably been prisoners since that first attack." He was sitting on the edge of his cot reloading his revolver when Captain Caitlin saluted and departed unnoticed.

On the Petersburg mound on the morning after Angelica's death, the first rays of the summer sun were reflected by the lenses that Willie had tied high in the trees on either side of the battery.

CHAPTER 8

Conscience of a Commander

It was nearly three hours past midnight. Canvas covered the windows of the small farmhouse in the trees that had been used for a field dressing station and emergency surgery for the past five days. Outside, ambulances and commandeered farm wagons moved off in sporadic, bone-jarring journeys to railheads, from which the wounded would eventually be transported to hospitals in Washington and Philadelphia. Other wagons carried the dead to another of the broad cemeteries that documented the price of the Virginia campaign.

There had been little sleep for Colonel Zaretski since the 48th Pennsylvanians had charged Petersburg mound. Because he had spent so much time visiting the wounded, he had moved his headquarters tent close to the farmhouse. The visit to Grant had been lucky. And now his thoughts returned to the zesty optimism of Lieutenant Curran.

"Remarkable fellow, that Irishman," said Colonel Zaretski to Major Harrington, his artillery officer. "Talks funny but seems to have savage battle instincts."

"Yes, sir. Did you know the sun will be coming up in about an hour?"

"Can't seem to sleep, I. . . ," his voice trailed off.

"Brave thing he did for us there, calling in your fire so the rest of us could slither out. We left so many. . . ."

"Colonel, I think the doctor said he left some sleeping draughts in your desk drawer. Why not try one to take your mind off the wagons for a few hours? Anton, if you don't let yourself shut it off pretty soon, we'll be having an ambulance case instead of a colonel."

Colonel Zaretski nodded. Before Major Harrington could leave he searched his desk drawer for one of the draughts, located it, then discovered that his hands were too unsteady to open the packet.

He motioned the major closer to the table to hold a spoon while he reached back in the drawer for the sleeping draught. His thick fingers got most of the brown-white powder into the spoon, then into his mouth, followed by a long drink of water from the canteen draped over the back of his chair.

"You must be good for the soul, Harry. Been trying to do that simple thing for six hours. Thank you—and thank you for what you did up on the mound. We're putting you in for a promotion. You've already been noted in the dispatches."

"Thank you very much, sir."

There was a pause as the heavy eyes closed.

"Forgive me if my mind wanders a bit. The creaking of those wagons out there gets shriller every night. But would you believe it's the silence that crashes in?

"Harry, Curran wants to move the dirt through here, this building, on stretchers and haul it away in the ambulances. We'll dump it in ravines in the forest."

"Impossible, sir! We'll have to find another way. We have never yet had a single Confederate shell land among our ambulances. I am not going to risk the lives of future wounded for one glorious explosion."

"I've been thinking about it all week. There is no other way. And would you bargain a debatable point of honor against the lives of what remains of the whole regiment?"

In the duel of eyes, the major's fell first. Since the stark rage of Cold Harbor and the grotesque confusion of Spotsylvania, honor had ceased to have much meaning to either of these men. The only thing important now was a victory that would end the premature dying of the best part of the nation both loved in its entirety.

"Well then, we're agreed. We'll exchange principles for time. The plan is clever enough to stand a chance. I think General Grant likes it. And now, if you'll excuse me, I'll turn in. You were right. I'm quite worn out with optimism."

"Good night, sir."

"Good enough. Lieutenant Curran is getting to me. You know, in my home town of Monongamesh they used to say that putting a stick in the hands of an Irishman was the most dangerous game in town. I guess that includes a shovel."

CHAPTER 9

Anton Zaretski

For Anton Zaretski the recounting of his family's journey from Poland to Pennsylvania was a bore. The multiple agonies of the long voyage aboard the heaving sailing ship were too intense in the vivid awareness of a six-year-old boy to bear any retelling. The ignominy of being dumped onto the docks of Philadelphia like a commodity stung even in his mature remembrance. The strange noises and total confusion of all the passengers were epitomized by the stomach-turning bewilderment of his father, Jacob, who was trying to find the home of a second cousin. The frustration of that day, when neither immigration official, hack driver, nor policeman could understand Polish, with no shipboard friends who could speak for them, and no waiting relatives, was seared into a compartment of the past that he preferred to leave closed.

Full despair was dispelled only by the basic good humor of his father who often concluded the recounting of that day with a knee slap. "There was no cousin, either! Shot dead by the cops two weeks before. Probably deserved it. His father before him was hanged by the czar."

Funny in retelling, but at the time the discovery was like learning that the sun would not come up in the morning.

In the blur that followed landing in America, his resourceful father somehow got his wife and small son settled into an apartment and set out to find a job. But there was no work in Philadelphia that year for a premier pottery craftsman. He was also a premier consumer of schnapps, and he soon discovered several friendly Polish taverns. There he learned that American pottery was coming from a triangle bounded by Pennsylvania, Ohio, and Virginia. Philadelphia was for merchants, lawyers, and politicians. He headed west with his family eleven days after landing

in America. North of the unpronounceable Monongahela River they
found the lush valley community of unpronounceable Monongamesh.
They also found superb clay and great demand for Jacob Zaretski. He
soon settled into a good house with dozens of neighbors who spoke
Polish, German, Hungarian, and Serbian. He also made his most important discovery about America: the law was for all the people, even
non-English-speaking immigrants.

The knowledge came some years later while Jacob was carrying
home a box of factory seconds. The box obscured his vision as he
walked across an intersection, where he was ridden down by a pair
of high-stepping carriage horses. Jacob's right arm was broken, his ribs
were cracked, and his right ankle was dislocated. The carriage owner
demanded damages for injury to his horses. Tavern cronies suggested
to Jacob that he hire a lawyer and file countersuit. Which he did and
which he won, to the amount of five thousand dollars. It was such a
staggering sum that Jacob nearly killed his lawyer, who had promptly
claimed half of it for his fee. However, even twenty-five hundred
dollars made Jacob a rich man by all his previous standards. As his
bones mended, Jacob had his one important father-son conversation
with his teenage son.

"Anton," he asked his son in the corner of the tavern where he was
propped up for comfort and convenience of easy hospitality as he received
an almost endless line of thirsty well-wishers, "does this teach you anything
about such an amazing country?"

"Of course, Papa. In America a poor man is still a man with much
power because of the law. They told us such stories back in Poland."

"Yes, that's exactly what we were told. But people like me don't
believe such stories. But now it's true; I am worth more than a carriage horse. But that's not the lesson I had in mind this evening for
you. What else did we learn from this?"

Anton went blank. As he pondered the question he thought of the
glory his father was enjoying because of his new wealth. Anton grinned.

"Well, for one thing it's an expensive Polish custom to win money."

Jacob slapped his son's shoulder and then hugged him awkwardly.
He, too, laughed.

"Exactly, exactly! No, no, I don't mean buying a few drinks for your
friends who want to share your happiness. I mean really expensive."

"I don't understand, Papa."

"Anton, twenty-five hundred dollars makes me richer than I will ever
be again on one night. Believe me, I do not intend to hurl myself

in front of fancy horses every time I need schnapps money. But the crafty little lawyer who won this fortune for me also got twenty-five hundred dollars. He didn't have to break any of his bones doing it, either. And he does things like this all the time. Every month, Anton. I'll bet he gets paid something even when he loses, or maybe he doesn't even have to bring his aching client into a courtroom. Now to your slightly drunk father this seems like a wonderful way to make a living. Help yourself while helping others. So, you understand?"

"Not exactly."

"Then listen like the good son you have always tried to be. Tomorrow you are going to stop working in the mill and you are going to start reading law with Mr. Hurlwicz. In three years you, too, will be a lawyer."

Jacob Zaretski was beaming. Anton was numb. It was like getting on that pitching ship in Bremen. He had the same sinking feeling.

"Papa, I'm not sure I'm smart enough. And three years will take too much money now that you have—"

"All my money is something I earned for being careless. This is God's will. Money is only a tool for digging out of one hole into a better one until God has enough of small games. One day you will try to explain this to your children, and it will help to be a little drunk yourself. They will think you are crazy anyway. I give you Mr. Hurlwicz's card. He is expecting you at nine in the morning. So you will have to get a haircut, a bath, a shave, and two suits of clothes. Whatever Mr. Hurlwicz demands in payment, I will pay every month for the three years. Then my son, the attorney, will begin his distinguished career."

"Papa, it's too much."

"New pots for old, Anton. Just new pots for old. A good bargain when there isn't a cousin, eh?"

Then they both laughed, and friends went out with Anton to help him pick out two suits and to tell the barber to heat up the bathwater.

Issac Hurlwicz, an inspiring advocate for social justice, was a total autocrat in his own home. Food just so, rooms just so, guests greeted just so, and, above all, no unexpected crises. Order was the altar upon which his professional time was offered up. The two servants always seemed to speak in gentle whispers, shuffling soundlessly on unseen endless belts in harmonious efficiency, as if reading their master's thoughts. It was no wonder he was a bachelor.

Hurlwicz's office was an addition to the large frame house, which seemed to cry out for the excited shrieks of children in spite of the devotion to calm. It was too big for one man. Clients entered the office by way of the library, where they waited. An enlightening experience.

Anton waited there the first morning of his new life. He forgot his anxiety, however, as he walked along the shelves, taking in the strange and wondrous titles of plays, novels, histories, and poetry. He noted German as well as English authors, and several languages he didn't know. There were volumes of Greek classics and Jewish philosophy. There was nothing about the law. He was so busy looking at the literature of the Western world that he failed to hear his teacher enter the library from the study.

"Ah, good morning, Zaretski. You enjoy this room?"

"Good morning, Mr. Hurlwicz. Yes, sir, I do like this room. I've never seen a whole room of books before."

"You are welcome to anything here when you feel you have the time, or feel the need for diversion. The law can be dull. This is my storefront. As long as you are going to pay for your legal education, I shall make my confession to you early. It's a sham. Do you know the definition of an educated man?"

"Someone like yourself, sir. An educated man is someone who has gathered in all the knowledge of previous men."

"Let a tired and pragmatic man suggest something less obvious. Scattered through this room you may have noticed a few clever Greeks. There is also Shakespeare and Voltaire and the Bible. These hold all the deep thoughts, confusion, humor, beauty, tragedy, and truth a man can bear. An educated man, Zaretski, is one who knows the value of this truth, beauty, humor, and wisdom in whatever form he may find them. He knows their value because the more he learns, the more deeply he savors the really good thoughts and honest emotions.

"Now then, while you are ruining your breakfast digesting that shibboleth, let me begin our relationship with a simple promise and a few rules. The promise is that I shall teach you the law; justice you will have to seek on your own. You will read law with me every Monday, Wednesday, and Friday morning from seven-thirty until nine-thirty. From ten o'clock until 1:00 P.M. you shall serve with me as a law clerk in my office. From one until two you may dine with your family. From two until six you shall occupy the spare room in my office area as a study. You will have a key to the office so that you can study there in the evening as well. On Saturdays you will clerk from nine until six. You will also be able to assist me whenever I have to appear in court.

"I shall examine you twice each four months, orally and in writing. If you begin to fall behind, you shall be dropped. The fee for the three years is twenty-five hundred dollars. Your father has already paid me. If you fail, a pro rata share shall be deducted and the balance returned to your father. Your summers are your own. I suggest you spend them doing anything but the law, such as earning money for your partial support.

"Upon successful completion of your studies, we will go to Harrisburg for review by a council of judges. If the council passes favorably upon your studies, you shall be granted a license to practice law in Pennsylvania, and we shall see to finding you an appropriate shingle. Do you like the law, Zaretski?"

"I don't know, sir," he answered, overwhelmed by the thought of three years of such tyranny and by the size of his father's payment.

"Does this arrangement seem satisfactory?"

"I don't know."

"Come, lad, what do you know, then?"

"Clay, sir."

"Clay?"

"Yes, the good clay from which the factories of this valley draw breath. I understand clay."

Hurlwicz stepped back and swept an arm toward his open office doors.

"Come, then. A lawyer's time and advice are his principal assets. I think we are going to do very well together. Adam began as clay, you no doubt remember."

The year went quickly for Anton Zaretski, immigrant pottery apprentice, law student, and clerk. His father and mother saw little of him. His head often ached from the endless challenge of torts, opinions, counteropinions, interpretations, procedures, rules of evidence, contracts, deeds, trusts, estates, taxes, civil obedience, mortgages, and precedents. He had never dreamed that the fabric of society's backdrop could be so finely woven.

His first semester's examinations were perilously close to disaster. At the end of his second semester, he was almost a respectable scholar. He even had one glorious moment in court when his observation that a major witness was left-handed turned the case unexpectedly in favor of Hurlwicz's client. He found a hundred-dollar bill and a note saying "Well done, Anton" in an envelope on his desk the next morning.

The summers were good times of hard physical work in the pottery. There was not much need to think, and there was lots of time to discuss philosophy with his father and the other workers.

But it wasn't philosophy that awakened Anton to life during the summer; it was a brawl. He had just joined in the singing of two verses of a traditional Polish bar song on a carefree Saturday evening in the tavern when a group of tough German miners made so bold as to compare that singing to the creaking of the wheel used by effeminate potters in the artistry of creating chamber pots. In the following nonverbal exchange, Anton managed to smash one jaw, break his left hand, demolish one table by hurling two Germans onto it from the bar, and shatter one front window by being flung through it by the two Germans. It was the glass that started the blood flowing from his neck. When it wouldn't stop, they suspected he needed help beyond bar ice. He fainted outside the doctor's office. When he regained consciousness, he was in a strange, foul-smelling room, and his throat hurt. A young woman was leaning over him doing something to his neck.

"Very nice," he said, but the words came out like a wheel rolling over gravel.

She smiled.

"So you finally decided to rejoin the world, Polish, German, and otherwise. The two Germans are next door with their own share of broken bones. Your neck was nearly sliced through by the window glass. A near thing. You may never feel much like talking again. That's fine for a young lawyer. I'm Maria Rokoshy, your nurse. I'm Hungarian. The loss of one brawling Pole is no cause for tears. Keep your head as still as possible for the next week, and we may yet save you."

It took his throat ten months to heal, but it only took him two weeks to ask Maria Rokoshy to marry him. She demurred.

"Anyone with your temper is as liable to tear up a home as a barroom. My father's a big boozer and as fast a talker as yourself. Although I love him, I moved out. Who would ask for more of the same? Read how much comfort the law gives a brawler's wife, and find a sweet angel elsewhere to hold your head."

It was the worst setback of his life. Losing his voice, possibly his career, possibly his father's investment, and the girl he wanted to marry made his second year of study almost unbearable. It was hard to face his father, and Hurlwicz offered prickly solace. Work, the development of a real skill in preparing briefs, turned into an unexpected asset. Since he couldn't talk, the material had to stand up by itself on paper. In May of his second year, Hurlwicz complimented him.

"We may have a judge by the hand," he said concluding the second year of formal study. "These briefs are a trifle shallow, but the dedication shows talent for hard work and a clear grasp of fundamental issues. Treat yourself to a long, quiet walk in the hills."

His throat had healed enough to permit a "thank you," and he went for a walk in the crisp spring of the foothills. He hadn't had a drink in seven months. But Maria was still not seeing him, and his world appeared thoroughly mixed-up and confusing.

"You've been avoiding me of late," Maria said from under a tree near his path. She gave him a private smile and a direct look, leaving his soul bereft of covering. "The hospital has been quiet, the taverns orderly, and your studies brilliant. Don't be more modest than necessary. Congratulations. I hope you like cold pheasant; my father is a good shot. I think you should be able to handle some chilled light wine, and if your hand still hurts at domestic tasks, I'll pull the cork for you while you spread the tablecloth."

"Did Mr. Hurlwicz cook this up with you, Maria?" he asked, taken aback by the surprise encounter on the hillside.

"Of course. A girl can't take care of everything these days. Besides, why should a law student be opposed to a little conspiracy? Some things are best settled out of court."

He grinned as he spread the tablecloth. But he ate in silence. His throat still hurt too much for casual talking, and his heart was beating so fast his thoughts couldn't keep up. Why? his eyes asked her. But she avoided answering. She took off her bonnet to let the wind catch her hair.

"Anton Zaretski, you are spending too much time by yourself."

"I've tried—" he began.

"And you are thinking of too many theoretical problems with that old swindler, Hurlwicz. Look up from your books for a moment and gaze out over this valley. What do you see? Grass, trees, farms? Good! Now I'll tell you what you should be looking for. Do you remember that I told you I left my father's house because he drank too much? Well, he wasn't always drunk, and once, when sober, he told me there

was enough coal in this valley to fuel half of America. When you get
your shingle, I'll show you how to get your fortune."

He understood her talking, but he couldn't understand her timing.
"Why—?" he began once more.

But again she interrupted his painful speaking efforts by placing her
hand gently over his mouth. Then she took his hand and pressed it to
her cheek. While he sat numbly, she quickly put the dishes and food
remnants back into a basket and suddenly was gone. The fragrance of
her hair lingered longer than the scent of the spring blossoms.

Anton went back to the pottery for the summer, but now Sunday
afternoons found him wandering the hills until he found her. One drizzling
afternoon in late August he found her standing uncomfortably under
an oak near a small barn that belonged to a friend of his father's. He
was puffing slightly from the wet and slippery climb up the hill to the
tree. Maria was just reaching out her hand to help him when lightning
struck the far edge of the tree. He felt nailed to the earth, unable even
to reach out for her as she crumpled at his feet with a helpless whimper even as the thunder exploded over their heads and nearly half the
oak splintered to the ground.

It seemed hours before Anton could move his legs, but he knew his
senses were less than reliable even as he found the strength to pick a
nonbreathing Maria up and carry her out of the rain into the barn. In
his terror he suddenly remembered an unusual technique he had seen
practiced on a drowned man by the doctor on the ship that had brought
them to America. Gently lowering Maria onto the floor on her back,
he breathed into her open mouth. Nothing happened. He tried again,
trying to get the natural bellows of her lungs working again by forced
draught. And still a third time. This time she responded. The momentarily paralyzed lungs began with a painful slowness to inhale and exhale
on their own. Her eyes flickered. She looked up at him wildly, and
suddenly she screamed. Like a newborn infant, he thought. It was a
beautiful sound.

Tears rolled down her cheeks as the terror of the lightning poured
from her. She moved her head, then her arms, then her legs. Her left
leg was numb, and her throat couldn't form words. She reached for
his hand and pressed it to her bosom. Then she fainted. It was only
when he was carrying her to the doctor's that he became aware that
every bone in his body felt stepped on.

Maria was two months in recovering. She favored her left leg slightly
for the rest of her life. At Christmas she accepted his offer of marriage.

He completed his training with Isaac Hurlwicz in May, sat before the learned judges in Harrisburg in June, and was accepted as a member of the bar in August. As a wedding present, Hurlwicz offered him a junior partnership.

"We'll have one grand plan," Maria said on their honeymoon to Virginia Beach. "We will own as much of the land as possible across the whole valley."

"Don't you want to have a family to help dig the coal when your husband gives out after ten years of that kind of living?"

"Children come without a plan. God decides important things like that. I'm only talking about comfort things, like decent shelter, running water, dependable transportation, a few clothes, good friends—"

"The American dream. Consider it done. And don't forget secure old age. And speaking of old age, do you know I haven't made love to you since breakfast?"

"But, darling, we're having breakfast in this huge bed right now."

"Exactly, Mrs. Zaretski."

"My God, what a goat! No wonder Polish weddings take three days. It's to tire the groom out so the bride has a chance."

"You're spilling the coffee."

They returned to the ocean every year. They always had breakfast in bed. And they had six children to remind them of many perfect weeks.

Anton Zaretski's big chance came almost casually, like the mailman to the door. While working at his desk several years after joining Hurlwicz, he noticed several families clustered with their belongings on wagons in the city park. There was something unusually aimless about their being in the park so early in the day. They were nothing at all like the amiable, determined westward-bound settlers who occasionally passed through Monongamesh. He wandered out into the hot sunshine to talk to them. He was surprised to learn that they were but lately dispossessed from farms less than twenty miles from the valley. One of the new railroads had shown papers, a sheriff had appeared, signatures were forced onto more papers, and the work of half a lifetime vanished in less than an afternoon at prices well below market.

The story nibbled at him. It was too much like the life his father had described in the land they had left. There should be no such brutal transactions in the America he hoped to build. He informed the perplexed travellers that he was a lawyer and asked to see the papers that cost them their homes. The five families were quick to show them.

The papers, much as he feared, proved to be in perfect order. Still there was an anxious gnawing within him. He asked all the families to be his guests for the night and to stay until they had caught their breath. He prayed that Maria would understand. He then presented himself to Isaac Hurlwicz.

"This stinks," he said to his senior partner, laying the papers on his desk, "but I don't know why. I feel I'm getting into a sea of legal custard, and I can't find enough of the dish to put my feet on."

"Your feet may be on good instincts. Now let's find the law," answered Hurlwicz. "By the way," he added as he got up to begin searching through his law library, "I don't suppose they're able to pay?"

"I forgot to ask."

"Fine. I just wanted to be really sure you understood the basic difference between principles and capital." Hurlwicz began to hum.

By the end of the afternoon, with papers and books thrown about the room, the two lawyers had learned very little that could be of any use.

"Let's go back to your instincts, Anton. We're looking in the wrong library. We want the one where they keep the daily papers."

"What will we be looking for when we get to the other library?"

"If I knew, would we have to go? By the way, what's your wife having for dinner?"

"Twenty-eight people."

It was a small item in a four-month-old weekly that gave them the clue they needed. The paper held a small announcement of a proposed railroad that would come through the valley in the next two years.

"That's it, Mr. Hurlwicz! The railroad is coming through the valley. Probably the south flats. That announcement makes sense. But these people all live along the north ridge. That makes no sense."

The older partner paused to let his eager associate's words gather the patina of reflection before he answered.

"That railroad will fight like Billy-Be-Damned if we're right, my boy. You won't believe the way they'll fight. But it's not the first time a railroad has surveyed the wrong section of ground. We will have precedent. Let's go to Harrisburg for a word with the surveyor general's office, a cup of tea with the senior counsel for the railroad, and perhaps a longer winter ahead than either of us realizes."

"Have you ever heard of a missurvey suit winning?"

"No. The railroad always manages to win. A good legal department can tie some suits up for twenty-five years without even breathing hard."

"Then we'll need allies, Mr. Hurlwicz."

"Such as?"

"Such as the people: those who have been wronged and those who could have been wronged. The great, helpless, immigrant-rooted American sprawl."

"How will you ever assemble such a blessing?"

"I think a good place to start is our newspaper editor. We'll tell him what we're about and ask his help."

"A good theory, but you probably have heard the rumor that the railroad enjoys such favorable coverage because it pays the editors along the right of way to print the right news."

"You know what you've always taught me about hearsay evidence. Our editor has never given me any impression of being in anyone's pocket. Maybe the railroad has considered him too small to notice."

"Let's sound him out, then. If he's too much one way or the other, we leave him be. If he's as angry and confused as we are, then he's our man."

"Agreed."

He was their man, and soon editorials on the front page were being picked up by other papers around the state. Presentation of obvious facts to the railroad's senior counsel led to an out-of-court settlement in two months. The property along the improperly surveyed route was restored to the former owners and generous settlements paid to all concerned. The two lawyers found themselves famous and were soon traveling as much as two hundred miles to argue cases they usually won.

A year after the railroad settlement, Issac Hurlwicz was asked to become appellate judge for western Pennsylvania. Anton Zaretski was asked to run for mayor of Monongamesh, population now 6,240. It was a total victory; both of the other candidates dropped their campaigns in the face of Zaretski's undeniable popularity.

Since being mayor was only a part-time position, Anton Zaretski was encouraged to continue his legal practice. Although he painfully avoided any conflict-of-interest cases, he soon found himself with more work than ever, and he was the happiest he had ever been. People instinctively turned to his broad shoulders for help and leadership. The firm added four partners in the next two years. Just when life was really settling into a joyous pattern, Jacob Zaretski died, Isaac Hurlwicz was shot down by the father of a hanged murderer, and Kills-the-Hawk brought Indian troubles back to the valley.

Kills-the-Hawk's war was unexpected. By 1842 the Indians of western Pennsylvania had come to grudging terms with the hardy white settlers who made pots, built cities, farmed hillsides, and dug the coal. Those Indians who could not come to terms had moved on to the west. From time to time, young braves would hurl their spears into the ground in front of the chief's tent and go raiding. After some minor but heady successes, the firebrands generally discovered they were not fit for long-term war management. They were usually tracked down and executed by white settlers, or they, too, vanished across the Mississippi into the endless plains.

Kills-the-Hawk was only slightly different from the other hotheads. He had a compelling way with words, a feeling for tribal history, and a noble bearing. He was also insane. Consequently he attracted not several, but dozens of bored and resentful warriors, half-breeds, and white renegades. Worst of all, he proved to be a good manager, delegating numerous responsibilities, rewarding and punishing justly, and permitting well-debated choices in major decisions. News of the prosperous camp, the successful raids, and his elusive marches soon brought him hundreds of new fighters. The news also brought terror to the settlers.

As the largest settlement on the frontier, Monongamesh knew its duty. The city levied money for a fighting force of one hundred men for ninety days of service and offered Anton Zaretski a major's epaulets and a silver sword to take command of the militia.

"We'll give you a few professional soldiers," the city council told the protesting mayor, who didn't even own a musket. "But most of your troops have been potting redskins since they were big enough to tamp home a slug. What they need is a leader with courage and common sense."

"What sort of authority will I have to back up the orders that will have to be issued?"

"Once sworn in, the militia becomes a part of the United States Army. You'll have life-and-death authority for ninety days."

"They're good men. I guess someone has to do this thing."

"Someone very special, Major."

Major Zaretski refused to permit sudden high rank or a lifetime of inexperience in warfare to take the life of a single recruit. In his judgment, three months would permit just enough time to get ready for one good fight. With luck, one good fight would end the war. He called a meeting on the first morning after the federalization of the militia.

"Men, we're all in this madness up to our armpits. Madness or not, the valley does need us, so here's our program of training for the next three weeks—"

"Three weeks!" hissed incredulous voices up and down the ranks, followed by such additional strategic observations as, "Those redskins will be able to murder dozens of families in three weeks," and, "Let's go now!"

"No, we'll begin training first, and tonight I'll show you why. The schedule of priorities is as follows: first, physical conditioning; second, discipline and drill; third, tactics. Now I need a couple of hill-country scouts, some men who have fought renegades like this before and know how they like to fight. I'd like to see them first thing in the morning. The sergeants will now take command for the remainder of the day. Dismissed."

At dinner with his staff that evening, Major Zaretski announced the second day's training, which included a five-mile run, two hours of close-order drill, two lectures, and a second run of two miles. He then rolled a map down over the back of a chair.

"I've been meeting with quite a number of people since this morning, and this map is the result. The Indians and renegades have attacked all the areas shown on the map in red. You can see that they seem to concentrate their activities within a fairly small circle north of us. I'd estimate the circle at no more than fifty miles in diameter. This tells me two things: the Indians have no horses; and Kills-the-Hawk, unlike most war chiefs, doesn't mind fouling his own nest. He probably has no tribal support, and once broken he will stay broken, or at least he will depart this area if we aren't lucky enough to kill him. Kills-the-Hawk must be trying to prove something to someone in broadax terms. I propose to make that drive his undoing.

"Next to the Xs, which symbolize attacks, I've listed dates and put in dots to represent the number of people killed. You'll note right away that brave Mr. Hawk likes lonely farms or small families in single wagons. More significant for us, he likes to group his attacks in bunches, waiting about four weeks between encounters. This is his third month of operation; we intend to make it his last. Since his last known raid was two days ago, I figure that three weeks should just about get us ready. I had hoped for three months, but this map has made me realize that time is a luxury. Any questions?"

"Can we get some horses, sir?"

He grinned privately at the "sir," but answered with a straight face.

"Yes. We've ordered some cavalry. No need to tell that to anyone, by the way. If they don't come, no one will be disappointed. If they do come, they should be good morale-boosters for some very tired men who have probably begun to hate me thoroughly."

On the note of tired men, Major Zaretski's staff made their excuses about early starts and took their leave.

Maria was laughing when the door closed.

"That's why they like it so. They're like little boys. And now they're getting ready to fight the other little boys who have been playing the bully with farmers' lives. Well, I hope the better school wins, but I wonder if the Indians aren't laughing at us, too?"

"Is that what you think of me? I have the lives of a hundred men and the safety of the entire valley in my hands, and I wish to God I was more like a little boy. Little boys have a way of sleeping through anything after the excitement."

"Anton—"

"Some other time, Maria. I can't be very inspirational to my men when my wife is laughing at us behind the curtains."

"Why don't you find out what Indian renegades are most afraid of and get some. Knowing this and having an answer will take you out of the coon-hunting mentality."

He stopped on his way up the stairs to the bedroom. He then let his head sink to his chest while he started to chuckle. He nodded his head and then, without looking back, beckoned with his arm for her to join him. Together they looked in on the children and then, still arm in arm, went to their own bed.

The next morning, after their five-mile run had scattered the company so completely that it took over half an hour to reassemble, Major Zaretski felt that his men must have made a mistake. The scout looked about nineteen. His eyes and calm manner, however, put that worry to rest. He wore rough clothing. A heavy knife hung at his side, and he carried an old-fashioned long rifle. His feet were in moccasins.

"Good morning. We need a good scout to put an end to Kills-the-Hawk. Interested?"

"Yup," answered the frontiersman, looking him straight in the eyes.

"Just like that? Don't you want to know the terms? You'll be signing up for ninety days and serving, like the rest of us, under the rules of federal military service. You'll have the rank of corporal. Your meals, quarters, and clothing will be provided for you. You—"

"No need, Major. I'm in. I want the sonovabitch, and I need your help. I know you need mine. Let's get on with it."

Major Zaretski offered the dour pioneer a chair and sent for some coffee and enlistment papers.

"What's your name? Why are you so anxious to catch this Indian?"

"We're not going to catch him, Major. We're going to kill him. My name is Wendermuth. I was born on a farm up in the hills about twenty miles from here. Indian troubles have been finished for fifty years. But last month those bastards killed my mother and father, sister and little brother. I was away at the settlement store. Only the worst kind of Indian kills children, Major, especially when he knows them. I grew up with Kills-the-Hawk. He's a coward, and like most cowards, he's cruel. My father was caught in our stable. He never had a chance to get to his gun, but he killed seven of those bucks with a singletree and the knife I'm wearing right now. My mom killed one and so did my kid brother. What they left behind of my sister I don't think you'd care to hear about. Anyway, by the time I got home there was just the burying. I burned the farm. Hawk had left it for me, you understand. When I burned it he thought I was moving out. But I was declaring war. So here's my signature; now tell me what you think you want me to do."

No wonder the eyes seem old, thought Major Zaretski. Maria was right. His hundred men were playing games of an honorable and dedicated sort, but this panther of the forest was in for the kill. Over coffee that had grown cold, Henry Wendermuth joined the federalized Pennsylvania militia.

"Corporal Wendermuth, I want you to prepare a lecture of about half an hour for this afternoon at four on what to expect in the fighting of Indian renegades and suggestions on how to combat them. Describe the way they travel, the way they like to fight, their attack and retreat procedures, what happens to prisoners, and so forth. You will report directly to me for future assignments. For the present, I would like you to undergo daily training with the rest of the company so they will learn to trust you. One last thing: from a military sense, what do these Indians fear?"

"They're like children in a lot of ways, Major. They hate routine living as we know it, but they can stand without twitchin' a muscle for twelve hours to catch a deer or ambush an enemy. But most of all, militarily, I'd say they're afraid of cannon. They ain't seen much cavalry, either, but then there ain't too many places where you can use horses around here, anyway. And . . ." he paused as if his next observation would sound frivolous.

"Go ahead, Corporal Wendermuth, please."

"Well, sir, these Indians can't stand being laughed at. If I were in charge of training, I'd give over ten minutes a day to training these men to laugh on command. No matter how tired they are. This whole mess started when one of Kills-the-Hawk's chiefs laughed at him for wanting to be a war chief. He's trying to prove to us that he's worthy of praise and respect. He's crazy, you know."

"How long do you think it will take us to catch up to him?"

"I have a fair idea of where he is or may go. Once you stop all this ball-banging you call training and get into the hills, we ought to be facing him in eight to ten days. See you this afternoon, Major."

Soon after the scout left, Major Zaretski dispatched telegrams to Harrisburg confirming the arrival date of twenty-five cavalrymen requested earlier and sent his aide to Pittsburgh with orders to beg, borrow, or steal two or three pack howitzers and their crews. He gave the aide ten days to complete the round-trip journey. The aide had the feeling that failure to secure the guns would be a good reason for continuing westward to the end of the Ohio River. Major Zaretski then called in the officer he had placed in charge of training.

"Don't laugh, Pete, but starting this afternoon, I want you to devote at least ten minutes a day to conducting laughing classes. That's right, laughing exercises, upon regular military command. At odd times. And one more thing. I want you to train the men to dig shallow body pits, say eighteen inches deep and six feet long. Buy spades on my account for those men who can't bring them from home. Have them saw off all but two feet of the handle so the spades can be carried on a field pack. I'd like to see the first results by tomorrow afternoon. They've got to learn how to dig those pits in under three minutes."

"Yes, sir."

"Oh, and one more thing: see if you can find, or get someone to find, enough noncombatants to form a band. I want the men to be able to march around the square every evening to some lively tootling."

The spades were no problem, although there was no joy in the exercise of digging body pits. The band proved more difficult, but help came from an unexpected quarter. When the weary troops began their first march around the square several evenings later to the brisk rhythms of Scotland, Britain, Ireland, and Germany, the vigor of the musicians in their unexpectedly crisp uniforms was a welcome stimulus to all.

"My compliments, sir," Major Zaretski said to the bandleader during a pause in the music, offering a brisk salute.

"We try to please, sweetie," answered Maria from under the shako of the bandleader. The band giggled. They were all women. Major Zaretski, outflanked, withdrew.

"Christ, Lieutenant," he said to one of his staff, "why didn't you warn me? Never mind. The band is great. Dismiss the men after the turn. The body pits, by the way, were too narrow this morning. We'll try again tomorrow. And tell the training officer to make it an eight-mile run in the morning."

"Eight miles, sir?"

"Wendermuth tells me an Indian can do over thirty in a day. We've got to build up to at least ten before we head into the hills. You know, this really scares me."

"The Indians, sir?"

"No, our tootling womenfolk. One day we'll have 'em in the army on a regular basis. Maybe they just like uniforms or something. All right, go down and dismiss the men."

Actually the band had been the idea of Wendermuth the scout. He pointed out to Major Zaretski that the Indians had probably heard of the Monongamesh company. Somewhere in the low hills surrounding Monongamesh an Indian was watching every bit of the training. By playing music every night, the band could probably confuse the real evening of departure by as much as twelve hours. One evening soon the fires would all be fakes; the men would assemble in the dark and follow Henry Wendermuth into the forest. By dawn the Indian scout would realize he had been fooled and would hurry, in disgrace, to report that the white man was very tricky, in a clumsy sort of way.

A telegram from Harrisburg brought welcome news to Major Zaretski. A troop of cavalry was on its way from central Pennsylvania. The commander was a horse breeder named Captain Kalanyi. Major Zaretski sent a runner to intercept and hold the cavalry troops five miles east of Monongamesh and to ask Captain Kalanyi to ride in alone in civil-

ian clothes. It was three days later that the cavalry troop arrived. It
was nearly a disaster from the beginning.

The trappings and uniforms of the horsemen were parade-ground
replicas of equipment worn by hussar units of Europe, complete to half
jackets worn off one shoulder and tall hats with waving plumes. There
were nearly thirty spirited mounts. When given his holding orders by
Major Zaretski's messenger, Captain Kalanyi twirled his luxuriant
mustache, allowed his horse to prance impatiently, and then said to
the lone messenger:
    "Your Major Zaretski is obviously a fool. These are the finest horses
and riders in the state. This troop has won ribbons throughout Pennsylvania and New York. We go where we want. Our sabers are here
to taste the blood of red savages, and they will not be sheathed until
victory or death. Do you understand, young man?"
    "I'm not quite sure, Captain. But I do understand that Major Zaretski
ain't no fool, and he don't ask folks to do things 'cause he's simpleminded.
Now I ain't no fancy Hungarian nobleman on a skittery horse. I'm just
a Polish private named Bielecki with a job to do. So why don't you
park your men here for a little rest and change them fancy duds, or
I'm going to shoot you right out of the saddle before your saber can
taste shit, and then I'll take the next in command to see the Major.
Plain enough, Captain?"
    The snick of the heavy musket being cocked was argument enough
for the dashing Kalanyi. He doffed his plumed shako and cape, handed
his sword to his aide, and accepted a long cloak. He ordered his men
to make camp and wait. He then followed Private Bielecki, who ran ·
the five miles back to Monongamesh for practice. The horse was wheezing
when the two approached the Zaretski home forty minutes later where
Maria was waiting on the porch. As Kalanyi dismounted, Maria said
softly to her tired husband:
    "He's the Hungarian circus rider we saw ten years ago in Philadel-
phia. Why not let me handle this? He looks peeved. We're having a
good dinner tonight, and we'll make him feel so special that he'll even
listen to a Polish major. Trust me. He is important, isn't he?"
    Major Zaretski nodded. The dinner went well. As a matter of fact,
it went so well that he felt twinges of unbelievable jealousy as Maria
seemed to revel in Kalanyi's casual charm and cordiality. When dinner was over and Kalanyi had accepted his invitation to spend the night,

Major Zaretski led the debonair cavalryman into the sitting room while Maria excused herself to supervise the guest room. Over port and cigars, Major Zaretski eventually got to his point.

"We're new at this war business, Captain Kalanyi. Have any of your riders been in battle before?"

"Ah, Major, you have found our one weakness. I'm afraid we are parade specialists. But I assure you, there are no braver cavalrymen here or in Europe."

"We will need each other. I would like you to practice wheeling and charging maneuvers in a limited combat area, because we are going into the deep woods to find these Indians. With luck, we will find a meadow. If not, a grave. Practice away from the village. If you have messages, send them to me by a foot soldier. Three evenings from tonight I want you to lead your troops into the hills to the north. I have prepared a map for you, and I will send two scouts to serve you. Your mission is almost suicidal, but with courage and luck, your men will make the difference in a fight in which we are sure to be outnumbered."

The two studied the map together, noting the timetable and distances.

"Captain Kalanyi, you are now the only person who knows our destination with the exception of our scouts, my staff, and myself. Share this information with as few of your staff as necessary. The Indians have only one use for prisoners, and I have none."

Kalanyi's face clouded. He reached for the port.

"We believe," continued Major Zaretski evenly, "that the Indians are afraid of horses. If you can keep hidden on your way to our rendezvous, marching silently with good field discipline, we are going to give Kills-the-Hawk the surprise of his life. Oh, have any of your horses ever been subjected to the noise of artillery?"

Kalanyi smiled.

"All good circuses have cannon. You are in luck, Major."

"I believe I am, Captain Kalanyi. Now, I have made arrangements for you to outfit your men tomorrow with green or brown clothing and walking shoes. The way through the forest may have to be taken on foot. I want everything that jangles removed and left with the people of the village where you are now staying. I will not have the march jeopardized by some fool's jingling spurs. Once committed, you will be in command of your forces, which I see as flankers. Should the Indians steal your horses, you must send one of the scouts to let me know."

"No one can steal our horses!"

"The Indians are very good at stealing horses, much as they fear them. When you head into the hills, I expect your men to be exhausted from the zealous nature of your training during the next three days. I expect them to be bone-weary from the climb to the high meadow through these woods. But I also am counting on you to inspire them to be the cavalry force that will win this battle. Can you do that much?"

To Major Zaretski it seemed as if Captain Kalanyi was looking at him with what might pass for respect.

"Where did a country lawyer learn so much about military tactics?" he asked quietly.

"Xenophon, Julius Caesar, Tacitus, Francis Marion, and Henry Wendermuth. 'Til the morning, Captain."

But when reveille sounded the next morning, Captain Kalanyi was already on the way back to his elite command. It was a good sign.

That afternoon Major Zaretski's aide returned from Pittsburgh with four pack howitzers, their crews, and ammunition. Major Zaretski ordered the artillerymen made comfortable in the city park and placed the howitzers, covered with canvas, under the trees.

"Good work," Zaretski complimented his aide. "How are the crews?"

"First rate, sir. They are all regulars and know their business. The commandant of the Pittsburgh garrison sends his compliments to you. He says he's sorry he can't come with us."

"So am I. Tell the gun crews I'll inspect their equipment right after parade this evening. Do caution them about keeping in the trees."

That night, Major Zaretski found the fifteen men and four artillery pieces awaiting his arrival. The cannon mouths seemed ridiculously small for the game he had cut out for them. Not much with which to terrify some four hundred Indians. But the cannon looked sturdy enough on large round wheels that unbolted easily for mule-portability. The men appeared fit; the rest of the equipment looked clean, oiled, and ready. The ammunition was dry. A husky sergeant seemed fully in charge and ready for any sensible orders, even from a civilian. Major Zaretski asked for a loading demonstration.

One of the howitzers was rolled out in front of him. The barrel was tilted slightly, a small cask of black powder was dumped down the muzzle for a prescribed count, a heavy wad of paper was tamped home on top of the charge with a bulbous stick that had a cylindrical wire brush on the other end, a cannonball was then punched down on top of that, and the piece was returned to firing position. The sergeant placed a sextantlike instrument on the top of the barrel, which was elevated with a rachet device on the side until the sergeant commanded a halt. Powder was sprinkled on the touchhole, and a man appeared suddenly with a brightly glowing stick. The sergeant stood back.

"There, sir, we have optimum range of fifteen hundred yards, ready to fire."

"Very, very well done, Sergeant. Can you put out that torch and stand easy? After we chat you can unload the piece. How often can you go through this in one minute?"

"We can average about two rounds a minute, sir."

"Fine. But fifteen hundred yards is much more than we'll need. These cannonballs are small. I notice I can even hold one in my hand. How do you explain their great reputation against the Indians?"

"Mostly the noise, sir. But these cannonballs are special. They explode on impact, and they sure tear up a charge."

But Major Zaretski wasn't quite satisfied.

"Did you bring grapeshot as well for close work?"

"No, sir, we did not. We brought a hundred explosive rounds and twenty-five solid rounds, but no grape. If, sir, you'll permit me to visit the blacksmith in the morning, we'll soon have all the grapeshot you want. How much do you need?"

"Enough to kill four hundred Indians."

"I'll look to it, sir."

"A final question, and then you can get to the rest you deserve. How do you control fire?"

"Through a forward observer and flag signals if we're firing over a hill, for instance. In direct contact, we can see the enemy for ourselves."

"I'll be back about noon tomorrow, Sergeant. I'd like you to practice unloading the piece from the mules into combat position with a round home for firing. I'll need your absolute minimum time to get ready. By the way, how far does a load of grapeshot carry and how wide a pattern can I expect?"

"Grapeshot can kill effectively at up to about seventy-five yards, and these guns give good account of themselves in a forty-degree pattern at that range, sir."

"Is fifty yards better?"

"Much, but we're talking about something like two seconds' difference in the distance a man can cover before he's beyond where the guns can do him any harm. Part of the artillery's duty is to keep the attacking force down and away from your own front."

"Is grape slower to load?"

"No, sir, just the opposite. There's no sighting and a minimum of tamping. These crews can get off three rounds a minute of grapeshot."

"Thank you again. I'll notify the blacksmith of your visit. By the way, what's your name?"

"Sgt. Sean Terry, sir."

"Mine's Zaretski. We'll be getting to know each other very quickly I'm sure. You may dismiss the men when you're ready."

Sergeant Terry saluted and Major Zaretski headed back for his house.

"I do believe we're getting there," he confided to his aide during the walk back home. "But fifty yards . . ."

The following afternoon Major Zaretski marched the company to an area of open ground midway between Monongamesh and the village where Captain Kalanyi was conducting limited-space maneuvers with his troops. There the company found the four pack howitzers, with crews at the ready. Spontaneous shouts of approval burst from the marching company.

Major Zaretski drew the men around him.

"My good friends and fellow citizens of Monongamesh. This is the last time I shall be able to speak to you in this way. From now on you are the men of the company, and I am the one who has to send you into impossible dangers objectively and impersonally. It is my greatest burden, but you have learned, as have I, that there is no other way. As you may suspect from this little speech, we are about to stop parading and training. Before you know it, we shall be into the hills, and we may all wish we were back here in comparative safety and comfort.

"We are going to do what we were commissioned to do. You are tough and ready, but the enemy is, too. We are going to beat him because we must. If we lose, the whole valley will be in flames the next day.

"We have a few surprises, but the main fighting force is this infantry company working in harmony with cavalry and artillery support. Yesterday the cannon arrived. The day before, a troop of cavalry joined us. You won't see the cavalry until the right time, but they'll be there. I've asked Sergeant Terry to meet us here this afternoon to help us find out if our firing discipline is what it should be. We don't have much powder to spare, but we are going to invest it to prove the pudding.

"I am going to return you to company-front formation in just a moment, point out the direction of the enemy, and order you to dig your firing pits in a prescribed time, the best time you have managed to date, incidentally. Then I will order the cannon to fire grapeshot at knee level. Anyone still standing, or even kneeling, after I give the command to fire will probably be killed. You are not to fire your muskets, just go through the drill. Above everything, remember to keep low. The command to fire will be this whistle given to me by Sergeant Terry of the gun crew."

As soon as the men were reassembled facing the cannon, Major Zaretski shouted: "The enemy is directly behind you. You have ten minutes to dig shelter and load weapons. Fall out!"

With an aide keeping a close look at the time, Major Zaretski watched as his men threw off their packs, broke into the two lines facing the enemy, shook out shovels and bowie knives, and began digging. He noticed bare hands helping where shovels had been forgotten or seemed too slow. Before the diggers could believe it, they heard the command "Prepare to fire!" followed almost instantly by the piercing screech of Major Zaretski's borrowed whistle.

Screams burst from six men still standing when two of the cannon fired. Clustered near the center of the company, they had been distracted by unknown causes so that the warning registered too late. It said little for their sergeant. They were also in the one area where the two grapeshot patterns overlapped.

"You sonovabitch," Major Zaretski heard from the flank as he walked to the wounded men, who were still screaming.

"Hold your positions," he called as men began getting out of their body pits to help the wounded.

Standing over the wounded, he spoke so that all could hear him.

"It's only rice, boys, just grains of rice, and the charge had more noise than force. It'll sting for a while, but you'll be marching around the square with us tonight. Imagine what grapeshot would have done at this range. And that's the way we're going to fight. When I say hit the dirt, I mean dig deep fast. But ten minutes is all you're ever going to be able to count on. So remember what happened here this afternoon."

Major Zaretski walked off the field. The holes were filled in, and the men marched back to Monongamesh. There was no small talk.

The scout, Henry Wendermuth, was waiting at Major Zaretski's home as ordered when the major rode up from the cannonade exercise.

"Hank, when the new pair of Indian scouts takes over this evening, kill them. When you get back, we'll follow you into the hills. The company is as ready as it's ever going to be. Incidentally, you were right: ten minutes is shaving it awfully close. But they'll keep their heads down, I promise you. We'll have to think of something to distract Kills-the-Hawk for ten minutes when the time comes."

"Yes, sir," answered the scout, leaving the veranda of the big house. That night the word was passed to leave fires lit but to pack gear. The wives, sisters, and mothers of the company made their way noiselessly into the compound to feed the fires as planned and to say good-bye to their men. There were no tears.

In silence, the company faded into the forest after Wendermuth. Only Major Zaretski knew of the two Indian corpses now dangling from one of the trees high on the northern slope of the valley. In the morning the women gathered whatever personal items their men had left behind. Suddenly the excitement of playing soldier had grown as cold as the camp-fire ashes.

For Captain Kalanyi the situation had become desperate. His horses had been run off, and two of his riders were dead. Fear of ridicule and seething fury brought together in him the leadership qualities he had always assumed were his by virtue of profile, family, and press agentry. He assembled what remained of his disheartened unit.

"Gentlemen, the Indians don't know what they have, but Major Zaretski gave me a fair idea of where they're going. They'll have to bob and weave a bit to get there, so we'll arrive first by going directly. We'll save the surprise of our horses being circus horses for the vital minute, but those red bastards will wish they had never heard of us.

"Leave your saddles here. Take only your boots, food for three days, your water bottles, pistols, ammunition and, above all, your sabers. Leave the scabbards. It's a little harder to slice a man in half without stirrups, but we'll have to sacrifice saddles and bridles for speed. You'll ride better than you've ever ridden before when we recapture our mounts, or you'll die. With luck, we'll be back to pick all this up in a week."

The troopers quickly did as directed. They then followed their galvanized, though horseless, leader up the slope of the mountain that Captain Kalanyi alone knew ended in an arena-sized meadow.

Kalanyi's scouts had also told him of a good campground midway between the place where the Indians had stolen his horses and the meadow where Kalanyi expected to meet the full Indian force. The scouts described the campground as a small clearing made by the S curve of a small stream. Captain Kalanyi stumbled into the edge of the clearing after two days of hard climbing that had cost him three more men and left the survivors barely fit for breathing. Keeping the men away from the water was difficult, but the hope of recovering the horses quelled all arguments. He shared his strategy with his exhausted men.

"Unload your pistols and leave them in your boots; you're going to leave them in the places I assign in a minute. I am gambling that the Indians will pass through here, even though their tracks show they left us going in the opposite direction. They want to show off their prizes, our mounts, as quickly as possible, and this is the only route for men with horses. The B unit will make its way around to the far side of this place and vanish into the underbrush as cleverly as Indians. That's where you leave your boots. The A unit will stay on this side in similar discomfort. When the thieves come, we must let them all get into the glen. Hopefully, they will be stupid enough to be riding. Being Indians, the riders will be hard on our mounts, and our horses will be angry and tired. This will be good for us. I will then perform the Kalanyi whistle, the horses will perform by habit, and we shall all charge with sabers. But no shouting. It will be difficult, but you must kill in silence. Be speedy, not gallant. We must kill them all. All, gentlemen.

"Most important, we must save the horses. The savages may attempt to kill them if they smell defeat. So you know why I say we must come in total surprise, swifter than the belles of Philadelphia to my bed. Run as if the devil himself were scorching your nuts. Very well, now that we agree on the plan, let's pray we have arrived before them and take our positions. No lights, no talking, no sleeping. When I whistle, strike!"

The men went to their positions on both sides of the small glade in silence. Captain Kalanyi posted one man at the entrance of the glade and another on the uphill exit. He then took up his own position behind a large log in thick grass commanding a good view of the glade from between low branches.

Waiting was not Kalanyi's game. Fortunately for the cavalry commander, his prey came into sight only three hours from the time of his own arrival. He smiled. Kalanyi's men would think him a true Magyar clairvoyant and follow him into combat with high spirits. Also as predicted, the Indians had become so confident of their ability to throw off pursuit that they were riding the stolen horses. The Indians looked like smoked jerky to Kalanyi, lean and tough. He noted that the horses seemed tired but somewhat better than he had feared. He crossed himself and asked St. Stephen to grant the horses good memories. As the last horse nudged his way into the glade, and before the first Indian could dismount, Captain Kalanyi put two fingers into his nearly dry mouth, sending the piercing command of the Kalanyi whistle into the glade. The Indians sat upright; the horses' ears pricked forward. Several snorted. When the whistle was repeated, with three warbles on the end of the signal, complete chaos erupted in the glade.

The horses all remembered. As if they were one animal, they began a furious bucking, prancing, circling, leaping, stomping, spinning, arching madness that hurled Indians in every direction. Those hurtling through the air wished they were on the ground; those on the ground desperately tried to dodge the slashing hooves. Even as the startled, terrified Indians crashed to the ground, sabers were upon them. With a vengeance they never dreamt they felt, the unbloodied circus riders hacked, sliced, and thrust with such swift ferocity that there wasn't a single Indian alive in the glade less than a minute after Captain Kalanyi's whistle.

Another whistle calmed down the swirling horses so that their respective owners could get near them to comfort and examine them for damage. Nearly all the mounts showed savage whip marks. Two of the Indians, Kalanyi noted, had died beneath the slashing hooves. Kalanyi nearly wept from relief as he put his cheek against the snorting head of his own horse, speaking soft words of deep affection and stroking the long nose.

As soon as the horses were calmed down long enough to drink, he led them to the stream, letting them browse in the glade. The troop cleared out the corpses, hurling the despised bodies into the thickets like carrion.

"Retrieve your boots and pistols and then follow me," said Captain Kalanyi when the glade was quiet. "We are only a day late thanks to the foolishness of our enemies and our good luck. Only one horse is lame from all the hard treatment. We can still make our rendezvous in two days if we keep our wits about us and go as softly as shadows. Do not expect to sleep very much, since half of us will always be on sentry duty to prevent any more horse theft. But at the end of all this marching, I promise you action that will have these hills singing your names for a hundred years. Your fortunes lie in front of you. A great victory here will make us the most sought-after circus act in the country. We won't know where to bank our money. Women will hurl themselves under your mounts or faint in the arena. In the meantime, we have the real excitement ahead of us, only this time I want lots of shouting. The Indians will think we are three times our real size, and there will be no rest from the time we begin until you hear the recall bugle from Major Zaretski, a man who appreciates us, believe me. Let's go!"

The troop headed out of the glade in single file, leading the mounts. Behind them only a few small feathers and some splatterings of blood on the long grass lingered to suggest for a short while that steel and revenge had ravished the most peaceful of the mountain's resting places. That night, when the forest animals came to drink, they made a wide passage around the thicket.

"The crazy thing about all this, sir, is that he knows we're coming; he's just sitting up there waiting for us."

Henry Wendermuth was talking to Major Zaretski on the evening of their seventh day out from Monongamesh.

"He knows our numbers, and he must know about the cannon. I suspect he's already run off the horses. Tonight he'll probably kill the mules carrying the howitzers. It wouldn't take much. He means to prove he can fight us as the white man fights and beat us for all the world to know."

"Do you know if he's ever faced grapeshot or exploding shells before?" asked Major Zaretski, ignoring his patient scout.

"I don't think so. Most of his targets have been too small. But some of his warriors or those white renegades may have warned him. If he outnumbers us four to one or better, he doesn't really care about a little grape. With us gone, he'll become war chief for sure, and then—"

"You really think he'll be there tomorrow?"

"Yes, sir. Tomorrow."

"Then it'll be simple. If we can have ten minutes to dig, we'll outfirepower him. Do you think he'll settle for a powwow?"

"Can't be sure. He's unpredictable. I'll try to think of something else. But I believe that as soon as we step into the meadow he'll attack."

Major Zaretski nodded and sent Wendermuth on an inspection of the sentry positions, doubling every post and tripling the guard around the mules. The powder was buried for the night as an extra precaution. Major Zaretski then went to sleep praying only for a dry day.

It was close to midafternoon of the next day when they marched onto the meadow. Warned by Wendermuth, they bunched ranks and popped out at one end of the meadow, like the cork from a bottle of champagne. Major Zaretski noted no signs of Kalanyi, but that was as planned. The cannon and crews were still totally intact. The gunners were given orders to assemble the pieces just before the company entered the meadow. Wendermuth had assured the major that there were no hostiles behind them.

The meadow was about three times the size of the village square of Monongamesh. The grass was lush and sprinkled generously with mountain wildflowers. Birds flitted, bees hummed, and Major Zaretski wondered why he was noticing such graceful things when less than three hundred yards from him stood at least four hundred of the most savage-looking warriors he had ever seen. They carried an assortment of good weapons and seemed restrained by the barest of threads. The Indians smelled victory. The major determined not only to prove them painfully foolish but also to survive the lesson. He stood erect and silent as the company split into two ranks in company-front formation. Upon command they threw themselves on the ground and began digging two long rows of body pits. Major Zaretski was grateful for the long weeks of drill that permitted this maneuver of slivering the earth. He knew his men must be as hollow as himself before the awesomely grim lines of Indians, painted, close, and silent. Like well-trained hunting hounds, the Indians seemed to be quivering for the chase. Which one was Kills-the-Hawk, he wondered. Would they give him ten minutes? Would he have enough voice to shout "Commence firing"? The wheels were coming off the mules, but the howitzers were still on the packs. Where had the Indians picked up so many muskets? The bowmen seemed lined up like artillery. They, too, had practiced, waiting thirstily for the day. He noticed a wavelike ripple building up among the braves, and he knew they were about to charge. The men weren't ready. At the same moment a piercing Indian cry broke from the center of his own ranks, and Henry Wendermuth stepped out in front of his double lines. The pulsing movement in the Indians' lines stopped.

Wendermuth had taken off his buckskin shirt. His knife rested in its ornate sheath. He walked toward the center of the field and began laughing. He held up the ends of several clumps of his red hair and then pointed toward a young chief who stood in the second line of Indian warriors. Then he sat down. The one at whom Wendermuth had pointed whipped off his warbonnet and stepped out in front of the Indian lines. Through his telescope Major Zaretski noticed that several red-haired scalps hung from the Indian's belt. Henry Wendermuth rose, smiling. The two advanced toward each other, each carrying a heavy frontier knife.

They circled. There were a few feints and a preliminary jump or two, a slash and a parry, an attempted sudden kick, then more circling, each trying to back the other away from the sun. The Indian warrior dodged cleverly and slipped under Wendermuth's guard to draw blood in a long, deep cut running the length of the frontiersman's rib cage. There were many grunts and shouts of approval from the Indian ranks.

Again they circled, Wendermuth conscious only of the danger of losing too much blood, not of the pain. The Indian taunted him. His blood was the color of the hair that would soon complete the Indian's scalp belt. Wendermuth faltered for a fraction of a second, dropping to one knee. As he howled his triumph, the Indian flung himself on the weakened scout. But even as the Indian flew at him, Wendermuth threw himself onto his back catching the outstretched knife arm at the wrist. Wendermuth levered his legs up over his hips, kicking them both straight up at the exposed belly of the halted-in-flight Indian. He gripped the wrist with the strength of a cougar as the Indian's body arced high over his head. Just past the top of the arc, Wendermuth twisted the arm away from the direction of the fall. The tearing of the dislocated shoulder was heard by many; the scream was heard by all. Ferret-quick, Wendermuth was on top of the crippled warrior the instant he hit the ground. Wendermuth lifted the stunned head toward the Indian lines for a second before he whacked off the scalp in two savage chops. After tying the scalp to his belt, Wendermuth picked up the form of the man who wore the scalps of his mother, father, and sister, and held the groaning, dying man over his head. As he walked slowly to the Indian lines, the braves parted before Kills-the-Hawk, at whose feet Wendermuth dumped his victim.

"We are waiting, woman-killers," he sneered. Turning his back the scout walked slowly toward his own lines.

Suddenly it all came together for Major Zaretski.

"Laugh, dammit, laugh!" he commanded; and even as the spastic coughs, grunts, nervous giggles, guffaws, and finally roars of laughter

ranged his lines, he ordered the cannon to fire explosive shells into
the bunched Indians.

"There's our ten minutes, and God bless you, Henry Wendermuth,"
he shouted to the bleeding scout even as the four shells roared overhead, exploding full into the center of the bunched marauders. But they
had heard cannon before and charged toward the dug-in company without
hesitation.

From behind the chargers came a hail of perfectly coordinated arrows that just fell short. The soldiers knew there would quickly be others.
The artillery fired again, but the exploding rounds hardly daunted the
shouting attackers. Musket rounds from the Indians were premature
and wasted. With the second flight of arrows, Major Zaretski's casualties began. He ordered the cannon to change to grapeshot and the
men to prepare to fire.

"Fire all!" he commanded. "And keep on firing." The major drew
the heavy bowie knife from his belt and cocked his pistol. He also lay
down.

As he watched over thirty Indians go down from the first musket
volley, Major Zaretski suddenly felt all the air sucked out of his body
from the concussion of the four cannon firing the heaviest possible
charges of grapeshot full into the attacking mob. He could hear the
eerie whistling of the tumbling shards of grape as they passed overhead. He could even see some of the lethal chips of metal screaming
end-over-end toward the attackers.

The effect was appalling. To him, it looked as if a gigantic scythe
had sliced through the front ranks, spilling hundreds of wounded men
into the paths of those behind. But the attackers' momentum was too
overwhelming to be stopped by casualties in the front ranks. Those
behind leaped eagerly forward for the honor of crushing the white men's
skulls. The entrenched company made miserable targets: their musket fire became deadly, and then the cannon exploded death and pain
at the Indians again.

But by the time the cannon could fire a third time, the attackers were
less than twenty yards away. While the blasts actually hurled some back
into the throng, the nearness of the Indians severely curtailed the spread
of the pattern. Many of them reached the front lines. Major Zaretski
pulled his trigger less than ten feet from a brave charging toward him.
The face seemed to vanish in the explosion at the end of his fingers.

"Sound the charge," he commanded his bugler, who somehow found space in which to stand and blare forth the call for the desperately needed horsemen. Almost instantly he heard an answering shout from the flank and caught the flash of waving steel through the mob flailing about him.

The cries of the cavalrymen and the snorting of the horses at their rear stunned the Indians, who had no knowledge of the swift and final message of charging sabers. While the main body of cavalry attacked the rear of the Indian force, five horsemen detached themselves to cut down the chiefs as they stood watching the action. Few escaped the initial pass, after which the cavalrymen rejoined the main troop as it wheeled and recharged the width of the blood-soaked meadow. Kalanyi's men flailed and thrust with such animated precision, riding with magnificent abandon, that Major Zaretski never knew until it was over that not a man had a saddle or bridle. By the second swing through, there was so much blood on the field that Captain Kalanyi was to say, in later years, that he began to fear for the safe footing of his horses.

Henry Wendermuth made his way to Major Zaretski's firing position. "We have to go on the offensive, Major!"

Major Zaretski ordered retreat blown for the cavalry. He blew the whistle that warned his men to keep themselves on the ground and stayed down himself as the grapeshot screamed past his head again. He could see that the attackers had hesitated, that confusion was about to preempt command from the Indian leaders who were no longer in evidence.

"Charge!" the major shouted, leading his men into the hesitant Indian mob. The Indians broke in the face of the disciplined counterattack and raced back toward their leaders. When they discovered that the cavalry had killed Kills-the-Hawk and most of their chiefs, the war party evaporated into the woods in full flight. The infantrymen pursued them for a few hundred feet, then gave it over to common sense. The cavalry troop returned to the edge of the field to await new orders, the artillery pieces were moved into the center of the field, primed and ready, and the infantry began taking stock of its losses. The entire battle had lasted less than fourteen minutes.

The Monongamesh company had suffered sixteen dead and thirty-six wounded. On the field lay 218 Indians. There were no wounded. Henry Wendermuth found Kills-the-Hawk's body and brought his warbonnet to Major Zaretski. Two artillerymen had died and four were wounded, including Sergeant Terry. Two cavalrymen were dead, five were wounded. Two horses had to be shot. It took only three days to make the seven-day journey home.

Major Zaretski found himself the hero of western Pennsylvania and mayor of Monongamesh for life. At forty-one he became the father figure for the valley and the arbiter in so many things political and private that Maria often found cause for jealousy in the demands on his wisdom and patience, two virtues she had once found impossible to imagine in him.

Captain Kalanyi toured the major cities of the East and Europe with his "bareback hussars" and soon made the fortune he had predicted. He was made a colonel in the Pennsylvania militia and served often as a guest advisor. His book on close-field tactics was read with considerable interest on both sides of the Atlantic.

Sergeant Terry, recovering from his wounds in Monongamesh, decided to retire from the army and stay in the valley as a blacksmith. His wife and nine-year-old son soon joined him. The village presented him with the smithy in appreciation.

Henry Wendermuth also recovered from his wounds and eventually accepted Anton Zaretski's invitation to become sheriff for the valley. He carried only his hunting knife, but even that became unnecessary after a few months. Maria taught him to read and write, and he taught the children of Monongamesh the names of mountain flowers and the location of herbs and valuable mushrooms. Neither he nor the mayor ever talked much about Indians.

And so a lawyer learned about discipline from an artillery sergeant, about the psychology of attack from an illiterate frontiersman, about cold courage from a flamboyant circus rider, and about diplomacy from his wife. It was enough to prepare him for becoming the colonel of a regiment. From his senior law partner he learned to respect a new idea. But in the privacy of his own office he reminded himself that the great lesson of Kills-the-Hawk was that in battle there is no cousin.

CHAPTER 10

A New Commander

Brigadier General Edmund Service knew full well that Grant had kicked him downstairs for being too dedicated, too zealous in the attack. "Unacceptable losses" was not a phrase that made much sense to him; it echoed around him like "gutless leadership." He was a politically appointed general, but he knew that politicians face facts a lot quicker than most bureaucratic generals.

Edmund Service had more energy than Grant's combined staff. He was even shorter than Phil Sheridan and had begun to put on a bit of weight. He was seen as a dandy since he had begun exhibiting a preference for large horses, hats with nonregulation plumes, and well-cut long coats that tended to disguise his stomach. He never walked when he could sit astride a horse, which he did very well. When he walked, he tended to make people nervous, which he enjoyed.

He most admired General Sheridan, a tough cavalry professional. Service longed to lead cavalry charges. He hated the assignments that often strangled him with hay-footed infantrymen, and he hated the concussive cacophony of artillery, which numbed him of thought. Worst of all were these recent battles where both sides had begun digging trenches. What kind of a ridiculous war was that?

He regretted that he had not been at Gettysburg. That would have been the kind of action for him, and he secretly admired the gallantry of George Pickett. Had he been facing that charge he would have led his men out of their shallow trenches full into the Confederate ranks and settled things for real.

"When a soldier digs a hole, he stops being a soldier and starts being a survivor. Wars are never won by survivors," Service said suddenly to his aide as the two rode leisurely along the side roads of northern Virginia in the general direction of the 48th Pennsylvania Regiment.

Prepared for nearly any sort of unrelated commentary from his tempestuous boss, Capt. Chet Phillips handled the observation with one of the sure-fire answers designed to keep his general at bay.

"Yes, sir."

Without looking around him, General Service held out his palm in the general direction of his aide.

"It's thirsty work riding these dusty roads in June. Do you have my camp cup handy?"

Having long since anticipated the request, Captain Phillips had the four-ounce collapsible cup extended and was quickly filling it full of bourbon from the saddle liquor pouch, the most important part of his field equipment. The pouch, designed to look like a telescope case, held two bottles of whiskey and was generally good for two days. There were times when keeping the pouch filled was definitely more critical than getting enough ammunition for the troops.

"Lovely, Phillips, just lovely. You will go far. Have a snort yourself; it'll do wonders for your constipation."

"Yes, sir. Permit me to pass this morning, sir. The doctor says my eyeballs are turning yellow, and it might be best to hold off until tonight so they won't embarrass you."

"Bullshit, boy!"

"Yes, sir."

"All right, Captain. It's turning into a bit of a ride after all their talk of 'just down the road a piece.' Fill me in on the Pennsylvanians. What the hell kind of slackers did Grant foist on me this time? You know, ten minutes more of guts at Cold Harbor, and there would have been no doubt who won the field. I hate amateurs!"

After a respectful silence, Captain Phillips began reading from the notes prepared for him by General Grant's personnel department the previous day.

"Sir, the 48th Pennsylvanians are a veteran volunteer regiment of some six hundred men from the eastern and western part of the state. They're mostly coal miners and farmers. They saw limited service at Cold Harbor and Malvern Hill. Their colonel is well liked. They have their own artillery, which is supposed to be pretty good. Their field drill is not too good."

"We'll fix that in a hurry."

"Yes, sir. According to these notes, they appear to be brave and resourceful."

"What does 'resourceful' mean? Do those notes explain any of this mumbo jumbo?"

"No, sir. They just say 'resourceful.' I guess they want us to find out for ourselves. Come to think of it, I've never seen that word used for any regiment before. Must be something special."

"Probably means they're a bunch of cannon dodgers but they haven't been caught yet. Wanna bet?"

"Not against you, General. You have too much of my money already. The 48th is commanded by Col. Anton Zaretski, a former lawyer and mayor of a little town not far from Harrisburg."

"Zaretski! What kind of a name is that for an American? And an officer, too! Any previous military experience?"

"Says here he hunted down some Indian and white renegades about twenty years ago under a chief named Kills-the-Hawk. Ever hear of him, sir?"

"Of course. I believe he was kin to Fills-the-Glass. You'll oblige for memory's sake, please." He extended the empty cup toward the general direction of Captain Phillips, who dexterously swapped the personnel folder for the whiskey case and poured another full cup. At this rate his boss would be drunk by midafternoon. Perhaps it would be best to spend the night camped near the road. "Anyone else to note, Phillips?"

"Major Harrington, who commands the supporting artillery. Also reliable."

"Fat and forty, fat and forty. All artillerymen are fat and forty. You watch. They're full of numbers and excuses. Always pretend to be hard of hearing from the guns unless it's supper time. Fat and forty—and slippery. We'll have to watch him. Or promote him and let General Burnside watch him. Ha! Anything else? And do make it snappy. My kidneys need a little attention, and it should be getting close to lunch."

"Well, sir, it's a bit unusual, but I guess General Grant had a good reason for putting them there. Seems we have an all-Negro sharpshooter unit attached to the 48th. Led by a Colonel Ashley, a regular. The Negroes are also all volunteers."

General Service drew in his horse with a vicious wrench of the reins.

"Niggers?"

"Yes, sir."

"Sharpshooters, you say?"

"Yes, sir."

"You remember that mess at Mechanicsville? I don't want any niggers under my command!"

"You remember they paid kinda high for what they finally got, General. Over 40 percent casualties."

"You sticking up for niggers?"

"Just reminding the general of the figures."

"Well, Phillips, we took the objective, and that's the only number that counts. Ask General Grant. Now let's find a shady place to put down the lunch blanket while I go raise the river a foot. What else does it say about Ashley?"

"Indian fighter from the West, sir. Cavalryman. Served with General Sheridan."

"Hm. Bet he wishes he was back choppin' up Cherokees after this duty. Our army is going to hell. Excuse me."

"Yes, sir." Phillips's major hope for a return to amiability lay in the chance of a long nap after lunch. The fried chicken from General Grant's mess might even put General Service in a mood good enough to keep the war away for another day. The wine he had brought to go with the chicken wouldn't hurt.

Half an hour later, with the full picnic consumed and the wine bottle empty, the bones, fruit rinds, and bread ends buried, General Service's attempt to nap was thwarted by the furor of galloping horses and screaming cannon caissons on the road less than forty feet from them. Knowingly, General Service remarked, "Three-inchers on the roll make a hell of a racket. And here comes a supply train for a month's stay at Grandma's. Looks to me like someone's getting ready to earn his keep."

When the roiling dust had settled, General Service stood up to brush some of the road debris from his uniform.

"Any idea where they're going?" he asked, trying to catch numbers from the occasional flapping pennants.

Captain Phillips's noncommittal answer was crushed by another thunderous passage of field pieces. When he could finally make himself heard, he did so to the general's total astonishment.

"What do you mean, they're coming to us?" He was almost apoplectic with frustration. "Make sense, dammit!"

"The Pennsylvanians are charging the Petersburg mound in the morning, sir. Those guns are supporting the operation."

"That's some way to run an army. Give a man a command, then send it into action without him. Come on, let's get a move on. Maybe we can show Colonel Zaretski a thing or two before he ruins everything!"

"Sir, our orders specifically state taking command of the 48th at noon tomorrow."

"I know what the orders say, and I say I take over when I get there. Now let's get going, and keep an eye out behind us so we don't get run over by any more guns. And let's hope our maps are almost accurate."

But the maps weren't accurate. General Service didn't get to the headquarters of the 48th Pennsylvanians until late morning the next day. By then the guns were silent, and only the weakening cries of dozens of retreating wounded hung in the air. General Service knew at a glance that the glorious attack of the 48th had been a failure. Knowing in his heart that it was a lack of grit that had doomed the operation, he intended to grill Colonel Zaretski thoroughly for the exact answers.

A small farm building, which would have made an ideal headquarters for him, had been transformed into a first-aid station. As General Service put his head in the door to look over the building, a blood-drenched surgeon curtly ordered him out of the light. Exhausted stretcher-bearers knocked against him as they lurched by, taking their ashen charges behind the building, dividing them into fields of the quick and the dead. Dozens of former ammunition wagons were wheeling into the area, rigged now as ambulances, to take the most seriously wounded on the long, bone-jarring trip to the field hospital near General Grant's headquarters. Very few would survive the journey.

He found Colonel Zaretski sitting on an upturned ammunition box, balancing himself with a musket as he watched the long files of stumbling, shuffling, exhausted men passing to the rear and taking whatever meager comfort they could salvage from the knowledge that they were still alive. Colonel Zaretski's pride in the selfless courage of his men went beyond description. He now knew, from what he had seen of the Confederate trenches and the dug-in Whitworths, that a frontal assault could never carry Petersburg. His heart ached for the men still within range of the Confederate sharpshooters, and he blessed Major Harrington for the extraordinary covering artillery fire that had allowed most of the men in the regiment to get back to their own lines. The colonel had ordered the thick abatis put back into place in front of his lines by nightfall but kept the stretcher-bearers combing the flat for two hours after recall had sounded. He noted with some surprise that not one stretcher-bearer had been hit by a Confederate bullet. He was sure the 48th had taken at least 30 percent casualties. The regiment would be useless for at least a month. Colonel Zaretski caught a glimpse of the paunchy, plumed general officer riding through the trees toward him. He thought it best to be on his feet when his new commander arrived. He saluted.

"Welcome, General Service. I'm Colonel Zaretski, and this is all that's left of the 48th Pennsylvania."

"What's happening, Zaretski? Looks to me like there's still time to round these slackers up and try again."

"No slackers here, General. And too much digging in up there." He swept his arm slowly in a gesture that included the mound and ended at the farmhouse-cum-aid-station.

"It's impossible. Even with all the guns from General Grant, we couldn't break through in enough places to hold anything. They're dug in like badgers. We've lost somewhere between 20 and 30 percent. Sorry, General, we had hoped to present Petersburg to you as a welcoming gift."

"I'm flattered. But you're bleating out old women's talk. Turn these cowards around, and I'll lead them up the hill to victory myself. Can't be all that bad; you're under cover for half the attack. The goddamn Rebs will never dream we'll be coming at them again so soon. Get your paunchy artillery major up here on the double. We go in an hour!"

"Sir," began Colonel Zaretski, "these men are spent. They've given everything—"

"In an hour, Colonel. I'm not accustomed to repeating orders. Spent? They haven't even been trying. All it takes to win this war is a little gumption."

As a reluctant Colonel Zaretski turned to signal a runner to get Major Harrington, he noted a rippling, thudding sound behind him, then another, and a third. Turning back to General Service, he saw three bayonetted muskets sticking into the earth near the general's boots. Soon a fourth and a fifth musket ripped into the earth around the general's feet. He was symbolically penned in. Before he could take a step, the number had jumped to a dozen. The owners of the muskets, plus dozens of others, stared directly into the general's eyes wherever he turned, seared beyond ceremony. They had faced death all morning and were not going back for a peacock. He could rant, but on this day the survivors were telling him: the 48th was climbing no more hills.

"Arrest these men. Arrest them. I want their names. This is mutiny. I'll not have it, you hear?"

The muskets were withdrawn, and the men moved along to the rear. With soothing tones, Colonel Zaretski moved the general away from the returning columns.

"General, these boys will be all right by morning. If you want to lead a charge, we'll have to go by ourselves, 'cause nobody's following us anymore today. Now let me fill you in on a little secret in case headquarters didn't get around to telling you about phase two of this operation. The 365th goes in at dawn from the flank. If the Rebs are as bushed as we are, the 365th might just pull it off."

"The 365th?"

"The Negro sharpshooters, General," reminded Captain Phillips.

"And just who the hell authorized that damn-fool plan?" screamed General Service.

"General Meade, sir," answered Colonel Zaretski evenly. "It was General Grant who thought of putting the two attacks back-to-back. A lot has to do with the foggy mornings we've been getting this spring. And now, sir, I'd like to introduce you to Major Harrington, our artillery commander, and Colonel Ashley, who's going to lead the 365th tomorrow."

"Later, Colonel, later. Just show me to my quarters for the time being. I want an officers' call at four o'clock, and I'll introduce myself at that time. White cowards or nigger cowards, cowards are all the same to me. There'll be some changes made around here for sure. And the next time we're given a job to do, we'll do it."

Inside the command tent set up for him that morning, General Service wondered if, perhaps, he had been hasty. The eyes of the men were as exhausted as any he had seen. He unstrapped his sword and lay down on the camp cot. The sounds of the returning survivors of his new command brought up strange memories of his unhappy days at Columbia University, the loneliest time of his life. The heavy boots made a somber contrast to his days of equestrian glory.

It was at Columbia that Service made his first discovery in what he considered the essence of manhood. He found that he could ride better than anyone at the university. Immediately he convinced his family to contribute two hunters to the furthering of his education. The exhilaration of competitive jumping drove him slightly mad. He was able to compete with anyone, regardless of size, so long as he was well mounted. He was so good that he was elected captain of the equestrian team in his junior year; he considered it his due. He became a marked man for the competition. He was delighted.

When on a responsive horse, Service considered himself invulnerable to harm. In competition he saw himself preparing for future cavalry charges that would inspire thousands. That vulnerabilities are deeper than the physical occurred to him in his senior year when his father died and the horses had to be sold to keep him in college. The equestrian team dropped Service, and a source of deep personal satisfaction was suddenly snatched from his grasp. He discovered a fondness for bourbon and graduated near the bottom of his class. It was a bad year, but there were other discoveries ahead that would change his life.

He returned to Indiana, taking over his family's large, badly managed farms. Here he walked into his second talent: he was a very good farm manager. He became as competitive in business as he had been in the jumping arena. He discovered that the "responsive horse" was called money. Understanding that produce was useless until moved through the market, he attacked the restrictive practices of Indiana middlemen who squeezed the bulk of the profits from the smaller farmers. He hired ambitious, tough agent-merchants to market his corn, hogs, and apples directly to Chicago and eastern markets. He made arrangements directly with the railroads. He began calling his corn "Hoosier gold" and created a demand that guaranteed him bushel-price leverage. When feed prices dropped, Service bought a meat-packaging plant and shipped or stored product as it suited him. He also bought a dairy, but the storage problems became so intimidating that he formed a dairymen's cooperative to help keep the prices stable regardless of the play in the market. Everything he touched turned to profit, and suddenly he was in a social whirl that made him laugh. Short, chunky, and argumentative, Edmund was the darling of the cotillion set because he was also unmarried, "going places," and rich. He soon decided that he preferred the honest company of whores who made no pretence about liking him for his money alone.

Service organized an equestrian drill club and gathered together a small league, of which he became the president. The drill club became the nucleus of a reserve cavalry troop for the army. He quartered the team's ponies at army stables for nothing and worked out a harmonious deal on the feed. In return, he often paraded the team in splendid regalia on handsome, well-disciplined mounts. The unit was known as the Service Volunteer Outriders, and his honorary rank was captain. The parade unit became so famous that he was often approached to run for state office. But he was beginning to learn that he could get his way more quickly as a kingmaker than as an officeholder accountable to so many. He gracefully declined. He was, however, always ready to donate to party business. A series of good guesses soon built him a reputation for shrewd political judgment.

In 1857 the army called for cavalry reservists to help put down the maraudings of a fire-belching abolitionist named John Brown in Kansas. Service volunteered his Outriders for ninety days and was promptly promoted to reserve colonel. The Outriders were soon on a train to Fort Riley. Those were the most glorious days of his life.

Service didn't even mind being reduced in rank to captain so that he wouldn't outrank the regular army officers in charge of the operation. The one he admired most was Capt. J. E. B. Stuart. Stuart commanded respect by demeanor and example. He made his riders practice fundamentals until they were able to respond even after twenty hours in the saddle or when suddenly awakened in the middle of the night. Yet Stuart's men loved him because they knew he was a master of the unexpected. He was unorthodoxy at gallop speed. Once, near Osawatomie, where Brown's raiders had been particularly brutal against Southern sympathizers, Stuart found himself outnumbered some three to one. Stuart ordered a charge directly into the superior force.

"If the numbers make you nervous, Eddie, don't count 'em," was his calm advice to Service as they leveled sabers and hurled themselves across the prairie. It was so exciting that he wet his pants. The ferocity of the charge shattered Brown's strength, and his forces retreated. Even so, it might have been equally disastrous for Stuart but for the timely arrival on his flank of a reinforced patrol under the regimental surgeon, whose instinct for good timing matched Stuart's. Surprisingly, casualties were light on the army side. The surgeon, however, was killed for his timely courage.

"Turning your back and hightailing out is when the casualties start coming," Stuart told Service. "Surprise, quick and dirty, noisy too, is the best thing the cavalry brings to the party, Eddie."

Weeks later John Brown massacred an entire wagon train at Pottawatomie, sparing only the Negroes. During the pursuit, Service caught a round in his left shoulder which unhorsed him. The bullet broke his shoulder, and the fall crushed his ribs. John Brown left Kansas.

The Outriders returned to Indiana, and Edmund Service remained in
the Fort Riley hospital, with a hero's wounds. That's where he met
Kitty Willoughby, whose eyes seemed to reflect his pain and at whose
gentle touch he felt immortality. It made no sense to him, but he didn't
care. Kitty's husband had been killed during one of the charges at
Osawatomie, and visiting the wounded filled her empty days while the
army wondered what to do with the young widow.

The combination of broken shoulder and smashed ribs put Edmund
Service in the most vulnerable condition of his life. He remembered
Kitty through the delirium of the first few days and the terrible embarrassment of the nursing. But soon, as the worst of the pain passed,
he began looking forward to her compassionate, gentle banter. He started
noticing foolish things that he had never paid attention to before: colorful
ribbons, lace at her wrists or bosom, simple pieces of jewelry, the
extraordinarily clean lines of her face, the way she wore her hair, the
pleasing variety she achieved from a fairly meager wardrobe. Within
a few weeks he caught himself feeling jealous of the time she spent
with other patients, many of them younger and far better looking than
he knew himself to be.

Kitty's voice was soft, almost lyrical. He knew when she was by
his bed, even if he were sleeping. She had long, soft, brown hair, clear
gray eyes, and a sensitive mouth, which often seemed to smile privately for him when she spoke his name. And she always called him
"Colonel," as if they shared a respectful secret. Kitty brought flowers and listened to his accounts of the Kansas skirmishes and battles.
She wanted to hear every detail of Osawatomie. Had he possibly seen
the death of her husband, Capt. Thomas Willoughby?

She had begun taking his hand to check his pulse to help out the
orderlies. She said there was much talk of nursing as a career for women,
and she was deeply interested in taking up formal training in St. Louis.
She felt women were better in sickrooms than men. She had been told
how small her widow's pension would be, and she was determined not
to be a burden to any man. He liked the way her small chin held level
when she said that; he knew she'd go through with the training. Her
family hardly existed. There was a single brother who lived in St. Louis,
she thought, but he hadn't written her in six years, feeling she had disgraced
herself by marrying a soldier. This brother was the rector of a two-
thousand-member church with a budget rivaling that of many indus-
tries in the city.

"If you want to know," she let slip one morning, "I think my brother and his congregation helped ship some of those 'Beecher's Bibles' that John Brown used to kill my Tom!" They were walking the corridor and it all just gushed out as if she had been thinking about it for a long time. She was quick to return to her usual calmer self. "Oh, do forgive me, Colonel. I usually don't let myself get carried away by my personal feelings. My, you do seem a little stronger this morning; I can hardly keep up with you."

Service patted her hand as he shuffled stiffly beside her. This situation he could understand. He also understood that her petiteness looked good on him as they walked together. He liked her spunk, the attention she paid to matters of the world when he explained them, the fact that she had no children, and her kind, healing words for everyone in the ward. Kitty's anger with her brother was every fighting man's anger with well-meaning amateurs who caused more trouble than they realized.

He was nearly well when she failed to show up two mornings in a row. From inquiries Service learned that she had finally received her husband's death benefits and that she had been asked to leave the post to make room for an incoming family. It was the army way. He was able to track her to a modest hotel not far from the post where she had settled to sort out her life. Kitty was crying when he knocked on the door with his cane handle. She was overwhelmed at his coming to call. She invited him in, apologizing for the disarray. He entered thinking how beautiful and fragile she looked. Service had never known such feelings in his life. Fragile things had always been for smashing or avoiding, since they announced weakness.

"It's ironic, isn't it?" Kitty said when they were seated and tea had been served. "My husband had the bad luck to die for his country while we had our first home on post. So the first thing the army does is remove the embarrassment from view. I do declare, a widow woman must be more trouble to the cavalry than a whole party of Comanches!"

Her eyes were close to brimming up again when he took both her hands. His gesture, which he had meant to be calming, betrayed him when his hands started to shake. Hers, in contrast, grew strong, and she held them fast in her lap. He leaned forward to kiss her cheek, tasted her tears, and kissed her again. She turned to offer her mouth. Their lips met compulsively. Almost without knowing what he was doing, he was suddenly undressing her, leading her to the small iron bed, and then screaming in unbelievable fulfillment, burying his face in the pillow to keep from bringing in the management, responding over and over to her need for him until they lay spent and complete in each other's arms.

"Kitty!" was the full extent of his commentary. It was more than sufficient. The very motion of her breath against his chest started his craving all over again, a great rising of compassionate manhood to which she responded as if they were the last couple on earth.

"It's been so long, so terribly long," she murmured, kissing his ear and arching in orgasmic response to his now-perfect probing. Then she started to cry again, heaving great sobs as she clung to him fiercely. "My husband—" she started to say.

"Sh-h-h," he answered, "it's all right."

"Yes, it is; but I've got to tell you anyway. My husband treated me like a servant. I thought all men must be like that. I never once felt like a woman. Until now. Does that make any sense?"

"Not to me. I can't understand his not treating you like a woman, because to me you are a helluva lot of woman."

"How gallant! Thank you, Edmund. You also do wonders for the spirit. I really appreciate your effort. At Riley, as you know, we had lots of wounded and very few kind words. That's why the doctors only let us in for a few hours a day. Can't have a bunch of blubbering females sloshing around the corridors, can we?"

"Where will you go, Kitty, when you finally sort things out?"

"I've about got it figured out. Caring for a house is about all I know. You know that Tom and I never had young 'uns. His kin are dirt-poor farm people from near Cincinnati, and they don't want another female mouth to feed. My brother in St. Louis understands about my wanting to be a nurse, and he'll let me live in his house until I can get through training. So I'm going to take Tom's benefits and invest them in a career for me. With all the hostilities everywhere, a good nurse might just be very valuable soon."

It was so impetuous, Edmund couldn't believe he was saying it. The thought of her going away to St. Louis tore at his heart with burning hooks.

"Kitty, come with me to Indianapolis and run my life, my heart. I can't bear to think of you in any place where I can't be with you every day."

The delay of some twenty years was set straight in some twenty minutes. He made plans for Kitty and her belongings to travel to Indianapolis by rail the very next day and arranged for a suite of rooms for her at the Centre Hotel. He told her to make preparations for a wedding in six weeks. Putting her on the train was almost more pain than he could bear. His separation orders came through the next week, and he prepared for the return trip to Indianapolis eight days after that. In the meantime, he spent his days completing his reports on the Kansas fighting for the army and his nights writing to Kitty.

He received one letter from her almost as soon as she got to Indianapolis. It was written by the hotel stenographer. Kitty explained that she had slipped on the wet train steps while descending and had sprained her right wrist. The stenographer was helping her out until he could get home. Short but fervent letters began arriving regularly soon after. Sometimes there were three in one day. Time hung like a leaden albatross upon his heart.

The night before departing for Indianapolis Edmund gave a party at the Fort Riley Officers' Club for all the officers with whom he had served over the past five months. It was a lavish affair for frontier living, and his generosity was well received. After the hearty dinner of roast buffalo hump and smoked turkey, and the many toasts of appreciation and well-wishing, he found himself recovering quietly at the nearly deserted bar.

"Colonel, suh," said the bartender in a soft voice behind him, "these gentlemen would like to know if it's all right for them to have a short word with you?"

He turned to face half a dozen of the more senior captains who had ridden with him. He smiled accommodatingly and waved them closer. But they stared past him, or at the floor, awkwardly. Finally the most senior of the group stepped forward, turned Service so that they both faced into the bar, and ordered two whiskeys.

"Your very good health, Edmund."

"And yours, Jess. What the hell's going on?"

"Nothing much, nothing much really. However . . ."

"However?"

"Since we've been riding together and getting our asses shot off together, we thought, the others and I, that perhaps we could talk for a minute."

"I'm your guest in this club. Go ahead and talk."

"It's a mite delicate, sir. Well, some of the others have informed me that you and Mrs. Willoughby have been, ah, have been getting right fond of each other."

"It's true, and I'm proud to inform you I feel I am a very lucky man. We're going to be married in about four weeks. If there's any way you and any of your staff can get away, you're all invited to Indianapolis to share our nuptials!"

"Yes, sir; thank you, sir. Very good of you. But that's sort of why the others and I wanted to visit with you for a moment."

"Yes?" answered Service, still smiling at the other's discomfort.

The captain reached behind him, and another officer smartly placed an envelope in his hand. The captain put the envelope on the bar and opened it to a picture. He laid the picture next to Service's glass. The picture was of a young, tough-looking cavalry captain. He sported a long, thin saber scar along one cheek.

"This seems to be one tough customer, Captain. Glad to note he's on our side. You have a point to make about him?"

"Yes, sir. This tough sonovabitch wasn't a cavalryman, though. He was our regimental surgeon." The officer seemed to take a second breath as if resolving a momentous decision. "He was a Negro who loved to ride. Being a doctor was the only way he could get a cavalry commission. He was able to pass for white everywhere, but he told us about being black from the beginning. Mighty good surgeon, and he sure could ride. He was killed at Osawatomie when he brought up the reinforcements that saved us. Remember?"

"Of course, but I still don't see the point to all this."

"Yes, sir. This here's Capt. Tom Willoughby."

"Yes . . . ?"

"Kitty's former husband, Colonel."

The silence grew heavy with the great unspoken truth. The room wanted to spin and fall away from him. He felt strong arms reaching for him even as the solid mahogany bar turned to rubber. He fought for sanity.

"But she couldn't have married a nigger. The army won't let 'em marry white women."

No one answered him.

"They can't marry white women," Service repeated, feeling more like a fool every second.

"Yes, suh," answered one of the soft voices around his chair. "They can't. Kitty is an albino. Even down South they both rode in the front of the train cars. Mighty handsome woman, suh. Tom Willoughby, he was mighty proud of his woman. Sorry to have to tell you this way, Colonel. But we figured you ought to know before leavin' in the morning."

He stood up and tried to say thank you, but the words wouldn't form. He reached for his wallet to pay the bar, but hands intercepted and escorted him to the main door. When the door closed behind him, he knew he could never bear to see Fort Riley or those officers again. A letter was waiting for him in his quarters. He recognized the writing of Kitty's friend, the stenographer. He ripped it open and began reading.

Dearest Edmund,
You will soon be returning to Indianapolis, and I do believe it's time for the truth. First, Mrs. Peters is writing this for me, not because I've injured my arm, but because I can neither read nor write. Are you sitting down, Edmund, dear? There is worse to come. Perhaps this letter is a cowardly way to tell you so much, but you deserve some time for contemplation. Some days ago, I asked a few of Tom's friends to show you his picture. By now you know the great dark secret of my life: I am a white black woman. There has been no comfort for me in the black community and only a vicious lie in the white. I was never even welcome among Tom's fellow officers, but Tom thought we were strong enough to handle anything. We weren't, and when he was killed I wanted to die, too. Tom wasn't quick enough to beat a bullet, and I'm not devious enough to live a lie with you.

After Tom died, visiting the hospital turned out to be more healing for me than for the patients. I discovered a talent for helping sick people, who can't see a whole lot of color when they're hurting. I never dreamed, Edmund, that you would fall in love with me, or that I would grow so fond of you. That day in the hotel I needed you so desperately that I abandoned myself to feelings I had never known even with my brave and bitter husband. I agreed to come here to Indianapolis to wait for you, but I have had these three weeks to think; this letter is the result.

When you return, I will be gone. I have paid all my bills and no one will ever know that I was your intended, except Mrs. Peters, and she has become my friend. I am moving to St. Louis to live with my brother, to learn to read, and to go to nurse's school. I want to get into hospital work as soon as I can.

I do not believe, dear Edmund, that I shall ever see your face again. As you helped heal me, so must I leave you to heal in the spirit of this terrible truth. How often in our lives do we have the privilege of totally opening ourselves to another as have we?

You will always be treasured in my heart. I pray the Lord will
watch over you and give you the time to create a new life with
a new love, as you have re-created mine.

With deep affection,
Kitty

Beside the signature was a precise and petite *x*.

When Service arrived in Indianapolis he took a carriage to the Centre
Hotel and asked to see Mrs. Peters, the stenographer. He identified himself and soon learned to his satisfaction that she had revealed nothing
of Kitty's letters to anyone. He offered her the position of office manager
with his corporation at six times her current salary.

"If you can be circumspect, Mrs. Peters, you'll have a position all
your life. I know how to reward my friends."

"I accept, and I understand. Most hotel people are successful because they are circumspect."

"Hmmm. Do you think you could run this hotel? Its profit picture
isn't very encouraging."

"I don't see why not. And the profit picture is due to petty graft,
petty theft, and poor services."

"If you do well with me, I'll buy this place for you. And what's your
real name?" he added with a twinkle.

"Amanda Ramos. Miss Ramos."

" 'Amanda Ramos, sir,' " he answered with a hint of an edge.

She looked at him evenly as she picked up her stenographer's book.
"I can manage your office, run your hotel, buy your materials, ship
your goods, and cover your ass, Colonel. But I say 'sir' only to my
father, and he, thank God, has been dead for six years. You still want
me?"

He retreated with a wave of resignation. Bachelorhood looked better all the time.

In 1858 the politics of Indiana were the politics of all the states in
the North that had adjoining borders with slave states. Indiana was in
perpetual upheaval. In some counties there were midnight raiders, burnings, and lynchings. Spurs of the Underground Railroad ran through
many towns and farms, and everyone talked of war. Edmund Service's
goal as kingmaker was to harmonize the realities of the near future.
He threw himself into meetings throughout the state, sharing observations

and collecting viewpoints. One thread became evident in short order. The views of Abraham Lincoln of Illinois made sense to many voters in Indiana.

In the summer of 1858, Lincoln debated Stephen Douglas for the United States Senate. Lincoln lost the race; but in Freeport, Illinois, Lincoln summed up the entire American problem. Editors were quick to call Lincoln's arguments the "Freeport Doctrine." In the Freeport debate, Douglas had stood up strongly for states' rights, the right of any state to declare itself free or slave. This was a popular position for many in Illinois since the state abutted Kentucky and Missouri. Lincoln, foreseeing an inconclusive agony of artificial trade-offs and ruinous balances, declared that the United States had to take charge of its own destiny by announcing that the Union was no longer accepting any new slave states. This was a brave stand. It cost him the senatorial election but brought him national fame. People liked his strength, his wit, his biblical style. The Republican party, still reeling from the disaster of the 1856 election and the candidacy of John C. Frémont, turned to Lincoln in 1859 and asked him to represent the party in the 1860 presidential election. The Republicans wanted Lincoln to run on a platform of Union preservation.

To Service this was gold. Putting Kitty Willoughby out of his mind, he turned his full attention to the blazing promise of a man who publicly acknowledged the probability of secession and clearly portrayed the great choice that the North would have to make—allow the secession or be willing to march into civil war. To Service, war was inevitable, and an inevitable war meant an inevitable generalship. It was the best of worlds for a man who knew no fear and who couldn't be bothered with counting casualties.

Throughout the campaign of 1860, Service became the most influential planner and organizer in the state. He focused on Lincoln's log cabin and Indiana roots, idealized his honesty, shared his earthy witticisms, and showered admiration on Lincoln's lawyerly sense of reality. According to Service's plan, if there was going to be war, Indiana was going to be ready.

As he campaigned for Lincoln, Service saw to it that the Indiana volunteer companies recruited vigorously. He made certain state funds were in place and also supervised a rugged training program. He was always on hand for federal inspections. Service supervised, among other things, the entertainment of the political and military delegations. Feasts

at his home in Indianapolis became famous, even by Washington and
New York standards. Reports from visitors always glowed with the
efficiency and enthusiasm of the Indiana reserve militia.

One sour note crept into the reports. Élan was high, but transportation and supply were miserable. Service was driven by the dash and
daring of Napoleon at Marengo and Austerlitz, and he ignored the fiasco
in Russia. He referred to such findings as the "paltry sniveling of petty
malcontents." When the War Department staff welcomed him to Washington early in 1860 to review the growth of the Indiana volunteers,
the staff members were careful to compliment Service's high spirits
and personal contributions to the military. As a professional, however,
there was the matter of proper supply.

"It'll be long, we fear, this business of a civil war, Edmund," said
one staff officer. "Armies camp and carp as well as march. They also
bleed. Armies such as we're going to see can't live off the country or
out of saddlebags the way you did in Kansas. They need planning for
the million and one minor details of just getting to where they're supposed
to get. For instance, according to our records, your regiment, if it were
called to active duty tonight, would be starving inside of three weeks."

"We plan to finish off any Southern corn pones within thirty days,
gentlemen."

"Admirable. But we even have Mr. Lincoln thinking in terms of at
least ninety days. Let us give you two small cases in point before we
go off to luncheon. One, I see no provisions for coffins in your supply manifest. You should be thinking in terms of at least 8 percent
casualties. Second, although you take justifiable pride in lightning mo-
bility, there must be some preparation for defense. A time to dig in,
you know."

"Defense!" gulped Service. "We're cavalry and running infantry. Why,
you know we can march thirty miles a day for a week at a time. Your
regulars can only do twenty. We're—"

"We know, Colonel Service; your reputation precedes you. However, we lay before you a most professional possibility. The South is
filled with mountains, which are ideal for defense. You may have to
integrate at least one company of sappers who can dig trenches and
tunnels for you."

"Tunnels? Trenches!"

"A bit of a science, Edmund. Many of West Point's finest have done
their share of digging and blasting. Remember, the top of each class
goes into civil engineering—rivers, harbors, canals, railroad tunnels.

That's one of the ways we'll beat the South if it comes to that; we'll railroad 'em to death. You'll see, getting there together is as important as fighting bravely."

Colonel Service returned to Indiana after the excellent luncheon. A two-fold plan evolved during the rail trip to Indianapolis. First, he bought a small casket company through his agent, the now-ubiquitous Miss Ramos. He then secured a contract to supply the Indiana militia as well as the Ohio and Illinois volunteers with five hundred coffins each and "as many others as might be needed." He ordered the factory to begin building to stock and leased a warehouse.

Second, he issued an order that anyone caught discussing defensive warfare, including such terms as trenching, tunneling, and abatis, was to be brought to him for possible court-martial on the charge of cowardice in the face of the enemy.

"Anyone who digs a hole around here other than for a latrine is going to find it pulled down over his ears," Service said at a staff meeting.

It was during the final weeks of the presidential campaign in the fall of 1860, when things were going better than expected for the Indiana Republican organization, that Colonel Service made two significant discoveries, one discouraging, the other flattering. He could no longer hold his liquor, and women who had political ambitions for their men were finding him fascinating company.

"They want some of your power to rub off," said Amanda Ramos one afternoon over tea in her office at the Centre Hotel. Under Amanda, profits had jumped over 400 percent. In every business Service had given to her hand, profits had soared, including other properties, grain, hogs, and dairying. "Nothing says that while you're becoming a legend you can't enjoy yourself. If I were a man, that's exactly what I'd do."

The answer shocked him. Her answers were seldom what he got from others close to him. He found himself trying to anticipate her replies and usually coming up short.

On election day in November, Indiana voters turned out in huge numbers to elect the first prairie president.

Colonel Service was promoted to brigadier general and invited to the inauguration in March. He invited Amanda to go with him to Washington.

"I'd just crimp your style, General. Have a good time and tell me as much as you can remember when you get home."

Her refusal made him so angry that he began drinking on the train to Washington. He missed the inauguration, the reception, and all the lively dances of the night. He never even got a chance to wear his new uniform. Lincoln sent a note to his hotel wishing him a speedy recovery.

"When we have need for you, Edmund, I know it will always be Service without compromise," Lincoln wrote.

Edmund would have laughed if his head hadn't been reeling.

Within weeks of the inauguration, the South seceded, Lincoln called for ninety-day volunteers, and a reluctant Robert E. Lee resigned his commission to become a general in the army of the Confederate States of America. After Bull Run, the military men on both sides knew it would be years, not weeks, that decided the war. The Hoosier volunteers were called up and, true to Lincoln's prediction, saved the faltering Union flank at Shiloh in 1862.

"It was brilliant, absolutely fearless stuff," said General Halleck in Lincoln's study afterwards.

"What kind of losses did the Indiana cavalry take?" Lincoln asked.

"About 30 percent, sir."

"My God!"

"It was fish or cut bait. The Army of the West is still intact."

"Issue a unit citation, and I'll write to Grant and Service. Then pull the Indiana boys out of the line for a breather."

Edmund Service was made a permanent one-star general at Pokomoke Crossing when a daring use of massed artillery decimated a tightly bunched Confederate charge. Only Phil Sheridan and George A. Custer seemed to be building better reputations for getting things done in the Union army. Lincoln made the presentation of his permanent rank to Edmund at the White House and made sure the news was carried throughout Indiana.

The Union generals were terrified that the Confederate forces would carve their way up through Maryland and force the Union government to flee Washington. That might be all England would need to come in on the side of the South. The Confederate army fought violent and successful battles at Fredericksburg and Chancellorsville, but was unable to advance on Washington because the victories had drained too much manpower. Once again, the vigor of General Service's counterattacks covered the Union retreats so successfully that Lee assumed a Union strength that didn't actually exist.

The Indiana cavalry became known as the "Follow Me" brigade. Edmund had the words stitched onto the regimental guidons. However, the repeated heavy casualties brought him the name of "Bloody Service," which he considered a compliment.

He was sent home to recuperate from a bayonet wound in the spring of 1863. He learned that the South's ablest field commander, Stonewall Jackson, had died on May 10, 1863. When he was wounded accidentally by his own men, surgeons had cut off Jackson's left arm in an attempt to save his life. Hearing of his death a few days later, Lee was reported to have said, "General Jackson lost his left arm, but I have lost my right."

All the North had feared Jackson. Service took considerable pride in reminding anyone who would listen that Jackson had been a reservist like himself, who had been called to active duty when his country needed him. I'll bet they didn't bother counting his casualty percentages, he mused. He also wondered if J. E. B. Stuart had known Captain Willoughby and Kitty back at Riley. And how was Kitty getting along in St. Louis in the high glow of her new career? Was she reading about him?

During his recovery, Amanda briefed him on the continued prosperity of his business, particularly the casket factory and the hotels. Amanda advised him to buy coal mines and railroad stock, which he did. More disturbing, however, was the erosion of Lincoln's support and the undercurrent of sympathy for a live-and-let-live treaty with the South. His own casualty lists had brought less than rousing popularity for himself. As he healed, he began planning Lincoln's reelection strategy for Indiana.

Two big things were very much in Lincoln's favor, and Service meant to capitalize on them. First, Gen. Ulysses Grant had won three big battles along the Mississippi, which folks were beginning to call the "War in the West." Second, in thinking back over Antietam, Fredericksburg, and Chancellorsville, Service recognized that these had all been strategic stalemates. The South would have to take over significant portions of the North, or the North would have to conquer Southern real estate in 1863, before any positive shifting of the tide could be determined. Politics, the art of the possible, needed a positive image of Lincoln to follow. He would be ready.

The mending hero built his organization on the manifest explosion of industrial and transportation strength throughout the North. In spite of the occasional catcall of "Bloody Service," his was still an impressive presence in the state, and his experiences were respected. He began hearing favorable comments on emancipation and Negro recruiting and wrote to Lincoln of local sentiments.

England, which had abolished the "blackbird trade" some thirty years earlier, abandoned the idea of entering the war on the Southern side. As predicted, Negro volunteers began showing up at Union recruiting offices by the thousand.

In the spring, Service began another tour of Indiana. This time he asked Amanda to accompany him. He had discovered that she had swift instincts, politically as well as financially. In May he replaced several stalwarts because of her conclusions that they were (a) ineffectual, (b) hypocrites, and (c) thieves. She was right in all instances. Gossip quickly decided she was his mistress and a power to be feared. Service smiled at such rumors; after all, the problem was hers.

As his wounds healed, Edmund Service discovered he could drink again, even though Amanda told him his memory went to pieces suddenly when he did. He took to writing himself notes late in the afternoon so he could remember important decisions the next morning. This worked fairly well, and aides covered for him comfortably. Barely a year away from the 1864 elections, the political fences of Lincoln Republicanism stood in great need of repair. Great personal sorrows now burdened the gaunt president along with the conscience of the lacerated republic. The loss of their young son Willie was almost more than either of the Lincolns could bear.

Near Bloomington, Indiana, Service committed one of the two great blunders of his life. The second would occur a year later in front of Petersburg, Virginia. In an elaborate rooming house near Bloomington, after a successful day of political persuasion and a long evening of convivial drinking, Amanda helped Service up the stairs to his room. As she was about to drop him onto his bed, he suddenly revived with great energy and, shouting "nigger whore," he proceeded to rape her.

Amanda lay in pain and humiliation for some time after she finally pushed his spent and snoring bulk away from her. During the entire outrage she had refrained from screaming, knowing her entreaties would bring only guffaws. She thought about all the things she could do to Service, starting with murder and working down through castration, but gradually concluded that neither would bring enough satisfaction. She finally hit on a scheme that would accomplish castration without surgery, a scheme that only she could put together. Gathering up her bloodied underclothes, she retreated to her own room to soak them in cold water. In the morning Amanda saw a physician; in the afternoon, she took the train back to Indianapolis alone.

Service, remembering nothing of the rape, was startled to see her leave. He had begun to depend on her for the daily running of the tour. His associates kept their counsel. The remainder of the trip verged on failure as the buoyancy seemed to leave the meetings. Service blamed geography and the mixed loyalties of the southern part of the state. Many spoke frankly of replacing a bumbling president.

Some two weeks after Amanda's return to Indianapolis, searing allegations began seeping into the state's newspapers about Service's business activities. Editors sent top reporters to intercept his campaign train as it returned to Indianapolis. Soon the stories were compounded by cries for legislative and congressional investigations as more and more charges surfaced that were too detailed to be ignored. The large dailies of New York, Philadelphia, Baltimore, Washington, Cleveland, and Chicago were quick to enlarge and deepen the scandal.

The material was straightforward and simple. A cover letter asked editors, legislators, and congressmen why the parents and lovers of Indiana soldiers had had to give up their loved ones while "Bloody Service" made an enormous profit on the caskets used to bury so many of them? Accompanying the letter were photographs of the original factory, the huge expansion, and copies of balance sheets and owner-ship agreements proving that Edmund was profiting handsomely from death. The more deaths, the higher the profit. One cartoon showed him leading one of his "Follow Me!" charges mounted on a coffin with four skeletal legs churning. Profits were shown to exceed 1300 per-cent. The letter concluded, "Is General Service's high casualty rate, the highest in the Union army, tribute to his courage, disregard for our boys' lives, or an astute eye for profit?"

Pictures, drawings, and balance sheets from his iron foundries, coal mines, and railroad interests soon followed. Cries for investigation, torchlight processions of venomously furious parents and wives, hangings in effigy and burnings in front of his house took place nightly. An-other cartoon showed him directing the politics of the state on a plat-form of coffin covers. He sold the factory, dropped his railroad, iron, and mining interests, and donated to the widows and orphans fund for the militia. All to no avail. Editors refused to see him. In less than two weeks he went from hero to the most despised man in the state. He resigned from the militia.

Service recognized the sharp blade of Amanda behind his disgrace. He sent for her, only to be handed a note by messenger with the news that Amanda had left Indianapolis. The note referred him to the firm's legal representatives. In the lawyers' offices he was handed an accounting of all the possessions that she had managed so well for him. She had overseen even the final sales, without bothering to extract her traditional commission. She had left him disgraced, but rich. The lawyers had no idea where Miss Ramos had gone. All settlements with her had been in cash. They assured General Service that all accounting was "proper to the penny." They sincerely regretted her departure.

"Did she leave a letter or anything for me?" Service asked as he sat in the paneled offices, stunned by the completeness of her wrath.

"As a matter of fact, she did," said one of the lawyers, pointing to a neat package on one of the heavy polished tables in the office.

Service opened the package to find a room key from a boardinghouse in Bloomington, which he vaguely remembered. He put the key in his pocket. He looked at the lawyers in confusion. They shrugged in shared perplexity. They then bundled the papers into proper folders, tied them with string, and gracefully showed him to the door.

"I don't understand, I don't understand," Service mumbled as he shuffled down the corridor to his carriage. He held the small box with the key close to his side in a hand that trembled slightly. Aides drove him furtively to a friend's farm. That night crowds burned down his home. He stayed drunk for three weeks. When he finally sobered up, he found personal orders from Lincoln, ignoring his resignation and assigning him to General Grant in the Army of the West at the Vicksburg siege.

But even in disgrace Edmund Service triumphed. In July, 1863, the Union won its most important victory at Gettysburg; and shortly after, Vicksburg fell. With these two huge victories, the tide of the war turned, and hopes for a Union triumph soared. All Service's handshake-by-handshake campaigning paid off in support for a Lincoln now seen as less bumbling.

Lincoln had replaced General McClellan as commander of the Army of the Potomac after the debacle at Antietam in September 1862, but General Burnside did no better, nor did Generals Hooker and Meade. The Army of the Potomac did not pursue its advantages, and the war in the east settled into stalemate. Lincoln appointed General Grant to command of all the Union armies in hope of achieving success in the spring of 1864. McClellan resigned and became the peace-wave Democrat candidate for the presidency in the 1864 race, while Maj. Gen. Henry W. Halleck, McClellan's successor as commanding general of the army, agreed to serve in the role of chief of staff. Lincoln again considered resigning, but feared the consequences of an indecisive peace. Grant set out to capture Richmond by attacking straight through the wilderness area of northern Virginia. At the same time, Grant ordered his often-despondent friend, General William Sherman, to begin the long march from Tennessee to Atlanta and beyond to destroy the food basket of the Confederacy.

On his way to Virginia from Vicksburg, General Service again passed through Indianapolis. He was now tolerated, and he discovered his political network had grown even stronger. His letters to the White House reflecting staunch support in Indiana were answered promptly and with appreciation. There was still no word on the whereabouts of Amanda. After giving him three months to put everything to rights in Indiana, Lincoln again posted him to Grant, this time for the start of the Wilderness campaign in the spring of 1864.

The Union, under vigorous leadership, was ready to move south. The outpourings of the Union factories had been stockpiled to the bulging point. Recruits, white and black, had materialized from every Union state, and morale was high. The only things bothering General Grant were the tenacity of the Confederate troops and the ruggedness of the Virginia terrain, which was ideal for defense. The countryside was hilly and covered with hundreds of square miles of roadless woods and thickets.

Victory at Cold Harbor on the eastern edge of the Wilderness came at an enormous expense of life. The Union generals discovered that the Confederate troops had learned to dig deep trenches which protected them remarkably well during artillery bombardments and yet allowed them to jump up to fight at maximum strength when the Union infantry tried to move in to take possession. At Cold Harbor, General Grant found it incredible that an army could fight as well as the Confederates did after sustaining the hub-to-hub artillery barrage of his divisions.

As the Union casualties mounted, morale dropped. The miles gained were few compared to the number of lives lost. McClellan, in his campaign to unseat the sixteenth president of the United States, called for an end to the slaughter and recognition of Southern rights. Grant's reply echoed Lincoln's own view of the entire war: "I intend to fight it out on this line if it takes all summer." His victories convinced him that casualties were even more costly to the South than they were to him. The South had no replacements and was drafting seventeen-year-olds. Southern desertion rates, once practically nonexistent, were soaring, but surrender came only under the bitterest conditions.

At Cold Harbor General Grant ordered Service to coordinate the flanking reinforcement that carried the day. General Service led an infantry assault directly into the Confederate trenches. Good artillery support had allowed General Service's troops to get within a few dozen yards of the trenches before they were noticed. The surgeon who ordered him strapped to the table counted eleven bullet and bayonet wounds over his body, all superficial. The only thing that bothered the surgeon was the heavy stench of whiskey around his patient. The Indiana press made much of General Service's miraculously slight wounds and his heroism.

While he was recuperating in Indianapolis, important state Republicans came to him, somewhat in awe. When Service returned to Virginia three weeks later, General Grant gave him no further duties before assigning him to the 48th Pennsylvania encamped in front of Petersburg.

General Service's reminiscences were cut short by the arrival of nearly a dozen horsemen following a hearty leader whose loud laughter could be heard even as he cantered into the clearing near the general's tent. The party was recognized at once by nearly everyone in camp, and cries of "ten-shun" clattered through the trees.

The party reined in. The leader dismounted and tossed his reins to an aide. Even though he was putting on weight, the new arrival actually managed to strut over to General Service as he emerged from his tent. He returned Service's salute carelessly.

"Good afternoon, Edmund. I see you're settling into your command in good order. Probably want to have another go at Petersburg, right? Glad we have to see General Grant instead. This morning rather proves our point, doesn't it, Colonel Zaretski? At ease, everyone."

"Yes, sir."

Hardly pausing for breath, the senior general continued.

"Let's pray the shadows thing works in the morning. Probably won't. It's such nip-and-tuck derring-do, I never should have allowed it. How's Colonel Ashley?" he asked Colonel Zaretski.

"He's planning to be in the vanguard, General Burnside."

"Yes, yes. Well, they are brave lads. Braver than they know. I'll tell you about them sometime, Edmund. General Grant didn't want to burden you with too many details. Oh, I nearly forgot. I brought over a wagonload of picks and shovels for you, Colonel Zaretski. Courtesy of General Grant. I understand he wants them all back when you're finished. And he told me to tell you that he's shipping you four tons of black powder. Expect them at the railhead two weeks from today. He'd like to have the whole business finished by the end of July. Can we do it?"

"We asked for six tons, sir. But of course, sir. You remember what a special regiment this is for digging."

General Burnside nodded and then waved up the covered transport wagons. Colonel Zaretski directed them further into the shade of the nearby trees where the picks and shovels were dumped onto the ground.

"Thanks a lot, General. We'll put them to good use tonight. Lieutenant Curran suggested an excellent place to start, the house we've been using for our surgery. We kick out the back of the house and go right through the floor. The slope is very gradual and the soil sandy and easy to dig."

"The hell you are!" bristled General Service. "That building is going to be my headquarters. . . ." Catching General Burnside's eye, General Service sputtered into an awkward silence. Everyone ached to change the subject, but the silence hung over them like wet powder.

It's going to be a long summer, thought Captain Phillips.

General Service took General Burnside on an inspection tour with Colonel Zaretski trailing behind. The wounded were scattered throughout the woods behind the surgeon's hut to keep the enemy from knowing the extent of the damage. On General Service's orders, the surgeons moved from the building to a glade at the rear under tarps. Many of the severely wounded would soon be hauled in the small supply transports that, shortly before, had brought in the ammunition for the frontal assault. The small wagons, pulled by horses or mules, carried everything the army used on the march. White canvas tops covered most of the wagons.

"That's it, General Burnside."

"That's what, Zaretski?"

"Those wagons, and those stretchers. That's how Lieutenant Curran meant for us to move the dirt right out from under the Rebs' noses. We take the dirt out on stretchers at night, covered with blankets, and slip it into the wagons like wounded men. The Rebs will think our transports are ambulances and will be congratulating themselves on our devastation. He even sketched the little transports on the side of the plans. I thought he was doodlin' and didn't give the sketch any mind."

General Service then made a contribution.

"They'd better put camouflage drapes all around the new field surgery. The Rebs aren't that dumb."

CHAPTER 11

The Tunnel

With the help of a theodolite from Washington, Colonel Zaretski and Major Harrington were able to project a direct line from the former surgery to the mound. They estimated that it was a little over five hundred feet to the foot of the mound. Curran had said the earth was good for digging, but Colonel Zaretski was soon absorbed by two immediate problems. First, the tunnel would have to be shored up by pilings and cross members and, second, the tools from General Grant were the worst tools in the army and would have to be augmented. Even the picks, which were too big, had to be retooled by the blacksmith.

Colonel Zaretski now understood the need for Curran's twelve-foot tunnel depth. At twelve feet, the Confederate listening posts would probably never pick up the sound of the digging. To make sure, however, once the tunnel reached the midpoint between the lines, Colonel Zaretski instructed Major Harrington to fire several rounds into the Confederate listening post area and beyond every half hour to help distract any casual listeners.

Colonel Zaretski decided to go to General Grant's headquarters himself to ask for better digging tools. It was a hard six-hour ride, and he didn't care that much for horses. With nightfall, however, he discovered one good thing about General Service. Once quartered for the evening, the general was no longer a problem, except for occasional choruses of bawdy songs or melancholy humming.

"Perhaps you'd let me join you, sir," offered Captain Phillips.

"Gladly—especially since you know the way. Besides, headquarters makes me nearly as nervous as horses, especially since we'll be going there uninvited."

Reporting the details of the two failed charges was going to be painful.
Requesting the shoring and better tools was going to take a kind of
haggling he had once relegated to courthouse steps. In Colonel Zaretski's
judgment, Petersburg was untakable except at an enormous cost of life.
Lieutenant Curran's tunnel was the only answer as long as the Confederate troops had powder and shot. Using Lieutenant Curran's digging estimates, Zaretski felt he could tell General Grant the tunnel
would be ready by July 29. He wrote everything down and attached a
crude copy of the tunnel drawings showing the large powder magazine at the end (the glory hole). The blowing of this underground
magazine would neutralize the trenches on top of the mound long
enough for the 48th to pour through. Curran had estimated that a thousand
men could be punched through the gap in a furious fifteen minutes.
With this many Union soldiers racing through the Confederate positions, the havoc would be total. Other units from General Burnside's
IX Corps could exploit the penetration within half an hour of the blast.
Petersburg itself would be in Union hands before midmorning.

General Service took to his bed after an early supper. Colonel Zaretski
and Captain Phillips took to their horses, riding as hard as they could
before darkness fell some five hours later. Captain Phillips's doubts
were too close to the colonel's.

"What if the whole thing doesn't work?" asked Captain Phillips. "I
mean, suppose the glory hole blows and everything, but we can't get
enough men across in time? This is a first-time thing, isn't it? We can't
exactly practice for it. And what if Lieutenant Curran's plans aren't
right and the Confederate lines don't collapse?"

"I wish I had all those answers. And you're right; we are going on
faith. But I do have one fact for you. If it doesn't work, I won't be
around to debate the issue. I'm charging with our boys. We are giving this thing all or nothing. If we can dig to the mound, I have every
confidence in Mike Curran's design. Which is sort of amazing to someone
used to hard evidence. I've only known the man a few days. You should
have heard him describing the explosion to me. That room where the
explosion is going to take place is no ordinary bubble in the earth. It's
going to be shaped like an upside-down bowl—no shoring needed in
there. According to Michael, it's the shape as much as the black powder
that's going to tear everything to pieces for us. 'You'll see,' he said,
'they'll be picking up pieces of Whitworths in downtown Petersburg.' "

"I'd like to go along with the men," Phillips suggested.

"Seriously?"

"I have the worst job in the army. I'd like to feel like a man again. Seriously."

"If you can get around General Service, I'll take care of the rest."

"Thank you."

They settled into the work of the long ride to General Grant's headquarters. With luck, Colonel Zaretski hoped to be there before midnight to salvage an early morning appointment. He hadn't yet figured out what he would tell General Service when he returned. To Captain Phillips, the road seemed almost as busy at night as it had been on that leisurely ride with General Service only a few days earlier. The full moon made the going easier for all kinds of transport, including many of the ambulances from the 48th. It was not far from Blackwater Creek that the incident occurred which changed the significance of the impromptu journey.

Out of the shadows of the scrub forest lining the road suddenly appeared some twenty riders who surrounded them with the instant completeness of a very practiced cavalry patrol.

"Evening, gentlemen. Forgive the intrusion. We're lost and would sure appreciate a little help."

The speaker wore the eagles of a Union colonel and the short, full beard of a man who was used to getting his own way.

"We have some important information for General Meade. We understand he's at headquarters with General Grant. Could you help us get there; we'd like to reach the general by midnight if possible."

"You're welcome to ride with us; we're headed the same way."

"Thank you kindly, Colonel. But we've got to ride a little harder than you may want to. Time's a-wastin' for us. I'm sure you understand. Just point us proper, and we'll be gone."

"Very well. After you go across Blackwater Creek up ahead, turn north at the bridge. You'll then have about twelve miles of twisting road to go."

"Thank you again, gentlemen." He tossed a perfunctory salute in their general direction, wheeled his horse, and waved the patrol in an easterly direction. The riders were gone without comment in the swirling dust. Captain Phillips laid a soft hand on Colonel Zaretski's bridle. The two waited a moment for the dust to settle.

"Colonel, those horses had no brands. All Union mounts have *U.S.* on them, but those horses were unmarked."

"Maybe they're just out of remount."

"Maybe they're just out of Dixie, Colonel."

"Oh, my God! And we—that is, I—just gave them the route to General Grant's camp. Why didn't they shoot us? What can we do? We'll never catch them."

"Colonel, I think that was an assassination team. We were lucky. General Service and I came down to the 48th on a shortcut that can save half an hour if they haven't put too damn many sentries on the back roads."

"You lead!"

It was the wildest ride of Colonel Zaretski's life. Twice, one or the other of the officers was scraped out of the saddle by uncompromising branches, but they remounted and somehow completed the battering trip without really slackening speed. Once they heard, in the near distance, the piercing whistle the bearded colonel had used when the suspect patrol left them. Provost guards stopped them twice. Finally, Colonel Zaretski got to a provost captain and explained their fears. Displaying unusual perception, the provost captain grabbed his own mount and shouted, "Follow me, I can help on this one!"

Because of this great piece of luck, they were able to get to the headquarters area before anyone had heard of the coming patrol. Colonel Zaretski awakened General Johnson of General Grant's staff, who quickly took charge.

Colonel Zaretski and Captain Phillips watched squads of tough-looking infantrymen jog across the perimeter of the headquarters area silently and with remarkable dispatch. The officers could make out the large tents that probably housed General Grant and his staff. At the same time they watched General Johnson set up a camp table and two folding chairs at one side of the clearing. A turned-down lantern was placed on the table, along with two glasses and a partially emptied whiskey bottle. Soon a slightly disheveled General Grant joined General Johnson at the table. As the two generals began talking in slightly thickened tones, the patrol burst out on the edge of the area. The heavily sweating cavalry colonel stopped in front of a sentry. Gasping slightly for breath, the colonel gathered himself.

"Colonel Parker to see General Grant. We have critical intelligence for the general from General Sheridan!"

"Yes, sir. Sergeant of the guard!"

While the sergeant of the guard was running toward the sentry, the two generals looked up from their table. General Johnson, walking just a bit unsteadily, approached the horsemen.

"I'm General Meade. General Grant and I were just having a night-cap. You look like you've been riding hard. Care to join us, Colonel Parker?"

Even as the words were being uttered, the cavalry colonel's saber sizzled from its scabbard, and he turned his mount's head toward Grant's table. A single shot from across the perimeter pitched the colonel off his horse into his men. As the horse reared in panic, two other riders whooped instinctive cries of command to action. But even as they moved to spur their frantic mounts, they were torn out of their saddles by perfectly timed fusillades from the woods.

General Johnson now held a long-barreled navy Colt revolver in his hand and said in a low, calm voice, "Just stand easy, lads. There are ten rifles aiming at the front and back of every man and horse here. Now just dismount real easy and come toward me real slow. If you're holding weapons, put them on the ground. Right now would be just fine. Look behind you if you don't believe me."

The riders turned to find two solid lines of infantry walking purposefully toward them, muskets at their shoulders. There was no way they could miss. Two riders who were climbing down from their horses in the front rank suddenly vaulted back into the saddle and raced for General Grant. They were lying low along their horses' necks, each now carrying a revolver. They began shooting in the direction of General Grant, who faced them dead on, refusing to budge. Musket fire killed one of the riders. He fell under the feet of the other's horse, which shied, ruining the second rider's aim. He overshot his target, knocking over the lantern as he reined in his horse and turned for a final shot at Grant. The raised pistol glistened in the flickering lantern on the ground. As the pistol came up, a wall of bullets tore the gun from his hand and him from his horse. Then the horse went down, too. No one else moved.

"Get these damn fools out of here. One general more or less isn't going to affect this war now," said General Johnson to the provost marshal captain. "And thank the men for a damn fine job. We really ought to lynch the Rebs as spies, but just get them into the nearest stockade. Their families will be needin' 'em soon enough. Crazy! This war is crazy!"

Colonel Zaretski and Captain Phillips regained the edge of the perimeter, where General Johnson caught sight of them.

"Gentlemen, give your mounts to one of the lads who has a free hand and come with me. I'd like you both to meet General Grant."

Colonel Zaretski and Captain Phillips popped to attention and saluted as General Grant came forward to meet them.

"Oh, no, gentlemen. Oh, no," he said with a large grin. "Please stand at ease. We've had enough hard soldiering for the evening. Besides, I'm not General Grant. I'm just a slightly paunchy civilian who resembles a better man. I happened to be visiting tonight and, after your most timely warning, was able to convince the general to make himself scarce for half an hour. Not such an easy task. But when you're General Grant such incidents are bound to happen. We look after the president, too, but his look-alikes are harder to come by. Here comes the real General Grant now."

General Grant stepped into the light of the replaced broken lantern to clap his stand-in on the shoulder.

"You're a damn fool, Allan, but well done. And these two must be the gentlemen who saved the night. I do believe one looks like Colonel Zaretski of the 48th Pennsylvanians. The other will have to introduce himself. Never mind the salutes, gentlemen, please give me your hands. That was most timely action."

Both laughed nervously as Grant continued.

"And you possibly know Allan Pinkerton, here, whose main job is looking after our commander-in-chief."

More handshaking and laughter. General Grant noticed General Johnson grinning in the background. Grant turned back to Zaretski and Phillips.

"Gentlemen, we owe you something. I'm instructing this old warhorse, George Johnson, to get you anything you need for that tunnel. That's why you came, right? We're still talking about a month, right? Good. Give my best to General Service [here Grant winked] and I'll not stand in your way for a speedy return. I'll send General Service a note in the morning. And keep an eye out for all that black powder coming your way next week. Or, if you'd rather stay over—"

"We'd best be getting back, sir. And thank you very much. I believe we now have a very good chance for success."

Grant nodded, and then he and Pinkerton returned to a large tent in the shadows. General Johnson invited the two back to the table so he could make notes. And that's how Colonel Zaretski inherited a trainload of good lumber at the railhead three days later, as well as thousands of yards of heavy cotton cloth for cutting up and sewing into sturdy bags, which would become twenty-five-pound sausages of black powder.

Less than a mile from Grant's headquarters, the dead Confederate raiders were buried in anonymous, shallow graves. The remainder were sent to prison camps in New York and Vermont. Their horses were sent to nearby remount stables, branded, and distributed to Union cavalry units. The remount commanders all commented on the uncommon quality of the mounts, which suggested high-level hopes for success of the desperate gamble. But for the sharp eyes of Captain Phillips. . . .

If we ever go a-raiding, thought General Johnson after the camp had quieted down, we'll have to instruct our raiders to kill anyone who gives help or even looks at our boys funny. If the raiders had shot Phillips and Zaretski. . . .

General Johnson summoned the provost marshal and reorganized the entire headquarters defense. The new plan made it far more difficult for anyone to come within half a mile of headquarters, and it made hundreds of senior officers furious. However, there were no more incidents.

General Grant returned to the big tent and opened a bottle of whiskey for the tall and tired visitor, the reason for Allan Pinkerton's presence in the camp that night.

"To contingencies," toasted Abraham Lincoln. "You certainly know how to entertain your visitors, General. A bit humbling. I thought perhaps they were after me."

Grant knocked back the toast, poured another, and looked at his commander-in-chief.

"Sacrificing twenty good men for one is an honor I can do without, Mr. President. Furthermore, I don't believe Bobby Lee was behind this little jaunt. Smacks to me more like the Confederate equivalent of our own Eddie Service—all balls and no brains."

"Glad you mentioned him [Grant could have bitten his tongue]. You know, I'm really indebted to him. There's so much popular disgust with the war that I'm afraid my chances for reelection this fall are like the old lady's virtue: questionable. His support in Indiana may be critical—if I decide to run, that is. By the way, I sort of expected General Service to be around here someplace. Where have you stashed him?"

"He's about a dozen miles west of here, smack in front of our toughest target, the Petersburg mound. We can't seem to take the hill itself, so we're building a tunnel to help us blow a hole through the front defense. We should be storming through at the end of this month. That may help the election, sir. And, if I may say so, you must run, Mr. President."

"Thank you. I'll think on it a while. Well, we'd best get some sleep. Do mention me to General Service when next you see him, clicking testicles and all."

"Yes, sir."

"Speaking of sacrifices, can Sherman take Atlanta before the election?"

"I do believe so, Mr. President. Sherman is as mean as I am and twice as clever. His dispatches have gone from 'They're knocking the hell out of us' to 'We're now holding our own.' I expect the next ones to suggest we're 'knocking on the gates.' "

"Well, General, let's put it this way. Whatever Sherman can do about Atlanta and whatever you can do about Virginia will make all the difference in what I can do about McClellan and his peace pottage in November."

"Oh, very good, Mr. President."

"If I couldn't laugh once in a while, Ulysses, I'd cry."

"I know, Mr. President. I know."

The Confederate captain climbed down the external parapet ladder to the level ground where the evening patrols were being organized. The leader of the first patrol was a slender lieutenant who looked like he would trade victory for a decent night's sleep.

"Who are you?" the lieutenant asked casually as he inspected his men's weapons. His informal method was reduced to fundamentals, as was his own living. Who was alive, who was hurting, who was salvageable, how much longer could they all hold on?

"From General Mahone, Lieutenant. Captain Michael Curran at your service. The general thought I might be needing a little seasoning in the art of night-patrol leading. He said he'd be obliged if you would let me trail along."

The lieutenant looked the man over. Big, pleasant, yet with an air of being able to handle himself in a fight. A hint of a foreign accent. A weariness about the eyes that suggested a fair share of hard duty. He liked him.

"No dust on me. If you're crazy enough to follow, I'm glad enough to lead. You picked the blackest night of the month, so it should be quiet. Stay close, don't talk, listen for my signals, keep low. Crawlin' is best. We'll be out about two hours. If we get separated, freeze where you are, and I'll pick you up on the way back. We're heading north and then east. Got a compass?"

"No, but I think I'll be able to see you fair enough."

"On a night like this, you'll be better off if you can smell me. Forget the compass, then, we have none to spare, even for company. Stay as close to me as you can without getting personal. If you get shot, go quietly. Toss away that holster and carry your sidearm. There won't be much drawin' time if we run into something. If you need to, shoot and roll away. Best to play doggo, though; shots bring down all kinds of unwelcome interest."

"Are we lookin' for anything special?"

"Same old thing, enemy movement. And be assured they're out there waiting for us. General Mahone wouldn't mind a few prisoners. And one more thing."

"Yes?"

"My men are used to taking their orders from me."

The officer from General Mahone's staff nodded. He not only un-snapped his holster, he left his pistol in it. He slid out a wicked-looking bayonet. Belt and holster were dropped silently at the foot of the ladder. The lieutenant rapped softly twice on the bottom rung. Two faint answering taps were heard overhead, and the patrol headed out. A sergeant took the lead; the lieutenant brought up the rear.

The route was laid out to patrol the sides of an oblong box. The patrol was to go some three hundred yards north before making a hun-dred-yard sweep to the east, then south and west to return to friendly lines. On most nights there was an understanding between the Union and Confederate patrols as to territorial limits. Curran was counting on an undeclared, unclaimed area somewhere along the north-south line in which he would vanish from the patrol and head for the Union parapets to the east. He gave a silent prayer for the 48th to be in its same position after the disastrous attack. What to do about the gray uniform? He'd worry about that later. First he had to get through the Reb outposts.

The night was so still and close that it worried him. Sounds car-ried forever. But in his case, better sounds and no sights for the next hour. Yet, if some Union sharpshooter wanted to have some fun at his expense, he was pretty sure sound could do him in. He had never felt so alone or hemmed in, even at the thousand-foot level in Wales. Crawling on elbows and knees, without making any noise, and not knowing if the next second would bring a Union bullet into his face, was as much tension as a man could handle, especially one who had been living by his wits and good fortune for four days, during which he'd only eaten

twice. Right now he was having trouble keeping the heels of the lieutenant in sight.

From time to time the patrol stopped, and the lieutenant crept forward to check with the sergeant in accordance with the coded knocks
on the sergeant's musket stock. Once they crawled right over a Confederate listening post. Curran was the only one who fell in.

"Howdy, Captain. The sergeant warned us you might be droppin' in."

Amid muffled laughter, someone handed him his dropped bayonet,
and three sets of hands hoisted him back up over the lip, nudging him
in the direction of the patrol. Could he catch up? Without the patrol's
lead, he'd never know when to turn east for the take-off point for his
escape. He crawled frantically until strong hands halted him and a voice
breathed into his ear, "Slow down, man, the Yanks will think we're
sending a brigade through here tonight. This is where we turn; stay
close and breathe slower."

The patrol, seemingly lightened by his embarrassment, turned east
and settled easily into the rhythm of the crawl. Curran sensed that each
man was even more alert than before. If trouble struck, this would be
where to expect it. All crawling stopped every twenty feet or so as
each man tried to penetrate the night for any unnatural sound. Inching back slightly after each pause, he was soon beyond sight of the
lieutenant and nearly beyond sound of the crawling. He lay motionless, hugging the damp earth, forcing himself to breathe evenly, his
eyes trying to get a fix on anything that would allow him to steer his
own way. He carefully removed his jacket and cap, then his shoes and
socks. He began crawling east again. Everything hurt, but if he guessed
wrong, everything would hurt infinitely worse. However naked he felt,
however stupid he looked, however much the fool he might have to
play, he had to be inside the Union lines to take sightings at dawn. If
he could make it through, then maybe Willie and Bunko had done their
part, too. If they had, the Rebs wouldn't allow the rattling lenses to
hang in the trees for more than one dawn.

Remembering the brief tumble into the invisible Confederate listening post, Curran decided not to trust any sounds he couldn't identify. The start of any hole was to be avoided. He slipped out of his
trousers and continued in drawers alone. Was he the first spy in history who ever carried the fate of an army in such unglamorous dress?

The lieutenant crawled up to where the sergeant was waiting for him.
"The captain's skedaddled."

"Couldn't take us country boys no more, eh? Wonder what kind of a story he'll have cooked up when we get home?"

"None; he's a Yank. I found his uniform. We've been had. I think we'd better get back right now and report. I don't like this whole business." The patrol turned south, then west, and soon had the information on the night's strange activities on its way to General Mahone. Although records were sketchy, General Mahone's intelligence team tied the defector to escapees from the prisoner compound some days earlier. Word was sent to all units to be extra wary of other possible escapees, and the incident was soon forgotten. But General Mahone, who liked to credit the Union forces with at least as much initiative as his own, did not forget. He suspected the absence of some critical data and filed the report under his system for "Wait and See . . . Trouble."

Meanwhile, Michael Curran, making his way in his underwear carefully across the unclaimed area before the Union lines, ran into a painful surprise. The skunk was so fast he never even had time to gasp. The fine spray from the rodent's hind end caught him full in the face and chest with the worst of nature's defensive stenches. With a high-pitched snarl, the skunk leaped off into the dark, while Curran rubbed fiercely at his eyes to regain his eyesight and breath.

The irony of it, he thought, longing for buckets of water in which to douse the burning agony of his blindness. I'm trying to save my country and the lives of thousands, and I've been ambushed by a skunk. Well, time to think a minute; panic now will kill you. He forced himself to slow his breathing and to stop pawing at his eyes. As tears came to help him, positive thoughts soon followed. At least, he thought, I'm above ground, a plus in itself, since he had always known that death would never come to him in the open. And as he reflected, he concluded that the skunk had probably done him a great favor. All could smell him coming and all would know he was not approaching to do any harm. Everyone would wish to pass him along to the next command as soon as possible.

Which is exactly what happened. Because his eyes hurt so, he relied even more heavily on his ears, and within half an hour he found himself at the edge of the Union abatis, the spiky network of logs and lumber built up in front of the trenches. He called out in a husky whisper:

"Hello the lines. Hello the lines. Don't shoot! It's Lieutenant Curran from the 48th. Let me in. I smell like a skunk, and I'm half blind. Don't shoot! I'm all alone out here. It's Lieutenant Curran; the man with Jones's wig-wags. Someone answer me, and keep your fingers off the triggers, boys."

Curran could almost hear the muskets probing for him; he could sense the disbelief of the sleepy front-trench troops. Nothing like this had ever happened before. Nobody knew him, either. A sullen, confused, disbelieving voice searched for trickery.

"Who's there? Speak up so we can fill you full of conscience. What's going on?"

"It's me, Lieutenant Curran. Hold your fire, boys! I'm out here on me belly right in front of you. I'm alone. Don't shoot! I can't see too well, and I'm going to need help. I'm covered with mud and skunk piss. Hold your fire! Get the sergeant."

"Whew, skunk is right. We'd better shoot him in self-defense."

"Get the sergeant, dammit, man. I need to crawl into the lines right away. Please help me."

"Whew-ee, I can smell him now. You ain't coming through here, mister!"

"I say shoot him. He's got no business out there. Must be a dirty Reb trick."

"This is Sergeant Wendermuth. What's going on out there?"

"It's me, Sergeant Wendermuth, Lieutenant Curran. Remember me telescope? I've got to get into the trenches. Fast. I don't have any clothes, and I smell like skunk. And I'm freezing to death in this muck. Help me!"

"Come on in, Lieutenant. I recognize your voice. Help him in, boys."

Hands reached over the sandbags and opened the heavy wooden abatis to get him through to the trenches. Sharpshooters watched for any Rebels who might be hard on his trail in the dark. Those who touched him took their hands away quickly, moving as far from him as possible. Although he could sense that he was coming down with a chill, he had to laugh.

"Thanks for the lift, lads. And thank you, Sergeant Wendermuth, for remembering me. I thought for sure one of your lads would put a ball into me before you got here. Men, I assure you, it will all be worth it in just a few hours. Now, Sergeant, if your nose can take it, could you please get me to Colonel Zaretski's tent so I can reclaim me map and telescope before dawn?"

Someone tossed him a blanket, which he draped over his shoulders, but the shivering barely stopped. Names were tossed at him from all sides by men hoping that he could give information on friends who hadn't returned. He answered what he could, promising to return shortly to do better.

"What about the new kid, Bunko Terry?" came a voice from down the trench.

"He and a few others should be coming over just like yours truly in a night or two. Pray for him and don't shoot so fast for a few nights. Boys, I'll be back. Lead on, Sergeant."

"Keep the blanket, sir. We'll just have to burn it, anyway."

Sergeant Wendermuth had Lieutenant Curran in the area of Colonel Zaretski's tent within twenty minutes. Wendermuth woke up the sergeant major and then vanished silently into the night on his way back to the trenches. He wondered if he should have told the Irishman about the new regimental commander. Well, he'd find out soon enough.

Colonel Zaretski's batman approached after what must have been a brisk run and handed Curran his map case and telescope.

"Powerful glad you made it back, Lieutenant. Colonel Zaretski will be along soon. If the lieutenant will come back here after he does his sightings, I got some vinegar that might help—a little. We should probably bury you for three days, the way we do the dogs, but we sure are glad to see you."

Curran accepted the map case and telescope, gave the batman a wink, and hurried back to the parapets. When the sun broke through the mist a few minutes later, he was able to identify the glints from the two reflecting bundles that Willie had placed in the trees. They were just about one hundred yards apart, as agreed in the prisoner compound, and one hundred feet back from the front rim of the Confederate defenses.

"Beautiful, beautiful," said Michael Curran to himself and anyone who happened to be listening. "We've got Saint Pete by the short hairs now, that we have!"

Colonel Zaretski and Captain Phillips rode into camp with the dawn. Captain Phillips went to find General Service, and Colonel Zaretski went to find breakfast. Near his tent the colonel found Michael Curran being sponged down with vinegar by his batman. Stench and mud meant nothing to the colonel, who promptly embraced Curran and could only stammer in shock, "My boy, my boy." His batman went to find something for them to eat while Curran described his escape, the depth of the zigzagging enemy trenches, the skunk, and most of all, the significance for the tunnel of the sightings just completed.

"With luck we'll be seeing Willie and Bunko Terry soon. They did a brave job just perfectly. They'll probably try to come back to our lines tonight or tomorrow. But the Rebs will be watchin' for 'em. By now, I don't even know how I did it, either. And when Major Harrington

gets here with the theodolite, I can give him a corrected tunneling fix
that will drill the center of that pimple out there like the dart board
of the Drake and Swan in Dublin in me prime."

Colonel Zaretski, with equal delight, told him of the trainload of
lumber for the shoring, which would be arriving at the railhead in
three days.

"How did you make a convert of General Grant?" asked Curran.

"He wants a victory. And he wants to stop losing so many good men.
Your tunnel can give him everything. Yes, I guess you could call him
a convert. After Major Harrington gets here, we'll talk. Then we'll give
you a chance to get some sleep, and we can begin tunneling for real.
General Grant expects this to be finished by the end of July. It's good
to have you back—downwind, anyway."

"Sleep can hold off a bit more. Let's see to the correcting of the
tunnel right away. I see me theodolite bumblin' toward me right now.
If I could just get things properly started this morning, I can sleep through
the Fourth of July without feeling disrespectful. I'm so interested in
the reports that should be here by now about the soil we dug up for
those two false latrines that I couldn't sleep anyway."

Colonel Zaretski waved to Major Harrington to meet them at the
rear of the small farmhouse. Thanks to Major Harrington, Curran's
sketches, and the concept of the "ambulance" dirt carriers, the
digging was already progressing in easy synchronization. Even the
stretcher-bearers were placing their loads of dirt, covered by blood-
splattered blankets, in the ambulances with equal shows of exhaustion and compassion.

Michael Curran set up the theodolite at the rear of the house. He
then walked into the backless house and recorded the angle of the
beginning of the tunnel, already eleven feet long, and sloping downward to five feet. The tunnel itself was nearly six feet high.

"I've made a mistake," Curran said as he entered the angle of descent onto his plans board. "We don't need to make the tunnel six feet
tall; five will do. It'll take less shoring and we should be able to finish two days earlier. My angle of descent is two degrees too steep. When
I was crawling out there in the Reb muck I could see that we occupy
more like 60 percent of the in-between area instead of my assumed
50. We can go faster at the shallower angle until we reach our twelve-
foot bottom."

He knelt to examine the latest boxes of earth that had come up from the diggers. He let the sandy soil pass through his hands, compacting it a few times. He then looked up at Colonel Zaretski with a grin.

"If we dig night and day, and the Rebs don't catch on, we'll be there in three weeks for sure. Colonel, do you think we could ask some of the lads to begin making bunches of torches for the diggers? The kind that produce as little smoke as possible. Let's be sure we keep them dry and covered. The Rebs can see right into our mess tins from over there. Oh, Colonel, this is glorious grand, glorious grand!"

Whistling softly to himself, Curran wandered back to Colonel Zaretski's tent area, borrowed a blanket, and was soon fast asleep. Thanks to the mining experience of so many of the 48th's men, the tunnel soon began making progress that astonished everyone.

The men were assigned to digging duties in pairs that rotated every hour. The earth was shoveled into empty ammunition boxes and dragged to the mine head by eager hands. Bets were soon being made on hourly and daily production among rival crews. During the first twenty-four-hour cycle, the tunnel progressed twelve feet. During the second full day, as the miners fell into the rhythm and neglected muscles recovered from soreness and again became used to the pain, the distance extended to eighteen feet. On the third day, when the tunnel dipped through the six-foot-deep mark, the pace increased to twenty-three feet. On that day the shoring arrived. Curran learned that an old bridge had been torn up for the tunnel at General Grant's command.

The working crews were then broken down into mine-face diggers, the most honored position; earth removers, who worked with boxes and ropes; earth carriers; stretcher carriers and remote-site dumpers, who rode with the ambulances; and shoring transporters and installers. In spite of the fervor of the teams, the rate stalled at twenty-four feet a day. Curran's plans depended on twenty-eight feet a day.

Delays were the normal way of life for mining engineers. Curran had already factored in the difficulty of digging upward as they approached the mound, and the preparation of the great glory hole that would house the four tons of black powder in wooden magazines when the tunnel was finished. Something else was needed, something that eluded him.

Colonel Zaretski summoned Curran on July 10. "I tell you what, Michael, I think it's time to bring all the officers over here for a long-overdue briefing. Too many things are going to go astray if we keep any more of this to ourselves."

"Absolutely not, gentlemen!" interjected General Service, striding in on the last sentence. "Everything about this tunnel, this worm hole, is degrading. But I seem to have been overruled in everything. The one not-so-stupid aspect of the whole mess is the secrecy that seems to have prevailed. Bringing all the officers in on things will just increase the chances of the enemy's picking up something. They've got sympathizers everywhere, you know." He turned to look at Michael Curran.

"And I'll court-martial and shoot anyone who disobeys that order. Understand, Lieutenant?"

"As the general commands, sir."

General Service left the area with Captain Phillips hurrying after, holding up his hands to the heavens in resignation.

Colonel Zaretski sent Major Harrington and Lieutenant Curran to brief the individual company commanders informally, one by one, so that the work details, the ambulance relay, the outpost sentries, and the leaders of the future charge would all be ready as needed. All were sworn to silence. More than one caressed the handle of his revolver at the mention of the general's name.

Bunko Terry and Willie Washburn crawled back to the Union lines about 3:00 A.M. on July 11. Bunko was shaking from swamp fever and exhaustion in Willie's arms. By now the Union sentries were getting used to stragglers coming home, and the two had an easier time than Lieutenant Curran. However, Bunko's teeth were chattering so badly that he couldn't talk after he got inside his own lines. They wrapped him in blankets and stuffed hot-water bottles around him. They watched him while he tried to speak but collapsed. They watched him while he tried to sleep but leaped up, quite out of his head. About dawn he recovered enough to deliver his message.

"It's the guns, Lieutenant," he said to the small group of medical attendants and officers gathered around his camp cot.

"You mean the Reb Whitworths, Bunko?" Curran asked softly.

"Yes, sir. They seem to move them around most nights, sometimes as much as fifty yards. We've got to make the glory hole bigger so wherever they move 'em, we'll still get 'em when we blow the front lines."

"Bless you, my boy, you've probably saved the whole doings. Missing those batteries would have been the end of us, surprise or not. By the way, do they move the guns deeper to the west or just north to south?"

"Just north to south. Always about the same front-to-back. About the same as Willie and me showed you before with the reflectors."

"We got the signals perfectly. A tremendous job you both did," interrupted Colonel Zaretski.

"Thank you, Colonel. I must have caught some kind of fever a few days back. Hope I didn't babble nothin' while I was with the Rebs."

"You've both done your country a great service, Bunko," said Colonel Zaretski. "We'll put a tent around these cots, and the doctor will be looking in on you and Willie every day. We'll bring you whatever you need until you're back on your feet. You try to sleep, and we'll try to figure out a better glory hole."

The concerned staff backed away as the tent pitchers moved in to build a shelter over Bunko and Willie.

"Kee-rist," spat Curran, " 'tis a miracle they wasn't flattened by the conviviality of the cannon fire we've been tossing out there!"

"They came just in time, that's for sure," said Captain Phillips, who seldom passed up a chance to be with the planners whenever he could dodge General Service. Twice he had taken his place in the tunnel-digging cycle. The tunnel now extended more than a hundred feet.

Lieutenant Curran spread the cross-section map on the camp table brought out from Colonel Zaretski's tent. The glory hole on the map was shaped like an inverted porridge bowl.

"We'll have to extend the glory hole to about double the present plan and make it more like an hourglass or a kidney that's been squeezed in the middle. The area of the glory hole will be three times as great but only about a third as high. And it'll be narrower front-to-back. 'Twill still be a glorious gash, and the extra digging should only delay us two or three days. It will just have to do; we only have four tons of powder, remember. Fortunately, the tunnel has always been aimed dead center. We'll only be branching out north and south some thirty feet each. The men will be able to go faster through the wider hole we blast in the lines. You'll see, but we've got to knock out those guns. Thank God Bunko and Willie got back to us when they did!"

Curran then seemed to disappear into himself as he began the computations for the change. Within the week, Bunko was strong enough to return to duty. He was assigned to the fuze detail. Willie was assigned to Curran's staff as well.

General Burnside returned to General Service's camp in mid-July to check on plans and progress. It was late in the afternoon. General Service was too far under the weather to get to his feet in his tent for his commander. Captain Phillips took General Burnside some 50 feet into the tunnel to give him an idea of the intensity of the work and the extent of the penetration. The tunnel was just over 300 feet long. With a target length of 511 feet, plus some 60 feet for the elongated glory hole, General Burnside was able to report later to General Meade that the dig was on time. Burnside was astonished. Captain Phillips escorted him a few hundred feet into the thickets to review the "factory" behind the camouflage fencing among the trees. Here General Burnside found shoeless men bundling casks of black powder into long, slender, sausagelike cloth sacks, which they slung over their shoulders to transport to a number of small bunkers a hundred feet away.

"Another one of Lieutenant Curran's ideas, General," Captain Phillips explained. "By putting the powder casks into these sacks, a man can sling a pair over his shoulder and easily travel the tunnel. Lieutenant Curran can then arrange them in the special way he's been talking about, which he says he learned in Wales. Once the twin glory holes are dug, Lieutenant Curran estimates just two days to get all the powder into place. We'll keep you informed of every step through General Service."

"How about keeping me informed yourself, Captain Phillips?"

"As the general commands, sir."

"That wasn't exactly a command, Phillips, just a couple of soldiers talking about the perils of military communications."

After showing General Burnside the final part of the factory, the place where the long yards of cotton fuze were being twisted, hand-sewn, and tested, Captain Phillips returned General Burnside to General Service's tent. An hour later, General Burnside whistled up his own aides and, somewhat jollier for his visit with General Service, cantered off to his headquarters a few miles to the east.

The small hospital wagons continued to roll day and night with their mixed cargoes of men and earth. By mid-July they were carrying only dirt.

Captain Phillips looked in on General Service, again snoring contentedly on his cot in full uniform. Phillips then returned to Colonel Zaretski's tent to volunteer for another tour of digging into the night.

"You can do something a whole lot more valuable," Lieutenant Curran said from the plans table. Curran was dead serious, dead tired, and frayed at the seams. He shook now and then as if from a skittering chill.

"Name it."

"Find me a local who can tell us the truth about the weather here in July and August."

"That's all? The weather?"

"Right. I'm concerned about rain. The crops around here seem to like water, and we haven't had much this month. 'Pears we may be due. Heavy or light is all I need to know."

Captain Phillips shrugged, rounded up a small patrol, and soon had a fair cross section of answers. He was back before midnight.

"It seems your instincts are right, Michael." Did the man never sleep? Phillips wondered. "It's been unseasonably dry. Sometime in the next four weeks they generally get a gully washer or two. The roads are often impassable for several days."

"So, if we want reinforcements, we have to get them in place right now?" asked Colonel Zaretski, another insomniac.

"That's about it, sir," answered Michael Curran.

"I'll write to General Grant immediately."

"Please, sir," interrupted Captain Phillips, "perhaps this should go up the chain through General Burnside first. He was most insistent on such things when he stopped by. I could deliver the letter to him personally. Tonight if you wish."

"Wouldn't that have to have General Service's signature on it also . . . ?" Colonel Zaretski let the sentence die even as he uttered it.

"Certainly would," answered Captain Phillips, looking straight ahead.

Colonel Zaretski nodded and went to his tent to write out a letter to General Burnside requesting five thousand additional men and twenty pieces of artillery. He handed the request, unsealed, to Captain Phillips, who headed for General Service's tent and rode out shortly thereafter to the east.

Nearly an hour later, Lieutenant Curran came into Colonel Zaretski's tent with the oddest request yet.

"Sir, I'll be needin' a stonemason or two, a dozen carpenters, and a portable sawmill. I should have done all this last week, but there you have it. Me wits is muddled from high livin' and low purpose."

Rather than bother asking, Colonel Zaretski ordered Curran to saddle up, and the two made the long ride to General Grant's headquarters to find General Johnson. An order like that would never get beyond General Burnside. Even though it was just dawn, General Johnson was up. He hardly seemed upset by the request or by the warning that an official request for five thousand men would soon be coming up the line. He said that he could handle the reinforcements by noon, but that the portable sawmill, with its accompanying donkey steam engine, would take at least two days. Overwhelmed by such cooperation, Lieutenant Curran blurted out his explanation.

"Sir, it's for makin' a wooden pipeline. Up to now we've managed with nature herself. But the diggin' is nearly three hundred feet long, and we are about to run out of oxygen in the tunnel. We're going to sink a shaft from our forward positions down to the tunnel. Just alongside the tunnel, but connected to it, we'll build a furnace. A chimney will go back up to the surface. We'll keep the furnace hot, blasting smoke up the spout with the hot air. We'll also be building a wooden duct, or pipeline, just under the tunnel from the entrance. The duct will be kept open a few feet behind the diggers. The furnace will suck the cool air in as it exhales the warm air out. It worked at the Sand Patch Tunnel in Pennsylvania; it will work here. The Rebs will think the steam engine is being used to make lumber so we can enjoy winter quarters around Petersburg. They may miss the point entirely, bless their blistered souls. And the chimney smoke will look just like smoke from our regular camp fires, which we've already built all around it."

As the two were about to leave, with all the largess of the Union army in their hands, Colonel Zaretski asked General Johnson casually and politely, "Sir, is there any chance of getting the five thousand reinforcements that General Burnside will be asking for shortly sent into our rear area by the twenty-fifth?"

General Johnson answered carefully.

"My orders, and my heart, as you know, are dedicated to making this project succeed. I can have these reinforcements sent over to you. But I've received no hint of need from General Burnside, either for men or artillery. When did you say you asked?"

"Nearly a week ago."

"I'll take care of it. Tell me again where you need them."

"Directly to our rear, sir. We'd like to hide them in the woods. So they should arrive at night. We'll get food to them, so there should be no cooking fires. And if the commander could report to me when they've arrived, I'll tell him everything. When we break through the Petersburg lines, we'll have to exploit every inch all at once. Our calculations show that we should be able to hurl most of the thirty-five hundred men of the IX Corps through the gap we blow within twenty minutes, spearheaded by the 48th Pennsylvania. And we're very ready, sir. If some of those deep zigzag trenches should somehow survive the blast, that's when we'll need immediate reinforcements until you and General Grant can punch the whole army through behind us. We see it all as a matter of thirty minutes."

"So do we, Colonel Zaretski. We'll send the troops to the railhead. Arriving by night should be no issue." He hesitated again. "By the way, your reinforcements will be colored. Anything else?"

Lieutenant Curran smiled as he looked at the ground humbly.

"We could use a hundred pounds of the cheapest tallow."

General Johnson nodded, and the two left headquarters noting that the general was already writing terse memos and sending aides in all directions.

On the ride back, Lieutenant Curran confessed that he had one more good reason for requesting the steam-driven sawmill.

"It's time to make railroad tracks, sir. If we get a proper saw, and can locate a few good sawyers among our men, we can make enough wooden rails to get us all the way to the mound. It'll only take a few days of sawing. We can put in three hundred feet right away and add the others a section at a time. We can put wheels on the ammo boxes and build mine carts in the meantime. The wheels will be clumsy, but we can grease the wooden rails with the tallow we've just ordered. Removing the earth has been one of our clumsiest problems. With rails and carts we can lick it. I've got the plans for the rails and the carts on me bunk right now. With such a railroad we should be able to add at least ten feet a day. We can call it the 'Zaretski, Harrington, and Curran Short Line.' "

"Short, Michael? For the longest tunnel of its kind ever built?"

"All mine roads are short roads, sir. Ask the Welsh."

"Done, Michael. But I've been wondering, is there any particular need to finish by August 1, other than our promise to General Grant, important as that is? Would another week hurt us?"

"Two big reasons, Colonel. First, the longer it takes to build, the greater the chance of the Rebs getting wind of our creativity. Think of all the tongues babbling around our camps even now."

"And two?"

"Two is even worse: the weather. August around here is a time of heavy rain. If the earth goes to mud, we'll never get enough troops up the mound in time. Remember, we go on two major premises, surprise and speed. If either is compromised, the Rebs will bury us all."

"Very well. Now let's get back to braving the wrath of Generals Service and Burnside."

When the anger of the former commanding general of the Army of the Potomac descended, it came with the momentum of an avalanche. It came with bulging eyes, burning red ears, protruding throat veins, a rasping tongue, and heavy fists smashing down on tables that had to be replaced.

"By God, Zaretski, you went over my head! Over my head, Mister! And in disobedience of my direct order. Direct order! You hear me, sir?"

"Yes, General Burnside."

"Hold your tongue! I promise you that such disobedience is no joke, even if you seem to have friends in the highest places. And your pick-nose dog's body, Georgie Johnson, has got another think coming, too. This is my sector, and I run the IX Corps my way. I have friends, too. I've suffered Virginia for three years, and no bushy pup wearing shiny new eagles is going to mock that kind of service! Five thousand men, is it? Well, I have to accept them. I hope they bring their own rations. But, I promise you, Colonel You-rat-ski, they move on my command and no other. My command, d'ya hear? And if there are any more of these unauthorized visits to Grant's headquarters, you'll be relieved of your duties. Unauthorized means without General Service's permission. Now is that clear enough for a lawyer?"

"Yes, sir."

"Where's General Service?"

"Not sure, General. Wandering the rear echelons on his own. I believe he referred to it as 'Support Area Reconnaissance.' Some farmer's daughters, I understand."

"Hmmm. Well, ask General Service to call on me when he returns. Glad we understand each other."

General Burnside and his smirking staff departed. The smarting of the dressing down was partially soothed when Colonel Zaretski was notified that the sawmill and donkey steam engine had arrived. Under the energies of Lieutenant Curran, a competent crew was soon bringing sense to the command obtuseness. The lumber, saw blades, water, and canvas belts were quickly sorted out. Lieutenant Curran soon had wheels in production and had even devised a technique of running the carts up ramps onto the beds of the wagons. With fresh air, rails, carts, and revitalized will, on July 17 the tunnel advanced a record thirty-six feet.

At the 340-foot mark the diggers ran into marl where the earth became heavy with clay. The digging stopped. "We'll have to head back toward the surface and hope it turns sandier," decided Curran.

Within a foot of elevation, the earth turned sandier, and the tunnel was soon back on schedule. Close to the four-hundred-foot mark, the diggers stopped again as strange noises started above them in several places. They sent for Curran. "Sounds like something's crawling around up there," said one of the miners. Curran smiled.

"Well, the Johnny Rebs don't think this tunnel is all 'claptrap and nonsense.' They're probing for us with mines of their own. We'll have to stop for a few hours and then start up again on a little less regular basis. Well, it's about time rumors and common sense woke 'em up. The grand thing of it is, the Rebs will have to explore the other salients as well, and they'll soon tire of this game. Chances are they won't come this deep. When we hear them quit, we'll start again. Their chances of hitting us are pretty slim. However, it might be best to send along a few lads with their muskets when we start up again just in case they should tumble in here. I'll pass the word to keep up the cooking fires; I'd hate for a clever Johnny with a telescope to spot our draft chimney now."

As the tunnel crept forward on a stop-and-go basis, the threats of countermines increased. Curran longed to descend another five or six feet, but every exploration again hit clay. Digging shut down on the nineteenth as a Confederate probe came so close that the Union diggers could hear indistinct voices. The voices stopped, and the probing moved north. Curran estimated he had lost nearly two days when he returned to full schedule. He cautioned against any talking and made sure the little wheels of the wooden carts were well greased.

At 450 feet the air became so foul that he longed to sink another shaft for a second furnace. He remembered that the Sand Patch Tunnel had used four shafts for a shorter distance. Since the second shaft would have to be dug in enemy territory, he compromised by limiting digging to fifteen-minute bouts, with an hour's rest in between. Fortunately, on the twenty-third they reached the 511-foot mark; the tunnel was finished.

On July 23, the tunnel reached the foot of the mound and the short ascent began. As Curran had predicted, going up was easier than going horizontally. Within two days the miners had reached the glory hole level some ten feet beneath the Confederate trenches. Ladders were mounted against the vertical shaft up the innards of the mound as the miners began digging out the large twin chambers that would hold the sausage sacks of black powder. As soon as the first of the rooms was finished on July 27, Lieutenant Curran started the chain of miners scurrying through the tunnel with a sack of powder dangling fore and aft from each set of sturdy shoulders. At varying stages of completion, Curran and Bunko Terry arranged the long, thick ribbons of homemade fuze through the thousands of powder sacks crammed into a series of large wooden boxes without tops, which Curran called the magazines.

Privately, Michael Curran was terrified. Would his split-second calculations be false? Would the powder get damp while waiting in the wooden magazines? Would the fuze speed be other than estimated in the crude trials with Bunko earlier in the week? If the two explosions were not coordinated into a single massive detonation, the thrust of the blast would be wasted. As he sat at the edge of the first explosion chamber, he realized that the whole effort came down to a significant factor of about one and a half seconds.

That afternoon, as the second chamber neared completion, Lieutenant Curran broke into a drenching sweat. Then his forehead turned to fire, and he fainted.

"Swamp fever," said the surgeon as he stood over the sodden blankets that alternately covered Michael Curran or were hurled to the floor in delirium. "We can't help him much. Keep him warm when he shivers, and help him cool off with sponging when he's burning. And don't be upset by any rantings; he's already out of his head. The only decent news I have for you is that it's not very catching. If he can make it through the next forty-eight hours, he may make it all the way. Right now he needs nursing and total rest."

Colonel Zaretski felt as sodden as the blankets on Lieutenant Curran's bed when he rode with General Service to General Burnside's headquarters on the evening of the twenty-seventh. It was agreed that the attack would be launched at three o'clock on the morning of the thirty-first. The blowing of the twin glory holes would be the signal to launch the 48th Pennsylvanians, followed by the other two assault regiments.

The predawn darkness would be a major ally. The blast was expected to open an area some five hundred feet wide and wipe out the Whitworth battery as well as the trenches. With the five hundred feet between the Union lines and the mound nullified, fifteen minutes would be more than enough time for the IX Corps to capture the heights. Grant would be able to move his entire army around the neutralized mound and into Petersburg by evening. The five thousand reserves were to be sent into the attack within fifteen minutes after the last of the IX Corps regiments had departed. General Burnside said he would join General Service at 3:30 A.M. on the thirty-first.

"Only one thing bothers me in the plan, General Burnside," said General Service. He turned to Colonel Zaretski.

"We need surprise, right?"

"Yes, sir."

"And how do you plan to get the men through our abatis and into the attack?"

"We knock down the abatis during the night, General, as we've discussed."

"Fine, and what will the Confederates be doing while you knock down the abatis?"

"Nothing. We've often knocked down and replaced abatis before. It's all part of the plan."

"Well, I'll tell you what the Rebs will be doing. They'll be getting ready for an attack. They're not stupid. I believe you knocked down the abatis a month ago before your direct-attack disaster, correct?"

"Yes, sir, we did, but—"

"We'll not do it this time. We'll send the units through our single existing opening. The enemy will have no warning, and should he counterattack, we'll have the protection of the abatis in place."

"But, sir! It'll take half an hour to get the 48th through a single opening! Even at a dead run."

"Then we'll have to get them to run faster, won't we? Perhaps stack their shoes or run them in drawers? That seems to be how you get surprise. Dismissed! I'll be along in a moment."

"I hate amateurs," General Service said to General Burnside.

That same evening, as Colonel Zaretski was beginning to feel the prick of despair over the sudden change in execution, Bunko Terry stood by Lieutenant Curran's bedside. He longed for the burly Irishman to recover so they could check out the final fuzing details together. Amid all the grunting, ranting, and mumbling, Curran suddenly sat up and recognized him.

"Bunko, what are you doing here? What am I doing here? What day is this?"

"It's the evening of July 27, 1864, sir. All the powder is in place up in the mound, just like you told us. All the fuzes are laid, too, just like you showed me. You'll have a ringside seat."

"Never! I'll be right up there in the tunnel to light the little darlin's, and then I'll be in the charge afterwards. Remember, boyo, speed is the story." Suddenly Curran was sweating again; Bunko could almost see the fever glaze coming over his eyes. His speech began to falter. Bunko prayed he would be next to Lieutenant Curran's bed the next time he awoke to ask him about the fuzes right away this time. He could see that a few seconds is all he'd get.

"Bunko, Bunko . . . listen to me, lad. I forgot to tell the colonel . . . the colonel . . . about the tracks. Oh, this mucking cold! The tracks, Bunko, do you hear me?"

The tent was suddenly filled with Colonel Zaretski and members of his staff.

"Michael, it's all set. We go in four days. Three o'clock in the morning. Can you do it?"

"Yes. Yes. But don't forget the tracks. Chop 'em up. . . ." Curran lapsed back into incoherence, shivering again in spite of the July humidity. Even new hot-water bottles and new blankets were of little value. Strong medical orderlies knelt by either side of the bed to keep him from thrashing his way onto the ground.

"Bunko, what's he jabbering about? He never said anything new to me about any tracks. The tunnel's all done. Why is he trying to tell us something new at this stage of the game, or is he just floating away into the past from the fever?"

"I can't tell, Colonel. One moment he knew me, and the next I was a stranger. And I need him to tell me about our fuze pattern. Maybe he'll be better tomorrow."

"Yes, we'll all pray for that. How is the powder stacking coming along?"

"One room done, one to go. How much time do we have, sir?"

"We go on the thirty-first. Can you have everything in place by sunset of the twenty-ninth?"

"We'll just make it. Will you be wanting me to light the fuzes?"

"My God, the most important job in the United States Army, and I'd forgotten all about it. Well, yes, I suppose I'd better want you to do it if Lieutenant Curran doesn't snap out of this fever. How much time between lighting the fuze and the explosion?"

"Four minutes, sir. My only real worry is the Y branch where the fuzes go to the two separate rooms. If I haven't done them right, we'll not get our effect. I wish I knew what he meant about chopping up the tracks."

It was Major Harrington who reacted first.

"Did he say anything else about the tracks?" asked the weary artilleryman whose guns had lobbed more than twelve thousand shells into the field and mound in the previous three weeks. "You know Michael. It must be something that's bothering him fierce to come out of the fever so clearly."

"He just said to chop up the tracks."

"There had to be more," said Harrington. "Chop 'em up where? Chop 'em up how? Chop 'em up how long? Chop 'em up why? Something, for Christ's sake! He's trying to tell us something fairly obvious, and we're as dull as cows chewing cuds. What are we overlooking?"

But no one had an answer.

That night Colonel Zaretski had Michael Curran taken east to the small field hospital near General Grant's headquarters. It had started to rain, and the hospital was set up in a sturdy, dry warehouse. But the doctor was not very encouraging.

"Like I said back at regiment," he explained in a tired voice to General Johnson, "if he can hold on for another thirty-six hours, we have a chance. These damned fevers are so virulent that they burn up the patient, and themselves, in a very short time."

"I'm sure you're doing all you can. Have someone by this bed at all times. And pay attention the second he turns lucid. Over at the 48th they seem to think he has another crucial contribution to make."

CHAPTER 12

The Glory Hole

The rains expected in mid-August began on July 27. They were torrential. Nothing moved except the rivers. But Grant was not one to let the elements interfere very long with a good battle plan. By the time Colonel Zaretski was able to stumble back to Grant's headquarters to report the near isolation of his sector, he discovered that Grant had already put his engineers to work rigging bridges over the charging rivers. Grant told Colonel Zaretski to ignite the glory hole whenever he could, the sooner the better. He suggested July 30. Grant further cancelled the travel orders for the heavy guns and urged the commanders of the light howitzers to get the guns up to musket range, if necessary, to support the attack once it commenced.

The tunnel stayed dry. The powder magazines in two great inverted bowls under the Whitworths were half full of bags of powder by the third day of packing, July 28. All through the next day sappers continued padding through the tunnel, loading up kegs of powder and moving them up into the glory holes.

Colonel Zaretski, impatient to expedite the operation, did not know that his supporting artillery had been unable to move into position by the evening of July 29. The gun crews were already fighting mud that covered their ankles. Messengers dispatched to General Grant couldn't cover the distance, and the semaphore signallers were useless in the storm. Telegraph lines were down. Alternate messengers aimed toward Colonel Zaretski's headquarters fared no better. Every commander on the front knew the assault should be cancelled.

Every commander except Colonel Zaretski. He understood how the destruction of the Whitworths and the penetration of the Confederate lines would create triple confusion because of the devastating weather.

He knew that in the midst of confusion and limited vision, the side with the plan would win. It was a gamble worth taking. He had enough confidence in General Grant to know that Grant would get the reinforcements through.

"I don't understand it," said General Mahone to the few members of his staff who had braved the heavy rains on the morning of the twenty-eighth to join him on the parapets of the Petersburg mound. He was assessing the damage created by the thousands of cannon shells Major Harrington had lobbed over in the past several weeks. There had not been much damage because of the immediate repair discipline that had been the watchword of his command. He was grateful for the energies of his artillerymen who had moved the Whitworths every other day. But from the parapets he observed a totally random pattern to the bombardment, and he wondered if he could have done just as well by leaving the Whitworths in one place.

"Captain Caitlin, bring your drenched carcass up alongside mine for a minute and tell me about those longish sheds those damn Yankees are putting together over by the woods."

"We've been looking at them for about ten days, General, as I reported. But we can't rightly put a handle on them. Nearest we can figure, General, is they're barracks for settin' out the winter so they can try runnin' up here again in the spring."

"Well, we'll have to remember to be hospitable. Can you hit those buildings from here?"

"Maybe, sir. They're just about outta range."

"Does that strike you as being a bit odd?"

"Sir?"

"Captain, it means they know exactly where you are. I'm surprised those rich dandies haven't concentrated two or three hundred rounds on the Whitworths just for practice."

"We do get an occasional near hit, sir, but I've written it off to luck."

"When the weather eases up, I want you to try dropping a few rounds through every barracks you can possibly reach without hurting our guns. I want those boys to know we still love 'em, hear?"

"Yes, sir."

"One good thing about this rain. The Yanks aren't going to be sending any troops out in this mess. Another day of this, and we'll have a bog between us that even mules couldn't walk through. If I weren't so out of everything, I'd celebrate. Well, thanks for putting up with me again. You need anything, you just holler. You won't get it, but at least I'll know you're thinking of me. Your men are doing a mighty fine job of keeping up the trenches. How's morale up here?"

"Top notch, General. If you gave the word, these boys would run all the way to Washington for you."

"I'll bet. Well, no sense standing out here in the rain like damn fools any longer than necessary. Let's go get dry."

As Bunko Terry threaded the long lines of treated cotton fuze around the stacked bags of black powder in the magazines of the glory hole, he was careful to keep all chance of metal striking metal out of the equation. He had left his boots, belt, buckle, blouse with brass buttons, and cap in a pile in the short passageway between the two stopes. He was careful to count and note the exact footage of the fuze lines. His chief concern was following the instructions that Lieutenant Curran had given him weeks before. The glow from the single lantern in the passageway was barely enough to let him do what he had to do.

Even the experienced miners looked at him with respectful silence as he left them to take the heavy reels of coiled fuze into the blast areas. Many expected the whole mess to go up when Bunko climbed the ladders with the lantern. They had rigged a perforated metal shield around the lantern, but even that might not be good enough if very much of the black powder had spilled from the sausages. By midafternoon, however, both of the glory holes had been properly fuzed, and the two main fuze lines had been joined together equidistant from either room.

Putting his shoes and blouse back on, and watching carefully for any black powder scatterings, Bunko removed the lantern from its peg and began the short climb down the ladders to the main tunnel below. He unreeled the remaining yards of fuze carefully as he climbed down. He tied the descending length of combined fuze loosely to the ladders with slender cotton loops so that the fuze remained very close to the center of the shaft to the glory holes. When he reached the tunnel floor, Bunko laid the fuze along V-notched brackets driven into the floor between the tracks. This kept the fuze off the damp ground. He stopped at one hundred feet and wrapped the exposed end in cotton and canvas. He laid the fuze end on an overturned wooden box and held it in place with several large stones. He sat down and recalculated the time to

explosion from the exact footage of the fuze. He was relieved to find
the time came to one minute, three seconds. He would have plenty
of time to get from the bottom of the mound, where he would light
the fuze (and confirm burning), to the tunnel entrance before the explosions. His biggest worry continued to be the juncture of the two
fuze lines at the top of the shaft. He conceded that it would probably
make little difference if the two explosions were not perfectly har-
monized. As he looked upward for the next-to-last time, he appreciated Lieutenant Curran's engineering of the dual glory holes. Curran's
design allowed for just such a time contingency. Bunko ached for the
presence of the Irishman and wished him well through the mine fields
of the fever.

Moments later he reported to Colonel Zaretski that the fuze was in
place and gave the exact time of burning. The Colonel wrote the fuze
time into the master assault plan and requested his presence, along
with a goodly supply of matches, at his headquarters at 6:00 P.M. that
evening, July 29.

"Plan to spend the next two nights here, Bunko. I don't want to have
to go looking for you at three in the morning on the thirty-first."

For no apparent reason, several Confederate shells exploded in the
new barracks area that afternoon. Two buildings were hit and set on
fire. One of them contained the spare reel of fuze. The building went
up like kerosene-doused cardboard. Why now? What did the Rebs know?
Had they brought in new guns? Moved the old? Were the glory holes
going to miss their targets? It wasn't fair, Bunko reflected, to put so
much responsibility on a private's shoulders.

He crawled onto the bunk that had been reserved for him in the staff
tent and slid the remaining fuze reel underneath. He estimated that he
had about twenty feet left. He retraced the two fuze routes in his mind.
He wondered how the twin stopes were holding up under the hard rain.
His last look had showed everything to be dry. Was it still dry? The
earth had smelled a little different when he had laid the fuzes in the
stopes. Could rain be trickling in without anyone's knowledge? Wet
powder meant no attack. He sat up and reached for his damp socks.
He'd have to find the colonel right away.

Colonel Zaretski welcomed him into the ongoing planning session.
The colonel agreed with his doubts and directed Major Harrington to
check out the tunnel with Bunko once more.

"Begging your pardon, Colonel, I don't think Major Harrington can
get up the ladder to the glory holes."

Amid the muffled guffaws of the staff, Major Harrington showed his mettle.

"The lad needs someone who understands the vagaries of black powder, not ballet dancing. Since I am surrounded by ignoramuses, I have to go myself. But anything a miner can get through, I can get through. Beneath this bulk beats the heart of a true ferret. Let's go, lad; this is not the time for debate. If that bushy Irishman can get up those ladders, then don't worry about me."

There were no chuckles or winks when the two disappeared hurriedly into the tunnel, each carrying a screened lantern. Twenty minutes later they had finished examining the whole length of the fuze up the ladders. It proved a tight squeeze for Major Harrington, but true to his word, he kept up with Bunko. He and Bunko recognized the problem at about the same time as they wedged themselves up onto the narrow linking passageway at the Y intersection. The damp smell overwhelmed both of them. They glanced at each other and both reached up immediately for the low ceiling.

"It's starting to leak," said Bunko.

"We must have built a tad too close to the surface," said Major Harrington.

"Do you think it'll hold up for two more days?"

"Let's look around. We need some heavy facts before I can answer that one."

Bunko took off his boots and, barefooted, crept to the first of the glory holes. In the flickering of the carefully held lanterns, they could see reflections from tiny beads of water forming along the dome of the stope. The ceiling was at least three feet higher than the ceiling of the connecting passageway. Infiltrating rain would reach the glory holes first. He shed his blouse and belt again and gingerly crept along the crest of the stacked powder sacks in the first magazine. At the center of the room, he ran his hand along the top of the dome. He duck-walked back to Major Harrington and held up his hand. The major felt the fatal wetness of it with dismay. He nodded his head toward the second stope, where Bunko repeated the investigation.

"Still dry in here, sir, but it feels like the roof of the passage. What are we going to do?"

"We may just have to go a little sooner. Good-looking fuzes, by the way."

"Thank you, sir. I was powerful worried about them, even though Lieutenant Curran helped me do everything."

Major Harrington nodded and began the painful squeeze down the ladders. Bunko left his coat draped like a small tent over the fuze junction before following. He was glad he didn't have to worry about this one alone. When the two returned to Colonel Zaretski's tent, Major Harrington made the grim report.

"Bless the lad, sir. The powder rooms will be soaking wet in another twelve hours."

"Any recommendations?" asked Colonel Zaretski, knowing the only answer.

"We go at three tomorrow morning, the thirtieth, instead of waiting another thirty-six hours for the thirty-first."

"Agreed," answered Colonel Zaretski, accepting the nods of all the staff. With the surprising calm that sometimes comes forward in calamity, Colonel Zaretski dispatched his aides to alert General Grant and the various local commanders of the change in plan. He was grateful for all the "illegal" time he had spent with each of them preparing for such contingencies. He sent a runner to General Burnside. He alerted the reserve division to his rear. He asked Captain Phillips to inform General Service of the conditions and share the plan to attack a day early. Captain Phillips departed on the run knowing what a task it would be to awaken General Service by three the next morning. Major Harrington left to coordinate the artillery, fearful of their ability to shoot accurately in the mud. A final aide was sent in a roofed carriage to the general headquarters hospital to alert Lieutenant Curran and, if possible, to bring him back. The colonel urged Bunko Terry to try to get some sleep and promised a 2:00 A.M. wake-up. Instead of sleeping, Bunko wrote a letter to his father, his first.

Captain Phillips found the situation worse than anything he had yet needed to solve. General Service was drunk and belligerent. An empty rum bottle lay on the floor; another sagged in his hand. His cheeks were puffy; his bloodshot eyes squinted at Captain Phillips as if in pain. Was there any understanding left in them? Drunks are hard to predict.

"General, we're in trouble," the captain said, entering the command tent. "The tunnel is starting to leak. We'll have to go at dawn, instead of on the thirty-first. What do you think, sir?"

"Think? What do I think? I think you're an impertinent, backstabbing young bastard. That's what I think! My own aide, and you've deserted me and thrown in with those goddamn sod-sucking miners. But I'm still in charge here. Do you remember that, Mister?"

"Yes, sir. You're the general. That's why I asked—"

"None of your cheek. And don't patronize me. I don't care where they go. Or when they go. They're all going to hell anyway with that damn fool worm works. Have you told General Burnside of the change? We do work for him, remember? Good man, General Burnside. We understand each other. Must ask him what to do."

"The colonel has sent a rider to the general, sir. But it will help if you sign the attack order, and then we can get that over to General Burnside as well."

"Well, they won't get my signature tonight. The whole goddamn mess can wait. Wait for dawn. Wait for me to confer with General Burnside. Hate shooting in the blind. That's for amateurs. Channels are the arteries of the body militant, you sneaky bastard. Are those the attack orders in your hand? Here, hand them to me so I can tear them up and finish my nip in peace."

When General Service lurched to his feet to rip the orders out of Captain Phillips's hand, the blood left his head. As he reached out his hand, his body suddenly shuddered into an off-balance, catatonic freeze. Service pitched forward onto the floor, the bottle shattering against the foot of the table. With efficient, much-practiced ease, Captain Phillips lifted the general onto his bunk, gathered up the glass pieces and the empty bottle, and dropped them into the trash. Sitting down at the field table, he wrote the general's name at the bottom of the attack order. The general started to snore.

"In for a penny, in for a pound," said Captain Phillips softly as he rolled up the attack order and prepared to return to Colonel Zaretski.

"Any problems?" asked the colonel, arching his eyebrows.

"None, sir. Here are the signed orders. He's sleeping now. I'll have him up in time to see the fireworks."

"Let him sleep. Remember he wanted everyone to pass by him in single file. We've got to blast out of here all at once or we'll never take the mound. Let him sleep."

"Yes, sir, only the general was raised on a farm, and he's got a built-in rooster. And a hell of a constitution. Besides, after putting away a couple bottles of rum, he gets a powerful urge to piss, and it's usually around dawn."

"Oh, God."

"Sir, if it comes to that, why don't you have every file salute as it goes by. He'll get so worn out from saluting, he'll have to go back inside his tent, especially if it's still raining. And for every company you run by him, couldn't we quietly run two behind him?"

"Captain Phillips, how do you and Lieutenant Curran like running this regiment?"

Captain Phillips grinned. "Does that mean you'll let me come along?"

"Right. If we can't knock 'em out of those trenches, maybe we'll let you talk 'em out."

He offered his hand in gratitude. Captain Phillips returned to the command tent to look after General Service.

General Burnside, assuming it was General Service who had dispatched the runner to him with the new attack schedule, nodded approval and said he would be with the Pennsylvanians by four o'clock in the morning to coordinate his other two regiments and the reserves. He also sent a runner to General Meade with the change.

General Grant agreed immediately with the new assessment of the tunnel. He was thankful for the reserve infantry already in place. He turned to his staff.

"Get the 48th some more artillery. They'll need at least six extra batteries in place out there by dawn. Coordinate with Major Harrington on the scene. If Generals Service or Burnside give you a hard time, tell them General Grant is proud to be able to lend them a hand, as they direct, as long as the guns are firing. I'll get there as soon as I can in the morning. And, Georgie," he added, turning to General Johnson, "we'd best alert the whole goddamn army. If the miners can pull the plug on the mound, we'll want to be hustling right into Petersburg on their coattails. I was beginning to think I might have to sit here until spring."

He turned back to the messenger from Colonel Zaretski.

"Why don't you join that other fellow who's looking in on Lieutenant Curran? If he can travel, that man will want to be with the 48th at dawn."

Although the aide found Lieutenant Curran sleeping, the doctor said the crisis had passed. If kept warm and reasonably dry, the lieutenant could be taken back to his regiment. The two aides bundled Michael Curran into the light carriage with the good roof and fought their way through the muddy roads back to the 48th. Curran's only words during the entire trip were prattle that sounded like, "Break the rails."

July 29, 1864
Near Petersburg, Virginia

Dear Dad,
I'm so scared I can't even think of going to sleep like the colonel wants. I'm in charge of setting off four tons of black powder
in about five hours. If I do it wrong, a whole lot of good men
are going to die for nothing. Lieutenant Curran showed me how,
and you taught me respect for the powder, but I'm alone on this
one, and I miss you a lot.

I'm sorry for running off without saying good-bye and for not
writing you all these months. Things are in me that I can never
tell you about, at least I thought so until tonight. I have defiled
your home and I could never face tomorrow without begging for
your forgiveness. It was all my fault.

I know you have built wonderful plans for us for after the war.
I loved being a part of "Terry and Son." Now I'll probably never
know anything except the sweet sound of it. Tonight I miss Mom
a lot, too. When I hear some of the men around here tell about
their homes, I realize how lucky I've been. What I took for granted
were really the best of times.

This war has been terrible. The weather is terrible. The food
is terrible. But the men here have been unbelievable. You never
saw such uncomplaining sacrifice or such solid understanding.
The worst part of all of this is not being able to see you again.

Your loving son,
Bunko

The outgoing mail sacks on the morning of July 30 were the heaviest
in the regiment's history. The mail was picked up about the same time
the kitchen orderlies delivered warm porridge and heavy cuts of bacon with slabs of fresh corn bread to the companies huddled against
the rain. Unable to sleep, Bunko was also unable to eat. He was grateful
for the sight of the drenched mail orderly. When the aide came from
Colonel Zaretski, Bunko was ready. His pockets were crammed with
matches and extra lengths of fuze were wound around his chest. A dry,
rough stone for match striking was in his pocket, as well as his pocket
knife for splicing and trimming.

When he stepped into the command tent, Colonel Zaretski smiled warmly and handed him his pocket watch.

"This should synchronize us. We're counting on you to get the blast going by three-thirty. The glory holes and the sun should come up at about the same time. If the fuze fails, fix it as quickly as you can, but leave yourself time to get out of the tunnel. Extra fuze, extra matches? Good. God be with you, lad."

Outside Bunko could hear thousands of men slogging without comment through the thickening mud. They formed up in company fronts in the cold, sodden dark separated only by the abatis, and by some five hundred feet, from the mound. Muzzles were carried down in hopes of keeping the first shot dry. The staff had concluded that dry powder might not even be a consideration after the glory holes blew. It would be bayonets all the way; the Reb powder would be as wet as theirs. Bayonets would be fitted to the dripping muskets as soon as the order to advance was given.

Bunko found his safety lantern on top of one of the heavy boxes at the tunnel entrance. A regular lantern stood next to it. He lit them both and headed down into the mouth. Both matches lit on the first strike. It was a good sign, he thought. His watch showed five minutes after three.

The call of nature came with piercing intensity to General Service at about the same time. The first of the attack companies was wheeling into place less than a hundred feet from his tent. Outside, the chill rain helped clear his head so that he was able to make out Captain Phillips, fully dressed and shaved, and armed with a heavy service revolver in his belt.

"What the hell is going on, Phillips?"

"The 48th is forming company fronts to attack the mound when the tunnel blows, sir. About twenty minutes, General. Everything's going just as you ordered. Here comes some hot coffee, sir."

"Ridiculous! In this weather? And I never signed any such paper. Where's my shaving gear?"

"In your tent, sir. Hot water and everything. Yes, this is ridiculous, and that's why we'll make it. The Rebs won't believe it. Last night, you remember, the tunnel started to leak. We had no choice, that's why you signed the order that we sent on over to General Burnside, as directed. General Burnside sends his compliments. He'll be here around four."

"Looks to me, Phillips, my back-stabbing friend, that the worm-eating 48th is preparing to slog across this muck in company fronts that will get them royally mauled. And the tunnel will never work, hence all your wet excuses. I told Zaretski not to tear down the abatis, but to go out through the passageway in narrow files. If the Rebs should decide to come back at us, we'll need those abatis. Is he planning to disregard my orders? Is he?"

"No, sir. He'll be here in a minute to explain. The companies have been instructed to leave the area in single files at your command. Colonel Zaretski was planning to start them right here so you could inspire every file as it leaves."

General Service stepped back into his tent to shave and drink the coffee (to which he added a generous splash of rum) and mull over what Captain Phillips had just told him. He couldn't remember signing the order, and something about his aide was a trifle too precise for such a ridiculous hour. But if Burnside had approved and was coming, then General Grant must have approved. His orderly appeared without a sound and set a tray of cold ham and hot porridge next to the coffee mug. There were even fresh biscuits. General Service noticed his hands were shaking as he lathered. Suddenly the smell of the hot food caught him and his world took a nasty spin. He brushed past the orderly out into the rain and sought the bushes behind his tent where his stomach revolted against past abuse in spasms that drove him to his knees. Captain Phillips asked the orderly to remove all but the biscuits. A momentarily exhausted General Service returned. His face was white, but his reddened eyes were bright with distrust. He found the bottle again and added more rum to the cooling coffee.

"Too goddamn early to eat. Help me get shaved, Phillips. My hand won't settle down this morning."

The soap lathered easily in the warmed rainwater. Captain Phillips draped a towel around the general and went to work expertly and quickly.

"I'll be quick, sir. The tunnel is going up in about five minutes, and you'll just be ready to take the first salutes."

"Take it easy. Tunnels never blow on time—especially when amateurs make the tunnels and plan the attack and control the artillery and botch the cavalry and fight in the rain. These troops aren't going to see any action today, and one out of ten is going to die of pneumonia anyway, and they'll call me Bloody Service for doing absolutely nothing.

Justice is a blind whore, Phillips. All General Burnside will get for his morning ride will be black swill and maggoty biscuits. This regiment couldn't blow its way out of a whistle factory."

For all his speed and cleverness, when Captain Phillips swept the towel away from General Service's shoulders, his watch showed three minutes after the half hour, and there hadn't been an explosion.

At regimental headquarters, Colonel Zaretski tilted his head toward Major Harrington, who headed at a dead run for the tunnel mouth. One of the sappers had a lighted lantern waiting for him and joined the artilleryman as he lumbered down the tunnel. Both expected the earth around them to bury them any second.

"Bunko," called a breathless Major Harrington from the foot of the ladders leading up to the stopes. "What's happened? Can we help? I've brought one of our sappers."

Bunko's head popped over the rim of the vertical opening.

"The fuze quit at the junction. Soaked. I'm redoing the lines with the fuzes I brought with me. I'm making two separate lines this time. I'll be ready in about ten minutes. I can light both lines from where you're standing. Stay down there, there's not much room up here."

Bunko's head vanished, and the two could hear him crawling from glory hole to glory hole laying the new lengths of dry fuze.

"Stand back," he soon called, and the two lines of fuze tumbled down the ladder passage. The flickering shadows of Bunko's descending lantern quickly followed.

"Get ready to run, sir," said Bunko even as he hit the bottom of the ladder.

Major Harrington and the sapper ran some fifty feet, then turned to watch Bunko light the two new fuzes. At this stage, Major Harrington would settle for the success of either one, because he was sure the blasting of one would probably detonate the other. Major Harrington noted that his watch indicated 3:51 A.M.

Michael Curran climbed down from the carriage as if all his bones were broken. His skin felt as though millions of raw nerves were rubbing against each other, wirelike, and all were trying to break out of their covering.

"Michael!" Colonel Zaretski shouted. "My God, I can't believe you're here. You're just in time for one more miracle. The fuzes won't light."

Looking into his face, Colonel Zaretski suddenly felt guilty. The face was waxen and old beyond any young face the colonel had ever seen. There was a dry, unhealthy pallor to him. The fever-bright eyes, however, acknowledged understanding.

Curran turned to the tunnel where Willie Washburn had a lantern lit for him. Willie scooted after Lieutenant Curran without an invitation. Colonel Zaretski immediately sent along a second miner with orders to help the lieutenant out of the tunnel when he chose to return. There was no hesitancy.

Lieutenant Curran soon found Major Harrington and the first sapper waiting for Bunko to get the replacement fuze lit. Without even a greeting, Lieutenant Curran asked for the situation.

"We've had two failures. Can't seem to keep anything burning long enough to do the job. Bunko Terry's up in the stopes now trying to get something to work. The tunnels are so wet they're about to collapse up there. Michael, this could all be for nothing. I think Bunko's about used up all the spare fuze there is."

"A good lad, a good lad. Here, give me old bones a lift up this devil's rear passage. If someone will loan me a bayonet, I think we can still earn our pay."

A bayonet was placed in his hand, and Willie made a knee while another miner gave Curran the boost he needed up the first few rungs. Curran's squinting eyes soon made out the shape of Bunko Terry trying to salvage a few dry strands of the fuze for a third lighting. He felt driblets of water running down his neck.

"Bunko," he called. "Come here, lad. Forget the fuze!"

"Lieutenant Curran! Thank God you could get back. I'm about done for. Everything's soaked!"

"Don't worry. Help me off this ladder. Where there's powder, there's always a fuze. Now take your hat and help yourself to a handful of powder from each hole. One of these walls is fairly dry. I'll etch a passage along the floor with this bayonet connecting the two stopes and you fill the trough with powder. I'd say about twelve feet for each gash should just about do it."

As soon as the dry powder runs were ready, Lieutenant Curran had Bunko split bags of powder from the bottom of each mound to the top. By that time Lieutenant Curran was beginning to feel light-headed. He was hearing Welsh songs and the snorting of matched Morgans.

*   *   *

It was now four o'clock, and the infantrymen were soaked. General Service had managed to get into his full parade uniform. He was also in possession of a full bottle of rum that he had found stashed in his parade boots. He laughed and asked Captain Phillips the time.

"Four A.M., sir."

General Service laughed. "Amateurs, amateurs."

Lieutenant Curran gave final instructions to Bunko while dangling his feet over the top of the escape hole.

"You'll have about ten seconds from the time you light the first powder trench. That should just give you time to light the second and scoot down this hole. Run like hell when you hit the bottom. You'll see our lights just ahead of you. Don't stop to look back. Now turn your two lanterns up full and remove the chimneys."

Bunko nodded and put the lanterns at his feet. As he bent to remove the first chimney, he felt a powerful fist along the side of his jaw and then seemed to be sliding down a hill that went on forever.

"Catch him," Lieutenant Curran called down to the sappers waiting at the foot of the ladder. "He seems to have fainted in the close air."

"Michael, what's going on?" called Major Harrington.

"Run, man, run. And don't drop the lad. We're going up!"

Not waiting for an answer, Michael Curran removed the second chimney and then threw one lantern to his right and the other to his left, where they sprayed blazing kerosene into the powder channels.

"Cush," he asked, "do you think it'll be a boy?"

Curran hurled himself down the access ladder, crushing both ankles when he hit the tunnel floor. Willie hauled him up from the floor and ran with him at a speed that a man with two broken ankles can't reach. The pain soon became so intense that he collapsed, leaving it to Willie to drag him without help. Willie scooped him up like a loose side of beef and sprinted for safety, saying a prayer with each stride that brought them closer to the tunnel entrance.

The two explosions at 4:45 A.M. came so close together that most of those present thought they were one gigantic blast. They destroyed the whole top of the mound. The six guns of the Whitworth battery, the gun crews, horses, and ammunition limbers all disintegrated at the same time. Geyserlike, the earth spewed hot, jagged metal and torn flesh for hundreds of yards. Surrounding trees splintered and fell by the dozen. The trenches directly over the glory holes disappeared, burying nearly three hundred men. What remained was a hole some thirty feet deep, two hundred feet long, and sixty feet wide. A five-hundred-yard gap opened the way to Petersburg.

The blast knocked Major Harrington onto his face. The sappers carrying Bunko, and Willie carrying Lieutenant Curran, sprawled near the major, and the lanterns went out, torn from their grasp. In the darkness they felt the remainder of the tunnel shaking like a beached retriever. Earth and small rocks spilled all around them, but the shoring held together long enough for the six men to dig themselves out and continue what became a frantic race to the tunnel's mouth. With each stride they could hear sections of the tunnel caving in behind them. As they staggered up the final ramp, their eyes told anyone who cared to look that all had had enough of tunnels forever.

Even as they lay panting in the open air, Major Harrington rolled over to get a look at his watch. It was 4:49, nearly two hours late, and the thin sun had long since risen. From the woods all around he could hear men cheering. He dragged himself to his feet and headed for his own batteries. He slid most of the way on terribly unsteady legs.

Catching the expected nod from Captain Phillips, Colonel Zaretski ordered the one company standing outside General Service's tent to begin running for the abatis in single file. He dodged behind the tent and gave the "forward" arm signal to the other companies waiting there in silence. A whistle blast from the woods directed engineers to begin enlarging the opening in the abatis.

General Service emerged unsteadily from his tent in time to take the salutes of the second file racing for the gap in the abatis.

"Hold the men," gasped General Service a few moments later as he lowered a wearying arm. "I need another cup of coffee." He sagged back into his tent where he poured himself a full cup of rum before returning to his position. Captain Phillips tried one more time.

"General, look at the chaos on the mound! We need all of our men up there right now. This single-filing won't get enough up there in time."

"Yes, yes, Phillips. Admirable strategy. But did you ever consider how little damage the enemy can do to a single column? This is the safest way through. They'll all get there in good time, never fear. I've learned a thing or two about war in these three years. Now start the files up again."

"Forward by files from the right, forward march!" ordered the waiting company commander at Captain Phillips's signal, winking to him as he saw the remaining companies racing behind the General's tent toward the widened breach in the abatis. If he puts away another cup of ninety-proof coffee, I'll be with the men in less than twenty minutes, thought Captain Phillips.

"My arm is coming loose at the shoulder," said General Service moments later. "You take the salutes for a while, I'm going to lie down for a few minutes. Be sure you wake me before General Burnside is due—or if you hear him coming. He plays sneaky little tricks now and then. 'Ah, yes, ah, yes, 'tis best at times to guess . . .' " he started to sing softly as he returned wobbly-kneed into his tent. Captain Phillips heard the general's sword drag across the desk and chairs as the general fell onto his cot. He looked in; the general was unconscious, the contents of the coffee cup spilled over his uniform.

"Leave him," said Colonel Zaretski, looking in over Captain Phillips's shoulder.

The woods shook with the repeated shouts of "Follow me!" and "Forward!" and the cheers of hundreds of men of the 48th Pennsylvania who knew, finally, that their day had come.

The advance files found the agony of the thick mud easy going since there was no Confederate fire. They worked their way around the edges of the awesome crater of the glory hole and stumbled through the maze of trenches that lay just beyond the pit. It wasn't until several hundred yards beyond the crater that they ran into their first opposition, sporadic musket fire from several directions. It was then that the lead elements realized they might be too few to hold what they had gained if more of the regiment didn't get there quickly. Below and behind them all they could see was a grim single file slogging across the mud as they had just done. Artillery fire from their own batteries had been reduced to rare sounds as the mud defeated all attempts at controlled firing.

Within twenty minutes of the explosion, the mud was recognized as being more treacherous to the attackers than to the defenders. Given time by the single-file attack, the defenders were filtering back into the secondary support trenches beyond the effects of the blast. As more concentrated musket fire delayed the forward elements, the attackers sought protection from the growing strength of the Confederate reserves. Slithering backward, the leading elements of the 48th found safety in a surprising place, the glory hole, where Rebel musket balls couldn't follow. Urged to protect themselves by those already in the glory hole, the arriving files dropped down beside more knowledgeable comrades to decide what to do next. Without artillery, or thousands more of their own troops, they were helpless.

Within moments of finding safety in the glory hole, however, the subtle treachery of the pit became evident. Although offering shelter from shooting, the sides were growing so slippery in the rain that the men soon sank the thirty feet to the bottom of the crater, which was rapidly filling with water. Some of the men disappeared into the mud. Others tried to make human chains that kept breaking as the distance to the rim exceeded human endurance. Those in the pit began shouting for the newcomers to press forward or to go back for ropes and planking or ladders, only to find that their cries came too late as the Confederate fire intensified and the terrors of open-field exposure compounded. Those who paused to listen were sucked into the steep maw of mud with the screamers.

When Colonel Zaretski noted that the momentum had evaporated from the 48th's advance and that hundreds of men seemed to be dropping into the crater without coming out, he signaled the two reserve regiments of colored troops into the attack. The gnawing knot of doubt grew heavier as he realized the Union cannon had all but stopped firing. What he was hearing was the snarling, short scream of the Confederates' reserve Whitworths from the rear of the mound firing with unexpected regularity. Only the massive outpouring of the reserve brigade could salvage the victory. It was now 5:56 A.M.

General Service emerged from his tent just as Colonel Zaretski alerted the commanders of the reserves.

"Put the abatis back into place," General Service commanded. "Someone around here doesn't seem to know how to follow orders. Two minutes between companies. I hear Whitworths, and they're not ours, so be prepared for a counterattack. What's happened to all your miners?"

Thanks to the quick dispatch of the first reserve companies by Captain Phillips, nearly twenty-five hundred men were rushing across the field before the abatis could be reconstructed, reducing the reserves to the trickle of the original attack.

Maj. Gen. William Mahone of the Confederate States of America was one of the first to recover from being knocked into the mud well to the rear of the crater that leveled his defensive front. Even as he struggled to sit up amid the debris that told him all too much, he sent scouts to assess the damage. He began assembling whatever riflemen could stand and whatever cannon could still fire to make up a relief battalion. He sent them toward the crater with orders to shoot and advance until the gap had been closed. Runners were dispatched to either flank requesting immediate reinforcements.

"We've got to close the breach, boys," was his only exhortation.

The scouts returned from the crater with two facts: the front was destroyed for about five hundred yards, but the Union forces were attacking in single file.

"I don't get it, but they ain't coming through here like that. When they get up to that hole, bury 'em in it."

Even as the first Union soldiers reached the top of the mound, General Mahone was organizing a counterattack. The blast hadn't touched off his reserve ammunition. If he had to use it all up in one day—this was the day! Heaving with brute energy on dozens of ropes, the artillerymen of the reserve Whitworth battery muscled the four cannon to the remaining bit of high ground on the battered mound. If they could begin firing on the straggling file of infantry before the main Union forces could arrive, they could freeze the attack in the mud. The attackers would have to find shelter in the crater, and that was when he would bury them in the mud along with his own lost companies.

But some of the attacking Union forces found themselves on the edge of the crumpled Confederate trenches in short order. They plunged into what was left of the trenches and soon found themselves disoriented in the maze. Before they had penetrated another fifty yards, the Rebels had begun retaking their own lines. The superior Union artillery fell silent as the two lines engaged, and Major Harrington feared that his rounds would be dropping on his own men.

The farthest point of the Union advance was a shredded platoon under the leadership of Sergeant Wendermuth. Having chosen a fortunate area of the trenches, the platoon emerged on the flank of the Confederate reorganization, protected from the Whitworths. Twice they attacked the Confederate flank to draw away fire so the remaining troops could advance; both the attacks were cut down. With less than a dozen survivors, Sergeant Wendermuth gambled on a desperate tactic. He chose two privates and told them to get back to Major Harrington as quickly as they could.

"Tell the major to fire everything he has toward the top of the mound

until we tell him to stop. They're wide open to lobbing shells, especially the Whitworths. Right now we're the only ones doing any ducking.
It doesn't even matter if a few of the rounds fall short. Hop to it!"

It probably would have worked. The first of the two messengers,
however, was killed shortly after he started his run. The second was
shot by a member of General Burnside's staff for desertion in the face
of the enemy as he approached Major Harrington's command post.

Sensing the conditions as he watched the rim of the crater through
his telescope, Major Harrington ordered the maximum elevation of
his guns anyway and started searching for the Whitworth battery on
the top of the mound. Although he never hit any of them, the Whitworths were forced to pull back and the infantry had to stay down.
Sergeant Wendermuth's position was blown up, but some of the 48th
dug itself out of the crater and penetrated the Confederate's reserve
lines. Some two hundred and fifty Confederate prisoners were taken
and escorted down the sides of the mound to POW compounds. But
the penetration was quickly contained by the flank reinforcements, which
included a number of Virginia Military Institute cadets, and the forward elements had to retreat to the crater again. General Mahone himself
led the final countercharge that drove all the Union troops into the crater.

Sergeant Wendermuth turned his empty musket into a savage club,
littering the forward position with dead and broken Confederate soldiers until a musket ball grazed the side of his head and he fell unconscious. The Confederates tossed the Union bodies onto the rim of
the small depression that marked the high point of the attack and fired
between the corpses at the crater in case any Union soldiers should
make it to the top again.

General Burnside arrived at General Service's tent about 5:00 A.M.
He drew up with a flurry of his spattered, drenched staff. He watched
the reserve regiments march past General Service's tent and he saw
equal numbers running behind General Service's tent toward the restacked
abatis. At the time he could not see the abatis standing resolutely in
place, as ordered. He didn't bother to inspect. He stood aside as General Service took the salutes of the files for nearly a quarter of an hour.
He watched as the companies regrouped after the abatis and ran as
companies up the mound, where they disappeared in the smoke of the
hilltop battle. At last General Burnside dismissed his staff to get breakfast
and asked General Service to join him in Service's tent. They passed

the review duties onto Colonel Zaretski, who urged the reinforcements forward at a run immediately and silently. Colonel Zaretski ordered the abatis opened up. One of Burnside's senior aides approached him deferentially.

"Ah, Colonel Zawhiskey, if the general had wanted such an undisciplined mob, he would have so directed, wouldn't he, now?"

He found himself looking into Colonel Zaretski's revolver.

"You have two choices, Colonel. You can stay out here in the rain with me and shut up, or you can lead these boys yourself as fast as you can run, and you can make all the noise you want."

The staff colonel stepped back silently.

Inside the tent, General Service thrust a hot coffee cup into General Burnside's cold, wet hands, poured generously from the rum bottle, and toasted his superior.

"The miners attacked a little late because they couldn't make the fuze work. Amateurs, but that's how they wanted it. The blast seems to have been moderately effective. The artillery is slovenly, and you watched the nimble-footed reservists sloshing around. I stood here for nearly two hours in this downpour sending them off with some semblance of military verve. The important thing is that there's a chill in this damn air from all the rain, and your cup should be given a second chance to keep it out."

"Your good health, sir!"

Captain Phillips was beginning to realize that the crater had become a seductive shelter for the 48th Pennsylvania. His telescope also showed the ominous quiet of the crater rim once the 48th dropped out of sight. Then it hit him with the same force as the spotting of the unbranded horses.

"They can't get out! They're trapped in the mud," Captain Phillips shouted to Colonel Zaretski. "We'll have to get ropes and scaffolding up to them right away. Let me take a battalion, and we'll get ropes and planking up there on the double."

"Take these next few companies of the reserve over to Curran's lumber mill and get whatever you need. Head the men out as soon as you can. Take all the ropes and lumber you can carry."

Captain Phillips stopped.

"Sir, that's it! That's what Michael was trying to tell us about the ladders and the rails. Rails are ladders. He knew the crater's sides would turn to mud, and he wanted us to carry ladders on the first waves. I've been so stupid!" He saluted and was gone.

The two companies, loaded down with the desperately needed rope and lumber, were met by General Service, swaying slightly, as they prepared to thread the abatis.

"Halt, Mister!" he shouted to Captain Phillips. "What's all this carpentry, Phillips? You look like a bunch of ragged engineers."

"Sir, the division is trapped in the crater. These ropes and this lumber can get 'em out. Things aren't working, sir."

"They'll go with bayonets, not hammers, Phillips. All that paraphernalia will just slow everybody down. Look at them slop around now. Drop all that excess muck and head out like infantry should. You're going to kill 'em, not build 'em box seats. Right? And by the way, if you do go, don't bother coming back to my command. Understand?"

"Thank you, sir."

Captain Phillips ordered the ropes and lumber dropped and bayonets fixed, then he led the two companies on the dead run through the abatis opening. General Service returned to his tent to report insubordination and disrespect from his former aide and to seek another cup of comfort with General Burnside and Brig. Gen. Edward Ferrero, who commanded the colored reserves. Captain Phillips halted his men, went back quietly for the ropes and lumber, and then returned to the charge. By seven-thirty General Service was sound asleep on his cot. General Burnside went out in the rain to observe what he could of the nearly eight thousand men now trying to scale the mound or huddled in terror in the crater.

Bunko Terry, who had been sitting numbly at a window of the old farmhouse that housed the mouth of the tunnel, was nearly catatonic from the shock of the bad turn of events at the crater. He couldn't believe the Rebs could have turned the attack around so quickly. As he watched first the 48th, then the brigade's other two regiments, and finally the reserve division come under the killing fire of the Confederate survivors, it occurred to him that something was wrong closer to hand. It was the silence of the Union guns, practically useless in the heavy mud.

"Rip the shutters off this building," he snapped to two of the medical orderlies standing near him as he got to his feet, "and follow me."

With the orderlies in tow, Bunko snaked his way to Major Harrington.

"Sir, an old trick of my father's, once an artilleryman. Toss logs from the abatis into the mud in front of the guns. Dump sandbags on the logs, put the shutters on the sandbags, then lash the wheels of the guns to the shutters. The guns won't sink into the mud."

"Bunko, bless your father. You'll be an old man before this day is over."

Within a quarter of an hour, Major Harrington had six of his guns firing regularly; by eight o'clock two more batteries had built platforms and were roaring in support. Major Harrington put Bunko to work on one of the gun crews where he threw himself into the task with furious zeal and agility.

The single barrage fired into the Union lines by the remaining Whitworths exploded close to the left flank of the main battery. It took out three guns and the command post. There was not enough left of Major Harrington or his staff to identify or bury. For the second time that day, Bunko Terry found himself facedown in the mud trying to regain consciousness. But this time he knew his problem. He was deaf.

The attack seemed to gain momentum with the arrival of Captain Phillips's two companies and the renewed vigor of the Union cannon. Leaving one company to toss down ropes and wood for stairs into the crater, Captain Phillips led the remaining new arrivals into a point-blank charge of the Confederate positions, which they overran. They moved ahead so fast that General Mahone again feared for the Whitworths. After firing the one long-range barrage at the Union cannon, he ordered the position abandoned and the guns pulled another hundred yards to the rear. Again it was their point-blank rapid fire from this final position that turned the tide of the new attack, even as the main battery had crippled Willie's dawn attack a month before. Confederate infantry, running back through the remaining mazes, hounded the ground-hugging Union infantry, helpless in the direct blasting of the Whitworths. Captain Phillips ordered a retreat toward the crater. The Confederates left their trenches in another counterattack. Captain Phillips, trying to cover the retreat, was among the first to go down. A Louisiana farm boy splintered Captain Phillips's sword against his musket barrel and crushed his head with the stock. Two others bayoneted him as he fell backwards. Tossing bodies aside as they advanced, the Confederate infantry pulled the Whitworths to the edge of the crater and began firing directly down into the pit. Infantrymen soon joined in the slaughter from the rim. The thick mud slowed down everything except the dying.

Arriving with the last of the reserves, Colonel Zaretski was able to dislodge the gunners from the rim and to set up a base of fire that allowed the few survivors of the crater to clamber out at last. They joined the retreat to the Union lines, covered by the revitalized artillery under Bunko Terry. Seriously wounded while covering the retreat, Colonel Zaretski left his right arm by the crater and came back in the arms of Sergeant Wendermuth for the second time.

When the guns were too hot to touch, when the muskets were reduced to clubs, when the screams for surrender and mercy had faded into whimpers, when the curses became incoherent, when the groans and sobs settled into whispered prayers, when the blood ran as deep as the rain, the Confederate forces withdrew, and the last few Union survivors staggered home.

Standing by the shutterless windows in the farmhouse, a gaunt General Grant watched the retreat of the survivors and said to half a dozen members of his exhausted staff, "This is the saddest affair I have witnessed in this war. Such an opportunity for carrying fortifications I have never seen, and I do not expect to have it again. There will have to be an investigation. But blame can't give me back this lost opportunity or those poor lads."

Grant attacked only sporadically that summer, and the mound remained in Confederate hands until late March the following year. Then, overwhelming Union forces captured Petersburg and forced General Lee to retreat up the Appomattox River until his surrender at Appomattox Courthouse on April 9, 1865.

General Service was dismissed from the army in August 1864 by order of General Grant. The president did nothing to interfere. Edmund Service returned to Indianapolis briefly, then disappeared. He was found in November in a back alley of St. Louis in the violent, final stages of alcohol poisoning. He was screaming, "No-good nigger whore!" even as he was carried to the hospital, where he died in delirium the next morning.

General Burnside was ordered to a long term of recuperative duties. He was never again allowed to command men in battle. He served a single term as governor of Rhode Island after the war and, later, a single term as a U.S. senator from that state. He died at the end of the term, remembered more for his appearance than for his judgment.

The 48th Pennsylvania Regiment was removed from the table of organization of the Union army.

Colonel Zaretski was invalided out of the army in August 1864 and returned to Monongamesh where Maria hugged him so hard his ribs nearly cracked. She cried when she saw his empty sleeve. He laughed. "I'll be in greater demand than ever! Just watch—everyone wants a one-armed lawyer."

Maria wept. "I love you, stupid jokes and all. Too many women in our valley have no one to hug."

During field-commissioning ceremonies in September 1864, General Meade was accompanied by Sean Terry and Mary Elizabeth McAuley to fasten Bunko's second-lieutenant insignia on his shoulders. Sean hugged his son, and Mary Elizabeth stood on tiptoe to kiss his cheek, smiling and crying at the same time.

"Being kinda deaf is an advantage in the artillery, sir," Bunko said to General Meade as he returned his first salute as an officer.

General Meade stood particularly straight in front of the next new officer and affixed the captain's insignia on the broad shoulders himself.

"This is a significant moment for the Union army. Because of all your command experience, we're starting you right off as a captain. I want you to know that I salute you, not only for the army in general, but for Colonel Ashley in particular. Welcome, Willie, sir."

General Grant called on Mr. and Mrs. Michael Curran in Philadelphia after the war in the summer of 1865 to present Michael's Congressional Medal of Honor. He stayed for tea and played easily with the three Curran children. Grant noted that Curran used his cane with casual grace to mask a slight limp.

As he was leaving, Grant observed, "Michael is a remarkable man, Mrs. Curran. How come, if I may ask, he was a second lieutenant for three years?"

Gwen smiled. "My Michael has a way with words but not with generals."

"He had this one eating out of the palm of his hand for a whole summer. God be with you both."

"Thank you so much for coming," said Gwen.

"You have done us great honor, General," added Michael, accompanying Grant to the door.

Although it had started to rain, Grant declined his carriage to walk back to the railroad station. The drops grew heavy, and the wind cut through the thin folds of his summer uniform. He felt old and tired. He paid no attention to the sounds of the scurrying pedestrians or the heavy rumblings of delivery drays. His head was filled with the roar of frantic cannon and the shouts of thousands of infantry advancing in obedient files toward the maw of the mound. No rain would ever sting hard enough to wash away the memory of the four thousand men who vanished in the suffocating embrace of a tragic enterprise that had come so close to the slippery hand of victory.